BRILLIANT GENESIA

EVA BARBER

Copyright © 2026 Eva Barber
All rights reserved.
ISBN-13: 979-8-9946519-2-6

❋ Formatted with Vellum

DEDICATION

To my son, Marty, with all my love

ACKNOWLEDGMENTS

My words can't express the gratitude for all your help in making this and other stories come to life. Thank you for your love and dedication to my stories. And thank you for the encouragement.

Thank you, Bob, for all your help in weeding my book of redundancies, and thank you for cheering me on.

1

NOBODY WANTS A CRAZY WIFE

Quiet Art hung on the walls of the windowless waiting area. This type of art had become the official and ultimately became required for all Andalian mental health facilities. The studies had shown it helped patients process the stress of therapy or even the wait for therapy, as Zara was at that moment.

The girl sank deep into the soft cushions of the blue chair and studied the paintings, taking her time with each and finally choosing one whose deft perspective drew her. She let her body shrink and enter the green valleys and walk the path along the meandering streams leading toward the pale blue mountains in the distance.

The furniture and pastel walls matched the soft yellows, blues, and greens of the paintings and the doors that led to the examination rooms. Zara glanced at the yellow door in between experiencing the world of the painting, expecting her parents to emerge at any time. It had been a while since they had disappeared behind the door, assuring her there was nothing to worry about. She'd just talk to a nice doctor about the images she kept seeing and the strange words she sometimes said. Zara's visions, as they called them, were becoming more frequent, and it was time to make them disappear. The doctor she would meet today would make that happen.

The longer she waited, the more frequently she glanced at the door and the faster her foot tapped on the plush orange carpet.

At last, the door opened, and Mia, her mother came out, smiling in her usual easy way and straightening her robe with an inconspicuous move of her long-fingered hand.

"Come on, Zara. The doctor is ready for you."

Zara took her time to leave the safety of the chair and shuffled toward her mother.

"Don't be scared, darling. The nice doctor is just going to talk to you," Mia said, extending her hand to Zara.

She let the girl walk inside and then softly closed the door behind them.

Zara's gaze landed on a middle-aged man sitting at a translucent desk. Her father, Gilbert, sat on the right side of the doctor, with one hand resting on the desk and the other adjusting a silver necklace with an engraved family crest. The insignia of a crow resting on a tree crown, engraved in great detail, reached down to his breastbone.

"Zara, nice to meet you. I'm Doctor Spencer Mitchell. Please, sit down," the doctor said, pointing at a chair across from him. As he moved his arm, the light green material of his robe shimmered, caught by the light filtering through the window.

"It's all right, Zara. Listen to Doctor Mitchell," Gilbert said and glanced at the doctor.

Zara slid into the yellow chair that felt hard and uninviting. She sat on its edge, folding her hands on her lap, hung her head low, and as instructed by her mother, waited for the doctor to ask her questions before looking directly at him. Mia sat in a chair farther away from the desk. She also folded her hands, letting them rest on her blue robe and blend with its pale pink roses. She kept her head low too.

Dr. Mitchell shuffled some paperwork around his desk, then opened a blue folder.

"Zara Ramsey. Twelve-year-old female experiencing visions and possible mild aphasia or schizophrenia," he read from a piece of paper he had selected from the folder. He then slowly put the paper down and looked at Zara. "Do you remember when you started seeing the images?"

"Two years ago..." Gilbert said, and his voice faded under the doctor's glance.

Zara looked into the doctor's eyes, which seemed devoid of color or life. "I could see her since I can remember," she said.

"What? Why didn't you tell us sooner?" Gilbert asked.

Mia said nothing but didn't appear as surprised as her husband.

"Oh? Was there a reason you didn't want your parents to know?" Dr. Mitchell asked. "Not even your mother?" he added without looking at Mia. With just the inflection of his voice, he set the tone of the conversation, letting the parents realize who was in control.

Gilbert's fingers traced the outline of the crow.

Zara noticed her mother's face redden. "I didn't want to bother my parents. It was nothing," she whispered and lowered her gaze to her hands on her lap, which now set against her green satin robe appeared alien to her.

"Bother us?" Gilbert asked, his mouth remaining wide open after he'd asked the question.

"But you knew, didn't you?" Spencer asked Mia, glancing briefly in her direction. He didn't wait for her answer. Instead, he asked Zara, "Tell me about the first time you had the vision. Take your time."

Zara remembered all her visions clearly, but telling a strange man about them seemed too intimate. "I was little," she said.

"Can you describe her?"

"She was tall. Much taller than my mother. She had shiny black hair and very dark eyes."

"What was the woman doing in your visions? Did she say anything to you?"

"No. She said nothing the first time. She pressed her hands on the glass and looked at me and...seemed...sad. As I was turning away and leaving, she waved at me. Like she wanted to say goodbye or...see you later..."

"You said you were little. How old do you think you were?" Dr. Mitchell asked, taking a pen from a glass holder.

"I don't know."

"Do you remember anything else from that time? Anything that would help us establish how old you were?"

"I remember holding my brown bear."

"The bear?" Mia exclaimed. "How could you have? The bear disappeared when you were four years old."

Zara turned to look at her mother. "I remember the bear with the pink and gold vest he wore. One of his eyes was not right. It had a different color."

"Impossible," Mia and Gilbert said in unison. The pink roses on Mia's robe emphasized her paleness. Her hands moved up from her lap to the golden clasps that held the robe together. She unclasped and clasped them again while alternating glances between the doctor and Zara.

"Is it possible she remembers events from when she was so young, Doctor? I distinctly remember reading that children can't remember events before they're seven or eight," Gilbert asked, raising his chin.

"Well, it depends on the child and the event itself. Memorable and traumatic events can be so deeply entrenched that they can be recalled," Dr. Mitchell said. He asked Zara, gazing at her with unblinking eyes. "Were you scared of her?"

Zara thought about the question and shook her head.

"What about the next time you saw her or the time after that? Were you ever scared or uncomfortable?"

The girl shrugged and lowered her gaze.

"Zara. Answer the question," Gilbert said.

Zara looked up and noticed that Dr. Mitchell's eyes grew brighter as he glared at her father. Gilbert blinked to hold his gaze but soon averted his eyes, drew his brows together, and glared at Mia. And Mia, avoiding his gaze, looked at her hands, and realizing what they were doing with the clasps, stilled them.

"Was it always the same woman you saw?" Dr. Mitchell continued.

"No," Zara whispered but volunteered no explanation.

Gilbert shifted to the edge of his seat but kept his mouth shut and avoided looking at the psychiatrist.

"I think we'll end this session. We need to schedule another appointment for Zara. This time, I'd like to see her alone. After I examine her, I'll determine how to proceed."

"Alone?" Mia asked. "Can at least one of us be with her?"

Dr. Mitchell ignored her, checking his calendar on his desk. "I have an opening next week—Tuesday at one-thirty," he said and glanced at the girl's father expectantly.

"I can bring her in, I suppose," he said.

"That settles it then," Dr. Mitchell said, and stood up. "See you next week, Zara," he added, looking at the door.

As Mia and Gilbert ambled toward the door, Zara darted past them and waited by the exit.

On their way home, Gilbert kept glancing at Zara and Mia in the rearview mirror while flying his small four-person plane over the desert. Mia was quiet, holding and patting Zara's hand, evading her husband's gaze. Zara's gaze stayed glued to the window until they reached their adobe house.

Set against a rocky hill, the one-story house spread low to the ground. On any other day, the artfully designed groupings of cacti and red grass in front of the house would be a welcoming sight. On that afternoon, they appeared sharp and threatening. The blue-hued glass in large windows reminded Zara of an overcrowded aquarium ready to encase her inside along with the thousands of other unlucky guests. Even the yellow window frames and blue containers filled with fiery grass and the pale orange of the adobe walls were dull and foreboding.

Gilbert opened the door for Mia and Zara and waited for them to enter. Zara headed to her room, but Gilbert reached for her arm.

"No, you don't. We need to talk."

Zara stopped but didn't turn.

"Sit down," Gilbert demanded.

The girl sat on the white leather sofa and stared at the carpet.

Gilbert glanced at the fidgeting Mia and pointed at the couch. "Sit down, Mia."

She obliged, and he waited before addressing them both. Mia shifted in her seat and busied her hands with the clasps under his unrelenting stare. Zara sat motionless, looking down, and counting and recounting the yellow moons on the blue carpet.

"You want to tell me why I'm the last one to find out that you've been having these strange visions all your life? And you?" He raised his voice, looking at his wife and pointing a finger at her chest. "You knew all along, didn't you? Why did you keep this a secret from me? Why is the father and husband the last to know what's going on in his house?"

"I didn't, Gilbert. I swear. I suspected she was going through something but didn't know what. It didn't occur to me to ask. Remember when I told you the teacher called complaining that Zara was not paying attention or answering questions in class, just staring at the walls?"

"I do."

"Only after that time and after my asking several times, she finally told me about the woman. And then I told you about it immediately. It's the truth. I swear."

Gilbert sat across from his wife and daughter. He rubbed his chin and sighed. "Go to your room," he said in a low voice.

Zara skulked out without making the slightest noise or making eye contact with either parent.

"What are we going to do?" Gilbert slammed the arms of the chair with his hands, letting tiny dust specks dance in the beam of the late afternoon sun that shone through the large windows. He continued talking, staring at the moving specks.

"She's cracked in the head. There's something very wrong with your daughter. She's never going to marry. Nobody will want her. Nobody wants a crazy wife."

"She's your daughter, too. Why don't we wait until Dr. Mitchell's diagnosis? Perhaps it's something really simple and easy to fix."

"I don't know. I'm not so sure he can help her. Why would he want to talk to her alone?"

"Isn't it normal, Gilbert? You read so much. You know so much about this. She is more likely to talk to a stranger about it because she doesn't want to worry us. And you know how secretive she is. Internalizing everything. He knows how to talk to children like her."

Mia kept talking in her soft voice, and Gilbert eventually calmed down enough to ask about dinner.

Meanwhile, Zara reached her room and closed the door behind her without making a sound. Then she pressed against the door, crossed her arms, and breathed deeply until her breaths evened out. She walked across the room on wobbly legs before collapsing on her bed. She couldn't hear her parents talking through the thick stone walls, but she suspected they were talking about her.

They had been talking about her for a while now, sometimes even in front of her, but mostly when she was in her room. She caught their worried glances and Gilbert's watchful eyes. Since her visions had become stronger and scarier, she couldn't keep them to herself anymore, with her waking up in the middle of the night, shouting. Lately, even during the day, the visions accosted her with their vividness and intensity. And now, they came with full sensory immersion —she could smell the pungent odor of decay and feel the touch of the woman on her skin.

Zara curled up on the bed, worrying that Dr. Mitchell might get all her secrets out. He just seemed capable; she sensed that in him. Despite the outward lack of interest in his bland eyes, she'd noticed his gaze growing heavy as if he were trying to read her mind. Would she be able to avoid telling him everything like she could with her parents?

2

WHAT'S BEHIND THE GLASS?

Zara sat in the back seat as Gilbert flew her to the appointment. Her father was quiet, to her surprise and relief. She opened her book and withdrew into it until the plane landed in front of the clinic. She sat in the waiting room and waited, gazing at paintings of landscapes and feeling grateful to escape into their comforting ambit, walking the pathways until it was time to go inside the examining room. A nurse in a white robe tied around the waist by a blue belt with shimmering tiny yellow gems motioned for her to follow. The nurse wasn't smiling but wasn't unfriendly either as she nudged Zara through a door.

Meanwhile, Gilbert sat across from the psychiatrist. "Will you tell us what you find?"

"Eventually. Not for a while, though," he said.

Gilbert narrowed his eyes and tapped his hand on the desk.

Dr. Mitchell added quickly, "I don't want you talking to her about it until I have a clear picture of what we are dealing with. It could slow or even derail her diagnosis and recovery. Do not discuss it with her. Avoid the subject altogether and try to distract her when it comes up."

"Even if she is having one of her outbursts?"

Spencer glanced at him sideways. "Outbursts?"

"You haven't seen her during one of those episodes. She looks like a ghost. Like she's not in the room with us, but somewhere else."

"Does she scream or cry?"

"That's just it, Doctor. Most of the time, she was very calm. Lately though, she started screaming."

Dr. Mitchell regarded him for a moment, then wrote something in a notebook. "All right. See you next week for another appointment. Goodbye," he said, waving one hand, still writing with the other.

Gilbert was reaching for the doorknob when the psychiatrist cleared his throat and asked, "Was Zara adopted?"

"What? Why did you ask that?"

"Well...I thought since she...looks different from you and your wife that perhaps you had adopted her."

"No. She wasn't adopted. She is our daughter."

"I'm sorry if I've offended you," Dr. Mitchell said, adjusting his bushy, graying mustache.

"You haven't. See you next week," Gilbert said, and closed the door behind him.

Gilbert left the clinic, not paying attention to the people passing by and nodding in his direction, and soon found himself on a path leading to the city park. Zara's examination would take two hours, he'd been told. It was too far to drive to work on the other side of town or back home before the examination was finished, so spending the afternoon in the park in solitude seemed like a great option. After all, he had a lot of things on his mind. The tall pines provided much-needed shade on this scorching afternoon, and the fountains calmed his nerves.

What Dr. Mitchell had said sent him back in time to right after Zara was born. He hadn't noticed that Zara had looked different when she was a baby, but lately he'd wondered about the origin of the almond-shaped black eyes or the wavy black hair. His family had only light blue eyes and mousy hair. Mia, with her delicate, nearly white hair and golden eyes, couldn't have contributed to her daughter's genome.

He trusted his wife and was as certain that she was faithful as he was that the sun would rise in the east and set in the west. But now, a tiny fleck of suspicion had surfaced and soon grew into a heaviness in his chest. Mia, his lovely Mia. Gentle, loving Mia. The love of his life. What he sometimes wasn't certain of was whether he was the love of her life. There were never moments in their life together that hinted at infidelity or her attention being drawn to other men, but sometimes when she sat by the window, thinking she was alone, her golden eyes were withdrawn into themselves so deeply and in such sorrow, he questioned whether he understood his wife at all. Why would she be sad? A good husband, a beautiful house and daughter, and plenty of money. Why would she be unhappy?

Zara felt her heartbeat in her throat as she followed the nurse into a cozy room decorated in pastels and flooded with ambient light. The nurse pointed to a bed positioned against an assortment of humming instruments, blinking with lights.

"Let's get you ready. I'm Amelia, and I'll take care of you before and after your examination. Do you want something to drink before we start? Water, lemonade?"

"No, thank you."

"Lie on the bed so I can get you ready."

"Why can't the doctor just talk to me? Why do I have to lie on the bed?" Zara asked, wiping her clammy hands on her light gray robe. Her own voice sounded alien, as if someone else had shrieked those words, pretending to be her.

"Oh, it's nothing to worry about or be scared of. The doctor wants to record what's happening in your brain as he asks you questions. Come on now. We must get ready before he comes."

"I don't want to lie down," Zara said. This was the first time in her brief life that she'd openly defied a request from a grown-up.

"There is nothing to fear," Amelia said, shaking her head and gazing at Zara.

Zara clasped her hands and blinked rapidly. She stood staring past the bed and the flashing lights, wishing she could disappear into the painting that hung above the wires tangled around the electronic equipment. Amelia left the room, and Zara stood in the same spot, watching the lights, until she heard the lock click. Her heart raced faster upon hearing heavy footsteps. Zara closed her eyes. *If I don't talk to him, he'll go away.*

The chair squeaked, and then Dr. Mitchell spoke.

"What are you afraid of? Here, why don't you sit down and tell me what's bothering you? Perhaps I can ease your fears by explaining why I want to record what's happening in your brain while you remember your visions."

Zara opened her eyes and glanced at him. Gone was his air of superiority, and gone was his indifference. He spoke with conviction and sincerity. Zara glanced at him simply to verify if this man was indeed the same doctor she had met when she was here with her parents. His mustache stretched as he smiled. His eyes sparked with curiosity and humor she hadn't thought he had.

He pointed to the chair opposite his. He waited for her to sit, shifted his tall frame on a chair that seemed too small for him, and puffed. "Yeah, Amelia ordered the wrong chairs for this room. I guess she underestimated my growing belly," he said, patting his round stomach.

"Why do you need to record it?"

"Right to the point. I like that," he laughed. "Recording it would let us distinguish the nature of your visions and tell us whether they're your dreams, or should I say nightmares, or something that you made up, or perhaps...something that you remember," he said. "Recent scientific advancements allow us to make that kind of distinction when examining the brain wave patterns with the WARA machine..." he said.

Zara's eyebrows raised slightly as she tilted her head. Dr. Micthell smiled and added, "which stands for Wavelength Analytical Resonance Appliance in case you're interested in knowing what the acronym stands for."

Zara heard only every other word, anticipating the condescending tone or arrogance he had shown in the presence of her parents to surface at any moment and dominate their conversation.

The psychiatrist continued, "Wouldn't you like to know that, Zara? I don't think you know what they are, and I think you are scared. I believe knowing what your visions are would make you less scared."

She glanced at him, parting her lips as if wanting to ask something, but changed her mind. Her gaze reverted to her hands.

"Have you ever heard of a patient-doctor confidentiality clause? If a doctor deems certain information may threaten a patient's chance of recovery if shared with anyone else, no matter their relationship to the patient, no one will ever have access to those files."

"Really?" Zara asked. Her face had lost some of its paleness and returned to its olive complexion. "Not even my father?"

"No one, I promise, if I deem it that way. I understand how you feel. I've had many patients your age over the years who have been brought to me by their families, sometimes against their wishes. Some feared that their dreams or visions made them wicked or crazy. After learning and understanding their experiences, they could manage them and go back to their lives without feeling inferior. Sometimes the truth is not as scary as we imagine it to be. Sometimes, we must search for answers that are hidden deep within ourselves because our conscience hides certain events to protect us."

Zara searched his eyes and, finding what she was looking for, nodded. "Okay. I'll do it. Will it hurt?"

"No. It won't. If at any time you are uncomfortable, raise your hand and we'll stop. Okay?"

Zara positioned herself on the bed and gazed at the painting while the doctor connected her to the machines. After a few minutes, she resembled a sea urchin, with multiple wires attached to her with round adhesive pads connecting her to the giant machine behind her head. Even her legs and arms weren't spared.

"Tell me about your visions. You don't have to go back to the very first one you remember. You can choose the one you want to tell me about today. Don't rush, as every detail is important. Sometimes it helps to recall an event that occurred that day or evening—someone's birthday, friends visiting, heavy rain. Anything. Don't worry if you don't remember everything. We'll get there eventually."

Zara closed her eyes and remembered the first time she saw the dark woman. Her pleading, sad eyes. Back then, the woman hadn't spoken yet, so Zara could only perceive her sorrow. She described her to Dr. Mitchell in the utmost detail. He didn't realize, and neither did her parents, that she forgot nothing. She could remember everything if she wanted.

Next she told him about the subsequent visions, which were mostly the same. The woman stared at her from behind the glass wall, waving. Then she said something, but Zara couldn't hear her. The seventh time Zara had seen her was in the afternoon, just after she'd returned from school and soon after she'd turned seven. The woman waved her arms and was yelling something. Zara shrugged and pointed at her ears to show she couldn't hear her.

After the seventh time, the woman's behavior changed. She looked thinner and paler, and her open mouth looked darker than it should. She hit the glass repeatedly. As she struck it, the glass rippled as if it were water. The woman tried but couldn't get through. She pointed at the wall and motioned for Zara to hit it from her side. And on a couple of occasions, Zara raised her hands but never hit the glass. The woman smiled when she saw Zara's raised hands, but the smile turned into an angry scowl after Zara backed off.

Dr. Mitchell listened, occasionally glancing at the flashing lights, numbers, and multicolored graphs that showed on the monitor as the girl told her story.

"Are you scared of her?"

"Not really."

"Are you curious about what's behind the glass and what she wants from you?"

"I am."

Doctor Mitchell waited, but she hesitated long enough to lose her concentration and the willingness to share.

"Zara. Do you know that woman?" he asked after looking at the monitors in silence. His tone was warm, gentle, but firm, carrying a sense of importance and urgency.

"I don't know her," Zara answered, and her voice quivered. "But I feel like I should. My stomach feels like I should know her. It always hurts as it does when I eat too much ice cream. But I've never seen her in...real life," she said and paused. "I sense she wants me to break it and set her free," Zara said. She glanced at the painting, but it didn't bring her solace this time. It looked uninviting and fake—like a flat image and not a path through the forest.

"You did well today. You must be tired. We'll continue next week. Amelia will take these pesky things off your body and clean the gel off your skin. Then you can go home."

Dr. Mitchell extracted himself from the chair with a slight grumble, and immediately after he left, Amelia walked in with her springy step.

"Hey, girl. It's all over now. Why are you trembling? These things don't hurt," Amelia said, removing the sensors from Zara's arms.

"I'm just a little cold," Zara lied. She couldn't tell her she didn't really want to go home and be interrogated by her father. She didn't want to stay either. In that moment, she wished she'd broken the glass wall and asked the woman what she wanted.

3

WHOSE DAUGHTER IS SHE?

Zara kept her eyes on her hands clasping her book, expecting her father to ask questions. Half an hour had gone by before she dared to open her book, and then another few long minutes before she started reading it. She tried to immerse herself in the book, but sensing her father's heavy glances, she kept rereading the same page, wondering if it wouldn't have been better to have a conversation with him instead. But she couldn't approach him—the rules of every household in Andalia were strict and unwavering, keeping everything in the established order for centuries. The daughter always waited for the father to speak first. Physical discipline of their children was not something the Andalian engaged in very often, and seldom with girls. But the repercussions of misbehaving could be grave for the very social Andalians. Parents deprived misbehaving children of social interaction for a time fitting the severity of their offenses.

Her father behaved differently that day. On another day, Zara might have had enough courage to signal with her body language that she wanted his attention. But not on that day. He breathed scorching insolence, and a tiny spark could cause him to explode and shout. Although she had never seen him explode into physical violence, she sensed a fierceness running through his veins. She never turned the page and wondered if he noticed.

From the plane, holding her breath, she immediately slithered to her room, fearing her father might stop her. When she reached her door, she was out of breath. She closed the door behind her and sat on the bed. Her mind couldn't come up with one coherent thought, and soon, she sank into a deep slumber. The thick walls shielded her from her father's high-pitched shouts that evening.

"Tell me the truth, Mia!"

Mia's voice was inaudible outside the living room. She sat on the sofa with her hands folded over her lap and gazed at Gilbert, repeating the same two words: "I am."

Red-faced and shaking, Gilbert paced the living room, not listening to what Mia was saying. "Zara came early. Weeks early. I should've known something wasn't right when your mother pushed for a quick wedding because of your father's cancer. But he recovered surprisingly quickly right after the wedding. As if it had never happened. Don't you think that was strange, Mia? Huh? Don't you?"

Gilbert stopped pacing and stood in front of his ashen-faced wife. "She is not mine, is she, Mia? Who did you fuck while we were engaged?"

Her golden eyes, glued to Gilbert, pleaded as she tried to push the sobs back into her chest.

"Answer me. Whose daughter is she?"

"Stop it. Don't do this. She's yours, Gil. I swear. Don't you remember I was a virgin?"

"You could have faked that. Your mother certainly knows a few tricks, marrying off all four of you. It couldn't have been easy," he said, albeit without his previous conviction and anger.

Mia was quiet. Gilbert sank onto the sofa, giving out a tremulous little whimper. "Why does she look so different from us and our families? How can you explain this?"

Mia shook her head. Large tears made their way down her cheeks.

"There is no one like her in my family. I don't think there is anyone who looks like her in your family. Is there?"

Mia shrugged and was now fully sobbing and staring at the floor.

"Fuck!" He left and returned with a box of tissues. "Here," he said, putting the box next to her. "I've got to get out of here to clear my head."

Gilbert left, slamming the door with a deliberate hard shove and a kick. Mia grabbed a handful of tissues, pressed them to her face, and curled her slim body into a ball.

Gilbert flew over the desert toward the setting sun. He landed by a rocky outcrop and set up the tent that he always kept in his plane. The synthetic light green dome inflated instantly after he pressed the yellow button on its side. He made a fire and sat looking at the dancing flames, thinking about his wife and daughter. His marriage, just like everybody else's in Andalia, had been prearranged between families—a tradition that dated back to ancient times. Nobody remembered a time when it was different.

The arranged marriages were not completely random. Financial and social standings were important, but equally essential were the physical preferences of the future couples and, most importantly, their genetic compatibility. Matching young couples usually took place over several years. Most families started planning when their children were still teens. When he'd first met Mia, Gilbert had been smitten with her. The way she looked at him from beneath her heavy eyelashes pushed his heart into a flutter. She never said much, comfortable with and fluent in silence. It had bothered him in the beginning, but he'd grown to accept and admire her quiet ways.

Zara was quiet too, but there was always something brewing in her solemn stare. Not interested in toys or clothes, she spent most of her time reading and writing in her notebooks. She had several of them stacked on the shelf in her blue bedroom. When she was five, she'd asked him to paint her room dark blue, like the night sky. He had, and then with the help of her mother, she'd covered her night sky with stars she speckled with silvery paint. That night, mother and daughter had been covered in paint, laughing and pointing at each other. He remembered the love in their eyes when they looked at one another. He realized that day that he would never be loved like that by either of them. But that didn't bother him for long. They loved him. Just not as much as they loved each other. A man didn't need that kind of love anyway.

As he sat hunched by the fire, glancing at the stars, he oscillated between anger and melancholy. Deep down, he was certain Mia had been faithful. Gilbert remembered the wedding night and the copious amount of blood on the sheets, her crying, and him comforting her, assuming she cried because it hurt. The little kernel of uncertainty, however, had wedged itself sharply in his subconscious. But then a sudden flash of realization, like a falling star, that maybe there was someone in her family or even his who resembled Zara filled him with hope. He didn't know her entire family. Gilbert wandered into his tent and slept without waking up once.

4

NOT A DIARY

"Well, how are we doing today? You're not scared of the wires anymore? Or the doctor?" Amelia asked, fitting a crispy white sheet onto the narrow bed.

"I wasn't scared. I just didn't want to do it."

"I see," Amelia said and turned her head away to hide her grin. "And now you do?"

"Now that I understand why he wants to record it, I don't mind it as much. I just wished they were not so prickly."

"Prickly? Really? Nobody's ever said that before. Let me see," Amelia said, and ran her fingers on the back side of the probe she smeared with a minty-smelling paste to attach to Zara's forehead. "You are right, girl. They are a little prickly. I'll try to make them less prickly for your next visit."

Once she was done getting Zara ready, Amelia hit the intercom button and notified Dr. Mitchell that his patient was ready. She left, waving at Zara. Zara lifted her wire-stuffed arm. Soon after, the doctor strode in and, after a brief greeting, went right into setting the instruments and starting the session.

"Choose the vision you remember the most and start thinking

about it. Try to remember it how it happened—from the beginning to the end."

Zara closed her eyes and recalled the first time she saw the woman because her face during that first vision was the most defined and the most chilling.

After she was done remembering and opened her eyes, Dr. Mitchell touched a few buttons, moved a few knobs, and sat staring at the blinking screen, tugging on his beard. Then he looked Zara straight in the eye.

"So," he said. "I analyzed the recordings of our session against the brain activity and I have inconclusive results."

"You don't know if I am dreaming or making it all up?"

"Oh, no. Not that. I know you are not making it up. That much is clear from the pathways your neurons travel. I can show you if you want to see it."

"Really? Yes. I want to see it," Zara said, and tried to sit up, flinching as the stretching wires pushed the nodes into her skin. She wanted to see it before he changed his mind, suddenly remembering she was a girl.

He played with a remote, and the screen brightened. Then he moved the monitor so she could see it, not being able to turn her urchin-like head. He zoomed in and used laser pointer to show her the neural network of her brain.

"See, this is your memory center. Not the sole memory center by any means. There are other memory-holding areas in your brain, storing other types of memory," he explained.

Zara traced the laser pointer with eyes opened so wide, they ached.

"This area is the most important, though. This is the recorded session when you were talking about the woman. See the green pathways? These are your memories. Now, the pink ones are also memories, but they are different."

"Different how?"

"They are traumatic memories. Caused by upsetting events. Do you see how the paths are fainter and more broken in these areas?

These are suppressed memories. We push our traumatic memories into the deepest parts of our brains to protect ourselves from the echoes of trauma. You have a few. Notice this faint area to the right? These are memories your brain has hidden from you. This thick pink line leads to the amygdala. It's where the memories have a deep emotional core. Your hidden memories have a strong emotional component."

"Oh," Zara mumbled. She opened her mouth to speak but closed it and pressed it into a thin line. *Shush. Don't ask questions. He probably forgot that I was a girl. If you say nothing, he can't later say you asked inappropriate questions.*

He continued, glancing at her with an odd expression, as if encouraging her to ask questions.

She swallowed, annoyed at the loud noise her throat had made. The moment was gone; she would not ask.

"Your parents have told me you keep a diary."

"No," Zara said. "Not a diary."

"Some patients I've treated have kept diaries to understand their visions or dreams."

Zara looked into his eyes, searching for signs of deception. Seeing none, she submitted to the sudden urge to share her secrets with another human being and shared with him what she'd never shared with anyone, not even her mother.

"There are ideas and thoughts I've had since I can remember. I write them down and organize them."

"Ideas about what?"

"About the universe," she blurted, and blushed. "I know it's stupid."

"Ideas and thoughts are never stupid, Zara. Is it something you'd like to share with me?"

The elastic band holding Zara's hair came loose as she shook her head.

"That's fine. You don't have to. You see, I kept a notebook just like that when I was a boy. It wasn't about the universe. My scribbles were about people and animals. I described their behavior and guessed what they were thinking. And you know what? Many years later, I found my scribbles, and instead of laughing at them, I found many of them insightful and even brilliant."

"But I'm a girl. I'm not allowed to…"

Dr. Mitchell took his glasses off and for a moment disappeared in a lingering stare as if trying to see through the space between them. "Have you told anyone about your ideas?"

"No."

"Good. Let's keep it like that for now. Someday, when you trust me more, you can share them with me."

Zara watched him with her mouth open. Why would a grownup, a doctor, want to read about her ideas? Was it a trap? He wanted to trick her into telling him and then get her in trouble. As a future wife and mother, her sole focus was on preparing for those roles. She heard stories from her terrified schoolmates of women who failed their first aptitude tests at thirteen and then again at nineteen, and afterward they could only be nurses or caregivers—their dreams of being wives and mothers shattered.

Her aptitude test loomed near, and conflicting emotions stole her sleep at night. At one end was the fear of social stigma if she failed. At the other end was the predestined path for her entire life. She couldn't decide which scared her more and wondered if other girls felt the same. Had her mother experienced similar fears when she was her age? Despite their closeness, Zara never shared her thoughts with her. She wasn't sure what had stopped her from doing so.

No, she would not tell him.

"When you trust me. Your secret is safe with me," he said and cleared his throat. "The reason I brought it up is that I want to propose hypnosis to bring your hidden memories to the surface. Perhaps it would help us understand why you have them. And you'd know what you're hiding from yourself."

Zara lowered her gaze. Her heart thumped in her chest, and she wondered if he heard it. She wanted to know, but she didn't want anyone else to know.

"Remember what I told you about doctor-patient confidentiality?"

How can I be sure you're not lying to me?

As if reading her mind, the doctor said, "My priority is my patient's health. If my patient thinks that the facts unveiled during our sessions would harm them if revealed to others, even their parents, then they stay sealed. Forever, if needed."

Zara looked up. He looked sincere, but she didn't trust adults. "I'm not sure," she said, grimacing.

"Tell you what," Dr. Mitchell said, looking at his watch. "We can do a trial session, just for a few minutes. I'll program the hypnosis pod for, let's say, five minutes and see if you are comfortable doing it."

Curiosity won. "Five minutes," she agreed.

"Okay. We're ready. Here is a remote. This thing is pretty small. It usually takes two or three times before my patients are used to it. If at any moment you're too tired or too scared to continue, press the blue button. The hypnosis will stop, and the pod will open. Are you ready?" he asked, holding the lid.

Zara found the button on the remote and gently put her finger on it. "Yes, I am ready," she said calmly, but her small chest moved faster as she took quick, shallow breaths.

The lid closed on her, and she was in darkness except for a faint bluish glow the pod walls emitted.

Dr. Mitchell's voice cut through the murkiness. "Are you okay?"

"Yeah."

After a second, a barely audible sound that started somewhere above her head grew in volume to a pulsating hum, neither pleasant nor unpleasant. She saw herself floating through and above the pod. But she was no longer in the examining room. Instead, she floated in a strange circular room with walls that were dark and seamless. She heard a noise and turned toward it. Inside a crystal tube stood a man who resembled the woman she was used to seeing. He banged on the tube walls. She floated closer to the tube, but he didn't see her and kept pounding. Her stomach tightened when she noticed his knuckles were raw. She floated so close she could touch the translucent container. When she did, she heard a woman's shriek behind her.

Zara's finger pressed on the blue button, and the pod opened.

Zara noticed Dr. Mitchell's eyes narrow as he saw her face, and his fingers immediately darted to his beard.

He helped her out of the pod, led her to a chair, and sat across from her. Then, he handed her a glass of water. "Drink it. One of immersive hypnosis's side effects is thirst."

Zara drank the water, barely able to swallow it through her constricted throat. She wasn't thirsty but procrastinated, deciding whether to tell him what she saw or keep it to herself. But then she glanced at the monitor that Dr. Mitchel had turned on and saw that the area, faint before, now burst with a pink knot of neurons. He'd know if she lied.

"You saw something new."

Zara nodded. "Not new. I had seen him before, but it was a long time ago. I saw a...man. And he was...he looked like the woman and... a little like me. He was stuck in a glass tube and kept banging on its walls. I touched the wall, but he couldn't see me."

"Interesting. Did you see anything or anyone else?"

Zara shook her head. She wasn't really lying. She didn't see the screaming person.

"The man. Did you recognize him?"

"I don't think so."

"You said he looked like you. Could he have been you grown up?" Dr. Mitchell paused and asked gently. "Have you ever wanted to be a boy or imagined what it was like to be one? It's okay if you do. It's quite normal. This is a safe place."

"Not a boy, but..." Her voice trailed off, and her eyes focused on her hands.

Dr. Mitchell observed her silently and added gently. "If you were a boy, you could do things you couldn't as a girl?"

"Why can't girls do things boys can?" Zara blurted, and her hand flew to her lips. She held her breath, expecting reproach.

But Dr. Mitchell turned his head away and rubbed his eyes.

"That's a tough question," he said. "Time's up for today. We'll meet next week and continue."

Zara thought his eyes looked even duller now, and the wrinkles around his mouth deepened and elongated. Perhaps it was the disappointment in Zara's eyes that made him add softly. "I can't explain centuries of traditions, norms, and research that led to the separation of roles between women and men right now. But I'll try next time."

5

WAS IT ALWAYS LIKE THAT?

For the next three months, Zara met with the psychiatrist once a week. There were more hypnosis sessions, followed by discussions. While reliving her vision during her fourth session, she turned to see the woman but found only darkness. If anyone was there, she couldn't see them. She had spent so many hours in the pod but hadn't gotten closer to understanding who the woman was and what she wanted.

Dr. Mitchell, true to his word, tried to explain why women weren't allowed to hold positions of power or hold jobs that required years of advanced studies but wasn't very successful at it. As he fumbled through explanations, glancing at her exasperated black eyes, his face would redden and his fingers would wander to his beard.

Zara had already guessed from his body language and the expression in his eyes that he had stumbled because he was embarrassed. Later, he admitted to her that when she looked at him with those piercing eyes, deep shame had stopped him from telling her the reason behind the inequalities. He made up for it by giving her books and magazines, which she hid under her clothes on her way home.

But when she arranged them on her bookshelf, she realized her parents would spot the large volumes of subjects completely unrelated to rearing children or making cookies. She would not get caught like the women she had read about in those books. She would not be rejected by society, imprisoned, tortured, or driven to suicide.

In her father's hangar, she found an unused plastic container, put the books and magazines inside, and closed the lid, planning to bury it in the desert. After a moment of hesitation and a deep sigh, she dropped her notebooks on top. She returned home flushed, with her hair sticking to her forehead, hiding her blistered, dirty hands in her pockets. But nobody saw her return the shovel to the hangar or wash her soiled hands and knees.

~

"Is it true what the books say, Dr. Mitchell?" Zara asked one day. "That women are not as smart and can't handle the pressure of work or studies?"

He waved his hand in a dismissive move, but his hand froze in midair. "Zara. If I answer your questions truthfully, I could be held accountable for what I have told you if our conversations ever made it past these walls. Do you understand?"

"If anyone found out, I believe your punishment would pale in comparison to mine. You hold my secrets too. Doctor-patient confidentiality thingy, right? I won't say a word to anyone about what you tell me or about the books, and you won't tell my parents about the notebooks. Deal?"

He said nothing for a long time, looking at the painting across from him. "If I tell you this, your life will change forever. You will not be able to live your life as other women do. Frankly, I'm not certain I should, but I'm not sure I can go on without telling you the truth. I began questioning the rules of society for a while, and now feel even stronger now that the separation of roles does not benefit our society. Are you sure you want to know?"

"Yes. I do."

"The books I've given you are not entirely true. The research proving that the mental capacity to comprehend complex scientific data and to use it coherently is all made up or severely altered," he said, glancing at her.

When she had shown no distress, only wide-open eyes and total concentration, he continued. "Remember when I told you I had a similar habit of scribbling in my notebooks? I observed both women and men, and even at an early age, I questioned that there was a difference in their mental acuity. When I observed women, they seemed more attuned to situations, moods, and needs, and were more perceptive. And in observing animals, I've always associated higher perception with intelligence," Dr. Mitchell said and paused to gulp water.

"Driven by the need to understand, I began conducting studies on boys and girls. Over the years, I determined that there is no detectable intelligence variance between the sexes. I've done it all in secret and kept my notes hidden. No one knows about it."

"Was it always like that? Were women always only mothers and wives?"

"There are no records of it ever having been different."

"Why spread such lies? Who's benefiting from this? The government?"

Dr. Mitchell shrugged. "The government changes, but this remains constant."

"Have women tried to change it? Prove they are as smart as men?"

"There have been a few rebellious and courageous women in the past who tried to revolt, but they were caught quickly and made examples of."

"How?"

Mitchell averted his gaze. "They were hanged."

6

THE BEAR

Gilbert's glances at Zara became more frequent and intense, and so did his crude remarks at the dinner table about the ineptness of psychiatrists who charge exorbitant fees. Zara guessed he was getting impatient with the lack of results from her sessions. He had only seen the doctor in passing. Most of the time, Amelia called for Zara from the waiting area.

One day, he snuck into Zara's room when she was at school and searched for her notebooks. Not finding any, he asked Mia.

She shrugged. "Maybe she grew tired of them? Decided they were childish scribbles, and she threw them away?" she said.

"She didn't tell you about it?"

Mia shook her head.

"Right," he said.

Minutes before the next session had started, Gilbert knocked on Dr. Mitchell's office and entered before hearing an answer, demanding to be heard.

Dr. Mitchel frowned but waved him in. "You can't just barge in. You must make an appointment first."

"This is important." Gilbert marched to Dr. Mitchell's desk, but his voice failed him, sounding weak and unconvincing.

"It's been months, and I keep wondering whether you've made any progress with her. I want to know what you've found."

Dr. Mitchell sat quietly for a moment, spinning a pencil on his desk. "Fine. Bring your wife next week, and I'll tell you everything I've learned."

Gilbert raised his arms, but when Dr. Mitchell's sphinxlike gaze landed on him, he dropped his arms, and quickly closed the door behind him.

Zara, ready for another session, waited in the examination room, glancing at the door and wondering what had made Dr. Mitchell break his punctuality, guessing her father was to blame. This morning, she overheard her father griping about the lack of a progress report or proper communication from the psychiatrist, bitterly professing his mistrust of the medical profession and especially psychiatrists. Her mother gently reminded Gilbert that it was he who, after weeks of research, had chosen Dr. Mitchell to evaluate their daughter. Her father replied by slamming the door behind him.

From her bedroom window, Zara saw him wandering aimlessly between the cacti and desert shrubs that extended their spindly branches full of thorns in a warning. One got him on his shin, and he kicked the brush several times. He must have felt better afterward, because his face was calmer when he returned.

On their way to the city, he started a conversation with Zara, asking what she was learning at school. She recited her classes—childrearing, food preparation, cleaning, home economics—in a monotone until she got to a writing class. Her tone changed, and her eyes shone when she described poetry lessons and how she was having fun weaving words into poems that had a rhythm and a flow, and how she was getting praise from her teacher, Mr. Grier.

"A wife's ability to compose poems for her husband is highly prized. Some have to work hard to create anything that makes sense and is worth reading, but you're a natural," Mia said.

Gilbert listened while flying the plane. "So, you are writing poems in your notebooks?" he asked.

Zara licked her dry lips. "Yes."

"Do you still have them?"

"I...didn't like them. They were childish, so I threw them away. I am...I'll start a new one now that I learned how to," Zara exhaled. Her father had inadvertently helped her explain the contents of the notebooks. But she deduced from the tone of his voice that he knew her notebooks were no longer in her room. Her forehead and her upper lip gathered beads of sweat as she grasped how close she was to being discovered. She had lied to her father and was stunned that she felt no guilt about it.

"I'm sure you'll write beautiful poems," her mother said. Zara glanced at her mother, and when her eyes landed on her hands, she almost gasped, seeing her fingernails bitten raw. Mia noticed her glance and slid her hands into her robe.

Zara stayed in the waiting area while her parents, directed by Amelia, disappeared into a small conference room. After they were seated, Amelia brought a water flask and three glasses. She set it on a table and left, glancing at Mia and Gilbert with more curiosity than she ought to have shown.

Minutes went by. Gilbert alternated between tapping his foot on the floor and his fingers on the table. Mia poured water for her husband and herself and drained the entire glass while Gilbert glared at her. Soon after, Dr. Mitchell strolled in, holding a large brown folder. He sat across from them and slowly turned the pages and read sections, emulating a believable-enough engagement. Gilbert's face reddened and his lips thinned into an almost invisible line, but he kept quiet.

"We've made progress. Your daughter, science, and me. I am now certain what's behind your daughter's visions and nightmares."

"You are?" Mia spoke. Gilbert scorned her with a twisted grimace.

Dr. Mitchell didn't answer. Gilbert coughed.

"Your daughter is a deeply sensitive girl who's been plagued with an extreme case of anxiety."

"Anxiety about what?" Gilbert asked. "She has no reason to be anxious."

Dr. Mitchell stared at him for a long time. He procrastinated, extending the revelation's impact. "About the aptitude test. As it's looming closer, she is getting more anxious, fearing she's not good enough and won't pass it."

"Oh, my poor thing," Mia whispered. "Why didn't she tell me?"

"That's it? That's all you found after three months of weekly meetings and thousands of titanium pieces? She sees weird people because she's anxious about some stupid test that thousands of other girls take every day in Andalia? That's insane." Gilbert spat the words so fast, tiny saliva droplets landed on the glass desk.

Then he stood and straightened his back. "We are done here," he hissed. "Let's go," he said to Mia without looking at her. "The sessions end today. Come on, Mia, we need to get her out of here."

"You are making a mistake," Dr. Mitchell said. "It takes a long time to diagnose a patient, especially such a young one. And even longer to treat her. If you stop the sessions now, you risk the situation getting worse."

Gilbert turned around, raised his fist up, and shouted, "Shut up! You are nothing but a con man. I'll do some digging on you, Doctor! We'll see what kind of dirt I can find on you."

Mia looked at Gilbert with her face as white as snow. "Don't you think you should listen to him—"

"Done listening."

Gilbert rushed to the door and pushed Mia out. In the waiting room, he shouted, "Where is my daughter? Bring her or I'll find her myself."

Amelia went to get Zara while Gilbert pounded on each door. "Zara! Zara! Come out!"

A few minutes later, Amelia returned with Zara behind her. When Amelia darted into the examination room, yanked the probes off and pushed her out of the room, Zara asked why, but the nurse brushed her off.

"Come. We're leaving," Gilbert said to Zara.

Zara scurried to Mia, slid her hand inside her mother's icy hand, and they both followed him without a word.

The flight home felt like a lifetime. No one spoke. Not even the fuming Gilbert. For the entire flight, he kept his eyebrows drawn together, his mouth shut in a tight grimace, and his gaze on the windshield. Mia clutched her daughter's hand. Zara lowered her gaze to her book, pretending to read it.

Mia knocked on her daughter's door and entered, hearing a weak, "Come in." Zara didn't even look at the food her mother made for her —her favorite grilled cheese with jalapeño slices on top—and pushed the plate away.

Mia set the tray outside the door and sat on the bed by Zara, who curled herself into a ball. She stroked her daughter's black hair and explained that her father had stopped the sessions because he was convinced that they were not beneficial.

Zara, fearing her secret had been found, broke the silence. "Why does Father think the sessions aren't helping?" she asked.

When Mia didn't answer but kept scanning the wall as if tracing a buzzing fly, Zara's heart raced faster, and she wondered if her mother had ever seen what was inside her notebooks. Why else wouldn't she answer? She never kept secrets from her mother.

Mia met her gaze. "The doctor said your visions are caused by anxiety about the aptitude test," she said, then found Zara's hand and stroked it gently. "He also said that you are a very...sensitive girl and you worry a lot about everything. Is that true, my baby?"

Mia's golden eyes seemed to have shadowed. In that moment, Zara considered telling her the truth—wiping her mother's sadness and worry away with one confession and telling her she wasn't all that anxious. Tell her all about her doubts, tell her about her notebooks—her cherished secrets, her thoughts about the universe. She drew a breath, opened her mouth only to close it. Didn't her mother understand her well enough to realize that it wasn't about anxiety?

Mia continued, holding her daughter's chin up. "Your dad thinks that the doctor is a con man because you're so calm and composed, even during your visions, and you never cry or seem nervous."

Zara released her breath. Dr. Mitchell was trying to protect her. The doctor was lying to protect her secrets.

"Is that true? Are you afraid of the exam?" Mia asked.

The knot in her stomach loosened, and Zara nodded, avoiding her mother's eyes. She couldn't lie to her mother—she would know immediately. But her mother didn't appear suspicious. She pressed Zara's head to her chest, and soothed her with her gentle voice, promising she'd help her prepare for the test.

"You'll pass it with the highest marks."

Zara noticed her mother's face was smooth and calm when she was leaving her room. *She believed me. Everything will be fine now.*

As soon as the door closed, Zara jumped on the bed and kicked her feet up in a triumphant dance.

Gilbert was waiting for Mia in the living room. "Did you talk to her?"

Mia nodded, smiling. Gilbert watched her lips and frowned.

"Everything will be fine now. Dr. Mitchell was telling the truth. She is terrified of the aptitude test. I will help her prepare—"

"You believe her?"

"Why wouldn't I believe her? Zara doesn't lie. You know that. She never could."

Gilbert's eyes brightened as he eased into his seat and relaxed.

Facing Gilbert, Mia took a step forward and kneeled before him. "Don't you think we should continue sending her to the doctor? He might help her."

"I don't think so."

"Why not? He was right about her."

"I'll think about it. There is something off about him."

"I think he's nice."

"Nice."

Mia rose from her knees and put her face close to Gilbert's.

"Yes, he's nice, and he wants the best for our daughter, not to appease you and tell you what you want to hear. Don't you want to help your daughter?" Mia spun around and, with straight shoulders and deliberate poise, strolled out of the living room without a glance at Gilbert.

He stared at the hallway with his mouth wide open. "How dare you openly defy me..." he started. His words sounded hollow and unconvincing and trailed off. He sank deeper into his chair, and the corners of his lips went up. "I'll be damned. I didn't think she had it in her."

Gilbert had already left for work at a local government office, where he was a chief accountant, while Mia cut fruit for the morning's breakfast, humming quietly.

Zara sneaked behind her. "What happened to the bear?" Zara's brusque tone cut through the morning air like a pair of rusty scissors.

The knife clanked on the stone counter, then tumbled to the floor and landed near Zara's feet.

Mia slowly turned to face her daughter and, seeing her eyebrows drawn together, swallowed. "What's wrong? Did you have a bad dream?"

"What happened to the bear?"

"Why are you asking about the bear? The bear disappeared years ago."

"He took it, didn't he?"

"Who? What are you talking about?"

Mia's hand found the counter, and she clung to it while her face drained of color.

"I remember the man who came to our house one day. He kneeled to look at me and stroke my cheek, and he took my bear. Why?"

Mia slid into a chair by the kitchen table and studied the walls of the kitchen as if trying to ask them for help.

"Mom. Who was that man, and why did he take my bear?"

"Zara. It was just a dream," Mia regained her voice. "There was no man here. The neighbor's dog took off with your bear, but I didn't have the heart to tell you. Sit with me, my love. You mustn't worry about the test anymore. I'll help you."

Zara had always thought her mother was incapable of lying, but she was lying to her now. Her mother's exaggerated cheerfulness rang an alarm in her mind, but she pretended she believed her and sat at the table.

Her mother gathered Zara's hands in hers. "Everything will be fine now. Your nightmares will stop as soon as you are more secure in your ability to pass the test. Starting today, I'll sit with you and tell you all about the test and what to expect."

Zara looked at her mother, seeing her in a new light. Her perfect mother had secrets too.

7
THE TEST

The day of the test arrived faster than Zara had hoped. The fear of failing ingrained in every girl's psyche since the day they could understand the test's importance peaked as they stood in line, trembling and mumbling the phrases they'd learned while waiting to be let into the examination room.

Zara, however, was calm and strangely unafraid, mulling over the thought that had emerged during her sleepless night. It never left but stayed stewing, scheming, and then firmly implanting itself in her mind. With the thought, her imagination took her on a trip into the future where she saw herself in a white nurse's robe, working in a doctor's office that looked just like Dr. Mitchell's. *It wouldn't be so bad if I failed. It wouldn't be so bad at all.* When she got up, she tried to dismiss the thought, but then gave up. *Why?* she asked herself as a sudden revelation lifted her spirits, as if a bright ray of sunshine had landed on her lap. *Nobody knows what I'm thinking. I can think of whatever I want. Whenever I want.*

She smiled.

Now, standing in a line of anxious teenage girls, she felt oddly superior, watching her trembling classmates. Her mother had done as she'd promised and sat with her every day to help her prepare for the examination. Zara had listened politely to her mother's teachings but had caught herself disappearing in her own thoughts, nodding absentmindedly as her gentle teacher spoke. The lessons, heavy on home economics, bored her. When her mother spoke of rules and restrictions that forbade women from speaking without being asked, going to town by themselves, flying planes, or holding their own bank accounts, she gritted her teeth.

The massive wooden door finally screeched open, and two teachers let the girls inside. Three examiners sat high on a podium facing a large, poorly ventilated room filled with rows of hard wooden desks with attached chairs.

The girls sat at their preassigned desks as directed by the solemn teachers. Before each student were a pen and a booklet. On each page, a question was written at the top, and the rest of the page was blank.

Zara leafed through the booklet, scanning the questions. She glanced at the middle-aged teachers sitting on the podium and staring at the girls through their glasses, moving their mustaches and beards as if they were chewing something.

"Cheating is not allowed and will cause an immediate fail mark," one beard announced.

The lessons her mother taught her seemed easy, but the questions turned out even easier than she had expected. She answered the first three, turned the page, pressed the pen to the paper, and then her hand stilled. She read the next question, then glanced at her peers and at the grumpy men at the podium. Her heart pounded while she deliberated. This moment would shape her life. She could finish the test and get a perfect score, or she could cleverly mess up the answers, but she couldn't just leave them blank or they would smell a rat. Her parents and teachers were aware of her abilities. If she were to fail, would her parents still love her, or would they think less of her? Were she to fail, would she be happy as a nurse? If she were to pass, would she be satisfied with being a mother and wife and forever closing her notebooks and shuttering her dreams? Why was she so calm when the stakes were so high?

Two hours went by, and the students—some teary-eyed, some wiping their brows, some flushed and wide-eyed—began to rise from their chairs and hand their booklets to the teachers. Zara was still sitting at her desk, writing. She was among the last girls to leave the examination room. With her eyes downcast, pale-faced and with a little nervous smile, she handed her booklet off. In the hallway, she stood with her back to the wall and exhaled before facing her parents.

Her parents waited for her outside the building. Mia was biting her fingernails and Gilbert was pacing, keeping his hands in his coat pockets. Mia smiled when she saw Zara leave the building and ran toward her.

When Gilbert saw her pale face, he tensed. "How did it go?" he asked.

Zara shrugged lightly. "I think I did okay. I answered all the questions."

"I'm sure you did just fine," Mia said. "You answered all my questions correctly when I was tutoring you."

Zara licked her lips. "I was nervous."

A week later, the test results arrived in the morning mail in a big yellow envelope. It was waiting on the kitchen table for Zara to return from school and Gilbert from work. Mia glanced at it throughout the day and touched it a few times but didn't open it. Zara saw it, but pretending she didn't see it, darted into her room.

Mia opened her mouth to say something, but Zara left before she could utter a word. "She must be so worried," she murmured, stirring the pasta in the pot. When the front door flung open, she glanced at the envelope and slid it in a drawer. "We'll open you after dinner," she whispered.

Gilbert kissed her on the forehead and peeked into the pot. "Spaghetti. Yum."

During dinner, Zara mostly played with her food, moving the pasta around with her fork and glancing at the spot where the envelope was. The savory smell of the spaghetti sauce, normally making Zara salivate, that day made her nauseous. She kept her mouth tight and turned her head away from the steaming pot. Mia observed her, and as soon as Gilbert pushed his plate away, she pulled the envelope out. "Zara's test results are back," she said, smiling. "Who wants to open it?"

Gilbert took it and opened it with a quick tear. He read the first page, and his face slowly paled. The page dropped from his hand and landed on a plate, where it immediately soaked up the red sauce. Mia fished the letter from his plate and read it. She slumped into her chair and slowly searched Zara's eyes. The girl met her gaze but only for a moment. A glaze over her mother's eyes made them appear distant, cold.

Gilbert stormed out of the kitchen, slamming the door, and returned a minute later with an ashen face and stared at Mia and Zara with crazed eyes. "What are we going to do? What now?" he asked Mia in a barely audible voice. "Why did it have to happen to us? A daughter incapable of having a family. Everyone will laugh at us. Shun us."

"Nobody will laugh at us, Gilbert. And there is still time. She can still pass the second test when she's nineteen, and everything will be okay."

"What happened, Zara? Why would you do this to us? Didn't your mother spend weeks with you helping with the test? Didn't you pay attention? Why would you want to hurt us like this? Why?"

Mia stood up and faced her husband with a calmness that tightened Zara's throat.

"Gilbert, she didn't do this on purpose. These things happen. I remember a girl who didn't pass the first time, then passed with a great score, married, and had two beautiful children. Dr. Mitchell was right. We should have listened to him and had him help her with her anxiety. She didn't need my help studying. She is smart. All she needs is to learn how to control her anxiety," Mia continued in a soft voice, while with an almost-imperceptible hand movement, gesturing for Zara to leave the kitchen. "We should take her back to Dr. Mitchell, so he can help her."

Zara rose without a sound, and like a ghost, disappeared from her father's sight.

8

YOU HAVE A CHOICE

The afternoon sun peeked through the blinds and landed on Dr. Mitchell's glasses. He took them off and rubbed his eyes.

"We're all pretty arrogant," he stated, cleaning his glasses with the corner of his white tunic.

"Who?"

"The scientists." He looked at Zara with an enigmatic expression. "Men."

She caught his look and waited, focusing on his eyes, sensing that he was going to say something so important that it would change everything. His normally watery eyes gained color and shine.

"We get caught in our insecurities and entangle ourselves in webs of deception and even outright lies. And all in the name of science and humanity we shout, but deep down we realize we're lying to everyone and to ourselves."

Zara sensed he had more on his mind and remained silent and unmoving, gazing into his eyes. Her lips parted as she listened to Dr. Mitchell's rant. She held her breath, waiting for more, waiting for the revelation that would change her life forever. But Dr. Mitchell was silent, staring out the window with eyes shining like slivers of ice.

"About what?" she whispered breathlessly, to not to ruin the moment with sound. She could wait no longer—she had been anticipating a revelation since she had been back in therapy. It had been a month since Gilbert had capitulated to Mia's harrying that Zara should continue her treatment with the same doctor. Her final argument—that any other doctor would need to start from scratch and charge them again to examine her—finally swayed Gilbert to take Zara back to Dr. Mitchell. Zara admired her mother's cleverness in playing into her father's reluctance to waste titanium for no reason. Dr. Mitchell graciously welcomed them back, holding no apparent grudge against Gilbert's past behavior.

Much to Zara's disappointment and surprise, they spent the last three sessions talking about anxiety and how to control it with a short hypnotic session at the end. The sessions revealed no additional secrets and no new beings. In her visions, the woman competed with the man for her attention.

Every time she came through the door, she expected to have a different conversation with the psychiatrist after he had lied on her behalf and after handing him her latest notebook after her first session back. Showing him she trusted him was her way of thanking him for lying to protect her, and she expected to discuss her notes the next session, but he just blabbered about anxieties. Had she been wrong about him? Now that he had finally started being honest with her, she would not stop questioning him until she had answers.

"The male scientists. Arrogant and boxed-in by centuries of duplicity and deception and arrogance...simple stupidity. Simple male shortsightedness."

Zara shrugged. "I don't understand."

"Because women could bring so much to science. Men believe that when women focus on childbearing and childrearing, the household chores take all their attention and brainpower, leaving nothing rational or coherent. They claim that if women were allowed to take part in scientific discovery, they could taint it with their emotions and distort it with their irrationality. But that's...a big pile of bullshit. Don't you agree?"

Zara's eyes widened. She froze. Goosebumps covered her arms. Dr. Mitchell had mentioned his clandestine research and his findings to her before, but more subtly, not as passionately. This time, she saw rage in his eyes, his reddened face, and the passionate tugging at his mustache. She worried he might tear it off. In that moment, Zara realized she was crossing a line and stepping into a different world from which there was no way back to her previous life. She had already taken the first step by failing the test. There was still time to take the test at nineteen and ace it. She could still do it. Or she could cross another line.

While she wrestled with her thoughts, Dr. Mitchell gazed at her intently, tapping his foot on the tiled floor as if waiting for her answer, her acknowledgment.

"Bullshit," she said, and her voice broke. She had never cursed before. "Bullshit!" she repeated, and this time her voice didn't falter. She exhaled deeply.

Dr. Mitchell laughed. His eyes turned into gray slits, his belly shook, and his beard ruffled.

"That's right, girl. It's all bullshit," he said after his laughter had subsided. But suddenly, his face became sullen, and his eyes became the tired and colorless wells they'd always been.

Her heart started pounding. "Is there a way to—"

"You have a choice, your own choice, and you'll know what you'll be giving up in either case. Marry the husband the System chooses and have children, or…"

"Or what? I'm still just a girl. A twelve—well, almost thirteen-year-old girl. What choice do I have?"

A mysterious grin spread across the doctor's face. "What if I told you there was something you could do?"

"Be a nurse or a caregiver to people I don't even know? I thought about it, as you already know, and even failed the test, thinking that being a nurse was something I'd rather be than just be a wife and a mother."

"But?"

"But it's not. I don't want to be a nurse. And it's not that I don't want to be a mother or a wife. I have nothing against that. It's just that I'm uncertain about what I want. Why couldn't women be both mothers and scientists?" Zara asked and pursed her lips. *Don't you dare cry.*

Dr. Mitchell stood up and approached her, touching her shoulder.

"Zara, my child," he said softly. "Look at me."

Zara looked at him, blinking.

"I read your notes. I gobbled up the entire notebook in one evening and through the night. Most of it went over my head. Although, like any other doctor of medicine, I have a well-rounded understanding of physics, my quantum knowledge is limited. But of the parts I understood, I thought they were brilliant. You're brilliant. A very talented young woman."

"Really?" Zara asked and gazed at him. Seeing only sincerity in his eyes, she smiled through her tears.

Dr. Mitchell walked toward the window and stood there for a long moment. Then he grabbed his chair and moved it closer to Zara. "You are so very young to make this choice. But I must ask you to make it. You see, I've lived my life the way I wanted. I've made my choices and am not worried about what will happen to me. Well, maybe a little. I don't think I'd enjoy prison. But I'm worried about you and somebody else, and that's why I must ask you to decide. It doesn't have to be today or tomorrow. But soon. Before your father gets impatient again. He researched the treatment for anxiety and knows how long it takes. Once he pulls you out, our paths will never cross."

"You are worried about somebody else? What do you mean? Who?"

"I can't tell you until you decide because I can't put my friend in danger if this comes out."

Zara stood up. "I will tell no one. I can keep a secret."

"I realize that. But things happen. You may say something in your dreams, or...you may be forced."

"I see," she said. When she sat back, her body felt heavier, weighed down by the realization that this was real and serious. "Tell me. I'm ready."

"There is someone who can help you in ways I can't. You'd be able to pursue your scientific dreams, but you'd be giving up your identity and motherhood. You'd be able to live your life the way you want to. Well, with certain precautions."

Zara shifted her gaze to the painting, but it provided no solace. It was just a flat painting today. Dr. Mitchell looked at the clock. "Our session is over. I'll see you next week."

Zara stood up and headed for the door, shuffling her feet.

"And Zara?"

"Yes?" she asked, turning her head.

"This is your decision, and I will respect it. Just know if you decide on this, you will not go back to your life. Literally."

"I know," she said, and snuck out the door.

"What's wrong?" Gilbert asked when he saw her leaving Mitchell's office, wrapping her robe tightly around her.

"Nothing. Fighting anxiety is hard, Daddy. I'm tired."

He grabbed her hand and squeezed it gently. "It'll be okay. You'll get through it."

9

THE SLAP

"You're quiet this evening. More than usual. Anything the matter?" Mia asked, poking her head into Zara's room. "You barely ate anything at dinner. Can I get you anything? A snack?"

"No, I'm okay. Just a little tired today," Zara said, and made room on her bed for her mother. Mia pressed her hand onto Zara's forehead. "You're a little pale, but no fever."

"I'm fine."

Zara laid her head on her mother's lap, and Mia stroked it in her usual gentle way. They stayed like that for a while—cherishing their closeness.

Until Zara asked a question she later wished she hadn't.

"Mother...have you ever wanted to do something else? Be somewhere else?"

Mia stopped stroking Zara's hair and raised her daughter's chin with a force Zara hadn't expected. Zara flinched. She's never seen her mother's eyes so full of...anger. Fury, really.

"Where is this coming from, daughter? Who'd put such a crazy idea into your head? Is it the doctor? Is the doctor feeding you such fables? Friends at school?"

Zara closed her eyes.

"Answer me!"

Zara opened her eyes. The hope that she had just imagined her mother's anger vanished upon seeing her golden eyes narrowing. "Nobody is feeding me anything, Mother. I was just curious."

"You're not to be curious. Remember that you are just a girl and soon to be a woman—a wife and a mother. You're not to be curious or desire anything else in this world except for what the System designs for you. Do you understand me?" Mia shouted the last few words, getting off the bed. Zara noticed her hands shook when she grabbed the doorknob.

"Who is the man who took my bear, then? Who is he?" Now it was Zara who was shouting. "Why don't you answer me?"

The flowers on Mia's robe blurred as she crossed the bedroom in two strides and slapped Zara's face. Zara's head twisted.

"I told you there was no man. There is no room for curiosity in your life, Zara. You must forget the meaning of that word, or you'll suffer all your life."

Zara glared at her mother. Her cheek stung, and she felt it redden and then burn. Mia gave her one last glare and slammed the door. Zara lifted her hand, which was heavy and foreign, and touched her cheek. Her beautiful, gentle, agreeable mother, who until now had only had kisses and hugs for her, slapped her. Slapped her hard.

Tears would not come. Zara lay in torpor all night; her fragmented thoughts couldn't make sense of her mother's outburst. One thought, however, buzzed in her mind and then morphed into a certainty: Her mother's anger was connected to the man who took her bear. Who was he?

But it was her fault. She'd stirred her mother's painful memories, and now she must fix it. Forget her curiosity and interest in science. Be an obedient daughter and pass the next test. Forget about the man who took her bear. She closed her eyes just before the twilight lit the night sky with its misty light.

Her mother usually poked her head into her room in the morning to make sure she was up and getting ready for school. Zara woke up and waited, glancing at the door, wishing yesterday hadn't happened. She'd alienated the person who loved her the most in the entire world. After the restless night, her stomach was rough, filled with the acid of worry and regret. What if she just stayed in bed and died of hunger? Her mother obviously would not check on her this morning. Maybe never.

What made her throw the covers off and lumber to her bathroom was the decision she needed to make. She stood in front of a mirror staring at her ashen face. "What do you want to do with your life?"

Zara entered the kitchen quietly, like a shadow. Her mother avoided eye contact, scrubbing the windows so they screeched, keeping her red and swollen eyes on them. Zara glanced in her direction and took a step forward, but seeing her mother's pursed lips and shoulders set in a straight and uninviting posture, changed her mind. She swiped the lunch bag off the kitchen counter and snuck out of the house.

It was only a fifteen-minute walk to the school. The morning breeze tousled her hair, which she'd forgotten to braid, and tugged on the corners of the day-old shirt she'd neglected to tuck inside her wrinkled plaid skirt. On any other day, she'd have been terrified by this carelessness. That day, she glanced at the flapping shirt, and instead of tucking it in, she took it out entirely, letting it flop in the wind. The breeze immediately found its way under her shirt, tickling her belly, and she giggled. The giggle morphed into full-blown laughter. She let her tears flow freely as she sat on the ground, laughing and sobbing, and watching the school building as it reflected the bright morning sun at her with its windows. By the time she reached the brown compound full of stressed teenage girls, she had made her decision.

10

ARAS

"What is he like?"

"You'll see soon enough," Dr. Mitchell said, barely glancing at her from the cockpit. He was drumming his fingers on the steering wheel. The yellow desert below them fluttered in the setting sun. The cacti and other sparse shrubs were slowly transforming into a white, glimmering expanse of nothingness.

"I don't understand why you're being so tight-lipped about it. I'm going to be living with him."

"Yes, I know, Zara. I realize you are anxious, and I can't imagine how you must feel. But trust me and have a little patience. You'll understand why I don't want to divulge the facts before you experience it with your own eyes. It's important, trust me."

"Whatever," she mumbled, working the seatbelt with her fingers. Her stomach grew tighter and her heart beat faster for the umpteenth time since leaving her parents' house with nothing but her notebooks the night before.

"You've probably wondered why we spent an entire month learning how to control anxiety instead of talking about your notebook. You must have been confused, secretly questioning whether you were really having anxiety attacks."

"Yeah."

"There was a method to my madness. There will be plenty of times when you'll experience extreme anxiety, and I wanted you to know how to cope and how to control it, letting no one realize what you're going through."

"Huh?"

"You'll understand soon. We're almost there," Dr. Mitchell said, maneuvering the plane onto the landing pad in front of a large adobe structure, flanked by monstrous flowering cacti on both sides.

"Come on, Aras is expecting us."

Zara took a small bag containing only her notebooks from the back seat and flipped it onto her shoulder. She followed Dr. Mitchell, who walked fast toward the building and then, to her surprise, used a pad next to a large metal double door to enter a code. The door opened, and he entered. Zara followed hesitantly, even though she had no other choice. She left her family home in the middle of the night, not saying goodbye to her parents, and joined Dr. Mitchell in his plane that was waiting for her in the middle of the desert.

She didn't think she could go back. Her mother was still cross with her, barely acknowledging her presence, while her father observed their interactions, shaking his head and mumbling something about women and their time. When he asked Mia why she was mad at Zara, she dismissed his questions and went about her chores, which she did with a ferocity neither Zara nor Gilbert had ever seen. No, Zara couldn't go back.

She entered the dark hallway, which led to a large room illuminated only by soft light emanating from lamps on small end tables by sofas placed artfully and strategically to create a cozy and relaxing atmosphere. All the windows were covered by blinds and curtains.

As soon as they entered, a figure shed from the window and walked toward them with an energetic stride and pointed to a lamp, which grew brighter. It must have signaled other lamps because they lit up too, and the room was soon suffused with soft light. Zara held her breath as she noticed a bearded man with bushy eyebrows and a mop of gray hair falling to his shoulders in messy locks. With his intense blue eyes behind the thick-rimmed glasses, he focused on Zara. Those eyes smiled at Zara as he greeted her with a pleasant and slightly higher voice than she'd expect from his hairy appearance. "Welcome to my home, Zara. Well, *our* home from now on."

He pointed to the sofa and chairs with an elegant gesture. On the table, centered between the sofa and chairs, stood a crystal carafe with ice water. He poured some into the glasses and waited for Zara and Doctor Mitchel to sit before he sat down.

"I'm sure Spence already told you we go way back."

Zara nodded politely, uncertain what to say. Dr. Mitchell told her practically nothing about Aras, only that he would take care of her from now on, which would include her education and inspiration, and that he was the most trustworthy person in Andalia.

"I'll be your mentor from now on," he said, taking a gulp of water. "Spence gave me your notebook. You have a lot of potential. What inspired you to write them? Have you ever read physics books?"

Zara shook her head.

"No, I didn't think so. You don't have the terminology, but your observations and ideas are…outstanding. Unbelievably insightful. I couldn't believe it when Spence told me you were only twelve years old. What an extraordinary gift you have."

Zara couldn't respond with a tight lump lodged in her throat. Could she ever dislodge this lump? This was the second time in the last month she had been told she was gifted.

"Do you want to be a scientist? A physicist?" Aras asked.

"How?" Zara replied after a pause. "I'm just a girl. I'm not allowed…"

Aras laughed, and Zara again was surprised by the high pitch of his voice.

Aras pressed his hand against his mouth to muffle his laugh. "I noticed. I'm old but not blind," Aras said, smiling and then added, winking, "So am I."

"Huh?"

Still smiling, Aras reached for his forehead, and with a quick move, pulled the messy gray mop off his head. Beneath the wig, his blond hair was slicked back and held with a band. He took the band off and tousled his shoulder-long blond hair, then he ripped his beard off. Last came off his bushy eyebrows. Zara's jaws dropped, seeing a woman in her fifties standing before her. Her blue eyes sparkled with mischief as she grinned at Zara.

Zara covered her mouth with both hands to dampen the shrill gasp that escaped her throat.

"I realize it must be a shock," Dr. Mitchell said, raising his hands. "Remember what I taught you about keeping calm when something shocks you? Breathe. Count. Breathe. You'll have to master these techniques, because in the beginning, it will seem like you're the center of attention, and you'll be hiding behind a disguise every day of your life, being a boy. It will not be easy. It will seem impossible and overwhelming, but you must play your part because your life depends on it, and Aras's."

Zara's eyes darted between him and Aras. The lump returned.

Aras touched her arm. "Hey, hey. You'll be fine. I promise. Don't let that shrink scare you. I've survived over thirty years and nobody has ever suspected anything."

"Really?"

"Yes, really," Aras said, handing her a glass of water. "Drink. You look like a ghost. You'd be surprised by how unobservant men are. They are practically blind."

"Aras will help you with everything—how to speak, how to walk like a boy. We won't throw you to the wolves immediately. Only after you've had training and are comfortable."

"I actually had fun pretending after the initial angst. You might have fun too," Aras laughed.

"I doubt it," Zara grumbled.

"Okay. I've got to get going now, but I'll see you in a few days. I'll send you a RAM," he said, which Zara knew to mean a rapid announcement message, "to let you know when I'm coming."

"Okay," Aras said, kissing Dr. Mitchell's cheek. Then she turned around to face Zara. "Hey, kiddo. You're probably starving. I know I am. But first, let me show you your room."

11

BEING A BOY

Weeks had gone by as Zara trained in how to be a boy, from when she woke up in the morning until she went to bed. She had never been so tired as she was now. She would never have suspected that pretending to be a boy could be so draining and so difficult.

"Are they a different species?" she cried out one evening after a long day of trying and failing to walk like a boy. "Why do they swear so much? And why do they have to spit and smirk all the time?" she asked Aras and slumped on the blue-green carpet and thumped her hands and feet on the floor.

"You nailed it—they are a different species," Aras said, and exploded in laughter.

Zara had grown to love this woman, whose spontaneous and very contagious laughter reverberated throughout her vast house almost constantly. Despite the age difference, they became friends immediately. Aras's affectionate attitude and sense of humor drew the girl close. She caught herself laughing along with Aras. There were those odd moments when her gaze landed on Aras's blue eyes lit with unhindered joy that she had the strange sensation she had met her before.

Aras turned out to be a tough but excellent teacher. Endowed with keen observational skills and an ability to adjust to situations, Aras told Zara that she had learned how to mimic boys's behavior in a few weeks but didn't go among them until months later. "Learning is not everything. You must practice so that it becomes second nature. I had the best teacher."

"Who? Dr. Mitchell?"

"No," she said and turned away. But before she did, Zara noticed the luster disappearing from her eyes. Aras headed for the door. "We had a long day. Time for supper."

Dr. Mitchell visited every few days, sending them a message prior to visiting through RAM and insisted on Zara calling him Spence, just like Aras did.

After observing him and Aras together, Zara realized they shared a more intimate bond than she had previously thought. Aras's blue eyes sparkled when she looked at him, and his eyes and face gained color. They both looked years younger in each other's presence.

One day, Spence came early, and while he sat surrounded by pillows on the plush sofa, Zara showed off her walking and talking like a boy. He laughed and clapped his hands.

"You are doing amazingly. Aras must be proud of you."

"Yeah. She is a great teacher. Who was her teacher?"

Spence stopped laughing and tugged on his mustache. "It's been a long time."

"Who was it? Something happened, didn't it?"

"Yes, something happened," Aras said, entering the room. Her eyebrows were scrunched as she marched to the sofa.

Zara's arms dropped. She tried to make herself smaller, realizing she had stumbled onto a painful subject.

"Oh, you might as well know. You probably should know what you're getting into. It's a dangerous world out there that you will soon be a part of."

"Come on. She's just a kid."

"No, she's not. I was only two years older when it happened to me. She should know."

"Tell her, then," he said, then rose from his chair and headed for the door.

After Spence left, Aras slumped into a chair, her face crumpling into a grimace. In that moment, she looked both older and younger—the deep grooves had aged her, but the lips curved downward and made her look like a sad girl.

"Matilda was my teacher. The best teacher one could have," Aras said. "Matilda Sterling was my teacher and my...mother. She taught me everything about pretending to be a boy, fitting into a society that I wasn't supposed to fit into, and, most importantly, giving me a love of science. Sharing with me what she knew."

Zara got up and put a glass of water into Aras's shaking hand. Aras thanked her with a tiny nod.

"She was such a good teacher, in fact, that her student felt so empowered, she became careless, reckless, stupid." Aras hung her head. "She died because of me, protecting me and taking the blame for my recklessness after I left a wig in the lab bathroom where we worked together. Those bastards murdered my mother. They hung her on a tree like a piece of garbage, and they let her stay like that, ravaged by weather, pecked by birds, slowly consumed by bugs until her flesh was gone and the bones started falling off. I did that to her. And Spence never forgave me for that. She was his mother too."

"I'm so...so...sorry," Zara whispered and on impulse reached for Aras's hand. When Aras didn't remove her hand, Zara patted it gently. "I did not realize. Forgive me for asking. I will never become reckless. I promise," she said and asked after a pause. "Nothing happened to you?"

"No, thanks to Spence. He had hidden me in plain sight. I worked in his office as his nurse. He created a fake nursing certificate and cleverly falsified my hiring date."

"And Amelia?"

Aras smiled. "Amelia would never betray Spence." Aras pressed her finger to her lips. "They have been together for a while now."

That night, right after dreaming about the woman, Zara dreamed about her mother. In her dream, the dark-haired woman pointed through her crystal prison into the distance. Zara turned her head and saw Mia smiling. Zara woke up and wept until the gray light of dawn broke through her blinds. But then she remembered her mother's eyes the evening before she'd left in Mitchell's plane—cold, unforgiving, and distant. Just one question had changed the dynamics between a loving mother and daughter. She still blamed herself for it but sensed there was also another underlying reason behind her mother's anger. And now, she might never know.

Woven between the lessons of impersonating a boy were science classes. Zara excelled in all her classes with Aras, her least favorite being botany. During physics classes, she entered a different world—her world. Every lesson, every new concept, every word, every detail Aras had shared with her, Zara inhaled with all her soul. She was in awe of the knowledge Aras possessed, but perhaps even more in awe of the unknown—the knowledge that was still out there, to be discovered...by her. With each passing day, with each new lesson, she grew more and more convinced that she had made the right decision running away and joining Aras. This was her destiny.

That was what she thought until it was time to enter the real world and start pretending. Not in front of the mirror but the entire scientific community. For the rest of her life.

12

EDMUND

Her heart pounded and her mouth was dry as she made her way from the stone steps, through a hallway full of boisterous teenage boys, and into a classroom—a huge, drafty room with wooden desks and vaulted windows with stained glass depicting famous scientists. All male, of course.

Although Aras thought Zara was ready to work with her in her laboratory, she couldn't just hire her as a research assistant; she had to navigate through proper and not-so-proper channels. First, Zara had to finish eighth grade and pass all the tests with a score of at least ninety percent. That was the proper part. The not-so-proper involved nepotism. Over the years, Aras had built her relationships in the highly partial and nepotistic scholastic world, handpicking the more agreeable and open-minded fellows to do her bidding, sometimes unknowingly. There were a few who owed her favors for helping write their papers, for which she was famous, who would make sure Zara was assigned to her lab.

Aras developed a special stain that contained tiny hair shavings and applied it to Zara's upper lip as a fake youthful shadow mustache and nearly completely shaved her long wavy hair to mask her natural beauty. Zara insisted on cutting it instead of wearing a wig, fearing that it would slide off. Afterward, Zara laughed, looking at her reflection in the mirror. "Hi, Edmund. Nice to meet you."

Under the name Edmund Stone, Zara blended in with the boys the very first day. They couldn't have suspected that her heart was pounding, her palms were sweaty, and she was a little lightheaded when she first sat at a desk with another student and responded to him in someone else's voice. For the first few minutes, her neighbor's face was blurry and his voice faint.

It wasn't long after that she started taking part in their pranks, getting into skirmishes, races, verbal fights, and wrestling matches. She discovered she was as strong, and even stronger than the boys and could outrun them. Noticing their reaction to her speed, she slowed down. As Edmund, her goal was to be mediocre, to fit in and avoid suspicion. During classes, she held her hand down on her desk to stop it from flying up and being the first one to answer teachers' questions.

The boys were transforming into young adults before her eyes. Their voices were cracking, and their arms, legs, and noses were elongating. Even with the fake mustache and bad haircut, she was a "bonnie boy"—a nickname coined by her closest circle of friends.

Zara discovered she liked the physical aspect of being a boy. Standing in front of a mirror, she admired her growing muscles. With her prowess in sports and her willingness to take part in brawls and other mischief, she soon belonged to the heart of the eighth grade's science-oriented Intermediate School of Talents. Isaac Norton, Aras's assistant, transported Edmund to school and back every day except for the weekends, when the school was out for two days. Slender and laconic, the brown-eyed Isaac never asked questions and, when asked a question, usually just said "yes" or "no," and occasionally "maybe." Zara wondered if he knew her secret. Aras said he didn't, but Zara observed him more keenly after catching his curious glances when he thought she wasn't looking.

And so, her life at school progressed with no major incidents.

Until the trip to the Museum of Flight in the town of Seneca, six hundred miles away. The trip was mandatory, but Aras and Zara tried to find excuses. Zara would have to stay at a guesthouse with her classmates for two nights.

"I can't go. They'll find out I'm a girl," Zara said.

"If you don't go, they'll question you and ask to speak to your parents. Go," Aras said, scratching her chin.

"What about..." Zara pointed to her chest.

Just after Zara had turned thirteen, her breasts had grown and bulged through her blue uniform. Binding her breasts with an elastic band added to her daily chores of hiding her identity.

Zara sighed. "How am I going to go to the bathroom?"

"You'd have to wait for the bathroom to be empty...you could bathe when others are asleep or eating."

"What if somebody walks in on me when I'm in the bathroom?"

"You don't have to use the urinals. Just use the stalls. Don't bathe. It's only two days."

"What about my breasts?"

"You're going to wear a shirt and never take it off," Aras said, nodding. "Yeah, that could work."

"Can't I pretend to be sick? I could start coughing right away."

"Not going to work, kiddo. They will require a doctor's note."

"Spence could—"

"Psychiatrists don't treat coughs, Zara," Aras said. "I can't produce reliable parents on such short notice. The fewer people who know about you, the better. You must go, but you must be careful. You can do it, kiddo."

Zara sighed. "Sure, send me into the alien's den."

The zeppelin was packed with the smells and energy of puberty, barely held from exploding by four bearded teachers (two at each end of the cigar-shaped vessel), all wearing black togas with white-and-blue lapels hanging from their stiff collars.

Edmund sat between two of his closest mates, Eric and Teo. Eric, a blond, blue-eyed, big-boned boy with a perpetual smile on his face speckled with thousands of freckles, sat by the window and exclaimed loudly each time he saw something he deemed attention-worthy. Teo, brown-eyed and dark-haired, made faces every time Eric admired something in the distance but allowed his eyes to wander toward whatever he pointed to.

Just before the Zeppelin took off, the oval door opened, and Mister Nappoli, the biology teacher, walked in with a boy in tow. "Everyone, this is Tirg. He was just transferred to our class and will join you on the trip," Mr. Nappoli said, pointing at an empty seat two rows from Zara and facing her.

The boy wearing a dark leather jacket ducked to avoid hitting his head and strode to the seat with the confidence and ease of someone much older than thirteen. He slid into the seat with equal parts poise and nonchalance. Then he scanned his classmates lazily with neither curiosity nor apprehension, as if arriving in the belly of a hot vessel full of teenage boys who already knew each other well, was something he did every day. The tiny smile dancing on his full lips froze when his gaze rested on Zara. She tensed when she saw his piercing blue eyes land on her. The surrounding air chilled and darkened. She had never seen him before, she was certain, and yet...when his eyes searched hers with a nervous impatience and boldness, they felt intimately familiar. She shivered.

A boy—Wayne Thompson, larger and more muscular than the other boys (repeating the class he failed last year), sitting next to Tirg —elbowed him. "Hey, weird name you got. Your parents couldn't spell Tiger?" he laughed, looking around the room. When nobody applauded, his eyes landed on Tirg's and immediately froze under the forceful blue gaze.

Tirg whispered something to Wayne, whose face immediately flamed, making his blond hair appear white. Tiger slowly shifted his calm gaze back to where Zara had sat, and his blue eyes flashed at the empty seat. Zara snuck out to the back of the Zeppelin, taking an empty seat in the dark corner, blurting out that she had to fart and laughing obnoxiously when Eric and Teo glanced at her.

She shoved her trembling hands into pockets and averted her gaze, struggling not to look his way. *Why are you being weird? He's just a boy you don't know. Why are you afraid of him?*

Zara sat in the corner, trying not to move, but the monotony of the smooth flight soon made her eyelids heavy. Her head slumped to the side, and she fell into a slumber, snoring lightly. Mike, the chubby boy sitting nearby, made faces making fun of Edmund's snoring.

"What's your name?" Tirg asked Edmund.

"His name is Edmund," Mike said.

"I didn't ask you, did I?" Tirg barked. "Get lost."

"What's your name?" Tirg asked again, tugging on Edmund's sleeve as he sat in the seat vacated by Mike.

"What?" Zara woke up, not remembering where she was. Seeing Tirg studying her with his piercing eyes and tugging on her sleeve, she moved her arm fiercely, freeing it from his long fingers. "What do you want?" she asked.

"I want you to tell me who you are. I know you, but I can't remember from where. Do you remember me?"

"Never seen you in my life."

"You sure?"

"Yeah, and I don't remember inviting you over to disrupt my nap. Get lost."

He didn't move. His blue eyes steeled as he glared at her, tapping his fingers on the leather of his jacket.

Zara glared back at him. "So, what's with your name? Not quite a tiger, almost a tiger, what?"

His chin moved as he gritted his teeth. "You do know me. You recognized me."

"You deaf or dumb? Not quite a tiger?" she asked, appraising him.

His tall, muscular body appeared strong, and his smooth stride reminded her of a cat getting ready to strike. But so was she—strong and agile. She tensed in her seat, clenching her teeth and glaring with her most daring look. Tirg's lips twitched, and throwing his head back, he laughed, and his laugh was as spontaneous as Aras's.

Then he stood up and brushed a strand of blond hair off his forehead. "I think you and I are going to be good friends, Edmund." He lowered his voice and added, "Tirg means tiger in my language." He left, strutting back to his seat up front, leaving Zara with her mouth open.

13

THE MUSTACHE

Zara threw her bag onto the lower bunk bed that stood in the corner of a gymnasium filled with dozens of aluminum bunk beds just like hers. Eric was already dangling his feet from above, and Teo's bag rested on another bed across from her. After the long flight and the strange and draining interaction with the new boy, she longed for a shower.

The smell of the fried potatoes seeped through the open door as Zara deliberated about her options for a bath. She inhaled the scent, trying to decide whether the sudden uneasiness in her stomach was caused by hunger or something else.

Eric jumped down. "Lunchtime!"

Meanwhile, pillows, shoes, and various pieces of clothing flew all over the room, and a couple landed on a substantial wooden table, scuffed with obscure messages and names of previous guests.

The air, stale before, now stank like a locker room after a long game. Zara fought not to gag at the bitter smell that forced itself inside her nostrils, permeating every pore of her body, and turned to throw the pillow that had landed on her head back at her attacker. When she saw who her attacker was, she sneered, grabbed the first thing her hand found—her bag—and threw it at him with a ferocity that surprised her and Eric even more so. Tirg, grinning, caught the bag in midair effortlessly. Mocking her? She noticed, frowning, that the most popular boys were crowding around the charismatic newcomer, grinning and laughing and encouraging him while glancing at him for approval.

How quickly Edmund has dropped off the popularity ladder, she thought. *All because of a foreigner with a stupid name.*

She shrugged. *I don't give a shit.*

"You okay, Ed?" Eric whispered. "Be careful; he is much bigger."

"I can beat him any day."

"You don't like him? Why?"

"What? No, I don't dislike him. I just don't give a shit! He's a dumbass!"

"Right," he mumbled. "Let's get some chow."

Teo, grimacing and wrinkling his nose, joined them at the door. "What was that all about? You know this new guy?"

"No, he is a fucking foreigner. How would I know him?" she said.

She waved her hand in the air to wipe the image of Tirg's blue eyes out of her mind while walking to lunch with Teo and Eric. Eric's nose and chest quivered like those of a bloodhound on a scent.

The smell of food, tea, and hot chocolate hung in the air of the enormous dining hall. Her mouth watered. She sat in a carved wooden chair so large her feet dangled. Teo and Eric sat beside her. As soon as his butt touched the seat, Eric shoved a steaming chunk of potato in his mouth.

She grabbed a chunk and moved it to her mouth but dropped it when she saw Tirg accompanied by three of the largest boys and also the biggest loudmouths come their way and take the four chairs directly across from her and her friends. Two boys who'd been sitting there nervously evacuated, taking their food with them. The wide table packed with napkins, utensils stuffed in tall metal containers, and condiments hid Tirg's face from Zara, but her eyes kept wandering across the table and then quickly retreating. Tirg interacted ostentatiously with his new buddies but threw glances across the table at Zara as she tried to spoon fried potatoes onto her plate, missing each time.

Teo grabbed his spoon and scooped a bunch onto Zara's plate. "What's the matter with you?"

"Nothing," Zara muttered, grabbing the hot potato from her plate and shoving it in her mouth, then turning it in her mouth to cool it off. It still burned her mouth, but she hid the distress.

"Here, have some patties," Eric said, throwing three round brown rings on her plate.

"What the hell is wrong with you, Ed? Can't you get your own food?" Sav, the boy to Tirg's right, asked.

Tirg's friends laughed. Todd, sitting on the left side of Tirg, picked up a patty and aimed it at Edmund's plate. The patty slid off the plate, hit her in the chest, and landed on her lap. She stood up and glared at Todd, then she grabbed her plate and threw it at him. The plate hit him in the chest, and the food landed on his lap.

Todd stood up and turned red. Tirg's buddies jumped up and clenched their hands into fists, ready for a fight. One picked up his full plate and aimed it at Zara. Tirg rose from his seat and intercepted the plate, grabbed a chunk of potato and threw the chunk across the table, grinning. The glob landed on her forehead, broke into pieces, and covered her dark navy uniform in greasy yellow specks. Zara stared at Tirg while everyone held their breath in anticipation.

A buzzing fly landed on the pile of potatoes and broke Zara's stare and the silence. Then, she grabbed a handful of potatoes and threw them at Tirg. Her face relaxed into a grin. Eric and Teo were already grinning and aiming handfuls at Tirg and his minions.

Soon everyone took part in the food fight, and the dining hall and all the pupils turned into a greasy mess, where brown-and-orange chunks mixed in midair and covered everything within throwing range in brownish goop. Amidst the laughter, shouting, and even some squealing.

That was how Mr. Tinburn, a chemistry teacher, found the room when he came to check on the progress of the meal, inadvertently receiving some of the food on his black robe and his bushy beard. "Stop it. Stop it right now. I command you!"

His soft shouts produced no results through the ruckus. When he turned around in a frenzy and shouted, more chunks landed on his red face and in his hair. The noise soon attracted the attention of the other teachers, and they came running into the hall with their robes flopping as they bellowed for the boys to stop.

Eventually, they ran out of food and, covered with brown goop, panting, flopped into their chairs or on the floor. The room was filled with hot breath and a steamy brown mess.

Zara's grin left her face when she realized that, in avoiding an actual fight and taking part in the food fight, she had put herself in danger. Her clothes and her hair were covered with food. She would have to bathe together with the other thirty-one boys. A bloody nose and a black eye would have been better. She scrambled to come up with a solution, but her mind was blank. She caught Tirg's curious glance and made a face at him. He didn't even blink and kept staring at her.

"What possessed you to do this, you morons?" Mr. Morre, the physics teacher, yelled. His stiff yellow beard bashed against his chest as he moved his head, bellowing, "Everyone take baths now! You've got five minutes to get yourself clean."

Zara darted to the bathroom as one of the first. She reached the first empty shower, fully clothed, and turned the knob on. The water was lukewarm, but she didn't care or show that it chilled her. It ran the length of her uniform, sloshing off the chunks of food.

"What are you doing, Ed?" Eric asked, breathing hard. "Are you crazy?"

"Well, they only gave us five minutes to clean, so that's what I'm doing."

Eric shrugged and joined her, and so did Teo after a moment of head shaking. The boys who got to the bathroom first and started taking their clothes off quickly put them back on and showered fully clothed, laughing and splashing water on the green-tiled floor and walls. The huge bathroom with long, narrow windows that nearly reached the ceiling reverberated with laughter and shouts as the boys lathered their clothes with soap and sprayed themselves with water.

"You've gone completely insane. What's gotten into you?" Mr. Tinburn shouted, standing in the doorway. His eyes bulged as he looked over the boys' soaking uniforms.

"You said five minutes. We don't have any other uniforms," Tirg said, emerging from between the group of boys.

"Oh, so it was your idea?"

"Yeah, what else were we supposed to do?" he asked, smiling. "Our uniforms are clean now."

"How are you going to walk to the museum like this? You'll make everything wet."

"We'll dry out. It'll be fine."

Mr. Tinburn threw his hands up.

The boys started heading out through the hallway, leaving soapy puddles on the tiles. Zara was wringing her clothes out with her hands when she felt a touch on her shoulder.

"Did you shave your mustache?"

She turned around quickly and saw Tirg staring at her lips with an odd expression. Her heart pounded as she fought the urge to check her face. The darn thing must have washed down the drain. She intercepted his hand. "Yeah, what's it to you? Are you jealous you don't have a mustache to shave yet?" she said and then moved past him, shoving him to the side.

"No, I just can't figure out how you did it so fast," he said, and laughed.

Zara walked away, but she didn't catch up with her friends. Holding her hands to her chest, she walked ahead, hearing the echo of his feet behind her. Did he suspect anything? Since he'd gotten on the zeppelin, he'd been watching her constantly. She deliberated, deciding whether to follow the plan she and Aras had come up with in case something had gone wrong or to continue as if nothing had happened. Zara had the RAM in her bag, and it wouldn't take long for Isaac to come to her rescue after she messaged him.

She weighed her options. If she called Isaac, she'd lose all the progress she'd made fitting into the male world and being able to do research with Aras. But if he really suspected her, she could end up in prison. His footsteps behind her reverberated in her brain as she hesitated.

As if he had guessed what she was thinking, Tirg breathed behind her. "No worries. Your secret is safe with me, Edmund."

Zara spun around. "What secret are you talking about? Is it still about the mustache? Get over it."

"I mean no harm. I want to be your friend," Tirg said, smiling. He extended his hand. His blue eyes sparkled.

His eyes were pulling her in. She fought it and narrowed her eyes.

"Really. I like you. Come on, let's go," he said, punching her in the arm and then grabbing and pulling on her arm to come with him.

Zara followed, questioning why her feet had stopped obeying her and carried her alongside him, and she questioned the sudden need to want to believe him. *Is it because he said he liked me?* From her arm, where his hand clutched it, a tingling sensation spread to her stomach.

Eric turned around, and, seeing Edmund with Tirg, he elbowed Teo and whispered something in his ear.

Teo shrugged. "Whatever. He seems okay," he added, looking at Tirg.

Tirg, followed by his three buddies, kept close to Zara and her friends in the flight museum. The curator grumbled, shaking his head in disapproval at the wet footprints on the concrete floor. Their guide was a tall man with a big red mustache that emphasized his long face, and he wore a funny red hat that sat crookedly on his large head and moved haphazardly every time he said something.

"Will you be attending our classes?" Zara asked Tirg.

"Yup. For a while," Tirg said and, seeing the question in her eyes, continued. "My father travels a lot."

"You said before that Tirg means 'tiger' in your language. What language is that? Where did you come from?"

Tirg stopped walking and hesitated. She waited, watching him lose his cool for a moment.

"That's okay. You don't have to tell me," Zara said quickly.

"I will. Later, when others can't hear. My father is a...diplomat, and I'm not supposed to talk about it."

"Well, then don't."

"I will. Later. When we're alone."

"Whatever," she said, and took one quick step forward to catch up with Eric and Teo, but Tirg's words and the way he said them echoed in her mind and slowed her steps. When *we're alone—not* if *we're alone*. He sounded so sure of himself, yet there was no threat in his voice, only a plea. Her stomach reacted to the word "when" and the urgency in his voice, fluttering as if it were a feather. She had to look at him. She inhaled, spun around, but he was gone. Vanished. Her mind felt as if a chilly breeze went through it as her eyes searched for him but did not find him. She exhaled and caught up with Teo and Eric.

"What was that all about? Are you his new friend now?" Teo asked.

"No. Just being polite. Let's go."

Throughout the rest of the afternoon and evening, the group of wet boys and the four teachers admired the exhibition of old air balloons. Zeppelins of all sizes, shapes, and colors, and older and newer planes. Zara marveled at the flying contraptions as she glanced around the room. Tirg was nowhere to be seen. In one moment, she imagined him talking to the head of the school, telling him he suspected Edmund of being a girl. In another, she remembered his eyes, and the certainty that they were not deceitful loosened the knot in her stomach. His eyes were mischievous, full of life and curiosity, but never mean.

She strained her neck, searching for Tirg's blond hair among the bobbing heads in the big room that served as the bedroom for all the boys. His three friends were getting their beds ready for the night. Everywhere she looked, her mates were taking their still-wet clothes and hanging them on their bunks. They still had some shouts and laughter left to give, but the excitement was dying down. One boy yawned, and the evening was over. After wandering through the giant museum for hours and after the donuts they wolfed down after dinner, they had little energy left.

Zara rearranged the blankets on her bed, took off her wet uniform and jumped into bed wearing damp shorts and a T-shirt. In bed, under the cover of her blanket, she checked the wrap on her chest. It was still there, but the wet band was rearranged and misshapen. She'd have to get up in the middle of the night and fix it. Eric climbed onto his bed and rolled over a few times, complaining that he was still hungry, stirring up dust. The white specks danced before her eyes, and she fell asleep soon after, counting them.

Ping! The sound woke her up. For a moment, she was disoriented, not remembering that she was among thirty-some boys.

Ping! Eric turned over in his sleep. She remembered she had to fix her breast band, and she quietly rolled out of her bed and tiptoed to the bathroom. In the stall, she rearranged her band and, satisfied, washed her hands while staring at herself in the mirror. A stranger looked back at her. Her face was tense, and she looked older. Her lips appeared redder, fuller, and her eyes appeared larger than normal, shining strangely under the murky light above the mirror. She splashed water on her head and started back toward her bed.

She slowed down, seeing a figure at the far end just before the entryway to the room where all the boys slept. The figure walked slowly toward her. Zara recognized his unhurried, poised stride. He kept his hands in his pockets and held his gaze on her. When he was near, she saw his eyes had the same mysterious glow as hers. His lips were curved in a smile that betrayed shyness—a trait she hadn't thought he possessed. She kept walking toward him; her pace slowed down even more. They both stopped walking when they were a few feet from each other and stood silently, motionless. Zara forgot to breathe, staring into his eyes. The way he looked at her lips made her dizzy, but instead of turning away, her eyes landed on his lips.

Lights flickered, and Zara inhaled and shivered from the chilly air of the unheated hallway and from the way he looked at her. Her bare legs and arms were soon covered with goosebumps.

He smiled and whispered, "I've found you. I was going to tell you about myself and where I come from. Come on. I found a place we can talk without being overheard."

Tirg pointed the way with his eyes. "There's a small staircase at the end of this hallway."

Zara's legs followed him, though her brain was telling her not to. He walked first but kept glancing back, making sure she was behind him. He disappeared on the small, dark staircase.

"Come on. You're not scared, are you?"

"Why would I be scared?"

"Kidding. I know you're brave." His voice sounded sincere and soft in the darkness.

Zara shivered again.

After a few minutes of climbing the steep, narrow stairs, Tirg opened a wooden door and grinned back at her.

She gasped at the sight. They were on the flat roof, where the night dazzled them with millions of stars. He walked forward and stopped just before an intricate wrought-iron balustrade. She joined him and gasped again, seeing the lights of the city spread below her.

Tirg was grinning. "See? It's a cool place, isn't it? I found it earlier today and sat here for a long time," he said and glanced at her. "You're shivering. Here, take my jacket. I'm not cold." Tirg took his jacket off and handed it to Zara.

"No, thanks. I'm fine."

"Hey, don't bite my head off," he said and chuckled.

It occurred to her he might be gay and attracted to Edmund. She felt her face redden and was glad for the cover of the night. Zara had known nothing about attraction between boys and girls, women and men, or people of the same gender. She had no brothers and had never been around boys. She'd had little knowledge of boys before she'd had to become one. Occupied with fitting in and spending every second on alert, trying not to make the wrong move or to say something that might sound weak or feminine, she'd never imagined herself as the object of their attraction. Or being attracted to them. Looking at his profile, she noticed his lips appeared soft and had an appealing curve, and she felt a sharp pang in her chest, and she realized it was resentment that he was attracted to Edmund, not her.

Zara gripped the balustrade and looked down. The streets were abandoned. A black cat wandered down the street, meowing mournfully, and in that moment, she wanted to jump down and join it.

Tirg wrapped his hands around the black iron too and swung his head low. "It's a cool place."

She nodded.

"You okay?"

"I'm fine. Yes, this is nice."

They stood in silence for a few minutes. Zara didn't understand what was happening to her and her body. It was as if his arms were magnets. She gripped the iron tighter.

"I wasn't making it up when I said that you look familiar. When I first saw you, it was as if I were seeing my mother or my sister. That type of familiar. I realize how it sounds, but here it is. And the more I look at you, the more familiar you look. Do you know what I mean?"

"Yeah," she said meekly, struggling to maintain her low, boyish voice. "I do. I don't understand it, but I know what you mean."

"I thought about it while I sat here, and then I remembered where I had seen your face. It was on one of the old paintings in my grandpa's castle. But that was a woman in that painting. A young, beautiful woman—"

"That's dumb. There are no paintings of people. Nobody paints people. You're making shit up. I've never heard of anything so stupid."

"What do you mean? Of course, there are paintings of people. What else would they be?"

"Landscapes. Only landscapes. Duh. You know, the Quiet Art?"

"I don't know what that is, but it's hard for me to believe you don't have paintings of people," he said, then looked down again and became quiet. Then, after a long pause, averting his gaze, he continued, "Where I come from, there are lots of paintings of people ..."

"Where do you come from?"

"Sinturija. Across the ocean."

"No way."

"I told you my father is a diplomat. He's on a mission in Andalia to exchange hostages. War prisoners, I think," he said and glanced at her. "You are the only one who knows. Now you know my secret, Edmund."

"Oh," she muttered and couldn't think of anything more to say. Visitors from Sinturija were uncommon, and some kids even considered them mythical creatures taller than buildings, but she didn't believe those stories. "Did you say 'war prisoners'? The last war was over two hundred years ago. Nobody lives that long."

"Yeah. I know. That's what I've overheard—there was a woman prisoner that my father wanted to get out of Andalia and back home. There could be a secret war..."

"A secret war?" she smiled. "That's silly."

"No, it's not. Like spy wars."

They talked until the stars grew fainter, replaced by the graying of the sky just before dawn. Zara shuffled back to the common bedroom and slipped into her bed, relieved to hear Eric snoring and Teo moaning in his sleep. She lay awake until the bell rang, thinking about the painting, Tirg's lips, the war prisoner, and the unspoken question that hung in the air between them. If there'd been any trace of distrust for him remaining, it had now been pushed deep into the furthest part of her brain. She couldn't wait to get up and look into his eyes.

They spent the next day at the Museum of Natural History, looking at the bizarre old animal bones towering over people. Some hanging from the ceiling, some lurking in dark corners, seeming to suddenly appear bearing their long teeth and reaching out with their talons. She walked around the immense rooms feeling strangely light, staring absentmindedly at the skeletons while her mind wandered to last night, remembering Tirg's smile and the way he looked at her. Today, his blond head, surrounded by the various colors and textures of his buddies' hair, moved ahead of her. The laughter and the surrounding conversations sounded subdued, as if they were filtered through thick fabric. Not once did he glance at her, and her heart grew heavier.

"You okay, Ed?" Eric asked.

"Yes, fine. Why?"

"Cause you look weird. Pale and stuff."

"I'm fine. Quit bugging me."

"Aren't you in a foul mood," Teo said, and punched Edmund in the arm.

14

HE IS GONE

Tirg attended the same classes as Zara. His popularity grew even more as the boys were attracted to his nonchalant personality. There were always boys surrounding him. Even the teachers couldn't escape his charisma and treated him with veneration as if he were the important diplomat, not his father. Zara observed him secretly, and as time passed, she no longer thought he suspected her. But as time went on and he did not even try to talk to her, she grew irritable and sullen, withdrawing from daily mischief with her friends. Eric stayed by her side and, holding his round pink finger to his chin, cracked joke after joke, but his friend not once acknowledged him.

Back at home, Aras noticed Zara's sudden petulance and bombarded her with questions. Zara shrugged, claiming she was tired. Spence couldn't get anything out of her either.

"Is everything okay at school?" Aras kept asking. "Did something happen?"

Zara kept shaking her head. "Everything is fine. Nobody suspects anything."

"You have only two months left before you're in my lab. I have everything ready and some exciting things to show you."

Four weeks before the end of the school year, Tirg bumped into her in the hallway.

"Hey," she yelled at him, but he ignored her.

She stared after him, squelching the urge to call out to him.

When she sat in her seat, she found a carefully folded note in her pocket.

"What's that?" Eric asked.

"To-do list. Things I've got to refresh before the final exams."

"Refresh? You? You don't need to refresh a thing. You always know everything."

"Don't be ridiculous."

Zara's slender fingers lumbered, unfolding the corners of the thin paper in the bathroom stall. Her hands couldn't shake more.

"Skip the geometry class and meet me at this location," the scribbles on the note said. Below the note, there was a hand-drawn map with directions to an "x" marking the spot of their rendezvous. She pressed her hand to her pounding heart. She counted the buttons on her uniform and let fate decide for her. *Go, not go? Go or not?* She knew exactly the number of buttons on her uniform, and that it was an odd number. The answer was always "go" if she started with "go," and she could not bring herself to start with "not go" or count something else.

"It's stupid. Of course I won't go," she whispered.

Just before geometry class, she darted to the bathroom and after a few minutes, her legs carried her to the meeting location, which turned out to be an abandoned shack, hidden from view by overgrown cacti and dried-out shrubbery.

He was waiting for her, sitting on a splintered wooden box, and jumped up when he saw her, grinning with a peculiar mixture of shyness and cockiness.

"Hi, Edmund."

"Hi," she said, and coughed, trying to make her voice sound more manly.

"Haven't seen you for a while."

"You are so popular..." she trailed off, and she admonished herself for sounding resentful.

"I have something to tell you," he said. A shadow landed on his face, obscuring his grin. "I'm leaving soon. My father's done what he intended, and we are going back home."

"Oh," she said. She slumped onto a wooden box and stared at her hands like she used to. "So, they freed the war prisoner? That woman?"

"Yeah," Tirg said, and cleared his throat. "Is there anything you want to tell me before I leave? You know my secret. I trusted you."

She slowly looked up at him and searched his eyes. She was about to tell him everything, then her promise to Aras along with the image of her friend's bones with chunks of flopping flesh hanging from a tree flashed before her eyes. Her own words echoed in her mind. "*I will never behave recklessly. I promise.*"

Zara closed her eyes and felt tears building behind her eyelids.

"It's okay if you don't. Really. I just want to be sure you'll be okay while I'm gone," he said and sat across from her. "Edmund. I will see you again. Maybe then you'll trust me."

"How? You live so far away. It's impossible." Her voice rose, but she didn't care.

"I'll find a way. I'll be back someday, on my own," he said, and reached hesitantly to touch her hand.

She shuddered but didn't remove her hand. Tirg took it and wrapped his hands around it. "I never told this to anyone. When I was a child, my great-grandmother called for me when the time came. When I sat by her bed, she grabbed my hand with a strength I didn't expect a dying old woman to have and said that I shouldn't be afraid of my fate. That one day I'd meet a girl in a faraway land who would become my destiny, and I hers. She said I would recognize her."

Zara felt the blood rush out of her face and coldness replace it and spread over her body. She stared at her hands nestled in his, wondering why they were still pink and not frosted over.

"I recognized her. She was hiding, but I found her, and now that I know who she is, I'll be back for her."

"I don't understand what you're saying," she whispered. "Who is she?"

"You know."

She rose from the box, aware but not caring that her voice quivered. "I must go back."

"I will be back for you. I promise."

He didn't follow her when she ran back, weeping. First tiny cries, then sobs, and finally her chest exploded in spasms. She hid in a depression in the ground and sat with her back against the earthen wall, hidden from view, considering staying in this hole until she shriveled and died.

That night, she screamed. Her throat and lungs hurt when she finally awoke from her nightmare. Aras stood at the foot of her bed, wide-eyed. "What's wrong, Zara? What happened?" She asked with a voice raspy from shouting at Zara to wake up.

Zara sat up in her bed. Tears streamed down her pale cheeks as she drew tiny breaths, extending her hands with her slender fingers now curved like claws.

"You had one of your nightmares, didn't you?" Aras asked. She walked to the nightstand and turned the light on and then sat beside her on the bed with its headboard carved into crescent moons.

Aras touched her hand. Zara twitched and shifted away from her hand, exposing her throat. Aras reached for Zara's neck. "What's this? Who did this to you?"

"Did what? What is it?"

"Red scratches on your neck. They look deep."

"I probably scratched myself in my sleep."

"Do you want to talk about it, or should I call Spence?"

"No, I'm okay. It was just a dream. I don't want to wake him up."

"You haven't had those in a while."

The next evening when Zara returned from school, Spence was waiting for her, tapping his fingers on the chair and tugging on his mustache. She sighed. Tirg was gone. The thought of talking about and reliving it made her stomach churn. She barely made it through the school day. The surrounding conversations melted into a meaningless, distant noise when she heard Mr. Tinburn announce this morning that Tirg would no longer attend the Academy for family reasons. And just like that, her hopes of being in the same building as him vanished. She had to pretend she didn't care while all she wanted was to hide in a dark corner and cry. In her pretense of not caring, she got into a scuffle with two boys and ended up with a bloody nose while gifting her two opponents black eyes in return. For a moment, she was better.

Zara had no explanation and no name for this sudden illness that made her want to weep and sigh or pound her fists into random objects. She'd never been as miserable as she was today. Not even when her mother had slapped her and pretended her daughter no longer existed.

"Hi, Zara. Let's have a little chat," Dr. Mitchell said, patting the chair next to him.

She sighed but obeyed and slumped into a chair beside him.

Aras brought them a pitcher clanking with ice cubes and glasses. She then promptly disappeared.

"Aras told me you haven't been yourself lately. And that your nightmares returned."

"Nightmare. Just one in the seven months I've been here."

"Aras said you were screaming your head off, and that you had even gouged your neck during your dream."

"No, it's not that bad. I'm okay."

"Do you want to tell me about your dream?"

Zara wavered. "Same old dream. The screaming woman."

Doctor Mitchel observed her while smoothing his mustache.

She knew him well enough to know that he didn't believe her. "Fine," she said, picking at her fingernails. "She broke through."

"Through the glass wall?"

Zara nodded. Still picking at her fingernails.

"Then what happened?"

"After the capsule shattered into a gazillion pieces, she left. She screamed at me, laughed at me, scratched me, and then just left."

"Did she say anything?"

Zara didn't respond.

Spence pointed at the tips of her bloodied fingers. "Is that your new favorite pastime now?"

She slipped her hands under her. "She said I freed her. That she was free because of me and that she'll come for me when the time comes."

"Do you know what she meant by that?"

"No! Of course not. And it was just a dream. I'm tired. I just want to go to bed. Can we talk about it at some other time? Please."

"Okay, but we still ought to talk about it. It's important."

"Thanks," Zara said and dashed to her room, where she collapsed on her bed, pressed her face into the pillow and wept. Cursing Tirg for leaving. Cursing herself for missing him.

Aras sat across from Spence. "She's hiding something. Something happened at school. I'm certain of it. Ever since she came back from the museum trip, she's been different. Silent, withdrawn, sighing all the time. But she keeps saying that everything is okay. I've not heard any rumors of anyone suspecting anything. I'm racking my brain trying to figure out what's going on with her."

"Nothing new at the Academy? No new study subjects? How about students? Have there been any changes to the students or to the staff?"

"I'm not sure, but I can ask Isaac."

"Do that. Something changed or happened at school that has upset her. We need to know. Not only for her sake," Spence said and lingered on her eyes.

A week later, Zara came home to Spence and Aras waiting for her in the living room. Aras was pacing, and Spence was cleaning his already-clean glasses.

"We need to talk," Aras said, and waved Zara in.

Zara's heart raced. "About what?"

"Sit with us."

Zara sat on the edge of the sofa and, like a cornered animal, shifted her gaze between Spence, Aras, and the hallway. She hadn't felt this way since she'd left her home. Something was in the air. She was about to be scolded.

"I've heard there was a new boy in your school and that he has gone back home," Aras said.

"Huh?"

"Coincidentally, the day you came home so upset was the day the boy left."

"So?" Zara studied her hands and started picking at her fingernails but stopped herself, sensing Aras's stare. She hadn't perfected lying yet. "I'm just tired of pretending I'm a boy all the time. It's hard. You should know."

"I do. But Spence and I are here for you. If pretending has gotten so hard it makes you cry, we need to talk about it and do something about it."

"I'm fine now. The school year is almost over. I'll be fine."

"Are you sure your crying wasn't about the boy who left? Tirg was his name?" Spence asked.

When she heard his name, Zara's face turned scarlet and her body stiffened.

"What's wrong?" Aras asked and moved to Zara's side and stroked her arm. "It's okay, kiddo. It's going to be okay."

Aras exchanged a knowing glance with Spence, after which he rose and left. Zara tilted into Aras's arms and sobbed for a long time. Aras didn't ask questions—just held her, let her cry, and gently stroked her head. For a moment, Zara imagined she was in her mother's arms and cried even harder. But eventually her sobs subsided.

Aras took her chin in her hand and looked into her reddened eyes. "You had a crush on a boy. It happens sometimes. To some people before the System marries them to strangers. But he's gone now, and you're safe. Does he realize you are a girl?"

"No," she said, and buried her face in her hands.

"Did he feel the same way about you?"

"I don't know what a crush is, but when he looked at me, I couldn't breathe, and yet I didn't want him to stop."

"And he thought you were a boy."

"Yes." Zara was glad Aras couldn't see her eyes. They would have betrayed her, because deep down, she knew Tirg saw through her.

"It will get better."

"What?"

"The ache. It will dull over time."

15

THE GOLD SUBSTANCE

The school year ended, and Zara stepped into Aras's laboratory for the first time and was awestruck. She felt an overwhelming sensation that she had reached a familiar environment—almost like returning home from a long trip. Swept into intense physics studies with Aras, she lacked time or energy to think of anything else but quarks, gluons, axions, and black holes. She collapsed into bed every night, exhausted but filled with wonder, excitement, and anticipation of amazing discoveries to come. The ache of missing Tirg lingered deep in her chest. His last words—his promise to return—she chanted them every night before bed, like a prayer.

Every day, Aras dumped a pile of papers and books on Zara's desk in a corner of the break room, then disappeared into her lab. Zara had barely seen her in the last two weeks. Aras was busy working on a secret project that Zara suspected involved the box that had been delivered a couple of weeks ago by several government agents in a military zeppelin that landed right in front of the lab, damaging a few cacti with its downwash.

Zara inhaled the reading materials, longing to engage in the research with Aras. But she had to be knowledgeable enough not to raise suspicions from other lab employees, who'd been hired by Aras solely based on their scientific knowledge and research prowess.

So, she read and read. Sometimes, the more she read, the less she thought she understood, but other times, everything seemed to fit into place, strengthening and validating her own ideas.

Weeks passed, and she still read. One evening, just before it was time to head home, Aras came running through the door, shouting and waving her arms frantically. "Come with me. I've got something to show you."

Zara knocked over the stack of papers, scattering them across the floor. She bent down to pick them up, but Aras stopped her. "You can do that later. Let's go."

Zara followed Aras, surprised at her speed while navigating the narrow, bendy hallway between the two parts of the lab. Metal doors lined the hallway on both sides, leading to rooms where they kept their supplies and additional equipment.

Aras pointed at the seat by the monstrous electron microscope, which took a prominent place in the lab that was equipped floor-to-ceiling with instruments, screens, and in the middle, a bench with more equipment. Zara inhaled the slightly metallic scent that hung in the air. The place had emptied a while back when the staff had gone home for the day.

Zara sat by the microscope, touched its metal knobs with trembling fingers, and looked up at Aras. "What am I looking at?"

"Just look at the slide and tell me what you see. The first thing that pops into your mind. Just guess."

Zara looked through the lens and saw a round, cell-like shape containing a golden kernel resembling a seashell folding and unfolding, changing its form.

"A golden seashell? What is this thing?"

Aras clasped her hands. "Is that what you thought? A golden seashell?"

"Yeah …"

Aras's hands flopped to her side, and she slumped in a chair by Zara. "I honestly don't know what it is. I've seen nothing like this before. This is just a tiny slice of it. When whole, it looks like metal. Like gold."

"Where did it come from?"

Aras hesitated.

"Is that what the government men brought in?" Zara asked.

Aras nodded.

"Where did it come from?"

Aras sighed. "Promise me this will never leave the walls of this lab."

"Of course not. Who would I tell anyway? I don't know anyone."

Aras inhaled. "This box was found in an ancient tomb on the very western tip of Andalia. On the Ghost Island."

Zara rubbed her forehead. "Is that where the supposed dark gods originated?"

"Same one."

"Whose tomb was it?"

"They didn't say. They just brought the box with a chunk of this gold substance and asked to analyze it and describe its properties. I signed a document that I wouldn't discuss it with anyone or take it out of this lab. I was afraid that they would make me sign it with my blood—they were so uptight about it."

"So you don't know what else was in that tomb? Have you read about it in the news?"

"Nope. I searched and searched and even called my colleague, an archeologist in western Andalia. I didn't ask him, but I remember how he likes to boast about his discoveries and taunt me with his success, and he said nothing about a discovery on Ghost Island. If he'd discovered it, he would've told me about it, and if he knew of someone else discovering it, he would have told me that too."

"Why would the government be involved in an archeological discovery? Is that normal?"

"I doubt it," she said, and scratched her head so vigorously that her wig shifted to one side. "I've been wondering about that, and the only thing I can think of is there must have been something in that tomb that got the attention of the bureau," she said, then suddenly jumped up. "I have a book about Ghost Island somewhere in my library. It was written by my friend Martin Brandon years back. Let's go back and look."

"Okay," Zara slid off her chair, and her stomach rumbled.

"Oh, my," Aras exclaimed, glancing at her watch. "It's late. You must be starving. Let me put that back in the safe, and we'll go home and have some food."

After a hasty meal of some leftover sweet potatoes and beans, Aras found the book on the top shelf of her library. Every inch of the large space was filled with bookcases crammed with books of all sizes. Aras maintained she had a system of keeping track of all the books, but Zara doubted it as Aras bombed at her attempt to explain her system.

They sat on the carpet in the middle of the room and read the pages together, tracing the paragraphs that interested them with their fingers.

"The dark gods were blamed for natural disasters, famine, plagues, and thunder," Aras read aloud. "Hebordes was the first dark god...his origins unknown. Spun his children out of his dark soul like a dark spider casting his treacherous web. The dutiful son was first, then came the bleak son, and last emerged the malevolent daughter, Azaria."

Zara pressed her finger to a spot on the page. "It says here that the dark gods were associated with several sun gods. They hunted... this must be a mistake. They hunted people together? The fiery-arrow-shooting Hepara and thunder-creating Hyrod, along with Azaria, massacred entire villages with fiery arrows and golden thunder," Zara said, and glanced at Aras, whose eyes shone. "You're not thinking this ancient story is connected to the golden substance?"

"It's been weeks, and I still haven't figured out what it is. It interacts with nothing else. I've tried everything I could think of. I'm stumped, and time is running out."

"Time? What do you mean?"

"They gave me a month to figure it out. If I don't succeed, they will take it away and have the Academy of Physics in Darwold examine it."

"Oh, no! Your nemesis, Dr. Sentrel?"

"Yup. And if he figures it out, I'll never hear the end of it. That asshole will make fun of me in the scientific world. Getting funding will be harder. This idiot has connections high-up."

"We'll figure it out," Zara said, and placed her hand on Aras's hand.

Aras smiled and ruffled Zara's hair. "With your help."

"Does it mean I'm allowed in the lab now?"

"Yes, kiddo. You got promoted," she said and giggled.

Zara wondered what had caused such a feud between two brilliant scientists who couldn't say each other's names without hateful comments and malicious grins?

They finished the book in the wee hours of the morning when their stiff backs finally rebelled, demanding rest, and not finding any more information about the golden substance, they shuffled to their bedrooms.

Zara fell asleep dreaming of the golden and dark gods raining arrows and boulders down on the world. It was afternoon when she finally awoke, covered in sweat. There was something in the dream that made her heart flutter, but for the first time in her life, she couldn't remember her dream. She vaguely remembered the dark shape reaching for her, but the more she tried to remember, the hazier it got.

Zara joined Aras in the lab. After a brief introduction to the fellow assistants, Zara delved into work alongside Aras. They tried every material and every type of radiation, but the gold substance was not interacting with anything. Aras's distress showed on her face despite the bushy beard and in her chaotic and careless movements when performing simple tasks. Vials, tubes, and glasses clanked and broke, crashing on the unforgiving stone as Aras strode through the lab with the corner of her robe flopping to the sides.

Assistants hunkered down and stopped offering suggestions and tried to make themselves scarce. Zara didn't pay attention to Aras. She sat holding the pen in her hand and an open notebook with a blank page, looking out the window, watching the wind bend the branches of the few scraggly bushes. A black bird flew by. Zara snapped out of her thoughts and started scribbling something quickly on the pad. After she covered the page with tight scribbles, she searched for Aras. She found her sitting on the break room floor, hiding her head in her hands and staring at the table as if there was something in its glossy whiteness speaking to her.

"Here you are," Zara said. "I have a theory. It might be totally stupid, but I think we should try as we have exhausted all other ideas. Do you want to see?"

"Huh?" Aras looked up at Zara with a face bearing two red marks where her hand had been.

"I have a theory," Zara repeated. She settled beside Aras, placing the notebook in her listless hands.

Aras glanced at her, with eyes surrounded by new wrinkles, and then, nudged by her young friend, started reading. As she read, her back straightened, and her eyes grew sharp and full of life again.

"My little genius. You are brilliant. Let's test it, shall we?" she said, rising and groaning as her knees popped.

"Do we have a strong enough centrifuge?"

"Downstairs."

Aras practically ran to the safe where they'd been keeping the samples, shouting instructions to Zara. On her way, she yelled at her senior assistant, Marcus, to join her downstairs in the accelerator lab. That's where they had kept their giant centrifuges and particle accelerators, the latest, most powerful one having been finished a few months ago. Marcus, a man in his late thirties, sporting a droopy mustache emphasizing his sorrowful face, too long for his short body, ran after his boss without a word. Zara was on his heels.

Once they had reached the basement, Marcus turned toward Zara and asked, "What's happening?"

"We have a new approach for interacting with the gold substance."

"Oh? What is it?"

"We'll expose it to a high gravitational field to see if it interacts with it."

They found Aras by a lit panel manipulating electronic buttons, knobs, and levers. Like a giant conveyor belt, the metal tube stretching far into the distance was entrenched in the cement floor of the long and narrow room, drowning in a tangled web of tubes and wires sticking out of tightly packed metal cylinders. Zara's jaw dropped as she stood tracing the wires. As Aras adjusted the controls, the screens above the conveyor belt lit and the giant metal monster started waking up, clanking, whining, and whooshing while its steel core trembled. The wires jerked and came to life like a nest of disturbed spiders.

Marcus approached Aras, handing her an electronic gadget, which she promptly attached to the back of a cylinder. Immediately, the small room filled with a massive hissing sound, the smell of heated wires, and flashing light throughout the tube and some smaller tubes on its top. Zara's heart pounded.

"Do we have permission from the president?" Marcus asked Aras.

Aras pinched her lips and glanced at Marcus, who pursed his lips and turned his head away. She then asked him to hand her the remote. He shook his head, grabbed the remote, and dropped it in Aras's lap. She glanced at him. "We are only using the centrifuge part of the accelerator to create a gravitational field, so we don't need permission," Aras explained to Marcus in a much gentler tone.

He waved his hands, accepting the explanation, but his lips were still pursed.

When she was done attaching the instrument, she looked at Zara expectantly. "Come on. Hand me the sample."

"Is it safe?" Zara whispered.

"We'll see," Aras laughed, with feverishly glinting eyes.

She placed the sample in the receiver and latched the door, then she drew a breath before pressing the button on the electronic panel above.

"Okay, kids. Let's go to the monitoring room," she exhaled.

On the giant monitor spanning the entire wall of the neighboring smallish room, they observed the pathway, and when a sudden bump appeared within the steady red line, Aras's face went pale. "Oh, my God. It's working. It reacted to gravity. Edmund, my boy, you indeed are a genius."

Aras embraced Zara in a tender hug, forgetting Marcus was there. Zara whispered in her ear, and Aras let go, smacking her on the back.

Marcus didn't appear to notice, staring at the screen and rubbing his chin.

Zara stared at the monitor, lost in thought and seemingly unenthralled by the results. Aras raised her eyebrows and bumped Zara's elbow with hers.

"That still doesn't tell us much. It's like dark matter. Only interacts with gravity," Zara said.

"That's huge," Aras said. She glanced at Zara, whose eyes were glazed over. "What's on your mind, Edmund?"

Zara fidgeted and glanced toward Marcus with her eyes.

"Okay," Aras said, stretching. "We've made progress today, so let's end it. Tomorrow, we'll continue. Great work, everyone."

"You want to tell me what that was all about?" Aras asked on the way back to the house. Zara was quiet, watching the cacti go by as Aras drove. She nodded but didn't answer.

"Zara?"

Zara sighed. "I'll tell you, but don't laugh."

"Laugh? Why would I laugh? Your idea was brilliant, and it worked. I'm sure—"

"I want to condense dark matter to see if it will interact with the gold substance," Zara blurted.

Aras laughed. Tears streamed down her cheeks. After a few moments of not hearing anything from Zara, she looked at her. "You are serious, aren't you?"

"We have everything we need." Zara whispered. The nanothermal chamber, the optical tweezers, and the paracentrifuge. Her eyes directed toward the window grew large. Her mind buzzed with a concept, which had formed a while ago and was now becoming clear in her mind.

Aras slammed on the brakes and stopped the car. She banged on the steering wheel in excitement, then paused and glanced at Zara. "It may work, but why? Why do you think condensed dark matter would interact with the gold matter?"

"The dark gods and golden gods," Zara mumbled. "I realize it sounds dumb...naïve..."

"No, no. That's all we've got. Besides, creating condensed dark matter would be so much fun. Maybe I'd rub his nose in it eventually," Aras said, and grinned.

"What happened between the two of you?" Zara asked.

"He's just a male chauvinist. He thinks he is the best scientist, the smartest man on the planet. Despicable human being," Aras said, and set her jaw, ending the conversation.

"Happy Birthday!" Aras bellowed, seeing Zara entering the kitchen for breakfast and morning tea.

"Oh, I completely forgot," Zara said through a lump in her throat. Aras, despite worrying about the golden substance, the potential funding cuts, and the president (of the Ministry of Science) breathing down her neck, still remembered her birthday.

"Here, have a cupcake. I didn't have time to bake you a cake, but I'll make it up to you this weekend. Spence is coming over, and we'll have a party!"

Zara blew out the two tiny candles that displayed the number fourteen.

"Did you wish for something?"

Zara nodded and looked away. Aras didn't pry and tiptoed to the kitchen to prepare breakfast.

Zara bit into the crispy cupcake, which smelled of lemon and honey, releasing its complex, nutty, and fruity flavor that exploded slowly in her mouth. The pang in her chest reminded her she was celebrating her second birthday since she had left home. She missed her parents. Even her father. A memory of him carrying her and soothing her in a gentle voice when she hurt her leg flashed in her mind. Her lower lip trembled as she fought tears.

Aras and Zara, with the help of Marcus, made preparations for their upcoming experiment. Aras kept the team small because experimenting with dark matter was not recognized as proper science. Some scientists even disputed its existence.

Aras was excited; her blue eyes shone while she kept murmuring under her breath and grinning, but Zara's face was tense and her eyes narrowed in focus. This was the moment she had dreamed of since her fascination with the most elusive matter in the universe had started when she read about it in the magazine Aras dumped on her desk when she first got to the lab. Now that her dream was about to materialize, doubts crept in. She was just a fourteen-year-old girl. Her ideas and calculations must be flawed, childish, dumb.

Marcus plugged numbers into the electronic section of an enormous glass tube, carrying supplies and equipment to the room containing the nanothermal chamber and the paracentrifuge while Aras was checking Zara's calculation, chewing on the end of the pen. Zara stood by, watching her, furrowing her brow, and keeping her hands in the pockets of her blue robe that was dotted with yellow stars.

Aras finally smiled and nodded. "Good job, kiddo."

Zara inhaled.

Marcus turned on the equipment, Aras manipulated the optical tweezers, immersing her silver-gloved hands into the glass tube, while Zara waited by the centrifuge for the chilled and manipulated sample. She willed her hands, dressed in thick rubbery gloves, not to tremble when she finally received the sample and carefully positioned it in the monstrous black tank. She closed the lid and slid the lever to the locked position and pressed the "on" button. And exhaled.

Aras shuffled toward her and patted her on her back. "Ugh! Now we wait."

"It's a great idea and good math," Marcus said.

Zara turned her head toward him. "Thank you." Her anxiety melted instantaneously.

"Happy Birthday, Zara!" Spence shouted, jostling his bulk through the door and trying not to drop the bouquet of yellow, blue, and orange cactus flowers he held in one hand and the package he had under his other arm. Soon after Spence plunged into his favorite chair, Aras emerged with a big grin from the kitchen, carrying a humongous chocolate cake decorated with golden stars and moons and topped off with fourteen burning candles.

"And how is the birthday girl today?" Spence asked.

"Good," Zara said, arranging the flowers in a glass vase.

"How's everything? Anything interesting happen?" Spence asked after the cake was half-gone and the present (a book on cosmology) opened and admired.

Aras and Zara exchanged glances and giggled.

"We made progress in our research. Thanks to this little genius," Aras said. "We have created a condensed dark matter element."

"Oh, that's exciting. What are you going to do with it?"

"We'll study it, of course," Zara said, jutting her chin up.

When Aras disappeared into the kitchen a while later, Zara asked Spence about the feud Aras had with Sentrel. Spence told her in a hushed voice that Sentrel was the one who figured out Matilda was a woman and reported it to the authorities, therefore causing their mother's death.

"They didn't know Aras was her daughter?" Zara asked.

Spence shook his head.

"He doesn't know why she hates him so?"

Spence assured her Sentrel had never figured out the reason behind the intense loathing Aras displayed toward him by dismantling his research.

"She always finds a reasoning flaw or a mistake in his research. All he can do in response is to spew lies about Aras's work," Spence said.

"But nobody believes him, right?"

"No, she promptly refutes his allegations, making him look like a fool again."

16

THE FOE

"Ready?"

"Yes."

"All right, then. Hand it to me," Aras said, and sat by the giant electron microscope.

Zara carried a small crystal box in hands outfitted with thick rubber gloves while Aras opened the glass compartment under one prong of the microscope lens. Aras drew a deep breath and glanced at Zara before opening it. The black element rolled out and into the center of the glass compartment. Aras opened another crystal box and, with tweezers, moved the golden piece near the black element while gazing into the eyepiece. The built-in camera was filming the event, and Zara stared at the screen, biting her lower lip.

They both jumped at the burst of golden sparkles and the flash of radiant blue light that followed. Aras saw it under the microscope and jerked her head out of the way, balancing her chair on two back legs. Zara saw it on the screen and gasped at the sight. The mere presence of the dark matter had transformed the golden substance into two golden globules.

"We still know nothing," Aras sighed. "They will take this away from us next week and give it to Sentrel, and he's gonna laugh at me. Oh, he's gonna have some fun."

"We still have a few days. What we learned today is big, Aras. This thing interacts with dark matter. Nothing else except gravity interacts with dark matter. If the current hypothesis is correct that dark matter makes the universe, then this means the gold substance must be part of it."

"You're absolutely right."

"What if we manipulated it?"

"Manipulate the gold substance, you mean?"

Zara nodded.

"How?"

"Excite it, spin it. I thought if we bombarded and spun the particles, we could collapse their quantum entanglement and separate them into different states. And then perhaps we'd find a state that could interact with something," Zara said and glanced at Aras. "What do you think?"

"And if we repeat it enough times, it may give us an idea of what this thing is," Aras said and nodded. "The reading you've done is paying off." Aras smiled and patted Zara's arm. "And what would that something be? Huh?"

"Sengali Prism," Zara said.

Aras's smile quickly faded. "But we don't have it. There's one at the Central Academy and one in the Darwold lab," Aras said, and shook her head upon seeing Zara's expression. "No, we can't. It would take days, which we don't have, to get permission."

"You wouldn't need permission if you borrowed it from Sentrel."

"No, absolutely not! Giving him the satisfaction of asking for a favor."

"They might give him the gold substance if we fail."

"I can't. You don't know what he's done," she said, but glancing at Zara's expression, she made a face. "Spence told you, didn't he, the bigmouth?"

"Don't blame Spence. I asked. I'm sorry. Forget it. It was a stupid idea anyway."

Aras left the lab, slamming the door behind her. Zara sighed and kept staring at the screen. Moments passed, but Aras didn't come back. Zara looked through the microscope and, manipulating its optical hand mindlessly, she pushed the slide with the golden globules closer to the dark matter element until they touched. The image blurred, and when it cleared after a few seconds, she saw just the dark element, and within it, tiny golden specks.

"Shit, what have I done?"

"What have you done?" Aras asked, sneaking up behind her.

"I didn't think it would work. I really didn't. I messed up. I moved them closer together, and they merged. Well, more like the black one swallowed the golden one. I'm sorry. We've lost the sample."

"We have more. I've reconsidered and will contact the old bastard."

"You sure?"

"Yup. Doesn't change how I feel about the prick, but I'm going to use him."

"Can I have some more?"

Aras gazed at her with an unreadable expression. "You have more ideas?"

"Maybe..."

"Wait. Do nothing before we talk about it."

"You're angry."

"No, I'm not. But we have little of that stuff left."

The very next day, Aras and Zara flew to Darwold, having previously confirmed that Dr. Sentrel would be in the lab and available to talk to them and collaborate on their project.

"Was he annoyed or was he gloating when you contacted him?"

"No, he sounded okay. Pleased, actually."

Expecting a monster, Zara was surprised when she finally met Sentrel. His full red cheeks and round belly, bushy white beard and mustache topped with snowy white hair and funny-looking spectacles, gave an impression of an amiable uncle, not someone destroying people's lives. He stretched out his hand and smiled, showing a full set of pearly teeth. Zara shook his hand, which felt warm and firm, searching his eyes for the evil.

"This young man must be your prodigy," Dr. Sentrel said, eyeballing Zara.

"Yes, this is Edmund. Edmund, this is Dr. Abel Sentrel."

"Call me Abel. I don't like my last name so much," he said to Zara and asked Aras, rubbing his hands together, "What's the secret you couldn't share over the messenger?"

"Let's go somewhere private," she said.

Zara observed Aras's hands clasping the bag that held the samples, imagining how difficult it must have been to be so close to her mother's murderer and not have gone for his throat.

Abel led them through a narrow hallway to his office, which was stuffed with books and papers in uncoordinated heaps with only enough space for a large, old, green sofa with worn-out fat arms, two side tables, and two chairs. Zara cringed at seeing the legs of a small coffee table bending under the weight of the stack of books on top.

"What I'm about to tell you cannot leave this room," Aras said, and drew a big breath. Zara noticed she was speaking in her lowest voice. "This is serious. Both of us could be in danger of losing our permissions to practice science and lead research."

"Okay."

"You must promise."

"I promise."

"I've been asked to evaluate a certain substance that was found in western Andalia. We've been studying it, dissecting it, and still don't know what it is, its origin, or its properties. It doesn't interact with anything we know of. We've tried everything. We thought we should try one more experiment before finally giving up."

"I see. Where was it found? Ghost Island?"

"How did you know?" Aras stirred in her chair.

"They brought me a sample too and, just like you, tried everything I could think of. But nothing worked, and I have no new ideas. So I'm not sure how I can help," he said simply, not trying to fib or sound important.

"They did?" Aras asked and pursed her lips. For a moment, seeing Aras's cheeks redden and her hand clench, Zara thought she might attack him and she readied herself to stop her if needed. But instead of attacking Abel, Aras continued in a strained voice, "See, my assistant Edmund had the brilliant idea of using the prism on the substance."

"The prism? You mean the Singali Prism?"

Aras and Zara both nodded.

"Why? It might destroy it. It *will* destroy it."

"It won't. I will alter it. Even if it does, we'll only be using a small sample."

"But why? What will you gain?" he asked.

Definitely not as smart as Aras. She should have the prism, not him, Zara thought, but then patiently explained their theory and why they needed the prism.

"Ah, that's clever. I'd never thought about something as crazy as this. But it's brave and creative."

"So, you'll help us?"

"Of course. When do you want to start?" he asked, but seeing their expressions, sighed. "I had planned to leave early tonight to appease my wife, who's been complaining that I've been working too much and whatnot. Oh, well. It won't be the first time I've disappointed her."

Zara was surprised again, seeing genuine distress in his eyes. *Loves his wife but sends a woman to her death.*

"We will also need the Quantum Splitter to segregate the particles afterward," Zara said, descending through an opening in the concrete floor down narrow metal steps, arriving at the lab that housed the prism and several other instruments mounted on the walls and embedded in the concrete floor.

"Yes, and the Computator. The largest you have," Aras added, rubbing her forehead.

"It's already here. This prism pays our bills. We mastered the technique of separating particles efficiently. Entire particles. That's all I've used the prism for so far. What you're proposing has never been done before, and it is...mind-boggling. You're proposing to split the particle itself."

"Is that a problem?" Aras asked. "Are you scared?"

Zara detected irritation in Aras's voice as she spoke, looking him hard in the eye.

"No, I'm excited. No reason to get mad."

"Sorry."

"I understand how you must feel, having the deadline looming and no prospect of solving the puzzle and whatnot. You must want to resolve this mystery more than I do."

"Perhaps I do."

Zara watched their interaction discreetly, ready to intervene. So much was at stake. If Aras lost her temper, she might reveal herself, and they'd both be sent to prison or worse.

"Does your splitter have both vertical and horizontal separators?" Zara intercepted the conversation, hoping that the focus on practical matters would keep Aras out of trouble.

"Yes, it does. This is the newest and improved version."

"Let's get to it, then," Aras said, frowning.

Zara removed the samples while Aras and Abel calibrated the instruments. Hearing no antagonizing remarks from Aras, only calm and encouraging responses from Abel, Zara relaxed and quickly prepped the samples.

After they started the process, they gathered around a large screen and waited for results. Aras stood with her arms crossed, tapping her fingers on her arms. Zara stood motionless, forgetting to breathe, while Abel stood relaxed, patting his round belly and nodding.

"Yes!" Aras yelled, pointing at the screen. "We've got them separated into...three...no, six...wow! I can't count."

"There are at least several hundred different quarks and leptons," Zara said.

"No," Aras said. "These are not quarks and leptons. According to my calculations, there could be up to forty leptons and the same number of quarks. These are the preons. We have proven the existence of a previously hypothetical subatomic particle."

Abel's voice deepened. "Amazing!"

Aras slowly turned her gaze to Abel's face, which showed no sign of malice. Only exuberant joy. Aras stepped back, still staring at him, and then raised her hand. Zara blinked. When she opened her eyes, she exhaled when the raised hand landed on Abel's back in a friendly pat instead of a punch.

"We should celebrate! Why don't the two of you join me for drinks at my house? My wife usually prepares dinner for ten people. She says you never know when a hungry person may show up and whatnot. That's my wife for you. And she's a damn good cook too."

"I think we should get going, don't you think, Doctor?" Zara asked, glancing at Aras, who seemed to waver. A sudden fear that Abel was onto them and was planning to trap them and contact the authorities overwhelmed Zara. She locked the box containing the rest of the gold substance with clammy hands, and turned toward the exit, glaring at Aras.

"We should talk about it and figure out what our next steps are and get the copies of the results, then run a second analysis to confirm our findings..." Aras kept talking, as if to herself, her blue eyes hazed over with excitement, gazing somewhere in the distance at something only she could see.

"Yeah, we can do it later through the messenger system," Zara said. The alarm bells rang inside her head. She clutched her stomach. "I don't feel good. I think I'm getting sick and wouldn't want to give it to Abel's wife," she said, piercing Aras with her black eyes.

"What's wrong?" Aras asked, coming down to Earth.

"I don't know. Maybe is something that is going around the lab."

"Okay, let's go back," she said to Zara and then glanced at Abel. "Will you send us the results?"

"Are you sure about this?" Abel asked. "My wife is good at curing all kinds of illnesses. She raised five kids who were always coming down with something, and she could always cure them with home remedies and whatnot."

"Thank you for your kind offer, but we must go," Aras said, and headed for the door. Zara exhaled. "Be in touch."

"Sure."

Before they left, Zara caught his glance and shivered. She lurched forward, pushing Aras with both hands through the door. Aras almost tripped.

"What was that all about? Why did you lie about being sick?" Aras asked after they'd safely extracted themselves from the lab and walked back toward the plane waiting for them.

"I had a bad feeling about him. Don't trust him. At all."

"Hmm. He seemed friendly and not at all possessive of the research."

"Exactly. Too friendly."

Aras tapped her on the shoulder. "I'm glad you were with me to get me out of my head while I was imagining the notoriety, the recognition, and the future research. So much older and so much stupider than a fourteen-year-old. Sorry, kiddo. I almost got lured into the enemy's den."

"In the lab full of assistants and other researchers, he couldn't do anything to us, but who knows what he'd planned for us at his home," Zara said. "Or maybe nothing. I didn't like the way he looked at me. Just before we left, he had a strange expression on his face. He reminded me of my father just before he'd bitten into his steak."

The next evening, Spence nearly fell over ramming through the front door, yelling, "What were you thinking, the two of you? Why didn't you check with me before going to Sentrel's lab? To be so close to him, he could expose you? That was really dumb of you. He could easily have revealed your identity. What the hell is wrong with you, Sara?" Spence wiped his reddened face.

"I shouldn't have told you, dammit. He doesn't know I'm a woman or her daughter."

"That's what he does. It's his thing. He has a sixth sense for this sort of thing. He hates women. I thought you knew that," he said, glaring at Aras.

"He didn't appear to be hateful. He talked so well about his wife, like he cared a lot for her—"

"Abel Sentrel is not married. Never has been."

"Are you sure?"

"Absolutely. You need to lie low now and not contact him. Stay in the lab and don't participate in any conferences or meetings or anything that would put you in the spotlight."

"But we have to get the research results from him," Zara almost whimpered at the thought of losing all that data.

"No! Forget it. It's too dangerous."

"Spence is right. We shouldn't have done it. I suspect he'll take the credit for our findings anyway," Aras said, and then, as if she had had an epiphany, she ripped her glasses off, staring at Spence. "If he suspects but is not sure, he might want to draw us in."

"So, if he contacts us, it means he suspects us?" Zara asked. "Wouldn't it be suspicious if we didn't contact him?"

"What do we do?"

"Do nothing for now. Let me ask around. I have some close friends who know him well," Spence said and grabbed his coat. Before he left, he shouted. "Stay put!"

After he left, Aras rubbed her eyes and retreated to her bedroom. Alone in the darkened room, Zara wondered whether Aras's real name was Sara. Second time Spence had called her that. Has Aras ever regretted not being a girl, a woman, or a wife? *Will I?*

17

DARK MATTER

Two days passed, during which Spence spent some time with his friends, searching for gossip, and then assured Aras and Zara that Abel did not suspect them—or if he did, he wasn't certain enough to start rumors.

The day before the deadline, before the agents returned expecting results of their analysis, Aras sat at her desk in her lab office, took a long sip of her favorite whisky, and waited for her voice to calm before calling Abel Sentrel.

"Well, hello there. I thought you were not interested in getting the results, Aras."

Aras pulled the receiver from her ear. Abel's loud greetings boomed through the holes in the metal earpiece. "Sorry. Edmund was sick and gave it to me too. It's the first day that my headache has finally been manageable."

"I was about to send the report to you. Not that it will make any difference to the government. We really learned very little about this gold stuff and whatnot. Who knows—they might extend our deadline."

"What makes you say that?"

"If the top two science nerds couldn't figure it out, who else would? I mean, who else is there? He, he, he."

Aras grimaced and yanked the receiver away from her ear and silently imitated Abel's laughter. Then she smiled to herself. "You might have something there. Thanks for sending the results."

Aras was about to hang up when Abel asked. "How about we meet and discuss the next steps? We could collaborate. You know what they say about two heads being better than one and whatnot?"

Aras's hand froze in midair. "I already have two heads," Aras gave out a forced laugh.

"Oh, yeah. How could I have forgotten your assistant? The good-looking lad? Edmund is his name, right? What's his last name?"

"Stone. Edmund Stone," Aras said, pressing her twitching hand on the receiver.

"Doesn't sound familiar. I don't recall any Stones in the scientific community."

"His father is a store owner. Anyway, I've got to go, Abel. Thank you again," she said and hung up. Then she slid into her chair and, banging on the desk, shouted. "Son of a bitch!"

"What's going on? Who were you yelling at?" Zara asked, poking her head in Aras's office.

"Abel. I think he knows something. He offered to help."

"But we will not accept it?"

"No, absolutely not! He seemed to think that they might extend the deadline."

"That'd be great," Zara sighed.

"Yup," Aras said and studied Zara's face. "We are going to have to come up with some kind of beard for you."

"Am I not a little too young for a beard? Nobody would believe it."

"Abel said you were a good-looking lad. We must hide your good looks somehow."

"There are many other boys who are better looking than I am. In my class, there was a boy—"

"A boy, yeah," Aras interrupted harshly. "You're not a boy, so you should be ugly. And soon your breasts will get bigger, and your face will start changing. We have to do something."

"You went through it just fine, didn't you?"

"I wasn't as pretty as you. You attract too much attention with your pretty face and your eyes."

The contract was extended, their supply of the gold substance replenished, and their compensation increased substantially. Apparently, the government was aware of their collaboration on the research with Abel and the results. Aras was surprised at the ease with which she had negotiated additional equipment. The authorities hadn't even blinked at her request of the Singali Prism and the Phantom Collider to continue the research.

"Your equipment will be delivered within the next few weeks," the black-clad officials told her and left.

"Ugh," Aras exhaled, slid into her chair, extended her legs out, and leaned back, laughing. "We've not only escaped danger, but our lab will be the best-equipped in all of fucking Andalia!"

Zara smiled, but her smile was strained, her excitement tempered by the memory of the look on Abel's face. That, and his lies about having a wife. What was he planning?

They plunged into ceaseless work, spending most of their days in the lab, eating most of their meals there. Despite their efforts and dedication, they failed to describe even its basic properties, such as its molecular weight, malleability, melting point, and conductivity (which was nonexistent). It interacted only with gravity and dark matter, but Aras was against disclosing the second piece of information to the government officials.

Aras prepared a report summarizing the experiments with the Prism and the Collider, describing the various states of the gold substance when separated into preons, then masterfully directed her discussion in the report to normal visible matter. The work with the gold substance, she explained, laid the ground for modifying metal, wood, or synthetics in the same way, enhancing their properties into superior matter. This, she claimed, would lead to its various potential technological applications in construction, aviation, and military applications, imagining that was what interested the government.

She was right. The government officials were very interested in pursuing the preon technology on easily obtainable, visible matter, and did not mention the gold substance even once. Zara and Aras guessed it was because it had failed to be the miraculous substance they had hoped it to be. Zara wished she knew what else they had found in the tomb to create this secrecy to begin with.

"My intuition tells me we're going to be working on this preon stuff for a while longer," Aras said one day. "I can already see its potential use in aeronautics and computing when enhanced by manipulating its state."

"Is that what you want to do?"

"We might have to, kiddo. You don't get government contracts for nothing. They expect something in return. Besides, it's fascinating."

"Aras, I need to ask you something."

"Sure."

"What do you think about Doctor Philione's research on the disappearing dark matter? Do you think he's right? Is he a credible scientist in your eyes?"

"Oh, Phillip Philione? He is brilliant. I'm surprised you found this article, as it was not considered mainstream science, and he received some backlash for it."

"So, you believed his findings?"

"Absolutely. If he published something, it means he checked, double-checked, and triple-checked his methods and results," Aras said, and seeing Zara's face, laughed. "I can introduce the two of you."

Zara worked with Aras, further manipulating the preons, but also continued her research and experimented with dark matter.

For five more years, they'd go back and study the gold substance. But since they'd not made much progress and their supply of it had diminished to the point of needing to conserve what remained, they'd locked it in the safe.

As Aras predicted, their work morphed into developing methods to manipulate normal matter to attain new properties, potentially revolutionizing aviation, computation, and even construction technologies. Funding was not a problem anymore. Aras beamed with pride and excitement, adding to the existing building to accommodate the expanding staff and equipment. Zara was involved in Aras's research, but still fascinated more with dark matter, spent part of her time working on her projects in a secluded lab with her friend's approval and quiet encouragement.

From time to time, Zara remembered Sentrel's probing eyes and would run into Aras's office asking about him. Aras would shrug, saying she didn't know and didn't care. Zara eventually stopped asking, but anytime an unknown delivery truck would show up, Zara tensed, ready to grab Aras and run for the desert. But as months went by and nothing had happened, she convinced herself that he had forgotten about them, and she stopped seeing his malevolent eyes at night.

18

THE VISITOR

"How are your dreams these days?" Spence asked after they had eaten dinner and sat in the living room, sipping their favorite drinks.

"Ugh," Zara sighed.

"That bad?"

Zara shifted in her chair.

"Do you want me to leave so you can talk like a patient and doctor?" Aras asked and rose from her chair.

"No, you don't have to leave," Zara said and motioned for her to sit. "They are different now. She's still in my dreams, and her presence is still as distressing." Zara played with her tea, stirring it in circular motions, before she added in a shaky voice. "She looks more and more like me. She could be my sister."

"Oh," Spence said after a while. "Have you ever considered that it could actually be you trying to bring to light your unfulfilled dreams and desires?"

"I have entertained that idea. Sure. It would explain a lot, and I wouldn't feel like a neurotic maiden."

"Nonsense," Aras snorted.

"But you don't think it is you?" Spence asked.

"No, I don't. She looks similar enough to give me pause, but her expressions are different, and so are her movements, her mannerisms. I'd never sway my hips like she does, barely touching the floor while walking as if she were being pushed or pulled by something."

"And you don't know what she wants from you?"

"No, just that she wants me to finish something in a hurry."

"Finish? Have you started doing something?"

Zara glanced at Aras, who nodded and said with a sigh, "You can tell him."

"I've been working on dark matter. I've already figured out how to condense it into a visible mass—a crystal-like black shard—and I've been continuing to work with it and uncover its secrets."

"Does anyone else know about what you're doing?" Spence asked, tugging on his beard. "You don't want to bring unnecessary attention to yourself."

"Nope. Just the two of us."

"What are you trying to accomplish by studying it? Are there any practical applications for this dark matter stuff?"

"Well, it's the stuff that makes the universe. We ought to understand it. Maybe eventually, if we can figure out how to produce it more efficiently, condensed and manipulated dark matter could be extremely useful. It's tougher than hell and very malleable. It might revolutionize how we build things."

"I thought that's what the preon technology is all about."

"Yes, they are connected. Dark matter would be manipulated similarly to produce the materials we want. But dark matter possesses extraordinary qualities that might be used for...travel. Traveling so fast you could take a peek into worlds beyond ours, and maybe even stay in one and observe," Zara said, and encouraged by Spencer's curious eyes, she continued. "You see, the dark matter particles remain connected to each other over great distances, which requires them to communicate faster than the speed of light, something we had previously believed to be impossible, which means...we could travel through time."

"Are you serious?" Spence rose from his chair, spilling his drink on his checkered robe.

Zara nodded and Aras laughed out loud. "Isn't she smart? She's doing it all by herself. I've contributed nothing to it. She checks in with me occasionally, but I've not helped her once."

"You're helping me just with your presence," Zara now laughed. "Your genius is rubbing off on me."

"You just have to promise me you'll be careful with this dark matter business. Both of you," Spence said. Noticing them grinning, he narrowed his eyes. "I mean it. Promise me. Professional envy is nothing to be ignored."

"We promise," they said in unison.

"According to some scientists, dark matter has been disappearing for a while. We should know why and whether we ought to be worried," Zara said.

"Sentrel had probably forgotten about us anyway," Aras said.

"He's been sick," Spence said. "Really sick, I've been told. He's been in and out of the hospital, but I've heard they haven't diagnosed him with anything. Strange thing."

"Couldn't have happened to a nicer person," Zara mumbled.

"I'm hungry," Aras said, stretching. "I'll bring us some snacks."

While Aras disappeared into the kitchen, Zara shifted herself to be closer to Spence. Her closed lips moved as if she were saying something, but no sound came out.

"What is it?" Spence asked.

"I've never asked before," she whispered. "But I always wondered. Do you know how my parents are doing?"

Spence did not answer immediately, studying her face. "Are you sure?"

Zara nodded.

"Your parents put out posters. They and the police thought Romanas kidnapped you. Apparently, people saw them in the area around the time you...disappeared. Well, I might've helped with the rumors."

"Why would Romanas kidnap me?"

"People believed Romanas traveled around just to kidnap babies and children."

"Who'd believe in such nonsense?"

Spence's hand adjusted his glasses and touched his beard before sliding down onto his lap. "To invigorate their gene pool."

"That's nonsense! And you helped propagate this stupid notion?"

"Only that one time."

They sat in silence for a moment before Spence continued.

"Your father came to my office one day. It was a month after you'd left. He...he came to ask if you ever confided in me about him."

"What do you mean?"

"He cried so hard, he could hardly speak. He thought you willingly went with Romanas because of him. Because he was too harsh on you."

"What did you tell him?" Zara whispered, gripping the sofa's cushion.

"I told him I didn't think you left because of him. I told him you loved him."

Zara looked him in the eye. "My mother?"

"Gilbert said she blamed herself for your disappearance. She never said so to him, but she withdrew into herself and rarely even spoke to him," Spence said and added, seeing Zara's lips tremble. "But that was a long time ago. I'm sure they're both doing better."

Zara sat in her little office in the lab's corner thinking about what Spence had told her about her parents, imagining herself in her mother's arms.

"You have a visitor," Marcus shouted from behind the closed lab door.

Zara jerked and jumped out of her chair. She adjusted her fake beard and positioned her thick-rimmed glasses on her nose. She opened the door. "Who is it?"

"He said he's your friend from school."

"Really?" She didn't keep in touch with Eric or Teo. How would they even find her? "I'm coming," she said while her mind searched for an excuse to send them away.

"There he is," Marcus said, pointed toward the large arched hallway, and left.

She saw a tall figure leaning against the column—too tall for it to be Eric or even Teo. When the tall man peeled off the column and walked toward her, her heart moved uncomfortably close to her throat. She recognized that lazy, nonchalant walk, the swagger of the slender hips. She held on to the wall. And when he was close, the blue eyes and the smile were all she saw. Everything else was in a fog, as if her mind had conjured it to conceal him. *He's not real. It's not possible. It isn't him.*

"I told you I'll be back for you."

"Tirg," she said. "It's really you." As she said it, her hand flew to her mouth. Her voice sounded so high and feminine.

"Yes, it's me," he said, then laughed and smacked her on her back, seeing two men walk by. "Edmund, let me take you to dinner, my friend," he bellowed. When the passersby were gone, he lowered his voice. "Let's go somewhere we can talk without being overheard and seen."

Zara reached for his hand, expecting it to go through him. But her hand found a firm and warm hand with skin kissed by the sun and smoothed by the wind. She retracted her hand quickly. Tirg smiled with his mischievous but warm smile, and she pressed herself against the wall when her legs stopped obeying her. Tirg grabbed her arm and led her out of the hallway. From behind, they appeared as good friends who were going out to have fun. From the front, the pale face of the young, bearded man with glasses that seemed too big for him was led, almost carried, by another man who, although not as pale, looked like he'd been struck by divine lightning. They left the building and walked to an awaiting plane.

"I've found a nice place, just a few miles up in the hills. It's cooler there and remote," he said. She heard a slight vibration in his voice as he strained to keep it steady. "Nice beard, by the way," he said.

"And the glasses are super nerdy. But they hide your beautiful face well."

A few minutes later, Tirg landed the plane in a small valley surrounded by hills. Although scraggly and sparse, the vegetation provided respite from the monotony of the cacti landscape that dominated most of this part of Andalia. She followed him to a rocky outcrop. He then turned around, faced her, and gently took her hands in his.

"I don't want to waste more time. I know I said that you can tell me your secret when you trust me, but if I wait any longer, my heart will explode. And you'll have a big mess on your hands," he said, and laughed. He drew a deep breath to continue, but Zara interrupted him.

"I trust you," she said, freed her hands from his and removed the glasses, exposing her big almond-shaped eyes, and then slowly ripped off her beard. Her skin was slightly reddened under the scratchy beard she wore most of the day, but she smiled, loving the breeze and sun on her face. The smile died on her lips when she saw his expression.

"Zara," he whispered. "I missed you."

"You know my real name. How?" she could barely speak as her chest couldn't gather enough air.

"I'm sorry I didn't tell you before, but I didn't want you to worry. When we went to school together, I took my father's plane and followed you home. I had to know the person who turned my world upside-down. I suspected you were a girl, but I had to be sure. Honestly, even though I am not gay, I entertained the idea of being with a boy because of how I felt. But if you were a girl, I had to be careful not to get you in trouble with this idiotic system. I've heard what they do to women in this country," Tirg said and brushed the hair off his forehead before continuing.

"Last time we had to leave immediately after we had accomplished our goal. This time, I can stay longer because I'm working for my government on negotiating another deal, which will take much longer. And," he laughed unsurely, "I'll do my best to be very slow."

"But how did you find out I was a girl? You wouldn't have discovered that by following me home."

"Remember who my father is. He has access to limitless information. Once I learned Spencer Mitchell was Aras's friend, I found all his patients, and what do you know? One of his patients was missing. A girl named Zara. A girl with haunting black eyes. I felt like shit for a while after that."

"Why?"

"As a man, I can do anything I want. I can study what I desire; I can travel, and yet I've complained about school and travel and all kinds of trivial inconveniences. And you," he paused and cleared his throat, "you had to risk your life to do what I take for granted. I felt unworthy of you, like an insignificant insect. But then, I thought to myself that I should be by your side and protect you. You can be yourself in my presence."

For a moment, Zara became lost in her thoughts. What he'd said was so true. She'd been constantly surrounded by people from whom she had to hide her identity and pretend to be someone she was not. Over the years, she'd become skilled at pretending and fitting into a masculine society and even envied them when they did what was natural and never apologized. Zara realized that during that time she also had become a woman but didn't truly understand what that meant, never having had the time or the opportunity to imagine herself as one. Long gone were the times of being groomed to become a perfect wife and mother. Now, a tiny part of her questioned whether there was something in that world that was missing from her life.

"In my country, women have more freedom and can pursue their dreams. They can be doctors, scientists, or bankers; they can fly planes and do whatever they want."

"You're joking."

Tirg shook his head.

"Sinturija is beautiful and rich in natural treasures. Filled with old trees, clear lakes, mountains, bears, and streams full of fish," he said, and lingered on her eyes until she met his gaze. "I can take you with me. You wouldn't have to pretend anymore."

"You sound like a travel agent."

Tirg laughed, thrusting his head back.

"You want me to leave Andalia? Forever?"

"You can come visit."

Zara kept her eyes on his, but her thoughts wandered off again. The possibility of leaving Andalia and never seeing her parents again stirred a longing to see them. Would they want to see her?

"You okay?" he whispered.

"It's been six years since I've seen my parents. I don't even know how they are doing."

"Maybe it's time you visited them?"

"Oh, it's impossible. I failed the test on purpose and went against their precious System. My parents would report me, and I'd go to prison."

"They would?"

"I thought my mother loved me, but just before I left, she became a different person."

"Because you failed the test?"

"Because I questioned her happiness."

"Perhaps you could see them from a distance."

"How?"

"I doubt they'd recognize you because of all the facial hair and the goofy glasses, and second, you are older, taller, and God...you're so beautiful..." Tirg said.

He gazed at her with such intensity she felt her cheeks getting hot as the blood rushed to her head. In that moment, she didn't care if he was going to turn her in. All she wanted was to look into his eyes and listen to his voice. Even if it was just for a moment.

"The first time I saw you, I thought you were the most beautiful creature in this world. And so familiar. Then I remembered the painting and remembered what my grandma said, and everything became clear."

"And how so?"

"Destiny. You're my destiny. And I'm yours. I saw the look on your face when you first saw me."

"I'm a scientist. I don't believe in destiny," she said, irritated by how puny her voice sounded.

"I didn't, either. But I do now. You are my fate, Zara."

"Did your grandma tell you whose portrait it was?"

"No."

"You didn't ask her when you went back?"

"She died."

"I'm sorry," she said and leaned toward him, and surprised herself with her boldness and touched his cheek. She'd never intentionally touched a man who was not her father. Tirg leaned his cheek closer, grasped her hand, and kissed it. Like serpents, sensations she had never experienced wove through her body. Her heart thumped somewhere in the distance as her eyes wandered to his. She knew what a kiss was, having observed Gilbert kissing her mother. But what she experienced as he pressed his lips to hers was not what she had expected. Her mother just smiled lightly afterward, but smiling was the furthest thing on her mind. She felt her body fade into his and the surrounding air to flow right through her as if she were an apparition. And then the blood rushed through her body like a river suddenly freed from a dam.

He pulled away and looked into her eyes. "We must go back now. If anyone saw us together, I wouldn't be able to protect you from the government. I'll find better ways for us to be together."

Her body wanted to be close to his. She grasped his hands. "I don't want to go back."

"Don't look so sad. You'll see so much of me you'll be sick of me," he said, and smiled, but his expression quickly grew serious. "Do you trust Aras and Spencer Mitchell? Completely?"

"Of course. Why do you ask?"

"You live with Aras and can't just leave and meet me somewhere without Aras knowing."

"Yeah. I'm not sure how they'll react to my seeing you. They'll think it'll be too dangerous for me and for..." Her voice trailed off as she remembered her promise.

"Oh, my God. What am I doing? I must be mad," Zara exclaimed and jumped up.

While her soul wrestled between guilt and the desire to fall back into his arms, he watched her. Then suddenly, a spark of understanding flashed in his eyes. "I know about Aras...that she is a woman."

Zara's hands flew to her chest. "You do? How could you possibly know that?"

"I told you I have access to information other people don't. I'm in the spy business, Zara.

"Who else knows about Aras?"

"What do you mean? Just me. I would never—"

Zara turned around and started running.

"Where are you going? You don't even know how to get back. Zara! Please stop. I've known about it for a while. Nothing happened, right?"

Zara stopped and waited for him to catch up but was still facing away from him.

"Ugh, you run fast," he said, panting. "I'd never betray you." He seized her hand and pressed it to his chest. "Look at me, please."

She turned around slowly, and he gasped at her terrified, ghostly face.

"They mean a lot to you? Aras and Mitchell?"

She nodded, finally looking him in the eye. She pulled her hand. "If you know who she is, you must've heard what happened to her mother. I'd rather die than see Aras meet the same fate. You had no right to spy on Aras," she said in a voice so icy it chilled the air between them. "You talk about trust and yet you spied on me and my friends when you should have waited for me to tell you when I was ready!"

"I'm sorry. You're right. But I had no other way of reaching you. I wanted to know more about you. You were on my mind every single day since I left here. I was going crazy, imagining you being found and imprisoned or worse, and I needed to know you were safe. Getting the little bits of information about you was what kept me sane all this time while I planned my return."

"That's not the way to do it," she said. Her tone was still cold but had lost its sharpness.

"I won't do it again. Forgive me," he said, and smiled his mischievous and irresistible smile as he extended his hand. "Come on. I'll fly you back to your lab."

"Does your father know about me or Aras?"

Tirg swiped the imaginary hair off his forehead. "I might have told him about the girl I was nuts about."

"Not that Aras is a woman?"

"I never told him," Tirg said, putting his hand on his chest.

"Wasn't he worried about you leaving on your own?"

"No, he encouraged me, thrilled that I had chosen the same career. He does not have a clue that the reason I did it was to find you. Being a spy wasn't something I wanted to do with my life…" he said. His words trailed off as he noticed Zara's probing eyes.

"What did you want to do with your life?"

"I'll tell you when I fully trust you," he said, and exploded into laughter.

Then he scooped her into his arms and kissed her. Instantly, anger, uncertainty, fear, apprehension—all vanished as his muscular arms gently wrapped around her—replaced by the ethereal sensation of floating in the air.

"You must stop kissing me like that," she whispered.

"Why?"

"I can't control my body."

19

THE DIPLOMAT

Tirg had waited for her every day in the hallway and had flown them to the same spot in the desert. He never pressed her to tell Aras, but she knew she had to. Four days had passed before Zara told Aras about Tirg's return.

Aras reacted to the news of Tirg's return as Zara predicted she'd have. Aras and Spence sat on a sofa in Aras's living room, studying Zara and listening while Aras, with her voice thick with emotion, peppered Zara with questions. "I still don't understand the spy business. How could he have found all that information from across the ocean? Is he telling the truth? You don't really know him. Maybe he is our government spy. I don't have to tell you how dangerous this is? For all of us."

"I can imagine how you must see this, but I trust him."

"So what? What are you planning to do? How do you think this is going to work? I thought you understood that playing the part of a male scientist, your life as a woman was over. There was no turning back, and there is no halfway. You can't be a woman and a man simultaneously. When emotions are in play, secrets escape," Aras said, crossing the room in hasty strides and wringing her hands. She stopped in front of Zara and looked her in the eye. "I don't want to see you dead."

"You won't."

"So, what are you going to do?" Aras asked, throwing her arms in the air.

"We talked about moving to Sinturija. Women can be scientists there. We wouldn't have to hide."

"Moving to Sinturija? Are you mad?"

"He said it's beautiful."

"Tell me more about him. You only knew him for what? Three months?" Spence said. "You haven't seen him in five years, and you're willing to gamble your freedom, your life, and leave your country, Aras and me, your research, and venture out into the unknown. What else do you know about him besides that he is a spy? Is he a good man? What about his family?"

"He comes from a long line of diplomats from a respected old family. You're right. I know little about his family, but I don't have to, because I know *him*. You probably think I'm stupid and irresponsible. From your perspective, this must seem like a foolish thing to do. But he is my destiny. The first time I saw Tirg, I knew it. I tried to dismiss this idea as foolish and forget him. Believe me, I tried, but I couldn't and won't," Zara said. Her lips quivered.

"What about your parents?" Aras asked.

"What about them? You two are more like my parents. You never tried to force me to be someone I wasn't. And my mother wanted nothing to do with me at the end. They probably don't even remember me."

"I don't think that's the case. Your mother loves you. Gilbert might be a little rough around the edges, but he loves you too. You can't blame them for not understanding you and your passion for science. How could they? Even if you had told them, they might not have understood it. And it wouldn't be entirely their fault, living in a society conditioned to shun any individuality in women."

Zara slumped onto the sofa, shutting her eyes tightly to force the tears to stay behind her eyelids. "I don't know what else to do. Since he came back, I haven't been able to focus on anything. Not even my work."

"Yes, I've noticed a dead person walking around the lab. You have dark rings under your eyes, and you've lost weight," Aras said. She sat next to Zara and embraced her.

Zara rested her head on Aras's shoulder. "I don't know what to do."

"Why don't you take it slow and don't decide yet? Learn more about him. You can meet with him safely because he is your friend from school. Don't jump into a deep hole without a rope. Do you think he'd be amenable to meeting with us?"

Zara nodded. "He'll do anything for me. Yes, he'll meet with you."

Aras and Spence exchanged heavy glances. Aras's face tightened. "Let's have him over this weekend."

The weekend came, and Tirg arrived at Aras's house and stood at the front door, holding a bunch of flowers for Aras in his damp palms before finally ringing the bell. Spence let him in and entertained him in the living room while Zara sat on Aras's bed, watching her friend struggle with preparing to meet Tirg. She clutched the gray mop of curls in her hands, glancing at herself in the mirror.

"You don't have to wear this shit," Zara finally said. "He knows."

"I know," Aras said, tossing the wig onto her bed. "It's been so long since anyone has seen my face except for Spence and you. I feel naked without my disguise."

"It'll be okay. Come on, he is here," Zara said, and beckoned for Aras to follow her.

As they neared the living room, Spence's beefy laughter grew louder. He was laughing at something Tirg said and toasting him, clinking an etched crystal glass filled with golden liquid when Aras and Zara entered the living room. Tirg walked toward Aras and extended his hand. He smiled, and his body relaxed, with a hint of unassertive confidence remaining in his straight shoulders and his focused gaze. Aras stared into his eyes for a long moment, not uttering a word. Until melting ice clanked in Spence's glass. Then she shook his hand. Zara exhaled.

Spence laughed at everything Tirg said and handed him drink after drink and kept toasting him. Aras bombarded him with questions about his family, his country, his likes and dislikes. He answered politely and with the ease of someone who has nothing to hide until she asked about his work.

"I can't talk about my work. I'm sorry," he said apologetically, and glanced at Zara.

Through the afternoon, dinner, and into the evening, Tirg told stories about his family and Sinturija. Spence was laughing loudly and clapping his hands in delight. Aras had not moved her eyes off Tirg, but her expression worried Zara. What did she think of him? Did she like him?

Tirg had impeccable table manners, using utensils like an artist with the hands of a piano player, but devoured his food like a hungry sailor. Zara said very little throughout the day, watching Tirg or studying Aras's expressions.

After Tirg left, an uncomfortable silence fell over the room. Spence and Aras looked at each other with unspoken questions hanging between them, but neither one volunteered to speak first.

"Do you want me to leave so you can talk about him freely?"

"No reason to get snippy," Aras said.

"I liked the lad," Spence said, glancing sheepishly at Aras. "Smart and funny. He seems to be very fond of Zara."

Aras nodded but remained silent.

"What? Just say it," Zara said.

"You know how deeply we care about you, and we're doing this to protect you. I think he is not telling us everything. But Spence is right. He's crazy about you. A man couldn't feign it unless he were a superb actor, and he doesn't strike me as one."

"Why do you think he's hiding something? I didn't pick up on that," Spence said.

"I didn't either," Zara said, and glared at Aras.

Aras sighed. "Fine. I'll be completely honest with you. I'm overprotective of you and overly sensitive to men hiding their secrets so well, they sometimes overplay their frankness so much, it is like oversweetened tea. And I pick up on that. Something about his work doesn't add up. He's way too young to travel across the ocean on a diplomatic assignment all on his own."

"He's smart, and he learned from his father," Zara said. "His father groomed him from a young age. Tirg said he comes from a long line of diplomats. Maybe he is a natural?"

"Diplomats? You mean spies. Does he know about your research? All the details?"

"I never told him, and he didn't ask, so I doubt it. He knows it's scientific research and that it concerns physics, but that's all I told him."

The mistrust in Aras's eyes waned. "You believe and trust him, don't you?"

"Yes. I do."

Aras released air in a deep sigh. "We'll help you, kiddo. Just promise you won't make any rash decisions before talking to us. He can stay here if he wants to. The house could use some enlivening."

20

SUNNY BOY

Tirg grimaced when Zara told him about Aras's invitation to stay with her. "I have a better idea," he said.

"What?"

"It'll be a surprise," he said. "I'll pick you up from the lab tomorrow and show you."

He wouldn't say where he was taking her. He flew the plane without his usual grin, silently staring out the window.

When he started descending, he asked her to close her eyes and not open them until he told her to do so. Then he scooped her out of her seat and carried her before setting her down. "You can open your eyes now."

"What's this? Where are we?" Zara asked, looking at a white adobe house, whose large windows reflected the setting sun.

"Do you like it?"

"Yes, but..."

"It's ours for as long as we want it. We can be together, not bothered by anyone. Only ravens, eagles, and snakes live here. People don't venture here because it's dry and desolate, the broker told me."

"How would I go to work?"

"That's another surprise. Come on, I'll show you," Tirg said, smiling as he led her through a door to a large hangar housing two small planes. "One is mine and one is yours."

Her eyes widened. "But I don't know how to fly."

"I'll teach you," he said. "It's not that hard. I learned, and I'm nowhere near as smart as you are."

"So, you mean we'll live here together…just the two of us?" she asked, and felt her face redden.

"Yes. What's wrong?"

"But we are not married. If anyone finds out…"

"Two male friends living together as roommates. There is nothing wrong with that," Tirg said, and embraced her. "In my country, men and women live together without being married, and nobody ever questions it. It's just a matter of customs and perceptions. What are you afraid of?"

"I am not afraid," she said. "It's just so new and sudden. We are from such strikingly different places."

"You're overwhelmed. I get it. I live here now, and you can live here with me or visit me. It's up to you. I'd never make you do things you don't want to do. But promise me if you don't want to live here with me, it's for the right reasons."

"And what would that be?" she asked, glancing at him sideways. "Oh, you think I'm a prude?"

"You said it," he said, grinning.

She punched him on the arm.

He quickly grabbed her hand and pulled her towards him and said half-jokingly, "Just imagine—if we lived together, you could punch me all the time. And since I'm from a long line of gentlemen, I would only give you the other arm and cover you with kisses in return."

"I'll think about it," Zara said. That's all she could say, while Tirg nuzzled her neck.

"Take all the time you need. Meanwhile, I'll be waiting, withering away, and soon will look like one of those poor, dried-out plants out there," he said, pointing out into the desert.

She waited only a few days, mostly because she dreaded telling Aras. She was ready to stay with him the first day and never leave. Only the tiniest part of her still hesitated. The part that was still clinging to societal norms. Giving in to him too quickly somehow seemed immoral. *Maybe I'm prudish*, she thought, and immediately decided to move in with him.

Aras embraced her for a very long time. "You can come back anytime. I won't ask questions. I hope you know this is your home. Forever, if you want."

"I do," she said and pulled away, glancing at Aras when a tiny tremor shook her friend's chest.

"Hey, you're not getting rid of me that easily. You will still have to put up with me every day at work. And I'll come to visit."

"I know," Aras said, sniffling and wiping her eyes in the sleeves of her robe. "Silly old me."

Zara didn't go to work the next day, or the day after, or the day after that. For the entire week, they stayed in one room: the airy bedroom with hardly any furniture except for the giant bed and two side tables, not able to separate from each other for longer than a few minutes, greedily exploring each other's bodies.

Emotions and desires suppressed by societal norms were suddenly freed, swelling within her, stripping her of modesty or guilt. She wondered whether she had entered a secret world unknown to her parents or other Andalians and questioned the Andalian societal rules again. Could the System ever match people in this way? Why did her mother appear unhappy then?

"What's this thing on your chest?" she asked, wrinkling her forehead. A memory flashed before her eyes. She remembered seeing this shape in the past, but couldn't remember where. Certainly not in her dreams. Then where? And why did it tug at her chest?

"It's my birthmark."

"Looks like a sun with rays radiating from it."

"Yeah," he laughed. "That's why my grandma used to call me Sunny Boy. I didn't like it when I was a boy, but I've grown to like it."

Zara finally returned to the lab, feeling only slightly guilty. It was her first vacation in over six years. For two weeks, she tried to immerse herself back into research, but her mind wandered back to Tirg. She stayed in the lab only because Tirg returned to work as well. She counted the minutes until she could fly back to him and to the quiet white house that was now filled with their love.

Everything changed one night when she woke up with an idea, and she realized exactly what she needed to do to move forward with her research. Now that she knew it, it seemed so simple. She slid out of bed quietly, staring at Tirg before she dressed and tiptoed out. She scribbled on a piece of paper torn out of her notebook, left it on the kitchen counter, and went to work.

Aras, also arriving early, noticed Zara's plane and rushed to her lab. "You're an early bird. What's the matter? You couldn't sleep?" Aras asked, glancing at her with a worried look.

Zara turned around, beaming. Her black eyes shone like two black diamonds. "I've got it. I finally figured out how to harness dark matter effectively and efficiently and create even more powerful fragments."

"You have? Want to tell me about it?"

"I realized one of the sub-particles differs from the others because it behaves like a gluon. I'll program the splitter to channel just those particles to the collector, and we'll end up having enough of them to stick to each other and form larger masses."

"Brilliant!"

Zara plunged herself into her work and did not once think about going back home, but when she returned home late but with her eyes beaming, Tirg leaped at her with bulging eyes, hugging her frantically. "I was so worried. You've never come back so late. And you forgot your RAM. Are you okay?"

"I left you a note about my brilliant idea and that I might be home later than usual."

"A note? Where?"

"In the kitchen. Right on the counter so you'd see it first thing when you woke up. I didn't want to wake you. You looked so peaceful and beautiful."

"Really?" Tirg turned around and dashed to the kitchen. Zara followed.

"Where is it?" he asked.

Zara glanced around and under the counters and the table, now set up with plates and utensils, but the note was nowhere to be found

"You didn't just grab it and throw it away?"

"No."

"You sure? I know how you are first thing in the morning. Did you put it in a drawer?"

"I'm sure. Are you sure you left me a note?"

"Of course, I am," she said, slamming her bag on the counter.

Tirg's eyes scanned the bright, uncluttered space, and then found hers. "I'm sorry. I believe you. You're here now. Safe."

For the first time since he had come back to her, she saw his face and body tense.

"What are you worried about?"

His blue eyes shadowed. "Somebody broke into our house. What were they looking for, and what else did they take?"

Zara gazed at him for a moment. "There could be a much less sinister explanation for it. My father used to fight with little critters in his hangar for as long as I remember. The little rodents would steal his manuals and shred them to pieces, building their nests."

"Hmm, I don't think we have rodents here."

"They fit into the tiniest places. You'd never even know unless stuff goes missing."

He smiled at her, but his eyes remained stormy.

"Or a previous owner could have wandered in. Maybe they are attached to their house. Who was the previous owner?"

"I never had a reason to ask."

She shrugged, inhaled the savory aroma erupting from the oven, and eyed the plates. "It smells divine here. You cooked dinner?" she asked, pointing at the oven.

"I wanted to surprise you."

She approached him and slid into his arms. "Don't worry about the stupid note. Mice ate it."

"You're right," he said, and kissed her on the head. "Let's see if we can salvage dinner."

For the first time in years, she thought of Sentrel and his malevolent eyes and shivered. Was he watching her?

∼

Later that evening, Tirg had another surprise for her. He disappeared for a moment, returning with a large, unknown to her, stringed instrument.

She eyed him suspiciously. "You can play this?"

"A little," he said sheepishly, and sat on the plush blue sofa beside her.

The large wooden instrument sang in his hands. The bittersweet melancholy brought on by the ballad took her by surprise. She closed her eyes and listened, imagining the story behind the tune.

"What are you doing to me, Tirg? You're bewitching me. I no longer belong only to myself," she whispered, more to herself than to him. He didn't hear her, his fingers dancing on the strings and his eyes on the frets. *I'll go to Sinturija with you. I'll go to hell and back with you.*

∼

Despite moving rapidly through the process of producing condensed dark matter fragments and fusing them with the preontechnology, she still couldn't wait to get back to Tirg. Her body tingled in anticipation of being in his arms. Her punctuality took a nosedive as she took her time getting out of bed to go to work in the morning, inhaling the slightly musky, vanilla scent of his body to last her until she returned.

One morning, she awoke later than usual. Tirg was already banging dishes around in the kitchen. The smell of brewing coffee, normally so pleasant, was foul and wrong. With her hand over her mouth, she staggered out of bed and started her daily ritual of wrapping her chest in a band. That day, the band just couldn't extend far enough, no matter how hard she tugged on it to stretch it. Tirg walked in on her standing in front of a large mirror, grimacing, wrapping and unwrapping her breasts. The band's ends flapped as she flung them around.

"Do you need help with that?" Tirg asked, embracing her and inhaling the scent of her hair.

She gave a little tremulous cry and tossed the band onto the light wooden floor.

"What's wrong?"

"It doesn't fit. It's gotten smaller."

"The band shrunk?"

She sat on the bed and grasped her breasts. With her face puckered, she looked like a forlorn child.

"Zara, my love, what is it?"

"I don't know," she whimpered. "They hurt and don't want to be bound."

Tirg sat on the bed beside her and wrapped his arms around her. "Hey, it's okay, my love. Let them be today. Stay home and let me pamper you."

Zara curled up on the bed and closed her eyes. A tear escaped from under her eyelids. "Maybe I'm just tired."

Tirg covered her up and watched her fall asleep. Then he messaged Aras that Zara was sick and wouldn't be coming to the lab.

Zara awoke in the late afternoon, wrapped a robe around herself, and roamed the house. When Tirg found her, she was circling the kitchen table in slow strides, holding her belly and grimacing.

Tirg paled. He intercepted her when she was coming around the corner, swooped her, and brought her chin up, holding it with his hand. "Tell me what's going on with you. Should I call the doctor?"

"A doctor? Are you mad? I can't see a doctor! He'll contact the authorities, I'll go to prison, and they'll kill you!"

Zara wiggled out of his embrace and backed away, staring at him with wild eyes.

"I wouldn't let them take you anywhere or hurt you. They can't do anything to me because I have diplomatic immunity."

"I'm okay. Don't fuss over me. I'm just tired."

Tirg's face tightened. "Zara, look at me. This can't continue. This country's rules are insane, cruel, and wrong. We can't stay here. People get sick, and when they do, they need doctors and medicines."

"Spence can get some medicine for us."

"Spence is a shrink!"

"I'm fine. All better. Let's drop it for now. Please," Zara said, and left the kitchen.

The next morning, Zara showed up earlier than usual at the lab and disappeared into her office. Later in the morning, Aras popped her head into Zara's lab and gasped, seeing her young friend sitting by her desk, bent over and holding her stomach.

"What's wrong? Are you hurt?"

"My stomach hurts. It feels weird and swollen."

"Where does it hurt? Show me."

Zara slowly stood up and pressed on her lower abdomen. "It hurts right here, and I'm so nauseous all the time. I can't eat anything without wanting to puke."

"Oh, my. I hope it's not your appendix. Come on, let's go to Spence. He'll be able to scan you with his machines and figure out what's going on."

"We can't do that. We'd be found out."

"Yeah, we can. I'll just message him to send the receptionist out on an errand. He did this for me when I had back problems. It turned out I had just pulled a muscle. With the pills Spence got me, I had a good time and was back at work in a few days."

∽

Amelia smiled, seeing Zara and Aras enter, and let them into Spence's office. "I'll go get him," she said and closed the door behind her.

"Are you sure about her?" Zara asked.

"Amelia? Yes," Aras said and lowered her voice to a whisper. "I told you they've been together for a while."

"They live together?"

"No, of course not."

"Lie down here on the bench," Spence said, opening a cupboard and taking out a handheld white instrument, which he plugged into a white blinking apparatus. Aras opened Zara's robe and pulled her white cotton shirt up.

Spence turned his gadget on and looked Zara in the eye. "You may feel a little tingling sensation, but it shouldn't hurt."

He placed the flat disc part of the gadget on Zara's belly, just above her sternum, and watched the monitor above while moving it across her belly. Aras held her hand, sitting on a stool by the padded bench. Spence's eyes turned into slits when he moved the disc onto the lower abdomen. He furrowed his brow and moved the gadget back and forth.

"What is it?" Aras asked.

He didn't answer, staring at the monitor.

"Spence, what is it? Tell us," Aras said.

"Let's go to my office," he said. He put the gadget away, turned off the machine, and, not looking either at Aras or Zara, left the examination room.

Zara and Aras glanced at each other and followed him. Zara's heart galloped.

Aras stroked Zara's shoulder. "It's going to be okay, kiddo."

Spence was standing by the window when they entered. "Sit down, girls," he said, still gazing out the window.

"Spence—"

"Sit down, Aras," he said, enunciating his words.

Zara sat, and Aras followed.

Spence tugged on his beard, drew a big breath, and sat across from them.

"What's wrong with me? Just tell me."

"Wrong? That's the incorrect term," he said dryly. "There is nothing wrong with you. You're pregnant."

"What?" Aras shrieked.

Zara's eyes widened. "What does that mean?"

"You're with child. You're going to be a mother."

Zara slumped in her chair and gazed at her hands that lay slack on her lap.

"What are we going to do?" Aras asked.

"She'll have to stop working before she shows. If her pregnancy is normal, she can give birth at home. Our mom did. If there are complications, we'll have to wait and see."

Aras and Spence gazed at Zara, who sat silently, resting her hand on her belly and withdrawn into her own thoughts.

"What if it's not normal?"

Spence sighed and rubbed his beard. "I'll do some research."

Zara kept her glazed eyes on her hands. *I am pregnant.* Her brain, sluggishly looped it, blocking everything else.

Aras grasped Zara's forearm. "It's gonna be okay, kiddo. We'll get through it."

Spence now had both hands rubbing his beard. His gray eyes steeled.

"I'm going to have to leave Andalia," Zara said, and rose from her chair. She was calm, and her voice was steady and firm. From her core, a realization, a sudden truth, arose and spread through her body as if it were a blissful wave. She realized it was the only decision she could make to keep them all safe.

"What? No, you don't have to go anywhere. We'll manage."

Spence said nothing, but exhaled, gazing at Aras.

Zara darted to the door. "I have to go now."

After Zara left, Aras looked at her brother. "She doesn't have to leave. We can protect her."

"It's not only her I worry about. It's you I'm most concerned about. If she gets caught, so will you."

"Not if we're careful."

"There is also the baby. Zara would not get the proper care, and if something went wrong, we'd both have it on our conscience. She's right. She has to leave. Tirg appears to be capable, resourceful, and very caring. He'll take good care of her."

Aras sat down, placed her elbows on the desk, and nested her head in her hands. "It's all my fault. I should have prepared her better."

Spence rose from his seat, walked around the desk, and patted Aras on her back. "I know it's hard, and I know you love her, but she'll be better off away from here."

Tirg wasn't home when Zara arrived. She dashed outside the moment she stepped in, declaring the air inside too stale to breathe. Holding her hand on her belly, she walked around the property, studying her surroundings and memorizing them. Soon, she'd have to leave it all behind and venture into the unfamiliar land, far from everyone and everything she loved. She sat on the ground with one hand on her belly and one on the ground beside her, drawing circles in the dirt, oblivious to the sun disappearing behind the hills and the air chilling.

That was how Tirg found her. "Zara," he said, "it's freezing outside. What are you doing here?"

"Oh, I hadn't noticed," she said, and looked around as if woken up from a trance. "Let's go back. I have something to tell you." She rose with a slight grunt and slid her hand into his.

His reaction to the news was that of a dog, happy after seeing his beloved owner returning after a long separation. Alternating between squeezing her tightly and then jumping around and running around the room, he shouted, "I'm going to be a father! We're having a baby!"

Tirg started preparations for Zara to travel to Sinturija rather than waiting for her to show. With the help of his influential father, who described her research to his government as important and benefiting Sinturija, permission for her travel arrived two weeks after Zara had learned she was pregnant.

She continued to work, mostly to copy her notes to take with her. The permission to leave Andalia had proven more difficult and taken longer. She was three months pregnant when she had her interview with the emigration agent.

Wearing her regular disguise and sitting in the murky hallway and staring at the name of the official engraved with large gold letters on a brown door, she bore her fingernails into the wooden bench, already scratched by previous nervous emigrants.

Just before her name was called, the letters started spinning. Later, she couldn't recall how she got inside, facing an old man with a long gray beard that almost touched his brown desk. She couldn't remember the entire conversation she had with him, only bits and pieces about building scientific collaborations with Sinturija. Aras, waiting outside, helped her onto the plane that was waiting in the far corner of the dreary parking area in front of an even drearier old building.

Straining his neck to see out of the back of the plane, Tirg waited, wringing his hands. "And?"

Zara looked at him blankly. "I don't know."

"I'm sure it went fine," Aras said, starting the plane.

Zara sat by Tirg and nestled her head on his shoulder and said to Aras, "Let's get the hell out of here."

21

THE EXPLOSION

Two days prior to their departure, Tirg left early for his office in the Sinturijan embassy to finish paperwork. Beads of sweat built on Zara's forehead as she stretched the band to bundle her breasts with it. They had grown so much. She threw the band on the bed and searched for a longer piece but soon gave up the pointless search in the house that was already mostly empty. After trying for a while longer, she finally succeeded and wiped her sweaty forehead.

She threw her bag onto the passenger seat of her plane, attached her pilot harness, and punched the buttons on the control panel, but it remained dark. She tried again and again, but nothing worked.

"What the hell?"

She found a manual in the compartment above her head and leafed through it to troubleshoot. Nothing she tried worked. The plane was not responding; not even the lights that usually came on when she entered worked. She hopped out and climbed on top to open the compartment to the engine. After hitting it repeatedly, the hatch finally swung open, and she stared at the engine parts, touching them and checking wires and their connections.

Did you think you would fix it just by looking at it?

She pushed the hair from her forehead, smudging black grease over it, shut the hatch, and jumped down.

Back at the house, she searched for the RAM but couldn't find it. "Tirg must have packed it."

Today was her last day at the laboratory and her only chance to say goodbye to all the researchers and assistants working there. Aras and Spence she expected to see this evening for a farewell dinner. *I hope Tirg returns in time for me to make it to the lab before they go home.*

She sat outside, wiping her dirty hands on her robe. Of all days, the plane had to break down today when she most needed it. After an hour, she went inside, organized her work notes and packed them into a small bag she was going to carry with her on the plane. She opened a secret compartment in her bag, took out a small box, opened the lid, and sighed with relief. The golden substance was still in it. The sensation of being watched resurfaced. She shivered and held the bag to her chest. *You're just being paranoid.*

It was mid-afternoon when she heard the plane. Thinking Tirg was home early, she ran outside only to be surprised by Spence getting out of his plane. She waved, wondering how he'd guessed she needed a ride, but her face dropped when her friend was close enough to see the hollowness of his eyes on his pale face.

She slowly lowered herself to the ground, not letting her eyes off Spence.

"No, no, no," she whispered with lips that were rapidly losing color. Her hands dug into the chalky dirt.

Spence kneeled beside her and wrapped his arms around her. Then he spoke with the voice of a stranger, distant and choked with tears. Zara said nothing, asked nothing. Even if she wanted to, she couldn't open her mouth with her teeth gritted hard against each other. Spence's words sounded garbled. She understood that something terrible had happened, something so horrendous that it would crumble her world. In that instant, she wanted to be a child, an infant who was incapable of grasping a tragedy.

"They told me the gas line under the lab exploded. Everything happened instantaneously. There was nothing anyone could have done to save the employees. The gas line and the lab flammables were a deadly mixture, the captain said. He assured me that everyone had died instantly and hadn't suffered."

Spence took Zara's hand in his and held it. He cried. She couldn't. Out of the confusion and shock, a thought materialized, clasping her core in an icy grasp. She was to blame for this. Somehow, it was her fault this happened. She didn't hear Tirg's plane land.

"What's wrong?" Tirg shouted, and losing his usual grace, tumbled out of the cockpit, and ran toward them. Zara sat staring at the ground.

Tirg slid beside Zara, raising a cloud of dust. "What happened? The baby? Did something happen to the baby?"

She didn't understand his question, looking at him with her black eyes that were as deep and black as the sorrow and the darkness within her.

Spence shook his head. "The baby is fine," he whispered. "She's in shock."

"Why? What happened?" Tirg asked, carefully placing both hands under Zara's shoulders. "Come on, my love, let's get you inside."

Tirg picked her up and carried her inside. After he made her drink water, positioned her on the couch, and covered her with a blanket, Spence told him what happened. Tears would not stop rolling down his face.

"I don't even know why I came here. I think I was hoping Aras was here unharmed, alive."

A long silence followed that neither man sought to break. Tirg kept his eyes on Zara, who was motionless, hiding the tremor behind her calm cheeks.

Then she broke the silence, speaking in a low voice. "The plane wouldn't start. It's broken. I couldn't find the RAM either." She paused and then looked Spence in the eye. "It should have been me in there, shouldn't it? Instead of Aras. But the plane was broken. It wouldn't go."

"What craziness!" Tirg kneeled before her, stroking her head. "You mustn't think like this. Spence said it was an accident."

"Was it?" she asked. "Was it really?"

"What are you saying, Zara? Where is this coming from?"

"We were close to getting it out there. To publish our research and to get grants for commercial applications. Sentrel was always envious of Aras. It's his doing! He did this!"

Tirg sat beside her and put an arm around her, but she didn't ease into his chest. Her body remained stiff in his arms.

"You're wrong. Sentrel couldn't have done it," Spence said.

"Yes, he did!"

"No, he didn't. He's in the hospital. This is what I was going to tell Aras today. That's the reason I went to the lab today."

Zara's eyes widened.

"His plane malfunctioned and crashed. The pilot died, and Sentrel has a slim chance of making it. I was hurrying to Aras to tell her that."

Zara's mouth formed a thin line as she jumped from her seat.

"Someone did this," she said.

"You think it was intentional?" Tirg asked. "That someone sabotaged his plane?"

"Two brilliant scientists have been attacked in one day. And both were working on the same secret government project."

"You don't seriously think the government did this, do you? That's insane. And the Ghost Island thing happened a long time ago," Spence said, running his fingers through his beard.

"I don't know who did it but I intend to find out. I want to go there now."

"Go where?" Tirg asked, raising his eyebrows.

"To the lab."

"The lab is gone. Only the fire crew and the police are there now, investigating it," Spence said, his voice faltering.

"I want to see it for myself. Who's going to fly me there? I need a ride—my plane is dead."

"I'll take you," Tirg said to her, getting up and facing Spence, touching his shoulder. "Why don't you stay with us tonight?"

Zara was silent during the flight. Tirg's face tensed as he glanced at her. His questions were met with shrugs and silence as Zara stared into the distance, still not crying. He finally stopped asking her but steered in silence, and landed a short distance from the lab. As he landed, a wall of smoke met them.

Zara reached for the door, but Tirg stopped her. "No! You can't."

"I must see it."

"You can see it from here. There is too much smoke—"

"I want to see it!"

"Zara, you're pregnant!"

Zara met his eyes. It was the first time he had raised his voice at her.

"There is too much smoke out there. You saw it. The building is gone. There is nothing we can do here. We should go back to Spence. He's lost his sister."

"I lost my mother!"

Tirg hesitated before continuing. "Aras was like your mother, but your mother is alive and well," he said. "You have your parents, and you have me. Spence has no one."

"He has Amelia," Zara said, throwing him an angry glance, but seeing his eyes, the angry words died on her lips. "You're right."

"I realize how much she meant to you and that you're hurting. All I can say is that I'm sorry, my love. I'd do anything to go back in time and save her. Anything."

Zara nodded, then looked at the wall of smoke and raised her hand. "I promise you I'll find who did this and make them pay!"

The next morning, Zara awoke after a night of restless sleep full of unsettling dreams, which, to her surprise, she couldn't remember. She found him outside, looking into the engine compartment of her plane.

"Where's Spence?" she asked, looking up at him.

"Finally asleep in the spare bedroom."

"Have you slept at all?"

"No, but you know me."

"What's wrong with my plane?"

Tirg wrinkled his forehead and looked away. "Nothing," he said, and jumped down, wiping his hands on his pants.

"What do you mean?"

"There is nothing wrong. It works just fine. It started for me the first time. I inspected the engine to see if there was something that might have disconnected temporarily."

"But it didn't start for me. Everything was dark, and nothing worked," Zara cried, and rubbed her cheeks. "I've tried and tried and tried."

"Hey, I believe you. It's okay. Planes are strange beasts. They have temperaments. It has happened to me before. The darn thing wouldn't start, and then when I was about to give up, it started."

"Right," she said, glancing at him sideways. The memory of the missing note surfaced. The dread and suspicion that she was being watched returned.

"It's my last day here. Before I go, I must do something."

"What?"

"I want to see my mother," she said.

"Are you sure she will not report you?"

"It's been years. I just want to see her one last time. I will not tell her I'm leaving or that I'm pregnant."

"You want me to fly you there?"

"Yes," she said. *Before I change my mind.*

22

I WILL NEVER FORGIVE HER

Tirg parked approximately a mile away from the house that Zara grew up in—the same area in which she'd hidden her notebooks from her father. Zara's eyes went to that spot as she jumped out of the plane. He stayed with the plane, trying to smile, but she saw his pinched eyebrows and the way he pressed himself against his plane.

Her stomach constricted as she walked toward the house that once was her home. It looked smaller and duller—the color faded from the walls and window frames, replaced by a patina of brown dust. What remained of the once robust cacti were blackened heaps of unrecognizable chunks.

Her mother should have been there alone now—cooking, cleaning, waiting for her husband to return from work. Zara walked carefully, trying not to make any noise, although her feet were unusually heavy and wanted to shuffle. She held on to the window frame and drew a big breath before finally looking inside. The living room was empty, so she moved to the kitchen, which, to her surprise, was also unoccupied. She tiptoed to her parents' bedroom, walking by her old bedroom and nearly passing it, but then stepped back and stared through the window.

"Mother...Mommy..." A cry escaped her pale lips when she saw her mother bent over the blue notebook with Zara's poems she had left behind. Zara guessed from her red and swollen eyes she had been crying. Zara darted to the door, but a hand stopped her before she tried to open it.

"You can't," Tirg said. "You're not wearing your disguise. She'll report you. You said so yourself."

"I have to. She's crying because of me. I have to!" Zara cried. Tirg scooped her up and started carrying her back. The front door opened, and Mia stormed out.

"Zara?"

"Mommy!" Zara shouted and extended her hands toward her mother.

Tirg kept running, carrying Zara. Mia followed.

Zara had never seen her mother run so fast. "Let me go! Put me down!" Zara shouted. "She's already seen me."

Tirg kept running.

Zara dug her fingernails into his arm, but he didn't react.

"Stop, Tirg! Put me down!"

It was the tone of her voice that made him stop and look at her.

"I don't think she will report me. She loves me, after all," Zara said. Suddenly, tears welled in her eyes. Tears she couldn't shed before now poured out when she realized her imminent separation from her mother.

Tirg hugged her. "Okay, okay, my love." Then he lowered her down slowly and gently. Meanwhile, Mia strolled toward them, whispering something they couldn't hear.

Zara noticed she looked so much older and thinner, and a jolt of guilt jabbed her in the heart.

"It's really you. You're alive. My daughter...my baby...you came back..."

Zara walked toward her mother, sobbing.

"Mommy," she wept when Mia wrapped her arms around her.

Tirg was watchful, but his blue eyes moistened.

Mother and daughter stayed in each other's arms, while Trig watched the road leading to the house.

At one point, Mia extended her arms and studied Zara's face. "You're so beautiful. The short hair suits you. So grown-up."

"Mother—"

"What happened to you? Did the Romanas kidnap you?" she asked, and pointed at Tirg. "Is he one of them?"

"No, I wasn't kidnapped. I'm sorry…"

"Shush, and no, I'm the one who's sorry for the way I acted. It's because I didn't want you to have a life full of regrets and shame I carried on my shoulders. I wanted to spare you. I didn't want you to hurt as I had. Long after you left, I understood I was protecting you for the wrong reasons and from the wrong foe. I was wrong to protect you from living your life. Back then, I believed you'd be happier living a structured life. I didn't know about your passion then. Only after I had found your notebook did I understand what you must have felt. I am so sorry."

"Why were you hurting?" Zara asked.

"I longed to be with the man I loved," Mia said to her daughter. "The man I loved the moment I saw him, but I let him go—shunned him because I wanted to be the good, obedient daughter-wife and didn't want to feel shame. But I still did. All those years I felt shame and pain, but the worst was the regret I felt. That man, Zara, was your father, and I should have run away with him."

"The man who took my bear? That man was my father? That's why he cried?"

Mia nodded and exhaled. "So many times I wanted to tell you. I wanted to bundle you up and search for him."

"Why didn't you?" Zara asked, searching her mother's eyes.

Mia's eyes softened, while Zara's hardened.

"I didn't want to deprive you of the life of a normal girl—"

"Deprive me? Normal? Mother, there was nothing normal about the life you wanted me to lead. That you led, and so many other women have, and do."

"But you would have been shamed, shunned by society, and

maybe even imprisoned. All because of my choices. I couldn't do it to you."

"Where did he go?"

Mia shook her head. Her hands trembled as she pleated them into painful knots.

"What do you know about him?"

Mia shrugged. "Not much," she whispered. "He said he woke up on the beach and couldn't remember anything. Years later, he somehow found me and tried to convince me to run away with him. I lied to him when he asked if you were his daughter, but he took one glance at you, and he knew. You look just like him."

"We have to go," Tirg said.

"You should go before your...Gilbert comes back," Mia said.

"Too late," Zara said, watching Gilbert's plane descend and land. Tirg motioned for Zara to go, but she ignored him, staring at the approaching figure. The man she'd thought was her father. Strict, demanding, temperamental, but fair most of the time. He approached carefully, watching the group, with his hands moving slowly away from his pockets as if grasping the air for support. The closer he got, the slower he walked, but when he realized it was his daughter standing before him, he crossed the distance between them in one long stride, picked her up, and kissed her cheeks. "Zara, my baby, my girl. You're alive. You're okay."

She wrapped her arms around his neck and nestled her head on his shoulder. "Father, I've missed you."

He spun her around, holding her tight. Mia's face reddened watching them. Tirg looked surprised. He tensed when Gilbert first approached, but now his body relaxed.

"Who's this?" Gilbert asked Zara, pointing at Tirg.

"My husband."

Zara expected an outburst of rage from both her parents, and she was prepared for it, crossing her arms in front of her and setting her jaw. There was a moment of severe silence as Mia and Gilbert alternated their glances between Tirg and Zara.

"How? Has the System—"

"No, Mother. No machine will select a husband for me nor tell me who to love or leave behind," Zara said and turned to leave. She didn't see Gilbert walking fast to Tirg, who instantly set his muscles ready to deflect the blow. But instead of a blow, an extended hand waited for Tirg's hand.

"You love her?"

"With all my soul," Tirg said, taking Gilbert's hand and shaking it.

"You look like a good man. You have kind eyes. Take care of my daughter."

"I will."

Gilbert turned to Zara. "I'm sorry for being harsh, Zara. I wanted you to be happy. I didn't know any other way," Gilbert said, shifting his weight from one foot to another. "I regretted it after your disappearance and promised myself that if I ever saw you again, I'd never treat you like that again. I love you."

"I know."

"You're pregnant," Mia whispered after studying her daughter. Her pale face, whitened even more, exacerbating her hollow cheeks, and the thinness of her skin.

Zara tensed and nodded. "We must go now," she said to Tirg.

Mia stepped toward Zara, but Zara was already on her way back to the plane. Her back was straight and uninviting. It was Tirg who lingered behind, glancing at Mia. When Zara didn't turn around, he waved to Mia and Gilbert and followed her.

"Zara?"

"Let's go."

"Don't you want to say goodbye to your mother?"

"I already did."

"She looks miserable."

Zara pursed her lips and increased her pace.

"Why are you being mean to her?"

"I'd never lie to my daughter and deprive her of a choice."

"She thought she was protecting you."

"I don't see it that way. She was protecting herself and her way of life."

"Zara, stop. It's not like you—"

"You don't understand," she shouted, turning her face, contorted with fury, toward him. "I will never know my real father."

"It's not like you never had a father. Gilbert was a good father to you."

"Yes, I realize that. It's about who my real father was. We share something special. Something I never had with Gilbert. The nightmares I have...the woman I keep seeing in my dreams and visions...she looks like him, my real father. There's a connection between us, a bond I don't understand, and now I never will, because she threw him away and didn't even bother to ask where he was going."

"Oh, my love. I didn't know. I'm sorry. But she is still your mother."

"She knew about the woman I saw in my dreams and that she looked like my father, but all that time, she said nothing. I will never forgive her. Never!" Zara shouted, sprinted up to the plane, and hopped into the cockpit.

Tirg started the plane and took off but didn't get far before Zara gripped his arm, gesturing for him to go back.

"I can't believe I left one of my notebooks. I thought all I left were my poetry books. My mother could have turned me in, and based on what was inside my notebook, the authorities could have found me. But she didn't."

Tirg grinned and turned the plane around. "That's my girl. I knew you didn't have it in you. Your mother loves you."

23

EMANESCENCE

"It's so green. So beautiful," Zara murmured, looking out the window of the car that carried her and Trig to his parents' house. The car and driver were waiting for them when they arrived at the airport. Zara's stare was arrested by the shiny gold buttons on the driver's navy uniform when he opened the door for her. The red flower with thick shiny petals sitting in the breast pocket of his jacket moved and released a fragrance that was both sweet and spicy, reminding her of cinnamon rolls her mother used to bake. The driver bowed deeply, seeing them emerge from the airport's exit and welcomed Tirg in a language Zara didn't understand but found beautiful. Tirg had taught her a few words since the time they'd decided to leave Andalia. She'd learned each word with worship-like attentiveness and care to pronounce them correctly.

The trees were turning fall colors she hadn't seen in Andalia. The reds were deeper, almost like blood, and the oranges and yellows demanded attention with their vividness. But the most startling were the skies. Reaching so far into the distance as if she were on a different planet, the dazzling blue skies were filled with emerald clouds shaped in ways that made her question her eyes.

"This time of year, the clouds amass a lot of moisture and

Emanescence from our bogs. That's why they look so different from Andalian skies," Tirg said, smiling. Ever since they had landed, his eyes shone with an intensity she hadn't seen before—as if the clouds and the air intensified their color and shine.

"The what? Emanescence?"

"That's what we call it. I'll show you soon," he said, kissing her hand. "Your nerdy scientific mind will love it."

She watched the tall and rigid trees lining the long road leading to the enormous mansion made of light sandstone, deliberating whether they were saluting her or warning her to stay on the path. The wings of the house extended far and bent out of view.

As soon as they arrived at the entrance flanked by two giant stone tigers whose bodies were painted orange and black, enormous doors opened and a group of people spilled out. Tirg jumped out of the car when it was still moving and dashed toward them, blending with them, and soon was hidden from her view. The driver opened the door and extended his hand.

As she ambled toward the moving group of heads, searching for Tirg's blond head, Trig peeled off and ran toward her.

"Father, Mother, this is my Zara," he said, taking her arm.

A woman, who looked barely older than Zara, stepped out and walked toward her. "Welcome home, child," she said to her in Andalian and extended her arms.

Zara shifted closer and soon was enveloped in a warm hug and the scent of the woman's dark blond hair falling down her shoulders. She inhaled its fragrance, which reminded her of pines and honey. Tirg's mother, approximately the same height as Zara, drew her closer into a hug, then pulled away, gazed at her, and finally kissed both her cheeks. She said something to Tirg in a melodic voice, and he nodded, grinning. Zara stood staring into her blue eyes and feeling the warmth they emanated. Zara had never met a woman with so much poise and imagined that's how a queen would have behaved and looked.

Meanwhile, Tirg's father was watching her, studying her intently as if learning and memorizing her every feature or trying to extract all her secrets. As tall as Tirg and possessing the same intense, curious blue eyes, he was shockingly handsome. In his eyes, she found something else that she couldn't identify. Zara ended up in his arms, in an electrifying embrace, not realizing how she got there. He held her while welcoming her into his country and family in perfect Andalian in a low and silky voice.

While she experienced the hypnotic embrace, Tirg picked up his mother and spun her around, kissing her cheeks. Then he did the same with a shy young woman, standing close to and resembling Tirg's mother. The other five people—three women and two men—stood still, politely waiting their turn to greet them. Zara gathered they were the staff.

After the greetings, Tirg, squeezing Zara's hand, announced his readiness to retire to their rooms and rest before dinner. Choked up by the warm greeting, Zara let Tirg lead her through the colossal doors, nearly running through countless hallways, all of them lined with old portraits. She thought of herself as an insignificant mouse, scorned by the painted faces of Tirg's ancestors. Tirg finally stopped, kicked the door open, carried her through the door, and dropped her on the bed.

The ceiling of their bedroom was covered with frescoes. The one above the bed was of a young woman with blond hair falling to her knees, sitting at a spring and gazing into the distance as if waiting for someone.

"At last. Home with my girl," he said, and kissed her. His eyes, passionate before, reached a new level that afternoon as if a part of him had been left in Sinturija and now reunited with him. They pulled her into a different realm and into the lovemaking, impatient and primal.

Afterward, Zara's senses were overwhelmed with unfamiliar sights, smells, and sounds as she lay on the bed gazing at a fresco of the young woman. Then, she felt herself sink into the bed as if her body had suddenly started shrinking, sucked out by emotions. She felt like crying, but her eyes were dry and sunken inward. As if sensing it, Trig embraced her tightly and kissed her forehead tenderly, slowly. "It's going to be okay, my love."

She believed him and soon calmed.

"You told me your father spoke Andalian, but I didn't realize your mother spoke it too," Zara said as they were dressing to get ready for family dinner.

"Everyone in my family speaks Andalian. My father made sure everyone spoke it, even the staff. He wants you to feel at home here."

"What are you wearing?" Zara asked, opening her eyes wide as Tirg put on a crispy white shirt, the ends of which were embroidered with gold, and a black velvet jacket also laced with gold.

"Family maryns."

"Huh?"

"We wear them for special family dinners."

Zara assessed her blue robe, which paled in comparison with Tirg's lavish attire.

"You look beautiful the way you are."

There was a knock on the door, and Tirg went to investigate. She heard him speaking to a woman.

He returned, grinning. "Apparently, my mother and my sister have been busy. They ordered a bunch of clothes for you until you get used to our customs and order them yourself according to your taste. But I think you'll find my mother's taste agreeable," Tirg said, walking toward a door at the end of the room. "This is your closet," he said, and flung it open.

"Oh, my," Zara gasped, holding her hand to her mouth. The spacious closet was filled with clothes, shoes, and hats of all colors and shapes.

"I think you'll need help to pick something appropriate for dinner," Tirg said, taking her robe off.

∽

The magnificence and richness of the house astounded her. Accustomed to simple, purpose-serving surroundings without much adornment, Zara didn't understand the reason behind the gold moldings, crystal chandeliers, rich frescoes, sculptures, and the intricacies of the furniture. She herself looked regal in the clothes Tirg had selected for her: a red velvet dress with black lace wrapping around her neckline, enhancing her breasts, which were already full, ready for motherhood.

Tirg sat beside his mother, and Zara sat beside him and facing Tirg's father. A mysterious smile played at the corner of his lips when she looked at him. She felt her face flush when he assessed her in her new attire.

"You look beautiful, my daughter," Tirg's mother said. "We haven't been properly introduced, my dear, as my son quickly snatched you for himself. I'm Elenora, and over there is my daughter Danuta. My dear husband's name is Zmey, which means dragon, but don't be fooled by his name; he is more of a teddy bear than a dragon. At the end of the table sit my sister Emily and her two daughters, Ola and Dora. Zmey's sister, Tamra, sits across from Zmey. You can't possibly remember all the names. It's a big family."

Tirg smiled at Zara. He knew she could remember everything, hearing it only once, but said nothing to his mother. Zmey, however, volunteered. "Zara remembers everything," he said. "That's why she was the top scientist in Andalia."

"Are you going to miss your work?" Elenora asked.

"She won't have time to miss it. There is a new lab set up for her and top scientists to assist her in her research," Tirg's father said, smiling and raising his glass. "Let's all welcome Zara to our home and our country."

"Welcome, Zara," everyone said in unison, raising their glasses.

"Thank you all," Zara said. Her voice broke. "What did you mean by 'new lab'?"

"Tirg told me how important your research was to you. Important enough to pretend to be a man for years and risk prison. We Sinturijans appreciate scientists, men and women alike, so I put in a good word for you in the Ministry of Science, and they set up a lab with all the newest equipment and a promise to get you more when needed," Zmey said. As he spoke, his enigmatic smile gave way to a serious expression and an excited glow in his eyes.

"Really, Father?" Tirg asked. "That's great. You'll make my girl very happy," Tirg said, and glanced at Zara.

Zara opened her mouth to speak, but she couldn't decide whether to thank him or be suspicious. In what world did the Ministry of Science bequeath upon an unknown woman, a foreigner, so many resources? A lab like that would cost a fortune. And how could a mere diplomat have convinced the ministry to do that? But the delighted expression on Tirg's face left her with only one choice: to be thankful and graciously accept the offer. She discreetly covered the forced smile with a napkin.

Danuta mostly picked at her food and kept glancing at Zara. Slender and poised, she sat upright, almost unmoving. Although she resembled her mother in all her features, she lacked her glow and charisma. Her blue eyes were not as blue, and her lips, although full and soft like her mother's, were not as red—as if there were not enough luster for both in the same room. Too shy to utter a word, she sat quietly and only answered when spoken to. For a moment, Zara thought she was back in Andalia.

Elenora told her they lived in the richest and most beautiful part of Sinturija, full of natural resources, mountains, lakes, and forests that stretched forever.

"And people are much nicer," Emily said with a laugh that thundered, carrying across the room. Her daughters nudged her on both sides. Meanwhile, new dishes, arranged like works of art on delicate porcelain plates, kept arriving without Zara's noticing when and how. Wine kept appearing in the same mysterious way. Her glass contained clear reddish juice from fruits she couldn't identify. Her tastebuds were exploding, tasting the food, whose smell and taste matched its appearance.

Back in their rooms (five giant connected rooms full of light and two full bathrooms), Zara collapsed on the bed, holding her stomach.

"Did you know your father set up a lab just for me?" she asked, yawning.

"No, but I'm glad he did."

"I am so tired. I think it's because I ate too much, but I couldn't help myself."

"Get some sleep. Rest before our wedding."

"Our what?"

"Our wedding is in two days. They've been preparing it for a while."

"I didn't even know we were engaged. I don't remember saying yes or you asking me."

"I'm sorry, my love," Tirg said, falling to his knees. "Would you be my wife?"

"I'll think about it," she said and turned away, placing a pillow on her head.

"You're not really mad at me, are you?"

"Furious," she mumbled. "For a moment I thought I was back in Andalia."

"No, never," Tirg said. "I'd never order you around or make you feel inferior, my love. And it wouldn't be possible. I worship you," Tirg said. His voice choked with emotion. "I'm an idiot and thought I'd surprise you. I'm so sorry."

Zara sat up and threw the pillow at him. "Don't you ever do that again."

"So you forgive me, soon-to-be Mrs. Igres?"

"Hell no," she said and threw another pillow at him. The corners of her mouth went up when she saw the pillow hit its target and then Tirg blinking his eyes and cupping his hands asking for forgiveness.

24

FOR GOOD LUCK

On the morning of the wedding, the fog lifted early, and the air filled with the sweet smell of freshly cut grass coming through the open windows. Zara's wedding dress arrived just as she woke up. Upon hearing a gentle knock, she opened the door and gasped, seeing the lavender extravagance. Adorned with gems, lace, and airy gauze, the dress dazzled as Maria, the maid, carried it inside.

Zara, staring at the dress, forgot to thank Maria before she left. Then she fidgeted, touching it with the tips of her fingers. "I can't wear that. That's crazy."

"Why can't you? You don't like it? I realize that in Andalia, the women pick their wedding dresses, but here it's the mother-in-law's job and privilege," Tirg said, standing in the bathroom's doorway with his face partially shaved. "Do you want a different—"

"God, no! I love it, but it's not me. It's too much."

"It's only one day in your lifetime."

The disappointment in his voice startled her. She glanced at him and, seeing his round eyes and his hand holding the razor in midair, she quickly added. "You're right. I'm sorry. I love the dress," Zara said and slid her silk bathrobe off her arms. She put on the dress, taking her time to unravel the gauzy layers, but still couldn't quite find the opening for the arms.

She felt Tirg's hand stroking her bare arm and the hot air of his breath on her neck. "Let me help you with that, my love."

"You're not helping Tirg," she whispered. "We'll be late for our wedding."

Sitting in a horse-driven carriage next to Tirg, who in his white suit looked like a prince from an exotic country, Zara almost believed it was all a dream. Tirg held her hand, and she felt his pulse race. Hers slowed down.

"We're almost there. Close your eyes. I'll carry you to the end," Tirg said when the carriage stopped. Then he picked her up and carried her along the edge of a crystal-clear stream.

Even with her eyes closed, she perceived a change in lighting and the air. The air became moist, earthy, electric. As Tirg carried her, tiny, cold droplets landed on Zara's face and arms.

He put her down on the ground. "You can look now."

The entire family and the staff were waiting in a semicircle amid rich flowery decorations. At the far end, flowers adorned the entrance to a cave. Elenora stepped forward, carrying two crystal glasses. She handed one to Zara and the other to Tirg. Then Tirg led Zara to the cave. Her heart pounded as she stepped inside.

A small spring squirted out of the floor of a large circular cave, creating a fountain of cascading water. Water reached the pointy stalactites, which scattered emerald droplets across the walls and then pooled in a deep indentation and soaked back into the ground. From the center of the fountain, a faint emerald light emanated, pulsing slightly.

Zara's mouth opened as she gazed at the show of colors. "Is this emerald water?" she asked, glancing at Tirg. "Is that what causes the Emanescence?"

"Yes. Right now, it's not as strong and colorful as it is in the spring."

"But what is this? What chemicals does it have?"

"I don't know. Nobody knows."

"Nobody's examined it? Studied it?"

"No," Tirg said, scratching his head. "This thing is sacred. People come here to wish for things sometimes, but most of the time, it is left alone just to be. We treasure our show in the skies."

"Sacred? Why?"

Tirg shrugged. "It just is."

"What makes the color so intense? There might be harmful chemicals."

"No, there aren't any."

"How can you be sure?"

"Nobody ever got sick drinking it. People have always believed it is sacred, and that it protects us, but it needs to be left alone, undisturbed. I understand it may seem strange to a scientist, but you can't really evaluate a belief in scientific terms. We don't have a real, established religion in Sinturija, but people believe that sacred things and places like this spring can bring good luck and happiness."

"Why are we here?"

Tirg bent and filled his glass with the water. "We drink it. Every couple in our family must drink from this spring for protection."

"Protection from what?"

"From anything bad that could happen. It's for good luck. Our tradition."

"You want me to drink this?" Zara asked. She stepped back and moved her hand holding the glass behind her. "I'm pregnant. I don't know what's in the water."

"Hey, love. It's okay. You don't have to if you don't want to. We can just tell everyone you did," Tirg said. He walked over to her and stroked her arm.

"You're disappointed. It's really important to you, isn't it?"

"You're more important."

"I'll do it," she said, filling her glass. "Are you sure no one ever got sick drinking it?"

Trig put his hand on his chest, close to his heart. "I'm sure."

"A sip will not hurt the baby."

The water tasted so sweet and fresh and cold that Zara drank more than a sip and, at the end, closed her eyes and worked her tongue on the roof of her mouth, trying to untangle its complex flavors. There was a hint of pine, honeylike sweetness, salt, and something lightly bitter that she had no name for.

Zmey and Elenora tied their hands together with a silky purple band, and then both spoke in their melodic language. Zara was calm until the band touched her hands—her body started trembling. She wondered whether Tirg was as nervous as she was but dared not look at him, fearing she might start laughing. Then Tirg's finger moved and tickled her palm. She glanced at him and, seeing his face, burst out laughing. Tirg made a face at her and laughed too.

"You two," Elenora said, suppressing a smile. Zmey remained serious, his blue eyes fixed on Zara. She stopped laughing soon after she saw his eyes.

They untied their hands and led them to a table, and a young woman approached, carrying a small purple case. When she opened it and took out a large needle filled with purple liquid, Zara shuddered.

"What's that for?" she whispered in Tirg's ear.

A small tattoo. We'll each have matching tattoos tying us together. You pick the design.

"I was hoping for a ring or a bracelet," she said, eyeing the needle. She suddenly felt her chest tighten, and she had a sudden desire to run. *Is he branding me?*

"It doesn't hurt...that much. It'll only take a few minutes. A ring or a bracelet you can remove and lose," Tirg said and glanced at her. "What's wrong, my love? We don't have to do it if you don't want to. It's just a stupid tradition. We can order matching rings."

She watched him as he waved at the woman, telling her to take the box not with a hint of dismay but with ease.

What's the matter with you? He is not branding you. He is not like Andalian men, and you're not in Andalia anymore. Haven't you noticed how much he loves you? When are you going to trust him?

Zara grabbed his arm to stop him. She drew a deep breath. "No, I don't mind. I want to be connected to you forever."

On their way back to the house, Zara nestled her head on Tirg's shoulder and whispered, "Do you think I'll ever be able to go back to Andalia and see my mother again?"

"I'll do everything in my power to make it happen, my love," kissing her head.

25

THIS IS MY LAB

Zara held her breath so long, she nearly fainted when she first set foot in the lab a few days later. She had never seen a building so extravagant in its colors, design, and boldness, with some parts defying logic and gravity and yet making perfect sense all together. The equipment exceeded her expectations in its newness and sophistication. She walked through the rooms, touching everything with the tips of her fingers as if testing if it was all real.

The family driver dropped her off at the entrance, giving her a little black box with buttons and a glass cover. "Press this button when you want me to pick you up. I'll be here twenty minutes after you press it."

In one large room, she found ten people sitting around a table. They all wore thin, shiny lab coats. When they saw her, they stood up and greeted her in Andalian.

"Welcome, Doctor Igres."

They introduced themselves one by one with a quick explanation of what they specialized in and what their roles in the lab were. The three women among the men behaved like they belonged to the team and were not there just to make Zara not feel alone or out of place. From their expressions, and with their eyes fixed on her, she gathered they were waiting for her command or directions. Her shoulders stiffened as she stood there facing their expectant faces, considering turning and running away and not saying a word.

I can't do it. I know nothing about running a lab.

She put one foot behind her, ready to turn when Aras's face flashed before her eyes. Her blue eyes twinkled with humor and excitement, mocking her. Zara imagined her saying, "Yeah, you went through all this to give up without trying?"

One foot was behind her, the other firmly anchored by the anticipation of continuing her research in this magnificent laboratory. There was also another emotion awakening inside her—a budding pride. A wave of self-esteem and the euphoria of being in charge kept the other foot firmly on the lab's shiny concrete floor.

As she scanned the faces of her new colleagues and saw no judgement, malice, or jealousy, only curiosity in the ten pairs of eyes, her breath evened, and her mind pushed the panic aside, and she spoke. The first few words as she introduced herself sounded detached, as if someone else were saying them, but as she started summarizing her work on the preontechnology and outlining the plan to continue and expand the research, her sentences flowed flawlessly, and the sound of her own voice wasn't frightening. Her speech animated as she noticed her peers nodding with approval and interest.

I can do this.

"How did it go?" Tirg asked after she'd returned home. "How did my brilliant scientist do on her first day? Did you show everyone who the boss is?"

"It went great actually," she said and looked him in the eye searchingly. "Was your father always interested in science and research? This lab is incredible. I still don't understand how he accomplished this in such a short time."

Tirg's expression grew serious as he sat on the chair across from her. "Our family is the oldest in Sinturija, and for centuries we served beside the rulers and gained rights and privileges and immense power. My father is even more powerful in certain ways than the monarch himself."

"Really?" Zara asked, tilting her head.

"Really. And family means everything to him. You should have heard him shriek with joy when he found out he was going to be a grandfather and that you were coming to Sinturija. He'll do anything to welcome you to our family."

"Yeah, but why the lab?"

"He knows how much it means to you. Why are you questioning it?"

"I'm not. Just trying to understand because…"

"Oh, I get it," Tirg said, grabbing and squeezing her hands. "You will not fail, Zara. You'll do great."

"Ugh."

Tirg stood up and pulled her out of her seat. Then, he embraced her and whispered in her ear. "Don't worry so much. Just have fun. I think that's what my father wanted."

"Tirg?"

"What, my love?"

"I told you about my secret project in Andalia. Does your government allow research on dark matter?"

He pulled out of the embrace and gave her a curious look. "Are you seriously asking me this?"

"Yes. I wasn't allowed to study it in Andalia; that's why I did it in secret."

"No, you can study and research anything you want. There are no restrictions on science. But I doubt dark matter was ever studied here. I doubt anyone even knows about it."

"Are you sure?"

"Yes, I'm sure."

"Could you…ask your father about it?"

"You could ask him yourself, but you don't have to because I already talked to him about it."

"What do you mean?"

"I told him about your secret project in Sinturija—"

"You discussed my secret with your father?"

"Yes, I tell my father everything. He was curious about you. He wanted to know everything about you, and he was fascinated by your talent and research."

"But that was my secret. I risked my career and maybe even my life."

"In Andalia you did, but we are in Sinturija now, and we don't prosecute brilliance."

"You still should have asked me," Zara said and shuddered as if the room got colder. "I'm going for a walk," she said, grabbing her coat and heading toward the door.

Tirg raised his hands. "I don't get why you're angry with me."

Zara threw her hands up, skirted out of the room, and walked to the stairs. *I'm not angry. I'm not angry*, she repeated to herself, skipping steps on her way down. She took the back door; she had discovered it the day before while trying to avoid Tirg's aunt and her daughters, who'd gathered around the front porch.

Breathing hard, she ran until she saw a forest. Never had she seen a place more striking than this birch forest. The sun filtered through the fall leaves and lay in bright streaks on the greenest grass she had ever seen. A delicate breeze wafted through the trees, stirring the branches slightly, and when they moved, their slender leaves whispered. The golden leaves dropped slowly and lined the path before her. The anger and suspicions evaporated, replaced by awe, as she drifted through the magical forest.

She stopped, seeing something she thought she had imagined as being part of the mystic beauty of this place. In a small clearing, on a large stone, a young woman sat reading a book. Zara stood watching her, expecting the apparition to vanish, but she turned toward her and smiled shyly and waved. She recognized her—it was Danuta, Tirg's sister. Zara walked toward her, uncertain of how a conversation between two shy people would work.

Danuta moved her pale blue dress, which draped the rock, out of the way, and invited her to sit next to her with a shy but welcoming smile. Zara sat and glanced at her. Something in her smile told her silence was an accepted and preferable form of communication. So they sat in silence. Danuta's face, now in the approaching sunset and with the trees casting long delicate shadows, was different. More colorful. She seemed more confident and peaceful.

"I'm sorry I haven't talked to you yet," Danuta said softly. Her Andalian had a strong Sinturijan accent, making it sound so much more melodic. "There is always someone with you. I wanted to tell you how much I enjoy having you here," she said and added after a long pause. "He loves you so much."

"I love him too."

"I know," she whispered and fell silent again.

Then she grasped Zara's hand and looked at her. In the sunset, her normally lackluster eyes were glowing as if on a blue fire. "Promise me you'll be careful."

The urgency and fear in her voice and eyes shocked and alarmed Zara. Was Danuta unstable? Or was she trying to warn her?

"Careful of what?"

Danuta searched her eyes. "Don't trust people. Some might say they have good intentions, but in reality, they are...evil. They are after one thing—power."

"I don't understand. Who are you talking about?"

The leaves crunched. Danuta's eyes lost their luster and shut.

"Here you are. What are you two doing here? It's getting dark," Tirg said, appearing from behind the trees. "Dinner is almost ready. Come on," Tirg said, and extended his hands to both women.

They both took his hand, rose from the rock, and walked back to the house.

"I see you were getting to know my little sister."

"Little? Hardly. I'm four years older. You're still my baby brother."

"Are you still mad at me?" Tirg whispered into Zara's ear.

"Maybe a little," she murmured, thinking about what Danuta had said.

During dinner, Zara kept glancing at her, but Danuta avoided her eyes. Unfortunately, she was seated too far away from her to talk freely, but she made a promise to herself to talk to her the next day after she returned from the lab.

"I hear you two were getting to know each other?" Tirg's father asked Zara, smiling.

"Yes, she's very nice and...perceptive."

"That she is," he said in a tone that implied he wasn't happy with his daughter's perceptiveness. "And very imaginative too."

Zara glanced at Danuta, who was stabbing her untouched food with her fork, keeping her eyes on her plate. Her complexion, so beautiful outside, now looked gray and lifeless as a stone, a marble with just a hint of pink under its smooth, white surface.

Elenora glanced at her daughter and gently stroked her hand, whispering something to her. Zara caught her quick, reproachful glance at her husband. With her eyes narrowed, she looked even more beautiful and poised. Like a queen admonishing her vassal. Zmey averted his eyes.

26

I LOVE SINTURIJA

Zara entered the lab, greeted everyone with a lazy hand gesture, and disappeared into her office, a large room, exquisitely furnished, with floor-to-ceiling windows spanning one wall and a desk that made her hold her breath when she first saw it. Made from a stone found only near the sea on the eastern corner of Sinturija, the desk was partly see-through, with knotty veins running through its center. When the sun from the giant windows hit it, it burst into a golden glow.

That day, Zara sat motionless, staring at the large desk drawer. A few times, she reached out to open it and then changed her mind, but finally opened it and took out her research notes and placed them on the desk. She stared at them for a while, then quickly gathered and carried them out to the main lab, dumping them on the counter with a loud thump.

"May I have everyone's attention, please?"

Zara scanned the curious faces and pointed at the scattered documents. "I brought my research notes and findings, as well as some other research from Andalia that you might find interesting, and because, besides preontechnology this is what we are going to be working on. I'll leave it to you to decide who wants to switch to this new project, but I'll need four or five people to help me get it started. Read it, and if it interests you, sign up for it. I'll be in my office if anyone has questions."

"What is it?" Serena, the youngest woman, asked, eyeing the papers. "Can you tell us about it briefly?"

"Sure. How many of you have heard of dark matter? Raise your hands."

Her colleagues glanced at each other and shook their heads. No one raised their hand.

"It is an invisible matter making up the universe, but it doesn't interact with anything except gravity. It doesn't respond to light or electromagnetic radiation."

"How do you know it exists if it's invisible and doesn't interact with anything?" Zak, a young man with curly brown hair and brown eyes that seemed too big for his face.

"She said it interacts with gravity," Serena said and rolled her eyes. "It probably makes stellar objects move and behave differently," she added pensively.

Zara nodded, already admiring the mind of the young researcher and hoping she would choose to work on dark matter. As if reading her mind, Serena reached for a stack of papers, and her hazel eyes immediately sparked.

"You want us to read it now?" Zak asked.

"Yes, if you will."

Soon after, all the papers were snatched, and a silence descended on the lab. Zara walked back to her office on slightly rubbery feet. There was no going back. The research on dark matter would continue in Sinturija regardless of whether it was lawful. She chose to believe it was. Even if it wasn't, Tirg's father would protect her. His intense eyes told her so. She exhaled, and her heartbeat slowed down.

You're in charge and can do anything you want.

She's never felt this kind of exhilaration as she imagined herself on top of the world, winning scientific praise and awards. The sudden longing for fame and recognition was a new sensation but powerful enough to send her mind into planning the research. And suddenly, all the pieces fell together perfectly, and she knew what to do. She would be the first woman to accomplish what no one else had, or attempted, or probably ever thought possible.

She passed the elevator and flew down the steps to the supply department, located three floors down. Once she burst through the metal door, she grabbed a thick book bound in black leather and flipped through the pages.

"Can I order this?" she asked the clerk, holding her breath while pointing to something on the page.

The clerk adjusted his thick glasses. "I believe so, yes."

"Really? I can order Fellurion?"

When he nodded, she jumped up and clapped her hands.

"I love Sinturija," she said.

The next several weeks became the most exciting time of her life.

Her team was energized with the prospect of uncovering the cosmos's biggest mystery and wanted to be a part of it. She had selected her team of five from the willing participants to work on dark matter research. She hardly spent time in the family home, planning her research, ordering supplies and more equipment. Tirg drove to the lab himself to extract her from the grips of dark matter to get her home in time for dinner, but she barely touched her food or responded to his questions, thinking about her research. Her eyes gained a feverish glow. Tirg begged her to cut her hours short, and she promised him she would once the research got going.

As weeks went by, she delved deeper and deeper into the dark world, disappearing from the living.

One evening after Zara returned from the lab, instead of Tirg, she found Elenora in her living room.

"Tirg is worried about you."

"Why?"

"Come sit with me," Elenora said, patting the soft green velvet on the sofa next to her.

Zara suppressed the urge to roll her eyes and sat beside her.

"You ought to be gaining weight instead of losing it now. He is worried about your health and that of your child."

"I'm perfectly fine. He shouldn't worry, and if he is, he should tell me this himself."

Elenora laughed. Her golden hair surrounded her face in waves. She really was beautiful, Emery noticed despite the irritation at the intrusion into her privacy. In truth, she couldn't stay angry with her mother-in-law. She emitted so much kindness with her body language, her eyes, and even her glowing skin.

"He told me he tried, but you're stubborn and do what you want. And I love that about you, except that in this case, I agree with my son. You're not taking care of yourself. You should be worried."

"I'm fine."

"When was the last time you looked in the mirror?" Elenora asked, grabbed her hand, and pulled her in front of a full-size mirror. "Look at the sunken cheeks and the feverish eyes. You're five months pregnant, but you're skinny. Think about your baby."

Zara drew a big breath to protest, but then she caught a glimpse of herself in the mirror and held her breath. A ghost stood before her. Elenora was right. Zara touched her gaunt cheeks, the pasty skin on her arms, and the hollow-eyed stranger in the mirror did the same. Zara shuddered.

"Do you see what I mean? Tirg is beside himself. He asked his dad to shut the lab down."

"No!"

"It's that important to you?" Elenora appraised her with unexpected coolness.

Zara walked back to the chair on unsteady legs. She arranged her hands in her lap and stared at them, like she used to when she was a child. It was the only thing helping her to quiet the voice in her head telling her she had messed up.

Elenora walked to Zara and touched her shoulder. "Come downstairs to have some food and let's talk. Tirg and Zmey will be back late from a meeting."

A plate of steaming food magically materialized on the table as soon as Zara and Elenora arrived.

Zara fought to swallow the first chunks of meat and vegetables through her dry throat, but Elenora's melodic voice telling her stories about Tirg when he was a child soothed her nerves, and she ate most of the food, and even chuckled a few times.

"I'm sure you can do both: work and take care of the life you carry within you."

Zara nodded. "Is he going to close the lab? Can he?"

Elenora planted her blue eyes on her, which grew serious and sad as she stared at her. "He can."

27

THE SANATORIUM

The next morning, Zara woke up late. Tirg was still sleeping beside her. He must have sneaked in late at night. She turned toward him and gazed at his face and moved a lock of hair off his forehead. I can be both a mother, a wife to this beautiful human being, and a scientist, she thought. She kissed his lips, and he woke up. His eyes moved fast from the clock to Zara's face.

He touched her cheek as if checking whether it was real. "It's nearly ten in the morning. Am I still dreaming?"

She smiled and kissed his hand. "No, I'm taking a day off."

He raised his head and supported it with his elbow. "Do you have a fever? Are you sick?" he asked half-jokingly.

"I'm fine. I had a pleasant talk with your mother last night."

"Did you? About what?"

"That you are worried, and that you solicited her help to talk some sense into me, and that you asked your dad to close the lab."

"I'm worried, but I didn't ask my mother or my father to intervene on my behalf. I was going to have a talk with you myself."

"You didn't ask her?"

"No, but I'm glad it worked," he said and grinned.

Waking up to Tirg's warm body and his smile reminded her of the reason she'd come to Sinturija. "Me too," she whispered and nestled her head on his shoulder.

Zara reduced her hours at work significantly and returned home in time for dinner every night. She couldn't quite convince herself that it was the fear of harming her baby and not because she feared Zmey might close the lab before her big breakthrough. She ate more and gained enough weight to see approval in Elenora's eyes.

One night at dinner, she looked around the massive dining table. Something wasn't right. Danuta wasn't at the table. Zara wrinkled her forehead trying to remember whether Danuta had been at the dinner table last night. She had been so preoccupied with her research that she hadn't noticed that Tirg's sister hadn't been dining with them for several days.

"Where is your sister?" she whispered to Tirg.

He cleared his throat. "She is in a sanatorium."

"Where?"

"I'll tell you later," he whispered and changed the subject, raising his glass and saying, "Zara has an announcement."

Zara swallowed. "We've reached a milestone in our preontechnology work. We've created a self-powered automobile."

"That's very impressive," Zmey said, putting away his knife and fork. "Completely self-powered? I thought that was impossible."

"It was until now. Not only does it power itself, but it also self-diagnoses any repairs itself. It only needs oxygen. But there is a drawback."

Zmey's eyes flashed.

"Any structures or machines created with preontechnology must be contained in dust- and water-free environments. We haven't been able to bypass this problem yet."

"So, they would have to be in a bubble in order to work?"

Zara nodded. "Our automobile is under a bubble with only oxygen pumped into it through nano filters."

"It is a monumental achievement. A machine that doesn't use any energy source," Tirg said, stroking Zara's arm.

"Of course it is," Elenora chimed in. "Congratulations, Zara. You certainly have been working relentlessly. We should celebrate," she added, raising her glass.

"How is the other project going?" Zmey asked, looking straight into Zara's eyes.

She felt her face redden and tighten. How does he know? Tirg must have told him, she thought, but then remembered she hadn't told Tirg about starting work on the dark matter project. "It's moving along," she said coldly. *He must have spies in the lab.*

Later that evening, while brushing her hair, Zara asked Tirg, "How did your father know I was working on dark matter?"

"You didn't tell him?"

Zara shook her head.

"He probably assumed based on what he learned about you."

Zara put away her brush and turned toward him. "Why is your sister in some kind of sanatorium? Is she sick?"

Tirg sighed. "She's been in and out of sanatoriums all her life."

"What's wrong with her?"

"The doctors aren't sure. They suspect schizophrenia but haven't committed decisively to the diagnosis. They said it's difficult to diagnose a mental illness that doesn't manifest itself frequently and convincingly enough."

"I found her quite normal and nice."

"She is. But she has these episodes of paranoia when she thinks everyone is out to harm her or someone else in the family. Lately, she became convinced that someone was going to harm you, so my father sent her to the sanatorium."

Zara's hands grew clammy, and she wiped them on her dress, but she said nothing of the conversation she had with Danuta among the birches. "I'm going to take a bath now," Zara said and headed for the bathroom, hiding her pale face from Tirg.

"Do you need help?" he asked, grinning.

"No, I'll be quick," she said and closed the door. She sat on the marble tub and turned the water on. She forgot to turn the fan on, and the room filled with vapor quickly, and she sat amidst the fog, thinking about what Danuta had said to her and how she looked when she said it. There'd been genuine fear in her eyes, and she hadn't appeared crazy or paranoid. Shy and out of place, but not crazy.

Zara was certain she hadn't told Tirg about the dark matter project. She noticed how close Tirg was to his father and realized it would be impossible for him not to share everything he knew, especially if asked. Her own reluctance to disclose it openly, she just now realized after learning about Danuta's sudden departure, was because of her mistrust of Zmey.

During dinner the next evening, Zara looked into Zmey's eyes and asked to visit Danuta at the sanatorium. "Could someone take me there?"

Zmey swallowed with some difficulty. "She is not allowed visitors."

"Why did you say that?" Tirg asked. "Mother just went to see her two days ago."

"I'm her mother. I can because my presence doesn't cause aggravation."

"Are you saying that my presence will cause her aggravation?"

"No, that's not what I'm saying. You're still a..."

"A stranger?"

Elenora's face reddened as she slowly folded her napkin and threw it onto her plate, covering mostly untouched food.

"I'll take you next week," Zmey said. "I'll check with the doctor first and take you myself."

"Why don't I take her? I'd like to see Danuta," Tirg offered.

"No need. I'd like to spend some time with my new daughter,"

Zmey said, and stood up, throwing his napkin on his plate with half-finished food.

~

After dinner, Zara asked Tirg if they could have their own house. "It doesn't have to be big or fancy," she said.

Tirg rubbed his chin. "Why? Don't you like my family?"

"I do, but I'm used to the idea of couples living separately from their extended families. You know, like in Andalia—like we lived together in Andalia. Just the two of us, and soon three."

"I see," Tirg said and sighed. "If you really want to, but I thought it'd be better here where we can get help with the baby. We have experienced nannies and grandparents who would dote on our child."

"Yes, I really want to."

He studied her face. "Okay. I'll start searching for a place for us."

"Thank you."

28

EMERY

The following week, Zmey had an emergency meeting and had to leave for several weeks, taking Tirg with him. Elenora wouldn't tell her where the sanatorium was, and Zara, not having interacted much with the other family members, had no one else to ask. The sensation that Danuta was trying to tell her something important intensified after she was sent to the sanatorium and even more after Zmey asked about the progress on the dark matter project. The one time she talked to Danuta, something passed between them while they sat silently among the birches. Zara saw in Danuta's eyes a reflection of her own isolation and then a nod of understanding and a declaration of friendship.

Remembering that day, an idea formed in Zara's mind, and she asked Elenora if she could help her set a stone in a necklace and secretly send it to Danuta for her birthday.

Elenora regarded her for a moment before pulling Zara close to her chest.

"She is so sensitive, that girl. I'm glad you are fond of her. I know she's fond of you, and I hope when she comes back you could be like sisters."

"I'm sure we will be," Zara said.

Elenora, alone with her young daughter-in-law, abandoned her royal poise and, holding on to her arm, led Zara from one boutique to another, and from one coffee shop to another, through the narrow sandstone-lined streets of the quaint town of Nariana. She babbled, picking out pastry for Zara, describing their origins and their secret ingredients, and giggled when Zara made faces at flavors she didn't care for. Zara heard tiny sighs flee Elenora's chest, and she guessed she was missing her daughter. Did she really believe Danuta was sick, or did Zmey sway her into believing it?

Zara plunged back into work. Her project had now reached the final implementation stage—the erection of the structures according to the model of her design. Zara was nearing the end of her pregnancy when the last panels and the power station under the chamber were installed. Now they only needed to be connected with preontechnology to form seamless walls to prevent dust from seeping through. The final product would be a seamless circular chamber for the antigravitational field to function properly.

Rubbing her belly in round strokes and whispering something to her unborn baby, Zara waddled into the lab every morning, checking on the construction.

Danuta had not come back yet. When Zara asked when she'd be back, Tirg said, "Soon." But that "soon" never came. Zmey rescinded his offer of taking her to the sanatorium before the baby was born.

Tirg spent every moment overseeing the construction of their new home on a piece of land that was part of the family estate, a few miles away, and only came back in the evenings to kiss Zara's belly and whisper to it.

Meanwhile, the baby room was prepared, baby clothes sewn, and nannies selected to care for the young Mister Igres's daughter.

Everyone prepared for a girl as Zara insisted she was having a daughter until it became reality.

The day arrived—Zara's water broke on her way from the lab, and the contractions started shortly after. Cursing, she notified Zmey to get her, realizing Tirg would not be back until the evening. Zmey arrived in a dust cloud, jumped out of his car, and ran up to Zara, who sat on the side of the road breathing heavily.

"Are you okay?" he asked, touching her shoulder.

She nodded and grabbed his hand. It trembled.

He picked her up as if she were a feather and carried her to his car, then gently lowered her in. "Just hold on, okay? I'll get you home in no time. Doctor Savado is on his way. Just hang on."

He drove fast, glancing at her in the rearview mirror.

Five hours later, Dr. Savado delivered an eight-and-a-half-pound healthy baby girl just as Tirg burst into the delivery room.

The moment she saw the girl's blue eyes and felt her little body pressing into hers, Zara did not once think about dark matter. Four weeks went by, and she didn't set foot in the lab, as if it didn't exist. The research that had been so important to her just a few weeks ago now gathered dust somewhere deep in her mind.

The young couple spent most of the time staring at each other and at their daughter, marveling at the perfection of her tiny pink fingers and toes, and her eyes.

When Elenora and Zmey visited, Zara reluctantly let Zmey hold her daughter, eyeing him with narrowed eyes when he held her.

"Her eyes!" Elenora exclaimed, looking over Zmey's shoulder. "I've never seen such beautiful and unusual eyes. They have golden and black dots all over them. How extraordinary."

"Just like her mother," Zmey said. "Extraordinary, like her mother."

"Have you decided what're you going to name her, or will you continue calling her 'my baby'?" Elenora asked.

"Emery," Zara said without hesitation.

"Emery, Elenora, Igres," Tirg said quickly.

"Ah, beautiful name. An unusual name. How did you come up with it? Is it Andalian?" Elenora asked.

"No, it's not. I'm not sure—it came to me," she said. "In a dream."

"Isn't she beautiful?" Tirg asked.

"When will you be going back to the lab?" Zmey asked. The tone of his voice was sharp, conveying impatience.

The silence that followed was thick, loaded with suspense. Zara glared at Zmey, who calmly waited for her answer, bouncing his odd smile on his lips.

"She just gave birth. She'll go when she's ready. The lab can wait," Tirg cut the silence in a voice with the sharpness of a razor blade.

"I've heard her crew is awaiting her approval of the chamber construction and ready to begin the testing."

"How did you find out about testing?" Zara asked, and her heart started racing. While waiting for his response, she was certain Zmey had planted spies in her lab. Tirg didn't know about the testing, so he couldn't have told him. But why would Zmey spy on her? It occurred to her he might have a stake in her research. Perhaps he was counting on selling the preontechnology when developed and getting rich, and that was the true reason behind the lightning-fast lab construction. It had nothing to do with his being a loving father-in-law.

Her icy eyes and pursed lips must have mirrored her thoughts as Tirg jutted his chin forward and glared at his father, waiting for a response. Zmey ignored the question and Tirg's stare. Zara glanced at Tirg, and seeing his expression when glaring at his father, felt a tingling sensation of adoration wash over her. She extended her hands to Zmey, wanting Emery back in her arms. With her husband by her side and her daughter's heart beating against hers, nothing else mattered. Her heart stopped racing.

Tirg stood up. "Zara needs rest."

Elenora glanced at her husband and moved toward the door.

Zmey stood up but did not move his eyes off Zara. "They really need you, that's all. I have to know everything about your research, Zara. It's part of my job."

"Part of your job as a diplomat? How?"

"Let's go," Elenora said. She pulled her husband out of the room.

"Are you okay, my love?" Tirg asked. "You don't need to go anywhere until you're damn well ready. You never have to go back if you don't want to. Our house is almost done. We can move, and nobody would bother you about anything. Just a few more weeks."

Zara kissed Emery's blond curls, trying to forget what Zmey had said. But the harder she tried, the more she wanted to go back, check on her team, and see her chamber. The tiny seed he'd planted had germinated and was growing like a weed. There was a reason he was the best diplomat in Sinturija and the monarch's right hand.

Two weeks later, Zara, Emery, and Trig moved into their new house and, at Zara's insistence, hired Alicja, their own nanny. A month after they moved in, Zara asked the family driver to take her to the lab. Just before reaching it, in a sudden panic, she ordered the driver to turn around. She ran to the house, expecting to hear Emery crying and the nanny nowhere to be found. Her eyes filled with tears at seeing Emery asleep in Alicja's arms.

After the incident, she convinced Tirg to teach her how to drive and to get her an automobile.

It didn't take long for her to learn how to control the machine. Having learned how to fly, driving was easy.

And on a sunny morning, Tirg walked her outside and pointed to a shiny dark blue automobile with oversized windows and light blue leather seats waiting for her outside.

"Now you don't need to wait for the driver."

"Thank you. I never really understood your family's need for drivers. Why can't they just drive?"

Tirg laughed. "It's a status thing. I don't like it either."

Tirg picked her up and kissed her. "Be careful out there, okay?"

29

LAST STEPS

Zara's team greeted her warmly when she showed up at the lab. While she was away, everyone except for Serena was working on the preontechnology, testing its applications in the real world and researching the dust problem. Zara asked Serena to oversee the chamber's construction in her absence, and the chamber welcomed Zara with its perfectly smooth walls already sealed. Her heart pounded as she followed Serena, who chattered about the progress and the last pieces of equipment needing checking while gawking at their creation.

Zara held her breath in awe of the unusual beauty of this chilly place. The walls gave off a slightly iridescent glow, bathing the room in an eerie light that cast oddly elongated shadows as she walked around. Soon after they walked in, the walls brightened slightly, as if welcoming them.

"Just as you designed. I still can't wrap my head around the fact that the walls respond to the change in static electricity and emit more light," Serena said.

Zak entered the chamber. "We waited for the Vortex Accelerator installation until you returned," he said. "Mister Zmey said you'd be back soon."

Ah, here is my snitch. "So how long have you been in communication with my father-in-law?" Zara asked, feigning amusement.

"Oh, no...not th...that long," Zak said.

Zara walked around, sliding her hand across the walls, stopping every few feet and pressing both her hands as if checking for a heartbeat. When she turned toward Serena, her eyes were moist. "Thank you. You all did an excellent job."

"When do we install and test the Vortex?" Zak asked.

"Not for a while yet. I have to run a few other tests first," Zara lied with a straight face.

Serena wandered around the chamber, inspecting the walls, but when she heard Zara speak to Zak, she spun around and opened her mouth, about to protest. When she saw Zara's face, she nodded and said, "I agree."

Zara left, glancing one more time at the walls, and Serena followed. Zara nudged Serena toward her office. "I want to install the Vortex capsule tomorrow and start testing, but I don't want to announce it to the entire world."

"I understand," Serena said and smiled, winking. "You want Zak gone for a while?"

"Yeah...how?"

"There's a new shipment of Fellurion waiting for pickup. Normally, I'd send an assistant, but we can make a case that this is too important," she said, and grinned. "It'd take him four days to go to Dantana and back. That'd give us enough time."

Zara nodded. "Thank you," she said absentmindedly, then walked to her desk and turned on her Computator. "After Zak leaves—and I am assuming he leaves tomorrow—let's meet in my office. You, the installation crew, and Alen and Toni. I've got to catch up on my notes."

"Of course," the young scientist said, and walked toward the door.

"Hey, Serena?"

"Yeah?"

"You're awesome. Thank you."

Zak left to retrieve the shipment early the next morning, and the installation proceeded as planned. Zara and Serena watched as the shiny crystal tube was carefully placed in its designated spot, followed by the console, which was a last-minute addition that Zara thought would help her keep her research recorded and organized.

The console was a hologram where messages could be recorded and played back, showing the person delivering the message as clearly as if they were in the room. It was something Alen, one of the young scientists in her group, had invented and then had built.

Zara oversaw the installation of the console and the Vortex Accelerator. Not everyone in the lab knew that the Vortex rotated at relativistic speeds to cause time dilation for time travel. Zak was among those who knew, and Zara now worried that he was waiting for it to be finished to notify Zmey. Thanks to Serena's quick thinking, they had a few more days to run their test before Zmey's spy returned. She glanced at Serena and sent her a warm smile. Serena's face lit up.

"Tomorrow, we try. We'll know if time travel is possible," Zara whispered. Alen and Toni left after placing the last two pieces, and they were alone. "Tomorrow, we'll attempt something that everyone thought was impossible. You know what to do?"

"Yes, I'll see you at my house tomorrow...no, yesterday," Serena said, and giggled.

"Let's program this thing."

Zara entered the narrow hallway that encircled the chamber outside and then descended the stairs leading to a small room underneath. Serena followed. The room's walls lit up with bright lights, illuminating the large monitors and instruments that started flashing blue as soon as they detected them. After programming it, Zara studied the panel for a moment, then grabbed Serena's hand, and they both left to go back to their homes.

Zara looked back and sighed deeply before opening her car with a shaking hand. Her speed varied on her way back home. When her thoughts wandered into a dark realm of imagining being stuck somewhere in the ether and never seeing her family, she slowed down, but then when her mind snapped back into believing her science was sound, she sped up.

Before Zara stepped into the living room, she stopped in front of a mirror and pinched her pale cheeks. She blinked, trying to vanquish the unhealthy glow in her eyes, licked her cracked lips, wiped her clammy hands on her coat, and searched for Tirg. She couldn't tell him what she was planning, knowing he would stop her, and she felt like a deserter. If anything happened to her, Emery would be motherless, and Tirg would be devastated.

Tirg was nowhere to be found, so she entered the nursery. Alicja was just putting Emery into the crib. "Master Tirg had some kind of emergency with some agreement with...I don't know. I can't remember what he said. But he said he wouldn't be home tonight or tomorrow night. He left you a note over there on the windowsill."

A wave of relief and disappointment traveled from her gut and wedged itself tight in her throat. No matter how she tried to hide it, he would sense something was up, and she would have had to lie to him. But if she were to die tomorrow...

She opened the note.

I'm sorry, love.

There is trouble brewing in the south with the Sovereign Nation of Morana, and I've been called to intervene. I hate to leave you and Emery, but I promise I'll use all my diplomatic charm to mend the peace and be back as soon as I can.

Love, your tiger

Zara folded the note and looked out the window, drawing a deep, painful breath. Perhaps it was the dark clouds that the wind pushed toward the house, or the disappointment Tirg was not here, that she suddenly felt as if the floor under her feet moved. She slid to the floor and rested her head in her hands. She so much wanted to be in his arms that night. The excitement she had for the upcoming time travel experiment faded as doubt and fear replaced it.

30

THE NIGHTMARE

"Are you absolutely sure you set your date correctly?" Serena asked for the tenth time as Zara struggled to remove her coat, eyeing the crystal tube of the Vortex.

"Yes. For the thousandth time. I'll be fine."

"I'm more scared for you than excited and cannot wrap my head around this time thing. If it works, you and I'll remember you spending the night at my home yesterday?"

"In theory," Zara whispered. "Will there really be two of you that day? What am I saying? Were there two of you in the past? I am very confused. This is just hard to understand."

"I don't know, but if everything goes according to the plan, I'll see you in my office in a few minutes. Then we go through the numbers, and we'll know more."

"And if it doesn't? Are you sure about this? Perhaps it would be better to send some kind of animal into the past."

"And how would we know we had succeeded? Would the animal tell us?"

"We'll have a memory of a mouse in our kitchen...perhaps you should let me do it," Serena pleaded. "You have a daughter."

Zara considered it, and for a moment, she almost agreed. For Emery. But the profound curiosity and the desire to be the first to do it won out. "I'll be fine," she said and stepped into the capsule. "You need to leave. The room will be pressurized and electromagnetized. Here, take my coat," she added, throwing her coat at Serena.

"I know," Serena said and caught the coat in midair. She waved and shuffled out of the room, glancing back.

As the door locked silently, a whiff of metallic air blew into Serena's face. She pressed her cheek and hands against the door, whispering, "I should be the one in there."

In Zara's office, she waited an hour, first sitting, then pacing the room, sitting back down, then pacing again.

"Damn. I don't remember her spending the night. Something is wrong. Something is very wrong," she kept repeating.

She bolted out of her chair and ran back to the chamber. The chamber was dark and empty. She entered and approached the crystal capsule. Empty. "No, no, no...this can't be happening. Think, think—what would she do if she went further back in time? Oh, no. If I can't remember, then it's possible she returned to a time before I even knew her."

Serena darted out of the chamber and to her white automobile and drove home. Dust flew around as she sped over the dirt road, yelling at the wipers as they smeared brown dirt on the windshield.

Serena's house was dark and empty. With her hand to her heart, she ran through it several times, shouting Zara's name. Not finding any signs of Zara, she jumped back in her car and drove to Zara's house. She stood outside, pressing her hands against the door for a long time before finally knocking.

Nobody answered. Serena knocked several more times, then circled the house, peeking into the windows, but the house showed no sign of life inside. "Oh, no," she cried, and drove back to her house, where she sat all night, staring at the front door and begging fate to bring Zara back. When morning came and Zara didn't show, she drove to the lab where she hid in her cubby and cowered, rocking in her chair.

It wasn't until after lunch that Alen knocked on her door and asked where Zara was.

Serena didn't raise her head, didn't look at him, just shrugged.

"Are you okay?" he asked.

"Yeah," she said.

"She must have stayed with her baby."

"Yeah," she said.

"Are you sure you're okay?"

"Fine. Go away."

Serena returned home and sat in a chair and waited, but her eyes, swollen from lack of sleep and crying, gave way and shut.

"Hey, wake up, Serena," Zara's voice penetrated her sleep.

"Zara, you're back!" Serena shouted. She jumped up and hugged Zara, covering her cheeks with kisses. "You're alright. You came back and you're not hurt," Serena cried. Tears flowed from her cheeks while her chest heaved with sobs. "I thought I'd lost you. What happened?"

"What do you mean? Everything went according to the plan, right?"

"No, you were supposed to be here the night before. This is the following night. Well, nearly morning."

"Nooooo," Zara whispered. "Are you sure?"

"Of course, I'm sure. I've been contemplating asking for help. If you hadn't shown up tonight, I'd have gone to your father-in-law."

"That means," Zara whispered and sank into a chair, "I must have traveled into the future, but I was certain I had entered the criteria correctly. But you know what?" she asked, her eyes flashing.

"What?" Serena asked, wiping her eyes.

"It means it worked. The Vortex worked. I traveled into the future. We just have to figure out—"

"Zara," Serena interrupted.

"We just have to figure out what went wrong and fix it—"

"Zara!"

"What?"

"When you didn't show up last night, I went to your house looking for you, and there was nobody there. I thought your nanny was taking care of Emery."

"Are you sure?"

"I knocked and knocked and knocked and nobody answered. The house was dark."

"Maybe they were asleep. She never opens the door to strangers."

"Go check on them."

"I will later. I want to check the parameters. It should be okay. I told Alicja I might not be back and not to worry."

Serena shook her head. "Suit yourself," she said, straightening her back. "I have to take a bath. I've been in the same clothes since you left. See you back at the lab."

Zara couldn't contain her excitement as she drove back to the lab. She was the first person in history to time travel, achieving what no one else had, as a woman. She just had to figure out why her parameters hadn't worked.

"I must have messed up. Maybe I was too excited and messed up," she said, checking to electronic panel. When she discovered it was actually set to move her into the future, she stood there for a long time, unmoving, with her mouth ajar. She finally shrugged. *Well, that's my fault then, and it is fixable. Next time, I'll triple-check.*

Zara went into her office, but she couldn't concentrate. Half an hour later, she was driving back home, increasing her speed as she grew closer.

"Alicja?" Zara shouted after unlocking the door. "Alicja? I'm back."

Zara started running, not hearing a reply. The house was empty. Alicja and Emery were not at home. Zara continued running, checking the same rooms over and over.

"Tirg must have come back and taken Emery to his parents. Yeah, that must be it," Zara said to herself.

She exhaled, found the black box, and started typing the message to Tirg.

"She's not at her grandparents if that's who you're messaging," a rich, melodious woman's voice echoed through the empty house.

Zara turned, dropping the messaging device to the floor when she saw and recognized the person talking to her. Tall and slender, the woman from her nightmares stood before her, smiling with her beautiful full mouth and oval-shaped black eyes. Her skin was now radiant, not chalky.

"Not now," Zara whispered, and pinched her arm hard, but her nightmare stayed and her arm hurt. "Who the hell are you? What do you want?"

"You don't remember me, do you?"

"Remember you? From where?" Zara asked, opening her eyes wide. How would she know she dreamed about her?

"Dammit, Olesya! We're just wasting time. You know who I am!"

"My name is Zara, not Olesya. I don't know who you are and what you're doing in my house, but I want you to leave. Now!"

The woman laughed, and Zara was shocked by her laughter. Her nightmare's laughter was natural and effortless, making her face seem even more striking. "If I leave, you'll never find your daughter," she said.

Zara felt the blood drain from her face and a wave of cold sweat cover her entire body. Every muscle in her body stiffened, including her heart. She attacked, reaching for the woman's throat.

"Now do you remember me?" The woman seized Zara's hands and threw her to the floor as if Zara were a mere fly. Zara flung herself back up and rammed her head into the woman's stomach. The impact sent them both to the floor. Zara landed on top and immediately reached for her throat. "Why are you talking about my daughter? Who the hell are you?"

Zara couldn't keep her pinned down. With her knee, the woman delivered a painful kick to Zara's kidneys and, after she was free, trapped Zara under her. Holding both her hands, she stared at Zara with a malevolent smile. "We're going to have to get reacquainted, my dear Olesya."

"You've got the wrong person. My name—"

"Your name is Olesya Solensky and I'm Zoe Brie. We knew each other rather well in another dimension. I was hoping you'd remember, but it looks like I'm going to have to explain everything. Will you behave if I let you go? This will be a long story, so I need you to stop fighting me."

"You're crazy," Zara whispered. "Where is my daughter?"

"I'm going to tell you everything, but you have to promise not to fight me. It'd be just a waste of time, and I assume you want to find your daughter sooner rather than later."

Zara nodded. If this woman was indeed crazy, and she had her daughter, Zara needed to appease her.

Sitting across from each other, the two women studied each other. Zoe started her story, gazing into Zara's eyes. Zara glared back. "I first learned of you when you were part of a team that discovered what dark matter was."

Zara made a face but fought the urge to interrupt. She pursed her lips while Zoe spoke of her childhood, finding the black shard, then helping Olesya find her brother, ending when Emery and Zoe disappeared into the capsule together.

"So my daughter pushed you into the capsule I designed, and then you traveled through hell and ended back in your dying world. Why would my daughter do that?" Zara asked, rolling her eyes.

"She thought I pushed you into the capsule first."

"Did you?"

"No, you went on your own. I just helped you."

"So you kidnapped my baby to punish her?"

"Don't be ridiculous! Of course not!"

"So why?"

"My world is dying, and your inventions could save it," she said, and added, "You really remember nothing? Even after I've told you the entire story? No memory flashes? Do you remember Peter?"

Zara shook her head.

"How about Sergi? The Russian guy with the incredible blue eyes. Do you remember him?"

Zara started shaking her head, but then Tirg's blue eyes came into focus.

Zoe saw the flash in her eyes. "You remember him," she said, and sighed. "Perhaps you're lucky you didn't remember everything; you've been free from all the pain and regrets and could start your life anew. Me...I've not been so lucky. I remember every single detail of my life. Everything I've—"

"Okay, cut this crap! I don't give a shit about your sappy life story. It has nothing to do with me or my daughter. Where is she?"

Zoe laughed. "You are as spirited as ever. As soon as you help me, you can get your daughter back and your little heavenly life back with your Sergi. Yes, don't look at me like that. Tirg is your Sergi, always was and always will be. In every dimension and every life, some things are just predestined to happen."

"What do you want from me?" Zara asked, struggling to contain the urge to dig her fingers into Zoe's throat.

"I need the dark matter shards you've created, and I need detailed notes of the process of creating preontechnology, so it can be recreated in my world. My world is dying—drying out."

"Why don't you just stay here?"

Zoe tilted her head, gazing at Zara with interest. "There are people I care about in that world, and I want to save it for them."

"You said we recur in each dimension and are basically the same in each one. Why don't you take care of your people in this dimension and give me my daughter back? This world is not dying."

"Oh, Olesya. If it were only that simple. I can't do that. If you want your daughter, you need to give me what I need."

"I must know where my daughter is first."

"I wonder—if you had to choose between your work and your daughter, which one would you choose, Olesya?"

"Don't call me that. I would always choose my daughter. If you really knew me as you say you do, you'd know that."

"I do know you, Olesya," she said, and a flare brightened her black eyes. "Okay, let's go to your lab."

"I can't take you with me. People will be suspicious, seeing a strange woman—"

"Cut the bullshit. You're the boss, so do whatever you want. No one will question you."

"How do you know that?" Zara stood up and moved closer to Zoe. "How could you possibly know that?"

"It doesn't matter. You want your daughter back?"

Zara nodded.

"Let's not waste any more time. Emery wants her mommy."

Zara flung herself at Zoe, who, expecting it, not only deflected the blow but grabbed her arm in a powerful grip and led her to the door. "You drive."

Zoe was wrong. Everyone stared at them, and especially at the stunning woman in a white dress walking behind their boss. But nobody questioned them or stood in their way. Serena was the only one who could have understood the situation and helped her, but she wasn't here. Zara's mind buzzed, trying to come up with a plan to overpower her foe. What certainty did she have that if she gave her what she wanted, Zoe would give Emery back to her? In her sick mind, she made up the story of Emery taking her into the capsule with her. Was she seeking revenge? But how could she possibly want revenge from a baby?

Zara led her to her office first. She pointed to a cabinet that was stuffed full of papers, neatly arranged into thick folders, each clearly labeled. "There you go. My research is all here. How are you planning to carry it out of here?"

"Is it all there? Are you sure?"

"Yes. Where is Emery?"

"Dark matter shards?"

Emery opened the safe and took out a glass box, with Zoe looking over her shoulder. Zoe smiled, seeing the black fragments inside the translucent box. She took the box out, pushing Zara aside.

"You've got everything you need. Now tell me where Emery is."

Zoe laughed, throwing her head back. "All in good time, Olesya. Let's go."

"Where?"

"To the chamber. Where else?"

"You're not taking my research?"

"All in good time."

"Where is Emery?"

"She is on her way here."

"You lying piece of—"

"I'm not lying. I swear. You'll see her in a few minutes."

Zoe, holding the box, pointed the way. Zara reluctantly started walking toward the chamber. How did this woman know about her research and the chamber? Had she been sent by the Sinturijan government? Andalian government? Were there government spies in her lab?

"What do you want from the chamber? I gave you what you asked for. Why are you leaving the papers? Isn't that what you came here for?"

Zoe pointed the way with her eyes. Zara stopped in front of the door to the chamber, but Zoe continued down the small hallway leading to the chamber controls.

"How the hell do you know about this?"

"Come on, don't ask stupid questions."

"Tell me how you know!" Zara shouted, stomping her feet. As her stomach twisted into a painful knot, she clutched it with one hand and halted, putting the other hand up. "Where is my daughter?" she asked, grasping for air.

Zoe stopped and looked at Zara. "You look like shit. Fine, stay here. I'll be right back," Zoe said and sprinted forward, disappearing into the corridor. Zara followed her, and her mouth dropped open when she saw Zoe manipulating the panel as if she had done it many times before.

"Don't be so surprised. You left such detailed instructions on how to program this thing, they've etched themselves in my memory. So, yeah, I know how to program your baby. Because it is your baby, isn't it, Olesya? It's always been about your baby. But which one, huh?"

"Was it you? Did you reprogram my time travel?"

Zoe sighed. "I had to. If I hadn't, you'd have ended up in a dark dimension, and all I went through would've been for nothing."

"Dark dimension?"

"Ugh, it's unnerving to answer questions about the things I should be asking you. I wish you'd goddamn remember everything already. You can't travel back in time—"

"Why not?"

"I'm not the genius here. You should know. You made it clear in your holograms. It had to do with some paradox thing. Grandfather something rather. Let's get going."

Zara's mouth stayed open for a moment while she considered what Zoe had told her before she asked, "And where and when are you going?"

"Back home. Where else?" Zoe said, punching numbers. Zoe stood up. "I'm done. Let's go to the chamber. Your baby should be here soon."

"How?"

"You'll see soon enough."

Zara opened the chamber, and Zoe walked in first, admiring the sight. "Just like I remember it. Splendid. Are these the only compressed dark matter fragments you have?" Zoe asked, pointing at the box she was pressing to her chest.

"Yes," Zara said.

"Hope you're not lying," she said and smiled, looking past Zara.

Zara spun around and uttered a joyful shriek. In the doorway stood Zmey, holding Emery in his arms. She was asleep, holding a thumb in her mouth.

"You found her," Zara whispered. "Good. We can send the crazy bitch to prison, then," she said to Zmey, and extended her arms for Emery.

But Zmey, smiling his odd smile, walked past Zara and stopped facing Zoe.

"You got them?" he asked Zoe.

"Yeah," she said, showing him the box. "A bunch of them. Your daughter-in-law has been busy," she said, opening the box and pouring half of its contents into his pocket. "Here, take some. Oh, and her research notes are in her office. Have your guy burn them all," she added.

"You know each other?" Zara asked, shifting her gaze between Zmey and Zoe.

Zoe and Zmey laughed like good old friends. Zara stood motionless like a pillar while her mind was racing. Why would Tirg's father conspire against her and his own granddaughter? Was Tirg in on it too? Suddenly, it all made sense.

"You're the prisoner," she said to Zoe and then glared at Zmey. "The prisoner you rescued from Andalia."

Zmey assessed her with his penetrating gaze. "You're too smart."

"I don't understand why you have to kidnap your own granddaughter. You could have all that without even asking me. I'm sure Zak would give you anything you wanted. Where is Tirg?"

"So, you figured out Zak. That's why you sent him away. Fortunately, I have other means of knowing what you were up to. We also needed you to set everything up and make sure it works. Even with your notes, no one could replicate what you've done. So, we needed your cooperation."

"You're goddamn crazy, evil liars, the both of you! I'm not going anywhere with you!" she shouted, and then, remembering Zoe telling her about special powers she supposedly possessed, she inhaled and thrust both hands at Zoe with all her strength.

For a fraction of a second, she saw fear in Zoe's eyes, but when nothing happened, Zoe relaxed and sighed.

"Ugh! As I suspected, you don't possess powers in this world," Zoe scoffed.

"You don't either," Zara said. "That's why you wanted the black shards."

Zoe grinned and in one quick stride crossed the distance between them, and with just one blow to Zara's neck sent her to the floor. Then she took Emery from Zmey's arms. Emery woke up and, seeing her mother on the floor, extended her tiny arms and cried out. By the time Zara collected herself and rose from the floor, Zoe was already in the capsule, holding a crying Emery, who was squealing and trying to get to her mother.

"Still a baby but spirited as her mother," Zmey laughed. "She's going to be trouble."

Zara scrambled to the closed capsule and pounded with her hands on its shiny surface. Zoe grinned at her.

"No! Open the door. Give me my daughter back, you goddamn bitch! You evil monster," Zara shouted as hot tears rolled down her cheeks. But Zoe didn't hear her, as the capsule was tightly shut and no sound penetrated its thick crystal walls. After a while, Zara couldn't shout anymore. Her chest hurt when she tried to inhale, and she collapsed by the tube but still held on to the cold crystal walls.

She felt herself being lifted and carried out. She tried to force her limp body to fight Zmey, but with barely any oxygen getting to her lungs, she could only wave her hand halfway toward his face, barely seeing it through a fog that formed before her eyes.

He carried her to her office and lowered her onto a leather sofa. "You need to relax and stop fighting this," he said, handing her a glass of water.

Zara sat on the sofa, drawing tiny breaths, each one deeper than the previous. The fog over her eyes lifted enough for her to see him. She knocked the glass out of his hand.

She rasped. "You fucking coward! Evil man! You just sent your granddaughter somewhere. You might have killed her. Your own blood. You killed my daughter! And I'm going to kill you too!"

She stood up, glaring at him with her black eyes opening wide and shining with the fire of vengeance.

He stepped back, still smiling, but tensing, readying for an attack.

"Where is Tirg? What did you do to him?"

"What makes you think I've done anything to my son?"

"Was he in on it? You never answered my question."

"Sometimes it's better not to know certain things. I need you to program the Vortex for another trip for us because we are going to follow Zoe and Emery."

"Follow them where?"

"To your world. To the world you once left behind and supposedly don't remember ... although I doubt it. The one that is dying now and needs your help."

"But this is a time machine, not something that can transport people into different dimensions."

"I guess you really don't remember," Zmey said and grinned. "Let me enlighten the scientist then. When the space-time continuum bends in on itself near singularities, it rips for a tiny fraction of time and opens the door between dimensions. If you know the location of the singularities, you can program your machine to travel to different dimensions."

"That's what Zoe told you? You believe her? She is deranged, crazy. How do you even know about her? How did you find her?"

"The Andalian government extracted her from the capsule and thought she was a spy. I traded many prisoners for her. Enough talk. Let's get going. Unless you don't want to help your daughter—she's now in a world that's dying of thirst."

"How am I supposed to prevent that?"

"With your technology. You'll do exactly what you did here: recreate your research and the chamber since you've already done it and we know it works. The preontechnology will save your daughter and your world."

"Why didn't you just take the research notes and leave us out of it? Don't you care about your granddaughter?"

"Zoe said the papers wouldn't survive the trip. I love my granddaughter. The love for my granddaughter is what motivates me."

"I doubt that. I doubt you know what love is. You're no different from all the Andalian men, seeking power and wealth, but I don't care about it. You can have your power. I just want my daughter and to know that Tirg is safe," she said and paused, studying his face. "It was you who stole my note and sabotaged my plane, wasn't it? You blew up the lab and my friend with it," Zara said with a cold calmness that scared her. Her nails dug into her palms as she fought the urge to scratch his eyes.

"Let's go. We can chat later."

"Just tell me Tirg is safe."

"Of course he is. Why wouldn't he be? Come on, walk faster," he said, pushing her inside the narrow hallway.

She didn't believe him, but she also couldn't believe he could harm the son who worshiped him. "What if I don't agree?"

"Your daughter will die of thirst and hunger."

"She is your granddaughter."

Zmey shoved her down the stairs. She tripped and scraped the palms of her hands. He extended his hand toward her, but she ignored it and sprang to her feet. He pushed her toward the panel. She extended her hands to stop herself from smashing her face into the control panel. The blood on her hands transferred onto the panel and looked purple in the eerie light.

"Hurry. Your daughter is waiting on the other side. She's probably hungry."

Zara bit her cheek, gritting her teeth. The iron taste of her own blood nauseated her as she programmed the Vortex according to the last coordinates. Zmey grabbed her and dragged her toward the chamber.

"Wait," she said as he pulled her into the Vortex. "I've got to get something."

"What?" he asked, eyeing her suspiciously.

"Something that might help with the research. Don't worry, I'm not going to hurt you or escape. It's right here, hidden in the console."

"Hurry."

Zara pressed the triangle on the console, opening a secret compartment. Zara grabbed a crystal box with Zmey looking over her shoulder and pressed it to her chest.

"What is this thing?"

"Something I need for my research," she said, ignoring his questioning eyes.

In the capsule, her father-in-law said his last words to her in Sinturija. "Zoe said you might not do it. She said you might choose the chamber and your research and not your daughter. She was wrong."

As the bright blue light came on, Zara finally was close enough and had enough strength to plunge her fingers into his throat. "You're evil. One day you'll pay for this!" But it was too late. Soon they started falling into the dark abyss, and she couldn't move, immobilized by the speed.

EMERY AWAKES

From millions of golden drops, I was born
The first thought was of you
Mother
As memories returned, I
I could tell you I mourned you
I didn't
I could tell you I tried
But that would be a lie
Not a single tear
I shed for you
In all those years I searched
Tangled in your shadow
In the darkest of darkness
I heard voices that told me
You were waiting for me
Are you?

31

OPEN SEA

She opened her eyes to blueness all around her. She blinked, but the blue didn't disappear. When her eyes opened wide enough, she understood that the blue-green abyss was water, separated from her by the wall of the crystal capsule. She lay curled at its bottom while the water battered the translucent barrier, trying to claim what was inside. She sat and studied the walls, breathing hard, and soon her chest hurt from her heart pounding against it. Her head hit the capsule when she jerked, seeing a fish piercing her with its cold, watery eyes. She pressed her hands against the walls of the capsule, searching for an opening. But the capsule walls were perfect—there was no opening, no lock, no handle. How long would the air last? Where was she? She stopped breathing, imagining she soon was to draw her last breath in this crystal prison.

Calm down. There is still air in here.

She drew a few even breaths and examined the capsule from top to bottom. That was when she noticed a faint triangle on the bottom. Before she pressed it, she looked out, searching for a light and the end of the abyss, and saw nothing but a deep blue void.

Maybe it's night outside?

She weighed her options: stay and slowly suffocate, or try to swim to the surface, however far it was. She couldn't remember, but her instincts told her she could swim, so she drew a deep breath and pressed the triangle.

The walls slid open, and water poured in and rammed her against the back wall of the capsule with such force that she lost almost all the air she'd just inhaled. She dove downward to avoid the force of the water, waited for the whirl to subside, and dove out of the capsule. With powerful strokes, she pulled herself up, searching for a light that would lead her to the surface and to air and salvation. Her chest hurt as she suppressed the urge to breathe and kept swimming up and up with no light in sight. The pain grew. Her eyes bulged, and blood pounded against her skull. This was it. Death was coming, and she just realized she couldn't remember her name and how she had ended up in this mess. She pushed up with one last powerful stroke. Then she said goodbye to life and, deciding to end the pain, inhaled.

She had assumed the water would taste salty and burn her lungs, not expecting to inhale air instead. Her lungs still hurt, but the relief of pulling air into her lungs put her in a state of euphoria. She had reached the surface and was still alive. She lay on her back, drawing short, even breaths, and opened her eyes.

Complete darkness and nothingness surrounded her except for a few faint stars blinking lethargically against the black sky. There were no lights anywhere, which meant no nearby land and no boats to save her. If only she could remember how she had ended up here, she might guess where there was land. But her mind was blank. The euphoria slowly ebbed as she realized she might still die, swallowed by this black, unforgiving water.

Am I being punished for something I've done?

She floated, staring at the ominous sky. The harder she tried to remember who she was, the tougher it was to stay afloat, as if the burden was making her heavier. So she just floated mindlessly, staring at the lazy stars, listening to the waves splattering around her, and eventually, she relaxed, calmed by the idle blinking and the soft splatter. As she drifted into the blackness, a tune popped into her head. She didn't remember the name of the song or its words, but it sounded familiar and soothing. She started humming the melody as she drifted, waiting for morning to arrive. As she hummed, a distant, foggy memory surfaced of dancing to this melody with someone dear to her in a giant room filled with bright lights and sparkling gems.

She drifted for a long time before the sun peeked shyly from beyond the horizon. Her body grew numb from the chill of the water as it sucked the warmth out of her. The sun, neither bright nor warm, made its way up and hid behind the gray clouds, wafting sluggishly. And when they covered the sun, her skin tightened from the chill, and her body seemed heavier. She searched the horizon. Still, no land, no boats. She was in the middle of the ocean.

I'm going to die here, after all.

She shut her eyes and drifted on her back. Tears squeezed out of her eyes and were absorbed by the salty ocean.

When they find my body, whose name will they put on my tombstone? Maybe no one will find me at all.

As she floated, feeling her body growing numb and heavy, she felt a thump on her head. She turned too quickly and swallowed a big gulp of salty water. And then she swallowed more when she saw a piece of wood that looked like it had come off a boat floating by her side.

"Where did you come from?"

What was left of the plank's blue paint had lost its intensity, bleached by the sun. She looked around, hopeful, but saw nothing else. She grabbed and inspected it—the plank was big enough to use as a float, so she slid onto it and worked her feet, and straining her eyes, pushed in the direction the straggler had come from. The sun now shone directly on her, and she could feel its tentacles reach deep into her skull and morph into a pounding ache. She tried to lick her cracked lips, but her mouth was dry.

It was getting dark when she saw it. At first, she thought it was just the reflection of the setting sun on the water, but when she was closer, her heart leaped into her throat. An orange ring buoy bounced on the waves. The setting sun made the orange pop, so it looked like it was on fire. She reached for it, expecting it to disappear. When her hand grasped the firm ring, she gasped and swallowed more water. She tried to slip through the ring, but her arm got tangled in a rope. Tracing the rope, she found an orange object entwined with the ring's rope and drifting along. When she reached for it, she thought she imagined it. The ring was attached to an inflatable lifeboat. With fingers trembling with excitement and slipping on the seaweed, she fumbled with it, swallowing more water, but finally found a yellow button amid the green slime and pressed it.

A round, orange boat materialized in front of her like a magic trick, bumping into her. She went under momentarily, crying out as she swallowed more water, seeing the boat float away. Her strength drifted away with it. A sudden wave came and covered her. She was drowning just when hope arrived. Then, the image of a dark-haired woman shouting at her not to give up released a powerful burst of energy and determination from somewhere deep down, powering her arms and legs as she swam to the lifeboat. Holding onto the yellow ropes on the boat's side, she climbed into it and wept.

Thank you. She didn't quite know who she was thanking—maybe the gods of the ocean. Searching the boat with her hands, as the darkness had already swallowed everything around her, she found several plastic pouches containing water. She emptied one in a few gulps, discovering the water tasted slightly sweet and tangy. She fell asleep shortly after and woke up when the sun was a third of the way up from the horizon. The buoy was still attached to the boat, bouncing behind it. Noticing the letters on its side, she brought it closer. The large letters spelled "Zoe." The name echoed in her mind as something she should remember, but it refused to surface.

For three days and four nights, she drifted. On the fourth morning, she woke up disoriented, realizing something was different. She wasn't swaying anymore. The boat had run aground on white sand.

On rubbery legs, she crawled out of the boat and walked, looking around. The white sandy beach stretched as far as the eye could see.

Peppered with occasional rocks and tons of golden-brown shells sparkling in the sun, the sand reached far inland and ended in grass-covered dunes. There were no houses, no boat ramps, no trails leading inland, no other signs of civilization.

Her eyes landed on a row of trees, and that was where she headed. She shivered and inspected her clothes. Her fingers went through holes surrounded by rusty stains in the frayed tank top. Shoeless and wearing only the top and underwear, she slowly made her way up the dunes and toward the gnarly pines. The ground covered with pinecones and sharp rocks slowed her even more. She walked through the sparse forest for hours until it ended abruptly at a road.

The surface of the road was full of multicolored shiny speckles that glowed as the road undulated through hills in both directions. The pines grew on one side, and unfamiliar, leafy green trees on the other.

"It probably doesn't matter which way I go."

She turned right and hobbled ahead on her sore feet, preparing for a long walk as the road seemed abandoned. She jerked when she heard the sounds of music and chimes. The tune grew louder. A giant truck covered with stickers and decked out in multicolored flashing lights strung all over its huge metal hulk was coming toward her. Colorful flags flanked both sides of the front and the back of the noisy monster. It didn't even occur to her to flag the driver because she believed the strange apparition was only in her imagination. With her mouth wide open and her arms in midair, she stared at the beast coming her way. Only when the rush of air swept over her as the truck passed her did she wave her arms and run after it, shouting.

"Wait, wait. Please stop!"

The tires screeched, and as the stench of burning rubber and brakes reached her, the truck stopped three hundred feet ahead. Next, the cab door opened, and a man jumped down and ran toward her. Short and round, the man panted as he jogged toward her. When he finally reached her, he rested his small, golden-brown arms covered with thick gold hair on his legs as he inhaled deeply whilst he appraised her with his curious dark brown eyes. She stood gazing at the stout man, as peculiar and flamboyant as the beast he drove. Once he regained his breath, his round, brown face lit up in a brilliant smile. His full lips stretched across his face, almost touching his ears, which were full of glistening, dangling earrings of different shapes and lengths. As he smiled, the tiny gems embedded in his teeth shone. Straightening up, he wiped tiny droplets of sweat off his brow with the red scarf he snatched off his head. Dozens of gleaming black braids with multicolored strings threaded into them spilled onto his shoulders.

"Hulla!" he bellowed and smiled again. "Oco dobish nutej?"

The smooth baritone of his voice broke her spell. She shrugged. "I don't understand you. Where am I?" she asked, startled at how squeaky and unsure her voice sounded.

"Ah, you're not Romana," he said and wiped his forehead again, studying her. "Are you Andalian?"

She shrugged. "I don't know."

"You speak it well, so you probably are," he said, looking over her clothes.

Her cheeks burned while he appraised her skimpy outfit.

He pinched the sleeves of his yellow jacket and stroked his protruding belly in round strokes. "Are you hungry? You look cold."

She nodded, probing his brown eyes. The man's kindness triggered a tsunami of sudden self-pity. Deep sobs surged through her chest as she stared at him, trying to answer.

"Oh, no, no, no. Ne puch. Don't cry," he said, almost crying himself. He made an inviting gesture with his hand, pointing at his dazzling machine. "Come, come," he added, smiling. "I have food and water, and I'll take you wherever you're going. Your feet are bleeding. Please. Let me help you," he kept saying softly, waving his fleshy hands in gentle, inviting gestures.

Her outburst of emotion lasted only a few seconds. Wiping her tears with her hands, she nodded and then followed the little man to his truck. It didn't even occur to her to distrust him. His goofy yet comforting mannerisms, smile, and eyes soothed her lonely soul.

More than food and water, she'd just realized, she longed for another human being. And this eccentric man seemed perfect. A flamboyant angel.

He jumped the steep steel steps to the cab as if they were a mere two or three inches. When he was inside the cab, he extended his hand to help her and then gracefully jumped into the driver's seat, his round belly jiggling as he settled in his bright red leather chair. Then he grabbed a lever by the steering wheel and raised it, starting the engine, which answered with a deep growl, and a bell sounded. While he revved the motor, he glanced over and pointed to a compartment in front of her. Its door was covered with stickers of various animals she could not name. She slid the compartment door open, and when she saw what was inside, her mouth watered. The large cabinet overflowed with snacks and bottles full of colorful liquids. She eyed a green bottle shaped like a cute animal with large ears. He glanced at her and grinned. "This one is really good. Kiwi. Try some."

She didn't need an invitation. With hands curved like talons, she snatched a bag and the green bottle and drained it with just a few gulps, belching loudly afterward. He giggled and patted his belly.

After she satisfied her hunger, devouring the contents of several packages of dried fruit and nuts, she scrutinized the cabin. With red leather seats and blue leather walls, the cab was both cozy and vibrant, with its glitzy golden tassels hanging from all corners, from the visors, the mirrors, and above the windows. All that glinted softly as colorful lights hung inside and outside blinked. On the dash, a line of varying sizes of yellow ducks with red beaks bounced their heads in agreement as the tires bounced along on the bumpy road.

Then he thumped his chest, repeating his name. "I'm Narius," he said while glancing expectantly.

Oh, he wants to hear my name.

She hesitated before finally saying. "I don't remember anything before I woke up in the middle of an ocean and then...." She stopped, seeing his friendly but befuddled glances. "I'm not making any sense to you?" she said and sighed. "Zoe. I'm Zoe. For now, at least. Until I remember."

What if I don't? She shuddered.

Noticing her shiver, Narius reached up to a cubby above his head and took out a red velvet blanket. A sigh escaped her lips as the blanket reached her skin. Soft as the fur of a puppy, the blanket enveloped her in gentleness and warmth. She slumped into the cozy red chair and closed her eyes to rest. As soon as her eyes closed, a myriad of questions crowded her mind. Who was she, and how did she end up in the ocean? Where was she? Narius's language when he first spoke was fast and overflowing with consonants, sounding like wind blowing through leaves in the forest, and was unfamiliar to her.

The screeching, puffing, and squealing sounds woke her up. The truck came to a stop. She rubbed her crusty eyes. Narius smiled at her, and the gems caught and reflected the bright early morning sunrays filtering through the windows. She must have slept for a long time. Narius stopped in front of a house dazzling with color and eccentricity. The sun made the bright yellow frames even brighter, and painted red poppies adorning the oval windows shimmered, appearing as though their delicate petals swayed in the wind. Whimsical butterflies were balanced on the flowering branches against a blue background.

An overweight golden dog jingling with tiny golden trinkets on his collar came running out of the door and gave a few loud barks and then showed all his ferocious white fangs in a wide smile, wagging his tail vigorously.

"Tamtam," Narius said, pointing at the dog and smiling ear to ear, just like his golden friend. He jumped out of the truck, and the dog jumped on his chest and covered his face with kisses with its big, sloppy tongue. After the dog was done greeting Narius, it looked at the truck and sniffed. She glanced at Narius uncertainly through the window. He grinned and motioned for her to join him. After the initial sniffing, the dog licked her hand and smiled at her. Seeing the dog triggered a memory of a big black nose and eyes. Her dog. She used to have a dog that had licked her on her face. But she couldn't remember his name.

"Come, come," Narius invited her inside. As colorful as the outside, the inside welcomed her with walls in yellow and orange hues, a jungle of plants, paintings, and sculptures. Her jaw dropped upon seeing the sculptures—half-human, half-creatures, the life-size wood-and-stone creations occupied all the corners of this large, bright area. The sharp morning light created deep shadows, emphasizing their strangeness, elongating and bending the already long arms and legs as if they were engaged in a dance or a ritual. The sculptures were as beautiful and mesmerizing as they were scary and disturbing.

"Hulla yo," a pleasant woman's voice interrupted her reverie.

A small woman, whose brown hair erupted in a volcano of braids full of tiny shimmering stones, smiled at her. She was drying her hands on a yellow kitchen towel while appraising her guest. Her knee-high dress was covered in layered bands of beads that swayed as she moved. Her feet drowned in oversized yellow shoes with red polka dots.

As soon as he got through the door, Narius flooded the smiling woman with words like a fast-flowing stream. Zoe stood there listening to him, mesmerized, transported for a moment into a forest where leaves could talk.

Then the woman spoke to her in perfect Andalian, rounding her words elegantly. "Narius tells me he found you on a road by the seaside. You were lucky because that road is not used much anymore. He seldom goes there, except that he had to deliver an order in that area. But it turned out that the address was fake, and he made that trip for nothing. Well, not for nothing. To find you," she said and waved her towel toward a hallway. "Come on. Our home is your home for as long as you want. We have several spare bedrooms for friends who visit us. We planned it that way, didn't we, Narius?" She turned to him and smiled.

"Are you...Andalian?"

"No, I'm Romana, but I learned Andalian working for the art council in our Romana community. What's your name?"

Zoe exhaled. "I don't remember. For now, call me Zoe."

"What happened to you?"

"I don't know. I woke up in a strange container submerged in the ocean and don't remember anything. After I freed myself from that glass thing, I found a buoy attached to a lifeboat as I was trying to stay afloat. Zoe was the name of that boat. It sort of sounded familiar."

"I see. Where are my manners? I'm Nora. Come on, I'll take you to your bedroom. Once you get some food in your belly and get a good night's sleep, you might start remembering," Nora said and gently took Zoe's arm, leading her to a room at the far end of the house. Tamtam followed, wagging his tail and touching Zoe's hand with his wet nose. She stroked his head, and he smiled.

"He likes you. You must be a dog person."

"I think so."

Cozy, bright, and colorful, the room welcomed her with its warmth and joyfulness. There were sculptures in the room, but smaller and of regular, human proportions. Nora handed her a handful of towels and then scratched her chin, evaluating Zoe's skimpy wardrobe.

"Hmm, you're much taller than I am, but I'll try to find something out of the clothes my friends left behind. Make yourself comfy here, and I'll be right back. Come, Tamtam. Let's get her settled before you beg her for attention, you big baby."

After they left, Zoe sat on the bed and exhaled deeply. The partially open door in the room's corner caught her attention. She opened the door and stood in the doorway admiring the enormous see-through bathtub surrounded by palms in painted porcelain pots. When she looked into a mirror with an intricate gold frame, the towels she was holding fell to the floor.

The wavy blond hair, tousled by the sea and the sleep, fell to her shoulders in messy waves. The big oval-shaped blue eyes sparkled with gold and black dots as she stared at the face of the stranger. Her full lips parted as she traced her face in the mirror, searching for clues of her identity. *Who are you? Are you Zoe?* The head in the mirror shook. *No, I'm not Zoe*, she sighed.

∼

"How are you?" Nora asked when Zoe, freshly showered, poked her head into the kitchen.

Zoe wore wide pants in a floral design and a white crochet blouse. Her wet hair dripped tiny drops onto the tiled kitchen floor as she walked toward Nora.

"Good. Thank you. I don't know what I would have done without your help."

"Oh, you are so welcome, hon. Sit down, or you can help me prepare lunch. You can cut the vegetables," Nora said, and pushed a cutting board and a knife her way. She pointed to a pile of round green vegetables. "Narius is unloading his sculptures from the truck. You know, the order that never got delivered. It shouldn't take him long."

"Is he the sculptor?"

"Yes, mostly, but I help. With inspiration," she said with a giggle.

"It's powerful and passionate. Beautiful, deep. I can sense their despair, hope, fear."

"Yeah. Narius has always had a great imagination. He used to paint landscapes, people, or flowers—until one night, about eight years ago, he had a dream. A nightmare, really, if you ask me. He dreamed of the dark monsters that fought with each other, and he started sculpting them; otherwise, they wouldn't leave him alone. I didn't even know he sculpted so well," Nora said, and shook her head. "He is very talented, that Narius of mine. Very special man," she finished softly.

Narius bellowed something when he entered the kitchen. He kissed Nora on the neck. She flung the kitchen towel at him. "Behave. We have a guest. We'll have torndilles and tampaniones today. Sit down. It's almost ready," she said, taking the cut vegetables from Zoe and tossing them into a giant bowl. "Did you wash your hands?" she asked, eyeing him and his hands.

He nodded vigorously.

When Zoe tasted the food, tears rushed to her eyes, and she stopped breathing for a moment. It was so full of flavor and surprising textures, aromas, and tastes. Zoe wolfed down her food, barely breathing. "Oh, this is soooo good," she said with her mouth full.

"Thank you," Nora said, beaming. "I enjoy making people feel good, and there's no better way than food."

In the evening, Narius and Nora conversed in their language and occasionally asked her questions to which she had no answers.

"We know someone who can help figure out who you are, if you agree. He finds people who have been missing for years, and he could figure out who you are. What do you say?" Nora asked, glancing at Zoe.

"Yes, that'd be great. Thank you."

32

FREDERICK

"Sam is here," Nora said, knocking on Zoe's door.

Zoe waited before entering the living room, studying the profile of the slim man talking to Narius. Both men stood before a sculpture of two man-creatures engaged in a wrestling match. Narius spoke in his usual fast, rustling way, waving his arms, pointing at his new creation. The man's wavy brown hair moved in the breeze wafting through an open window.

"Sam, this is Zoe. Or that's how we call her until she remembers and knows who she really is."

When Sam turned toward Zoe, she gasped. His face seemed familiar. His big brown eyes radiated unassuming kindness and intelligence as he regarded her calmly. She studied his chiseled face with high cheekbones and a royal nose and waited for a sign of recognition. But he didn't seem to recognize her.

"Nora told me about your predicament. A friend of mine specializes in finding people. I believe he's a magician of sorts because he finds people when nobody else can, and when all hope is lost."

"Who is he? Your friend?" Zoe asked. Her throat suddenly dried when she stared at him.

"He's a private detective. I can take you to him," Sam said, scratching his head. "He can't travel easily," he added quietly.

"Oh."

"You can trust Sam. He's been our friend forever. He is the gentlest soul in the whole of Andalia," Nora said, patting his arm.

Sam smiled and waved his hand. "Stop. You're embarrassing me."

"Andalia. Is that where we are?"

"That's where we are, sweet girl. In northwestern Andalia. Andalia is a large continent and a country. Our Romana community occupies a tiny portion of western Andalia."

"I'll go with you," Zoe said, staring at Sam.

"Of course. It's about an hour's drive. He's expecting us."

Sam directed Zoe into a small blue car parked outside. Zoe secretly wondered how he was going to fit his long legs into this tiny vehicle, but he managed just fine. He folded his slender legs elegantly and effortlessly like a dancer. He drove the car with equal elegance and poise, gesturing to points of interest with his slender fingers.

"See that giant building over there? That's an old gymnasium. Now closed because it partially burned down a while back. They built a new one that's big enough to accommodate the entire town of Romanovo. Here is Park Novetalis. It's the most magical place in Andalia. You find the oldest trees here," he said, and laughed. "That's what I think. Ask Nora or Narius to bring you here. Over there is the place where the Romana community holds its festivals and celebrations."

"You're not part of the Romana community?"

"No, I'm not. And neither is my friend Frederick. We moved here a while back, liking the community and its customs. We sort of fled our way of living because this one suited us better."

"You both did. At the same time?"

"Yes," Sam said, turning his face away.

Sam parked in front of a small gray house, well-maintained but lacking any personal touches, flowers, or ornaments.

Sam bent down and retrieved a key from under a rock. "We're here, Frederick," he said, entering the house.

Sam led Zoe through a hallway into the living room, which appeared comfortable but lacked decorations or softness. Facing away from them, at a desk set up by a large window overlooking a lush backyard, sat a tall, slender man in a wheelchair. Zoe tried to hide her surprise. She hadn't expected someone who finds people to be bound to a chair.

He turned. She couldn't see his face with the bright window behind him. He said nothing, observing her. After a long minute, he rolled the wheelchair her way. His intense blue eyes shone, and his face, the features of which looked carved in stone, betrayed nothing. His stare unsettled her. Something in those blue eyes sliced her heart, while her brain raced, searching for memories.

"This is Zoe," Sam said. "Zoe, this is Frederick, my best friend."

"Zoe? You remember your name, and it is Zoe?" Frederick asked. His voice surprised her. Deep and melodic. Gentle but carrying the weight of its message. Something in the timbre of his voice touched her heart softly. She wanted to hear more of it.

"No, not really," she said, and explained how she got her name.

"I see," he said, pointing at the sofa. "Sam will bring us something to drink. Malt for me."

"Got it. How about you?" Sam asked Zoe.

"What's malt?" Zoe asked.

Frederick smiled, and her heart galloped, seeing his smile. "It's darn good and refreshing on a hot afternoon like today."

"I'll try one," she said.

"So tell me everything from the beginning," Frederic said after Sam had left.

Zoe repeated her story. Frederick gazed at her, and although he tried to maintain a neutral and calm expression, the muscles underneath his skin were anything but calm. They twitched as she told the story, especially in the beginning, when she told him about her fight for survival.

"I see," he said through clenched teeth.

Sam brought three glasses sloshing with a golden liquid and handed them out. I've had this type of drink before, she thought, working her tongue against the roof of her mouth. She sipped it and licked the foam off her lips. Frederick observed her silently.

"So, do you think you'll be able to help her?" Sam asked.

"I'll do my best. I have a hunch it won't be easy."

The word "hunch" made her jump in her seat. Her heart rattled.

"You okay?" Sam asked.

"Yeah, thank you," she said, and took another sip. Much bigger.

Frederik smiled lightly. Sam furrowed his brow, shifting his gaze between Zoe and Frederick. The flash of recognition on Frederick's face when he saw Zoe seemed to have affected Sam. He observed his friend but said not a word.

Frederick promised to search for Zoe's real identity over the next several days. They stayed long enough to finish their drinks, and by the end, the conversation dragged. Frederick was silent most of the time, and Sam attempted to entertain her with the history of Andalia, but she paid little attention to his words, combing through her brain for answers. Why did the two men she had just met today seem so familiar?

What's the matter with me? Am I mad? Or am I so desperate to remember that everyone I see seems familiar?

"What happened to Frederick?" she asked on their way back.

A shadow crossed Sam's face.

"I'm sorry. I shouldn't have asked."

Sam said nothing. His eyes dulled. He remained silent for most of the way back.

"So, you met Frederick?" Nora asked. She sat at a kitchen table, painting a plate. Butterflies, just like the ones adorning the house.

Zoe nodded. "You're talented. These are beautiful. Like they are about to fly."

"Thank you. If you can be found, he'll find you," she said and paused. "You're probably wondering what happened to him."

Zoe looked up. Her expression must have answered Nora's question.

"I don't know the complete story. Only bits and pieces I gathered from their conversations when malt was involved."

Nora dabbed red paint from a small container and filled out the outline of a red poppy the butterfly was resting on.

"They came here from eastern Andalia because of what happened to Frederick. He was paralyzed while protecting a young woman. The soldiers who shot him thought he was dead and left him, but Sam found him and took him to safety. He saved his life, but sometimes I wonder if Frederick wanted to be saved. Poor gentle soul that Frederick is—he suffers so. I'm not entirely certain if it's only his condition he grieves or something else entirely. He seldom talks about himself."

"And the woman survived?"

Nora looked at her with an odd expression. She nodded slowly and hesitated before answering. "I probably shouldn't be telling you this. Yes, she survived. She's Sam's wife."

Zoe's hand flew to her mouth. "Why would someone try to harm her?"

Nora inhaled deeply, putting away her brush. "You see, they have strange customs in Andalia. We don't follow those customs, as we were once a nomadic tribe with our own sovereignty. And thankfully they left us alone, maybe because we don't quite look good to them. We are short and stocky with brown skin and kinky hair and wild natures. We marry who we want and when we want."

"And they don't?"

Nora studied her face before she replied. "They have the System selecting their wives and husbands for them. It's based on genetics, economics, family issues, and, they claim, compatibility."

"The System?"

"Yes, it's based on a computational system. All the information is plugged into it, and it spits out perfect matches. But as I understand it, there is some wiggle room for the parents to add certain qualities to the queries."

"How strange."

"Anyway, Anna, Sam's wife, was supposed to have married someone else. Someone the System had selected for her, but you see...she met Sam and fell in love, defying her parents. Her fiancé reported her, and..." Nora paused, rose from her chair, and filled two glasses with water. She drank half of her glass and drew a big breath before continuing. "They publicly beat her before her prison sentence. They tied her to a steel post and whipped her." Nora's voice faltered and her eyes moistened, but her lips pursed in an angry scowl. "Those animals whipped her so hard that she still has scars. If it weren't for Fred...I don't know what would have happened."

"That's horrible."

"Fred jumped into the plaza, untied her, and pushed her out, and then fought the guards that came after him following their initial shock. You see, no one had ever done anything like that, so nobody expected it, and Sam got her out on account of the turmoil and before the guards realized what had happened. And after he got her to safety, Sam came back to check on Frederick and, realizing he was still alive, hid him at a friend's house. You see, Sam is a doctor, and he nursed him back to health. Unfortunately, Fred's spine was severed below the waist, and he's been in a wheelchair since. But he is doing well finding people. He never complains," she said and shook her head, wiping her eyes with a yellow kitchen towel. "To do such a heroic act for a stranger."

"They didn't know each other?" Zoe's eyes became two huge marbles.

"No. They didn't. Frederick was just passing by and couldn't stand by while they beat a woman."

Narius ran into the kitchen, grabbed a handful of fruit and cookies, and ran out again, shoving fruit into his mouth with hands covered with black paint. His apron was covered in a chalky gray material.

"He's doing a new piece. He woke up two nights ago with what he said was the most powerful vision he'd ever had, and now he's spending every second in his studio. That man of mine has no sense. Can you believe he slept there last night?"

Two days had gone by, and Zoe had not heard from Frederick or Sam. She worried he couldn't find her identity or that he'd found something so horrible he would not see her again. The second option scared her even more. On the third morning, she couldn't wait, found Nora basking outside on the patio, and asked her if she had learned anything about the search.

"No. I haven't, sorry. I've been worrying about Narius so much, I forgot about it. But let me send a message to him."

She rose from her chair, turned on her heels, and left the patio. She returned shortly and shook her head. "No, he hasn't found you yet. He said it might take a while. He's finishing other jobs."

Zoe felt a pang of disappointment. She'd been foolish to assume she was his most important project. "Thank you," she said, and retreated to her room.

Before she got there, she stopped at Narius's studio, which, oddly (Narius always shut his door tight when he was working on a new piece, Nora told her), was left open. Propelled by intense curiosity, she tiptoed inside. Narius was not in his studio, which emboldened her to go deeper inside.

The entire southern wall of this enormous room was made of glass. The sunlight poured in, submerging the room in bright light. There was a giant structure positioned close to the windows, but she couldn't see it well against the light. She walked up to it, and when she finally looked at the sculpture bathed in sharp light, she gasped and pressed her hands to her mouth to stifle a cry. She stepped back, imagining for a moment that there was a real woman imprisoned in the marble, trying to claw her way out. The sculpture's mouth was open in a cry, and her large oval eyes were open wide in agony. None of Narius's other sculptures featured this much detail. And then a powerful vision, a memory, flashed before her eyes. Narius's sculpture awoke, stepped off its pedestal, and approached Zoe, whispering, "Emery, you're alive and all grown up."

Standing frozen and pale was how Narius had found her when he shuffled in holding a plate of food. "What are you doing here?" he asked.

She didn't hear him.

"What's wrong?" he asked.

Zoe's hand left her mouth and pointed at the sculpture. "I remember this woman. *She* is Zoe. She pushed me into the crystal capsule. My name's not Zoe. My name is Emery."

"You remember who you are now?"

Emery slowly turned her head toward him. "I only know it is my name because that's what she called me, and that she was the reason I ended up in that strange capsule. I remember yelling her name, and it was Zoe."

"But you said you were alone in the capsule."

"Yeah, you're right. I'm so confused."

"Do you remember anything else?"

"No. How do you know her?" Emery asked, pointing at the sculpture with her trembling hand.

"I don't know her. I dreamed of her," he said, and tried to move in front of the statue to block Emery's view. "Look, you shouldn't be here. I don't like to show my work to anyone before I'm done. I don't even let Nora snoop here before I'm finished because it interrupts my creative juices and distracts me—"

"But I know her," Emery said. "I need to know who she is because she is connected to me. Don't you see? Please tell me," she said, and grabbed his hand.

"There isn't much more. She yelled I need to set her free because if I don't, the world will end in horrible drought, famine, fires, and disease, and that everyone will die."

"Did she tell you to sculpt her resemblance? Is that what she meant?"

"She didn't, but I don't know any other way to set people free."

"What else did she say?"

Narius wrinkled his big, round nose. "I don't remember. She may have said something else, but I forgot. You know how dreams are."

"I need to see Frederick."

"Now?"

"Yes. Now. I remembered my name and hers. Frederick can use it in his search. Can you take me to him?"

Narius hesitated. "Sure," he said, taking off his dirty work apron, which had long lost its original color, covered with stains, paint, and dried patches of mortar or concrete. "I just need to tell Nora where I'm going."

"Why don't I take her, Narius? You can go back to your sculpture," Nora said when she found out Emery remembered her name and wanted to see Frederick.

"I dunno. It's been seen. It may be ruined," he mumbled, sending an accusatory glance toward Emery.

But Emery paid no attention to him, overwhelmed with excitement mixed with dread.

Frederick wasn't home, or he didn't answer. Emery pressed the bell in between knocking, but the house remained silent.

"That's strange," Nora said, trying to see through the windows. "I can't see anything through the blinds. He seldom leaves home because it's a hurdle for him to go anywhere," she said, wrinkling her forehead. "I know. Let's go see Sam. Maybe he knows where he is. He lives close by. I'm sure he has a good reason to be gone," Nora added, seeing Emery's pained expression.

Sam seemed surprised but flung the door open with a quick, graceful move.

"I don't know where he is. He said nothing to me and didn't ask for help. He could be on a case. Come on in."

"Where is Anna?"

"At school. She's tutoring kids who don't learn as fast as others."

"Of course. Typical Anna."

"I remembered my name, and I thought it would be important in the search…"

"Oh, that's great."

"My name is Emery," she said, observing Sam.

"What's wrong?" Nora asked, watching Sam's face turn ashen as he stared at Emery as if he were seeing a ghost.

"I should have known," he whispered.

"What? What are you talking about? Spit it out!" Nora said.

"We'd better sit down," Sam said, pointing to the white sofas and chairs arranged around a glass table with an overflowing bouquet of large white flowers with dark blue centers, whose sweet perfume permeated the room.

Sam waited for Emery and Nora to take their seats before he sat. "When Frederick was hurt—"

"I told her about it. I'm sorry. I'm such a blabbermouth," Nora said.

"When he was hurt and unconscious for days, Anna and I took care of him and prayed that he would live. Being with him day and night, we heard him moan and cry out names. Mostly one name."

"What name?" Emery whispered.

"Emery. He cried 'Emery' all the time. And that he would find her. But I asked him who Emery was when he was better; he claimed he didn't know. I believed him then, but when I brought you to him, I noticed you'd made an impression on him. I know him and his facial expressions, and when he is trying to hide something. He recognized you. Even before knowing your name was Emery."

"If he recognized her as Emery, why didn't he say so?" Nora asked.

Sam shrugged. "He is...complicated."

"Where is he?" Nora asked.

"I told you. I don't know where he is."

Emery slumped in her seat. She really was a monster whom he had known and recognized. He left because he didn't want to see her anymore. Maybe she'd wronged him somehow. She felt the energy drain out of her. *What am I? What if Zoe tried to kill me for a good reason?*

"I thought I saw something in your eyes too when you first met him. A hint of recognition," Sam said, gazing at Emery.

"His eyes," she whispered. "I remembered his eyes."

Emery disappeared into her room and threw herself onto the bed, letting tears flow freely and soak her silky pillow.

The next day she stayed in her room until the afternoon light shone into her eyes through the slits between the curtains. She shuffled into the kitchen and stood there, not sure what to do. Nora was nowhere in sight, so Emery made herself tea and sat at the table, holding her head in her hands. Through the open kitchen window, a few muffled sounds reached her. At first, the sounds were unclear, but then she started hearing words. "...strange...dangerous..."

She imagined they were talking about her, and in that instant, she felt alone in this strange world among the people she didn't know but who might know her and her dark secrets.

Are they all afraid of me? What am I to do?

She wiped her eyes with the palms of her hands, wrapped her fingers around the hot cup, and picked it up. Her hands shook when she brought the cup to her lips. The delicate porcelain cup slid out of her wet fingers, rolled onto the table, and clunked to the floor, breaking. Emery stood staring at the golden liquid spreading on the tiles, and all she could think of was its minty scent. Her hands flopped to her sides.

"Are you okay?" Nora asked, running into the kitchen, clapping her polka shoes on the tiles.

"I broke your cup. I'm sorry," Emery said, and burst out crying.

"Hey, honey. It's okay. I have many cups. It's not a big deal. I'll make you another cup," Nora said and tried to embrace her.

But Emery stepped back, overturning a chair behind her while tears ran down her cheeks. She felt their hot stickiness on her face. "Are you afraid of me? Do you want me out of your house?"

"What makes you think so?" Nora asked, eyes huge.

"Frederick left because of me, and you think I'm dangerous..."

"Is that what you think?" she asked, and when Emery nodded, she scooped Emery into her arms, ignoring her protests.

It was an awkward hug because she was much shorter, but Nora's compact body exuded so much tenderness and affection, Emery thawed and hugged her back, soaking her blue chiffon blouse with tears. Nora patted her gently on the head. "It's okay. Cry. Cry all you can. It helps."

After Emery calmed down, Nora sat her at the kitchen table, then quickly made tea and sat down, facing Emery. "Frederick didn't leave because of you, and nobody fears you. Definitely not Frederick. He's not scared of anything or anyone. He is the bravest man I know. I'm sure he had good reasons for leaving. Maybe it is related to your quest, maybe not. We'll just wait for him to get back. Nobody wants you to leave here, and I just love having another woman around. It will be okay," she said and patted Emery's hand. "I'll make you some food."

33

I MUST FIND HER

"He's still not back. It's been over a week," Emery said to Nora. Five minutes later, she said the same to Narius when he came for dinner. "Where is he?"

Narius shrugged.

"Is that normal? For him to be away for so long?"

"We don't know what his work entails and how long it usually takes to solve his cases. I'm sure he'll be back soon."

When she hadn't heard from Sam after three more days, Emery begged and eventually convinced Nora to take her to Frederick's house. To their surprise, Frederick opened the door. He waited for them to sit, then he looked at Emery. Nora shifted in her seat and gasped, seeing his serious expression.

"Sam told me you remembered your name, and that Zoe was someone who hurt you," Frederick said. "Have you remembered more since we last talked?"

Emery shook her head. "Did you find out who I am?"

"Yes," he said and fell silent, piercing her with his blue eyes.

"Well?" Emery asked, holding her hand to her chest to calm her thrashing heart.

"Your name is Emery Igres."

"My mother?"

"Your mother was Zara Igres, who was a brilliant scientist—"

"Was?"

"She disappeared without a trace twenty-four years ago. She lived in Andalia until she married a Sinturijan man and moved there with him. Soon after, she disappeared. I found out she moved there only because it was entangled in a tragedy that touched the entire Andalian scientific community. Your mother was developing a new technology that would've transformed the world and improved the lives of millions of people."

"Are you talking about the preontechnology?" Nora asked, raising her eyebrows.

"Yes."

"But her name was not Zara Igres. It was…Zara Ramsey," Nora said.

"Yes. That was her Andalian name," Frederick said.

"That was a huge scandal surrounding this tragedy, as I remember," Nora said.

"What happened?"

"The lab where she worked exploded right before she left," Frederick said.

"Some people even blamed her for the explosion. She didn't show up at the lab that day, so they speculated she blew it up because she wanted to destroy her research—"

"Why would she want to destroy it?" Emery asked.

"She was leaving for Sinturija. Maybe she didn't want—" Nora said.

Frederick shook his head. "She blew nothing up. According to the police investigation, a jealous rival researcher did it. They had evidence proving it, and your mother had sent a letter to the more progressive newspaper before she left, exposing the bigotry of Andalian culture, the hypocrisy of the scientists, and the absurdity of it all, blaming it for the death of her friend and the destruction of the lab and the research."

"I couldn't believe they actually published it. For the first time in

Andalian history, people went out and protested against the System. Your mom was a hero," Nora said. "The bravest woman who ever lived."

"I don't understand any of it. And what happened to the technology?" Emery asked.

"All was lost in the explosion. And after the explosion and the riots, the government deployed its army and squashed everything quickly. The scientific research was abandoned, and some of it even banned, and the funding for it was cut."

"How was she a hero then?" Emery asked Nora.

"She was a woman. Women are banned from jobs like that. She had to disguise herself, pretending to be a man to work in the lab. She could've been imprisoned or killed like—"

"But she wasn't," Frederick interrupted again, sending Nora a stern look.

Nora glanced at him, surprised.

"How did she disappear?"

"I don't know. Information from Sinturija isn't readily available in Andalia. I only found out about her disappearance because she married into a prominent diplomatic noble family in Sinturija, and for a while, that was all the media covered. She, her daughter, her husband, and her father-in-law disappeared."

"How do you know she was my mother?"

A shadow passed across his face. Waiting for him to answer, she watched his lips and eyes, and noticed they bore signs of lingering sorrow.

He spoke slowly. "Her daughter's photograph and the description of her unusual eyes were circulated everywhere, including Andalia, and her name was Emery. That was twenty-four years ago, and you look about that age. I have a strong hunch you are her."

That hunch again.

After a long silence, during which Emery sat staring somewhere in the distance, past Frederick's face, she finally spoke. "So, my mom and I disappeared, and then I woke up in a glass prison in the middle of the ocean. Sounds crazy. But if it's all I have, and if my mother was kidnapped and is still being held somewhere against her will, I must go to Sinturija and find her."

"You can't," Frederick said, echoed by Nora.

"Why can't I?"

"First, the ocean separating the two continents is enormous, requiring a special aircraft. You can only get on it with permission from the government. Mostly, prominent diplomats travel between the two continents."

"Where do they fly from?" Emery asked, unfazed.

"The very northeastern tip of Andalia—"

Frederick interrupted Nora, throwing an icy look her way. "It's heavily guarded to prevent unwanted passengers. They don't ask questions either but shoot the few who are stupid enough to get through the fences rigged with automatic machine guns."

"What's the big deal? Why don't they want people to fly there?"

"Sinturija is much more progressive," Frederick said, and lowered his gaze.

"You mean the System doesn't select husbands for women?"

Frederick nodded. "Women can work and have their own bank accounts. They're afraid of it spreading into Andalia."

While Emery listened to him, the gold dots in her eyes intensified. She fixed a heavy gaze on him and asked in a voice trembling with emotion yet forceful, demanding, daring, "Where do you know me from?"

"I don't know you. I just met you," Frederick said. His face reddened.

Emery pressed harder. "So why were you crying my name when you were in a coma? Why did I see recognition in your eyes when you first saw me?"

"I recognized you as the missing girl—"

"So why didn't you tell me? Why disappear for almost two weeks without telling me? What are you hiding?" Emery rose and crossed her arms.

Nora's brown face darkened as she watched their verbal battle.

The air in the room electrified with the intensity of Emery and Frederick's stares.

"I'm not hiding anything, and I don't have to explain myself to you."

"Yes, you are! I'm not leaving here until you tell me!"

"Suit yourself," he hissed, and turned his wheelchair around to leave.

Emery dashed in front of the wheelchair and stood there blocking his escape. "You're not going anywhere until you tell me."

"Nora, please take your guest with you," he said, avoiding Emery's eyes.

Nora sighed. "Frederick, I think she's right. If you know her, tell her, no matter how horrible the truth might be. She's not alone in thinking that you recognized her. Sam said that the way you called her name in your coma was heartbreaking—as if you were calling someone you had loved and lost."

"I don't know her. Leave. I want to be alone," he said, moving his chair with powerful thrusts of his muscular arms, pushing Emery aside. Emery drew a breath, about to yell in his face again, but his forlorn expression scattered her anger in an instant. She stood in silence with her mouth open while he maneuvered around her and left the room. Nora gently grabbed her arm and pulled her out of the house.

Emery shook her head. "Why doesn't he tell me?"

"I don't know. Maybe we're mistaken, and he really doesn't know you. Come on, let's go back."

Emery was silent all the way back despite Nora's cheerful chatter and her pointing to different landmarks and telling their backstories. Soon Nora stopped, realizing Emery was not listening, facing away from her.

Back at the house, Emery skulked to her room and stayed there until morning. She dreamed of a woman with sad black eyes and wavy black hair motioning for Emery to follow her, then walking away and disappearing behind a murky gray wall. When Emery reached the wall, it transformed into a tall building, the uppermost floor of which disappeared into the dark sky.

The dream awoke fragmented memories of the same woman in different surroundings. From the way her heart fluttered when the woman smiled at her, Emery assumed she was her mother. She jumped out of bed but couldn't stay still and paced her bedroom in circles. Her dream only reinforced the growing need to find her.

There was another person in the dream, hiding in the shadows. After her mother disappeared behind the wall, the building split, and a dark silhouette emerged from the blue light separating the structure. And as he walked toward her, the building faltered. She'd never seen Frederick walk, and yet she was almost certain it was Frederick.

Nora knocked lightly on Emery's bedroom door, and not hearing an answer, she cracked it open. Seeing Emery pacing the room in a frenzy, she set a plate with fruit, pastry, and pink juice on a side table. Emery glared at her wild-eyed, as if seeing her for the first time.

"You must eat something. You've been in this room since yesterday. Eat something and come out. Get some fresh air," Nora said.

"I will," Emery said. Her voice was hollow and raspy.

Nora left, glancing back.

Emery didn't touch the food and darted out of the room right after Nora left. She ran to Narius's studio, flung the door open, and blurted, "How can you tell north from south if there is no sun to guide you?"

"I don't know. Why?" Narius asked, raising both hands, one of which was caked with white paste and the other holding a wide metal loop on a wooden handle.

"When you deliver things in your truck, how do you know which direction you're going?"

"I've got a map, and I know the roads."

"When will you be going northeast next?"

"Not anytime soon. I seldom get orders there. It's not very populated, and people who live there don't care for art. Why?" he asked and cursed when the white blob fell to the floor, making a wet, squishy sound.

"Can I look at your map?"

"It's in my truck."

Emery turned around and darted out of his studio. Tamtam sat at the entrance door, evaluating her with his brown eyes. He barked at her when she opened it.

"Tamtam, you know, don't you? I must find my mother. She needs my help," she said, patting the dog on the head. He licked her hand and barked again.

She climbed into the truck and searched the cab. She finally found the old, yellowed map of Andalia, which she spread on the dashboard and studied. Andalia sat in the middle of an ocean, criss-crossed by sparse roads intersecting its middle and connecting the east and west, north and south in thick blue lines. Mountain ranges spanned the entire northern part of Andalia, while the south was peppered with thousands of lakes varying in size. Her finger stopped at the very northeastern tip. There were no roads leading to it, and the brown-colored area appeared steep and barren. And yet she smiled to herself. *I'm coming, Mother. I'll find you.*

34

TELL THE TRUTH

Frederick was just finishing his coffee when his doorbell rang. Dark rings under his hollow eyes and stubble on his cheeks and chin spoke of lack of sleep. He ignored the ringing for a long time. Long enough for Sam to pound on the door and shout.

"Why did you hide the key? We know you're in there. Open up!" Sam shouted.

Frederick pushed the cup away and maneuvered his wheelchair to the front door. "What do you want?" he yelled without opening the door.

"Open the door. Emery is missing, and we think she went to the northeast to try to sneak onto the diplomatic aircraft going to Sinturija," Nora yelled in a high-pitched tone.

Frederick's hands flew to the door and unlocked it with a quick, powerful move. "What did you say?" he growled, glaring at Sam, Narius, and Nora standing before him.

"She took my map, an old bag from the hanger, and some food and left in the middle of the night. The day before, she was asking me when I was going northeast next—"

"You didn't stop her?" Frederick interrupted, roaring at Narius.

With his unshaven chin and bared teeth in a scowl, he resembled an angry wolf.

"She left in the middle of the night. We didn't know."

"You know how dangerous it is? Why did you let her go?"

"She is a grown woman. They couldn't have stopped her even if they'd seen her leave," Sam said. His sharp voice cut through the air between him and Frederick. "We need to talk," he added, and pushed his way inside, wheeling Frederick back, ignoring his protests.

Sam positioned the wheelchair in the middle of the living room. Nora and Narius followed, glancing at Sam.

"I know you well enough to know when you're lying, Fred. I let it go before, but now that you've endangered a young woman's life, you're going to have to tell me what's going on and how you know Emery."

"You wouldn't understand or believe me if I told you," Frederick said with a deep sigh.

"You're just going to have to try hard to explain."

"We don't have time for talk. We must find her before she gets killed," Frederick said.

"Not before telling us what's going on," Sam said.

Frederick stared into Sam's unyielding brown eyes.

"What's happening?" a young woman's voice cut through the air, breaking Frederick and Sam's silent match of wills. "I got your note and came here as soon as I could."

"Thank you for coming, Anna," Sam said to his wife. "We have a situation. The young woman I told you about, who Narius rescued? She left for the military airport in northeastern Andalia to hitch a ride on the diplomatic aircraft because this numbskull told her that her mother disappeared from Sinturija—"

"Oh, no. She'll be killed, poor thing."

"She'll be killed before she even gets there. Women are not allowed to travel alone in Andalia. And this numbskull knows it, and apparently, he also knows her. I told you about his reaction when he saw her, and you heard him calling Emery in his comatose state. He knows her, but he refuses to tell us how. Maybe you can convince him?"

"Would his confession help to save her?" Anna asked, turning her warm brown eyes to Frederick.

"Probably. Most likely."

"Then you have to tell him, Fred," she said softly and clasped Frederick's hand. "You know you can trust us."

"I know that! It's not about that!"

"Then what is it about?"

"For fuck's sake! Why don't you just leave it be?" Frederick said. A large tear escaped his eye. "She is the love of my life. She is my Emery. I knew and loved her in a previous life, in another dimension, in another realm. She is my destiny. I knew you too, Sam, in my previous life. Your name was Thomas," Frederick said, trembling. "You and Emery were friends."

Anna slid onto the sofa and studied Frederick's face. Narius and Nora glanced at each other sheepishly. Narius shrugged.

"If this is true, why didn't you tell her?" Sam asked. He didn't seem shocked, nor did he display any signs of skepticism or acceptance.

"Look at me. How could I face her like this? In one life I was much older; in another, not quite a man; and in this, I am...broken. She's perfect, and I, in every life, in every reiteration, fail her. I can't tell her. And neither can any of you. Promise me you'll never tell her."

"Tell her what?" Anna asked. "You haven't told us anything yet," she said, and shook her head. Her light brown hair flew around her face. "Did you recognize Sam before you rescued me? Is that why you rescued me?" Anna asked.

Frederick nodded. "I didn't know who he was, but his face was so familiar when he stood there looking so forlorn, crying and trying to force his way out of his friends' arms to rescue you. While in a coma, my memories returned. All of them. I relieved Emery's disappearance and my death."

"And?" Anna flashed her brown eyes at him.

"Fine," Frederick said, and waved his arms. "I'll tell you. You'd better sit down. It's a long story."

Nearing the end of the story, Anna and Narius's sleeves were wet from wiping their tears. Nora kept her eyes on Frederick intently, as if she were waiting for more. Sam was silent. Frederick finished telling his story and withdrew into himself. He closed his eyes as his lips trembled.

"What a story!" Narius exclaimed in a voice thick with emotion.

"I believe you," Sam said.

Anna glanced at Sam.

Sam met her eyes. "When I first saw him, he seemed familiar. Like I'd known him before. I had dreams I couldn't explain. In those dreams, I saw glimpses of Frederick in a morbid gray city. He looked different, but it was him. Don't look at me that way. You know I believe in parallel universes, different realms. There are renowned scientists who believe it's not only possible but likely that there are many—"

"Well, I might believe in different realms, but how can mere humans travel from one to the other?" she asked Sam but looked at Frederick.

"I told you about the chambers and the capsules. That's how. Emery went through the capsule twice."

Anna kept her eyes on him.

"I didn't go through the capsule, Anna. The Minders killed me after Emery entered the capsule. Emery told she traveled through a dark dimension where people wait to be reborn by being pulled by a light. I don't remember any of it. My earliest memories of Andalia are of an orphanage, where I grew up. I never knew my parents. Later they told me I was dropped off as a baby with no name. And that's all I know about my Andalian origins. I couldn't remember anything of my previous life, not even my name, until I was in a coma."

"Does it matter anyway?" Nora had recovered her wits and voice. "Emery went on her own, and if we don't find her, she'll die," she said. "And I don't want her to die. I have grown quite fond of her."

"She's right," Sam said, and focused his stern gaze on Frederick. "We need to find her."

"How?" Anna asked.

"We know where she's going. I'll drive the truck," Narius said.

"I'll come with," Sam said.

"Then I'm coming with," Anna said.

"Me too," Nora said.

"I have room for two additional people. Frederick should be the one who comes along."

"He can't travel in your truck. He'd be miserable," Nora said.

"We'll take his wheelchair. Sam and I can help him in and out," Narius pleaded with Nora. "Someone has to stay in case she reconsiders and comes back."

"I'm small. I can fit too. You said she risked her life to save Sam's," Anna said, glancing at Frederick.

Frederick, who'd been silent for a while, played with a little black gadget with buttons that controlled his wheelchair and moved toward the window away from everyone. Anna fiddled with the buttons on her blouse while glancing at him.

Sam shrugged. "Narius, Anna and I will go searching for her. You two stay and wait. If she returns, send us a messenger."

"No," Frederick said. His loud and agitated voice reverberated through the room. "I'm going with Narius and Sam, but you have to promise me you won't tell her what I just told you about her and me. That part must remain a secret forever."

His speech was met with silence.

"Promise me! Everyone, promise me now!"

"Fine," Sam said, raising his hands. "I promise, but you're making a mistake. Emery is not a person who'd shun you because of your disability."

"I fucking know that!"

Narius and Nora were next to promise.

"Anna?" Frederick insisted.

"Why? I don't understand your reasoning. You'll have to tell her eventually. Why hide it from her? From what you've told me, she loves you. Who gives you the right to withhold it from her?"

The muscles in Frederick's face moved, and his eyes turned into blue icicles. To everyone's surprise, instead of anger, his lips twitched, and he smiled. "You're just like her. Willful, intuitive, and goddamn stubborn. I want you to promise me you won't tell her because I wanted to be the one to tell her if I'm ready."

"If you're ready?" she asked, adding a dash of sarcasm to her sharp tone.

"Anna," Sam said quietly.

"She has a right to know."

"Fine, when I'm ready. Happy now?"

"I promise if you promise to tell her… when you're ready."

"I promise."

"Then I promise too."

35

SEARCHING FOR EMERY

"She'd have enough sense to stay away from the cities," Sam said, thinking aloud and looking out the window of Narius's truck. Frederick, tucked into the back, was reading from a collection of books he had brought with him, which had been met with a silent glance from Sam and an eye-roll from Narius.

"Nora said that Emery didn't take enough food to last long. She'll have to stop somewhere for food."

"Except she has no money," Sam said.

"We can drive through the cities and towns and keep a lookout for her," Narius said.

"Do any of you know anything about the *Discovery*?" Frederick asked a while later.

"The ship?" Sam asked.

"Yes."

"Supposedly, it was the largest pirate ship ever and practically unsinkable. Some believed it could even cross the ocean and reach Sinturija, allowing the pirates to pillage from both Andalians and Sinturijans alike, taking them hostage or even killing them. However, some people swear it was a fairy tale and that no such ship existed," Narius said.

"What do you think?" Frederick asked Sam.

"I don't know. It seems far-fetched."

"This book describes her well, including dimensions, carrying capacity, and everything else."

"I believe it," Narius said. "I once met a sailor from *the Discovery*."

Sam didn't seem convinced. "Maybe he was just bragging."

"Maybe, but boy, was he scary-looking, and he had some even scarier tales of beheading people and kidnapping young women from Sinturija."

Sam turned toward Frederick. "Why are you asking?"

"If it were true, it might be a safer way to get to Sinturija."

"Are you serious? I thought we were on a mission to find her and talk her out of this crazy idea," Sam said.

"Well, you can try, but it will not work unless you imprison her. And she'd find a way out anyway. Emery will not change her mind, no matter how hard we try. She'll do anything to find her mother. She might be afraid and questioning her decision, but even then, she'd find her way to escape and travel to Sinturija." Frederick said the last words with a voice and eyes that conveyed both pride and sorrow. His eyes glazed over.

After a while, Frederik continued. "Supposedly, the *Discovery* disappeared fifteen years ago, and nobody knows what happened to her. Some say the government destroyed her."

"Then there's no point in even mentioning it to her when we find her," Sam said.

Frederick returned to his books.

36

OLY

Emery sat beside an old dirt road that had been partially overgrown by grasses and mats of orange flowers, munching slowly on a small chunk of cheese. She had little food, and her destination was still far away. She didn't know how far, unfamiliar with the map's distance units. But she breathed freely, knowing she was going toward finding her mother and learning her own identity. Frederick knew her, but he refused to tell her anything. Maybe she had done something so atrocious to him that was beyond repair and forgiveness.

A large black truck was approaching. The earth quivered with tremors as the black beast's giant tires drilled into the bumpy road. Emery jumped up, collected her belongings, and hid in the tall grass, watching the truck rumble by. What Nora had told her about the situation for Andalian women made her cautious of strangers. How fortuitous it was that goofy and sweet Narius found her and not Andalian officials. Or was it fate? After meeting Frederick, she was beginning to believe it was.

Another old truck drove by, puffing smoke and stirring up clouds of dust. After it disappeared into the distance, she continued walking, following the road. Despite almost continuous walking for three days and two nights with just a few brief naps under the cover of the trees, she wasn't fatigued. Propelled by the need to know and the yearning to belong somewhere and to someone, her fire only grew stronger, fortified by the certainty that she was heading in the right direction. Most of the time, the sun shone, granting her easy navigation. When it hid behind the clouds, like today, she stayed closer to the mostly empty highway that crisscrossed the land from west to east. For now, she was heading east until she reached the large river she had seen on the map, flowing north to south in the eastern part of Andalia. From there, she would follow it north.

Emery avoided the villages and cities, staying mostly in the forest, but when she assessed her meager food supply and when the hunger grew, she ventured closer to the outskirts of small villages. One small house had given her hope after she noticed its inhabitants leaving and spreading into the surrounding fields, picking corn. She waited a while, but finally her growling stomach won out over her fear of the strangers. Most of the way to the small yellow house, she crawled, then at the midpoint, she stood and ran bent over. Once she reached the wooden porch decorated with orange flower boxes, she pressed her hands and ear against the door. Hearing nothing, she turned the small brass handle and opened it. The hinges squeaked, which made her heart pound even harder, but in her hunger, she ignored the noise and danger and entered.

Only two small windows provided light for the small house full of sturdy wooden furniture, drying herbs, and clay bowls filled with fruit and vegetables. Emery smiled at the sight, already imagining sinking her teeth into the apples and pears and crunching on the thick carrots. She tiptoed to the table and reached for a red apple, but it rolled from her hand, plunging back into the clay bowl, when she heard a screechy male voice originating from the window alcove.

The skinny old man was so scrunched, he was barely visible in the wooden rocker. Covered by a checkered blue shawl, the man, almost bald with just a few sparse, oily hairs, observed her intently with keen black eyes. "Who in the hellish hell are you?"

Emery considered her options and decided to just grab some food and run. She reached for the fruit again.

The old man must have guessed her intentions. "You can ask for food if you're hungry. We gladly share with strangers." His voice had lost most of its coarseness and even sounded pleasant to her ears, but maybe it was because he'd offered food. Emery slowly reached for the fruit again.

"Wait. Not so fast. I share food with you, and you tell me your story. I bet it's a good one. A woman looking like you, wandering all by herself," he said, shaking his head and chuckling. "Don't you worry, I will not tell on you," he said almost pleadingly. "We don't get interesting visitors, and I'm stuck to this chair cause my legs don't work so good. I just want to hear something different to feed my soul. If you're running away from someone, I won't say anything to anyone. I swear."

Emery hesitated and glanced at the door, then at the frail man. He looked neither dangerous nor deceitful, and the plea in his voice sounded real. She approached his chair and gasped at his thinness and the intensity and intelligence beaming from his keen black eyes, enveloping him in a misty aura.

"I'm Emery, but I don't really have a story. I lost my memory somehow. I woke up in the middle of an ocean and don't remember a thing before that. A nice man found me... are you okay?"

The frail being appeared distressed by her story. His bony hands shook while he gasped for air.

"Do you need something? Can I bring you some water?"

He finally breathed in and shook his head. "Come closer. Let me look at you."

He studied her face and reached his bony hand to touch her cheek. She lowered her head so he could reach it. "Tell me more," he whispered. "Why are you here?"

"There is not much more to tell. Someone told me I was the daughter of a scientist who disappeared a while back. I'm going to find her. My mother."

"You look hungry and tired. Stay for a while and rest."

"I can't. Thank you; I have a long journey ahead of me, and I must continue."

He regarded her for a moment. "I understand. I'm Oly. That's what they call me around here. The name they gave me," he whispered, as if sharing a secret.

Emery gazed into the old man's eyes, thinking his mind was as frail as his body. But his eyes were sharp and young, shining in his withered body like black opals. "Who gave you your name?" Emery whispered back, following his cues.

"The children who found me at the seaside."

"Found you?"

"I remember freeing myself from a glass tube and drifting to the beach. Just like you, I remembered nothing of my life before."

Emery's face grew ashen. The limited food and water she ingested during the last few days and this revelation by the feeble old man, who suddenly seemed just like a shadowy apparition, sent Emery to her knees. She sat on the floor, looking up at him.

"I had formed new memories since then, and that time seemed like a forgotten dream. Until you came," Oly said.

I am not alone or mad. There are others like me. "Do you remember a dark-haired woman named Zoe?"

He shook his head. The veins in his neck bulged. "Your name sounds familiar. I think I knew an Emery."

"Ever wondered why you were stuck in that glass tube?"

"Every day, in the beginning."

"Me too."

"Stay. My grandchildren are good people. They won't mind."

"I can't. I have to find my mother. But I promise I'll be back if I find out who put me in there and why."

He sighed. "It may be too late for me. I might not be here when you get back."

"Then hang on until I come back. Our pasts might have intertwined."

"Take as much food as you can carry. Take the gourds hanging on the wall over there and fill them with water from the well. I will hang on and wait for you."

Emery filled her bag with fruit and vegetables and glanced back at Oly.

Oly pointed to the shelf by the window. "Take some bread. There is also cheese under that white cloth. Be safe, golden Emery."

Emery walked to Oly and took his bony fingers in hers. "I'll be back. Thank you, Oly."

37

THE WAVE

Sleep didn't come despite the fatigue she now felt. The sound of the night with its whispers, shadowy movements, and the image of the dark-haired woman that Narius had so masterfully chiseled into life haunted her whenever she closed her eyes, so she continued walking even in the dark, surprised she could see so well. She walked, and with her walked the mirages of the horrific crimes she had imagined committing before being locked in the tube and thrown into the ocean to die. Oly was probably a monster like her. But they both deserved to know what they had done to warrant such a horrible punishment.

One evening, her feet felt like boulders that refused to move. She collapsed near the thick trunk of an evergreen tree with long, delicate needles. The tree's long arms reached almost to the ground, which was soft from the accumulated needles. Hidden in the thicket, Emery relaxed and fell asleep to the sound of murmuring leaves, dreaming of her mother. She sat at the mountain's edge, looking into the distance at a sharp-peaked blue mountain, then she turned and gazed at Emery with affection and beckoned her to come closer. As she approached her mother, an enormous black bird flew from behind her and pushed both of them over the edge. Emery and her mother extended their arms to reach each other, but they were not close enough and drifted farther and farther apart.

"Emery," her mother cried. "Emery. Find him. Find your..."

"Mother," Emery cried, and woke up.

For a moment, she believed the moisture on her face was her tears as she felt her chest tremble in tiny sobs and shallow breaths. She soon discovered it was rain trickling through the canopy, gently washing the dust and salty tears off her face with soft droplets.

She wiped her face with her sleeve and shuffled forward, looking around in confusion for the first time since she'd started her journey, believing herself to be lost. The dream held her mind in a fog, and the dark clouds and the rain undermined her sense of direction and confidence. In that moment, she questioned her judgement, and even her sanity. How would she get through the fence and pass the armed guards with no weapons and no help?

She walked toward where she thought the highway was, but after two hours, she stopped and took out her map. She gasped. The moisture had penetrated her bag, erasing the roads, towns, and rivers, and the map now resembled a colorful rag.

"No!"

She crumpled the map, threw it into the brush, and walked away.

The rain wasn't letting up. The drops grew bigger, and the wind pushed them into her clothes, saturating them. Her shoes squirted water as she walked through the sparse forest.

She didn't see or hear them sneaking behind her. Suddenly, her arms were being pulled out of their sockets, yanked by powerful hands. The hands spun her around, putting her face right against a messy, wet beard and a large, flat nose, above which two little brown eyes scrutinized her with curiosity mixed with amusement.

"What we gaaat here?" a scratchy voice asked.

The beard opened, revealing a mouth full of rotting teeth. A fat red tongue followed, emerging from behind the black, yellow, and brown spikes, licking lips hiding somewhere in the wet brownness.

Emery shuddered but quickly realized that when the beard spun her around, her left arm had been freed. She planted a blow on his cheek. With her body twisted at an odd angle and with her arm held in a tight grip, she couldn't get a good swing or enough punch and inflicted hardly any damage. His face barely moved. But the blow was surprising enough for him to let go.

She was free. Backing away, she kept her gaze on her attacker, appraising him. Not much taller than her, the man's dirty, baggy clothes and a strange, pointy hat bore an old embroidered insignia that once might have been gold, blue, and purple, but was now sad and dirty, mocking the owner's better past.

From behind him, another man ran up but stopped two steps behind his buddy. A little taller, skinnier, and also dressed in rags, and a hat bearing the same insignias, the man, appearing to be also in his fifties, opened his eyes wide, seeing Emery. "What daaat?" he asked, pointing at her with dirty fingers, poking out of a hole in his black gloves.

"Not know."

"Romana?"

"Neaaaah, too pale."

Emery glanced from one to the other, backing away in imperceptible movements.

"Preedee," the skinny man said, extending his hand and moving toward Emery.

She jerked and backed away. The other guy jumped toward her with surprising agility and grabbed her arm with ironlike claws.

"Neaah, neaah, preedee gurl. Ya stay," he said, grinning. His breath, which stank of garlic, alcohol, and stale tobacco, reached her nostrils, and she gagged.

"Delicet gurl. Yummy."

The skinny man rubbed his hands and giggled. His teeth weren't rotten, but very few remained in his pointy jaw.

"He, he, he, we gonna have fun," the bigger guy laughed, and reached for her chest.

The blood rushed through her body like a cresting river after a heavy storm, and along with it came anger and fear. They built up inside Emery and were now too much for her to bear and hold inside.

One more second and it would have exploded. Her head throbbed, screaming to release the pressure. She gritted her teeth and, with strength she didn't know she possessed, pulled her arm out of the man's grip, and thrust her hands forward, screaming at the top of her lungs.

A silvery-bluish ball emerged from her palms and unfolded into a wide wave that hit the two men in their chests. They staggered and fell, the skinny one with a high-pitched shriek and the bigger one with something resembling a deep howl, dying in a gurgling sound. They remained on the ground, unmoving, while Emery alternated her shocked gaze between them and her hands.

Did I just do that?

With a throat locked in panic, she slowly kneeled by the bigger man. She uttered a tiny whimper, seeing his wide chest, unmoving, and his bulging eyes still, frozen in fear. She glanced at the other man. He was as still as his companion. Emery rose, picked up her bag, backed away, and started running, her feet splashing through the puddles. She felt nothing. No remorse, no relief, no guilt. As if the pent-up angst, anger, longing, when released as the strange ball of energy, took her emotions with it. A memory flashed of tall men in dark uniforms falling as the waves hit them. She'd killed people before.

Now I know why they locked me in the glass prison and dumped me in the ocean. I am a monster. I kill people.

38

THE BOAT

Emery stopped running when she realized she had reached the highway. It was empty. She sat on the hill overlooking the gray serpent partially hidden in the fog below. The sun was setting in the west, laying long golden streaks across the highway. She looked east and sighed. Frederick's eyes came into focus, and her heart spasmed when from the great depth of her mind, a faint memory emerged. She saw herself looking into his eyes and stroking his cheek while dancing to a familiar tune. The same tune that popped into her mind when she drifted through the dark ocean—her first memory. She remembered only how peaceful, how deeply loved she'd felt when in his arms, and a wave of love, regret, passion, and sorrow ripped through her body and wedged itself in her heart. "We loved each other," she whispered. "He must remember it too. Why, then…oh…"

The sudden realization of why Frederick hadn't told her the entire truth hit her. "You fool!" she shouted at the orange sky. "I don't care that you can't walk."

The size of the river surprised her. She could barely see the band of trees on the other side. Flowing lazily, bathed in the afternoon sun, the wide and lazy River Andarena was a spectacular sight. Emery spotted boats sailing in both directions on the almost flat surface of the blue-green water. She sat on the bank and rubbed her face and smiled.

"I made it. I really made it."

The uncertainty dissipated the instant she saw the water and inhaled the moist air. Hope cleared her mind of self-doubt and fear. She realized she had walked most of the way to her destination. What remained was perhaps only four or five days of walking, she thought. She felt the hunger grasping her stomach more frequently because she had rationed the food from Oly stingily. Now it was mostly gone, with only a few dried-out breadcrumbs and some chunks of moldy cheese remaining at the bottom of the bag.

Hollow cheeks, stringy hair, and wild eyes met her when she saw her reflection at the edge of the river. She recoiled, seeing her own ravaged face. Her once-colorful clothes fared even worse with mud streaks, frayed ends, and unidentifiable stains, giving off a stench of body odor and the moist earth when she moved.

I can't go among people, much less get to the airport looking like this.

She splashed water on her face, ate the few remaining breadcrumbs, and looked around in search of houses. During the last few days, she had seen no settlements, no houses, or other signs of human presence or civilization. She walked through the old forests, thankful for the lack of undergrowth and for the occasional purple berries she carefully ate. But now, she had to find clothes and food.

Walking along the riverbank amid old willow trees, she strained her eyes for signs of civilization. Soon, her eyes rested on a man-made structure located very close to the river or even on the river. As she skulked toward it, she realized it was a red and light green houseboat bobbing by an old wooden dock. It was getting dark outside, but the windows remained unlit. Emery guessed that the boat's inhabitants were not home, asleep, or liked the darkness. She sat behind a tree, watching the boat. Watching the windows. The skies darkened, but the boat stayed shadowy and lifeless.

Emery tiptoed to the vessel and stepped onto the deck. She had taken a few steps when a board squeaked. With one foot on the deck and the other frozen in the air, she watched the windows for lights, or for the owners to peer out looking for the source of the noise. She promised herself she would kill no one else with her strange powers. After the initial emotional stupor had worn off, the memory of their unmoving bodies and their vacant eyes haunted her. She studied her hands to see if they appeared different, unnatural, but they looked the same: the same slender fingers, now covered in scratches and caked with dirt around her broken fingernails.

She tiptoed forward and climbed onto the boat, stopping and waiting upon hearing squeaks and creaks from the tired old wood under her feet. The crescent moon provided just enough light to find the cabin door. She held her breath and opened it. The musty black interior welcomed her with deep silence. Once her eyes adjusted to the darkness marked only by the moonlight reaching inside with its silvery fingers, she walked inside slowly, breaking the silky spiderweb draglines that crisscrossed the cabin.

Spiders. Yikes. She grimaced and wiped her hands on her pants.

When she reached a wooden bench and a table, she noticed a lamp above. She pressed the switch, but nothing happened. From the smell of decay and mold, and the aura of abandonment, she guessed the boat's owners wouldn't be back tonight or ever. But that meant that she likely wouldn't find food, and searching this place in the dark made her skin crawl as she imagined big, hairy spiders crawling on her hands or immersing her fingers in substances that were the source of the foul smell. She considered leaving and coming back in the morning, but the fatigue had caught up to her, and despite the smell and the uncanny sensation that she wasn't alone, she curled up on the bench and was out quickly.

"Caw, caw, caw!"

The sound invaded her sleep, and she sprang up. A large crow sat on a lifeline, looking straight at her through the dirty oval window and cawing its head off.

"What? What do you want?"

The crow wasn't giving up. "Caw, caw, caw!"

"Is this your boat, crow?"

The bird quieted and cocked its head, watching her with its beady black eyes.

Emery stretched and looked around the cabin. The salon and the galley were connected. Besides the booth, there was another small table attached to the wooden walls and a black stove with pots neatly stacked above, draped in spiderwebs. Some other maritime paraphernalia and even a small bookcase with books about sailing were secured to the wooden walls. A painting of a large sailboat hung across from the booth. An engraved gold plate under the painting spelled *Discovery*. She read it aloud and shivered as her words echoed eerily through the abandoned air.

Emery hesitated before opening the cupboard, expecting to find it empty, or worse—a moldy black monster coming at her with the viciousness of rot. She squealed at the cans and jars stacked on the shelves. She seized one can and shook it, then cut it open with a sturdy knife she'd found in a drawer below. The sweet aroma of corn filled her nostrils, and her mouth instantly salivated as she saw the glinting yellow gems. One kernel held between two fingers slowly made it to her mouth, and then another. Not long after, she emptied the can, fishing the last with her hands, licking her fingers afterward.

She eyed another can, but her attention shifted to the partially open door at the salon's end, hearing a knocking coming from there. The hair on her neck stood up. She grabbed the knife and crept along the wall toward the door. Her sensible self was shouting to get off the boat; the nosy, curious, and reckless self pressed on.

The door's rusty hinges squealed. Emery tensed and held the knife in her outstretched hand, pushing the door open with her foot. The stench was slightly stronger here. Her eyes wandered to the most prominent feature of the room. On a wooden bed, a fully clothed man lay, clutching something in his hands. The knocking continued.

She raised her eyes to the window above the bed. The crow sat on the outside windowsill, pecking at the glass. When it saw her enter the bedroom, it cawed and flew away. The knife fell from her fingers, and her now empty hand covered her mouth, clasping it tightly.

Once she overcame her shock, she approached the shriveled body and inspected it. A dark green uniform speckled with mouse droppings was draped loosely over the bones. She gasped when she saw the embroidered insignia—they were identical to the ones the men she'd killed had.

She bent over the body and inspected the insignia and the buttons. The images were of a sailboat. His coat lapels had additional purple markings, which she interpreted as a higher rank than the men she killed had.

"I murdered sailors," she murmured.

The clothes she found in the closet hung on their hangers in a neat row. They were different iterations of the uniform the man on the bed wore.

If you take it, you'll remember your victims.

She selected the darkest one, whose color was between blue and green, and stood in front of a mirror enclosed in a thick oak frame embellished with a carved sailboat on top. Liking what she saw, she grinned. She topped off her outfit with a wide-brimmed hat stamped with the same insignia on the front. Her hair spilled from under the hat, covering the front of the uniform.

"That's not gonna work," she grumbled, and searched the boat for scissors. When she found them, she stared at her reflection with the scissors in her hand, hesitating. After a few moments, she set her jaw, quickly grabbed her hair in one hand, and started cutting it, letting it fall onto the wooden planks. After she was done, she put the hat back on and tilted her head, satisfied she could pass for a young man, hoping the hat shaded her face enough for a random passerby to take her for a male.

She packed the knife and a few cans into her bag and reached for the door.

"Aye, aye, Captain, rest in peace," she said as she was turning and leaving the bedroom.

39

SEBASTIAN

Emery walked at a brisk pace toward a town that spread almost to the river, separated from it by a wooden wall with an enormous iron gate, which now stood open. The tall wooden buildings bearing the dark gray, almost black patina of time lined gray brick streets on both sides. The town was waking up. Its inhabitants, almost as gray and dreary as their city, hustled as they went about their business. Some opened the ironclad wooden doors to their stores, some hastily walked to their destinations; some pulled wooden carts filled to the brim with vegetables, coal, chickens, and other things Emery couldn't and did not want to identify. Only brief sidelong glances passed over her as she walked, but she must not have raised suspicions or looked threatening, because after giving her perfunctory glances, they continued with their affairs.

Walking by a store that had just opened, she gasped. It was a bookstore, or at least a store with books and maps. With little thought, she entered and stared at a large map of Andalia displayed on the back wall. Just like on Narius's map, the military airport she sought did not show. The river, though, just like she remembered, originated in the mountains of the continent's northeastern corner. This map was more detailed geographically, showing elevations at five Bergel unit intervals (whatever the Bergel was). At the very northeastern corner of Andalia, there was a large, flat area. Her intuition told her this must be it, and her heart beat faster. She needed to cross the river to get there.

The store owner observed her and said something. He spoke Andalian, but with a heavy accent, drawing out each word. Emery shook her head.

He pointed at the map and asked. "Buy it? Want it?"

"I have no money," she said.

His eyes pointed at the door, letting her know window-shopping was over. Emery shrugged and left. She had already learned where to go.

After leaving the town, she entered fields of corn that hugged the side of the river. The river now narrowed and had lost some of its sluggishness. Emery glanced longingly at the eastern bank and the thick forest behind it.

Workers were picking corn and collecting it in large wicker baskets. When she reached an area that the gatherers hadn't harvested yet, she threw a few corn ears into her bag.

After two days of walking, the cornfields gave way to cottonwoods and willows, which grew in uneven rows alongside the banks. Then the conifers took over as the terrain became steeper and the river became smaller and noisier, whooshing over fallen logs and boulders. She ate her last corn before falling asleep by a giant tree. The next morning, the gold dots in her eyes glimmered as they rested on a welcome sight: a bridge spanning the river. Finally. The day before, she'd almost been ready to swim across.

To get to the bridge, she had to cross through a small town nestled alongside the riverbank. Not as dreary and gray as the first town, this one's houses were painted different colors and even boasted some decorations. She walked warily through the narrow streets. Just before reaching the bridge, she stopped as the aroma of food cooking, radiating from a green building with white shutters, reached her. She inhaled deeply as her feet carried her to the door. A big sign depicting a plate of food painted above the door suggested that this was a restaurant or an inn.

Inside, garlic, onions, meat, malt, and unwashed bodies mixed in a cacophony of smells. She nearly fainted from the desire and anticipation of cooked food. She was so hungry, she'd steal if she had to.

Several young men carried steaming plates and enormous jugs to rowdy customers, all of them men, sitting at wooden tables. Emery made her way to the counter, where a burly man with a head covered in silvery curls interlaced with tiny red streaks and an aura of authority around him poured yellow liquid into large clay jugs. From the hoppy smell and white foam topping spilling over the top of the jugs, she guessed it was malt.

She cleared her throat and spoke in the lowest voice she could make. "Could I work for some food? Clean the dishes, sweep the floors? Anything that could give me a bowl of food in exchange?"

"I don't give away free food. Go away," the man said, and waved her off with his large, hairy hand.

"Don't be mean, Rudy," said a man standing nearby, gesticulating with a hand holding a cup of malt. The liquid spilled on his clothes, and its rich aroma reached Emery's nostrils. She licked her lips and swallowed.

His neighbor looked Emery up and down and chimed in. "Yeah, Rudy, don't be rude to the young lad."

"Put it on our tab," the first man said.

"Whatever," Rudy grumbled, and asked Emery, "What do you want?"

"Whatever smells so good."

Rudy yelled something to one of the young men distributing food and then attended to other customers, but not before sending her a strange glance that blended pity with anger.

She sat at the end of the table, steered to it by her two benefactors. They flanked her, one on each side. She gobbled her food from the clay bowl, scraping its sides with a large wooden spoon despite the whiffs of body odor, malt, and stale tobacco coming from her neighbors. She avoided looking at their greasy hair glued to their red faces, their calloused hands, and their hungry eyes.

"Where are you from, lad?" one asked after she finished eating.

She cleaned the bowl with the last piece of bread and even considered licking it but just wiped her chin. "From the west. The town of Romanovo."

"Funny. You no look like a Romana."

Emery shrugged.

"Where are you headed?"

"Nowhere in particular. Just wandering. As you know, Romanas don't stay in one place long."

"Come with us. We'll show you a good time."

"Perhaps another time," Emery said, standing up. "Thank you for the food. You just saved a man from dying of hunger."

The man laughed in response, and his creepy, screechy laughter sent a rush of blood to her face. She adjusted her hat, waved, and strode to the door. When she was outside, she exhaled and sprinted for the bridge.

It was dark when she reached the bridge. She stopped in the middle to admire the glow of the full moon over the dark water. She didn't hear their approach. The sound of the water splashing on the rocks and the wind muffled their steps. One of them grabbed her from behind and wrapped his beefy arms around her throat. Panic set in when she saw stars in front of her eyes and couldn't breathe.

"He, he, young lad. It wasn't nice to refuse our polite invitation. We just wanna play and have fun."

"Yeah, don't you want to have fun with us?" the other man asked.

Emery couldn't talk and made a choking noise, so the man loosened his grip.

She coughed and rasped angrily. "What do you want from me? I have no money."

"Oh, you've got plenty of what we want, lad," her captor said, grabbing her arms and turning her around to face him. "Except you're no lad, are you? And where did you get the Admiralia garb? Who did you steal it from, girl?"

"I didn't steal it. It's my uncle's."

They both laughed. Then, when they stopped laughing, cruel grins spread across their faces. "No matter. We'll take it back from you. Let's go," he said, increased pressure on her throat, and pushed her. She mentally abandoned her pledge never to use her powers again, but she couldn't get free and could barely breathe. His grip was fierce. They led her to a building that, judging by the rank smell and the broken furniture, was abandoned and perhaps only used by vagrants. He pushed her onto an old mattress smelling of old and rust, then fell on top of her before she could get up. She groaned under his weight and started panicking. With his weight on her, he fumbled with his fat fingers to unbutton her pants, panting heavily. The other man squealed with delight.

"Two on one? That's not very brave of you two," a man's pleasant voice reached Emery as she struggled under the weight.

"Who the fuck are you?" the man on top of Emery growled but didn't bother getting off her. Emery saw a flash as the second man suddenly had a knife in his hand, holding it in front of him.

"Move along. There's not enough for three here. You can come later after we're done. He, he, he."

"I don't think so. Leave him be."

His voice was calm, but it carried a warning in the heaviness of its tone, though lacking in aggression, as if its owner wasn't looking forward to a fight.

The fat man finally rolled off Emery and, with a hateful grimace, faced the man who was spoiling all his fun. Ostentatiously, he drew a knife from its sheath and joined his friend in facing the stupid man who'd dared to barge in on their party.

Holding a hand to her throat, Emery slowly sat and looked up. A tall young man with hair as black as the crow she'd met on the boat and eyes just as dark stood facing the two men. He held no weapons and casually kept his hands in the pockets of his long coat.

He is incredibly stupid or an extreme optimist.

As if on cue, both men lunged at him. Emery readied to help, but by the time she got up, it was over. Her attackers lay on the dirty wooden floor with their arms outstretched and a look of utmost surprise pasted on their faces.

"Are you okay?" the stranger asked her in a deep, mellifluous voice. He bent down and picked up their knives and put them in his coat pocket.

Emery didn't answer, assessing him. Deciding whether she should run or thank him.

He didn't wait for her answer but waved at her to join him. "Come on, let's leave this place before they wake up. I don't feel like fighting these idiots twice."

His voice and the way he spoke set him apart from all the people she had met in Andalia. He didn't have an accent but had the air of a foreigner about him—someone who didn't belong. She grabbed her bag and followed him. To her surprise, he headed for the bridge. "I'm heading that way too," he said without turning around.

She caught up with him and looked him in the eye. "What do you mean, 'too'?"

"I was behind you when they attacked you."

"Oh."

"They didn't hurt you, did they?"

"No," she said and hesitated. "I could've fought them off, but thank you."

"I know you could've. No problem. My name is Sebastian."

"I'm Eme...I'm Emer."

At the end of the bridge, Sebastian turned north, and she followed. He turned and smiled at her. She held her breath, staring at him. It was the most beautiful and complex smile she had ever seen. Warm yet mischievous, spontaneous but knowing. His face beamed with extraordinary light, and it wasn't a reflection from the moon, but a glow from within.

"Are you following me?"

She shook her head. Why did his smile seem so familiar? Endearing and mocking at the same time and impossible not to reciprocate.

"I had a feeling you were going the same way," he said.

"How could you possibly know?" she asked, mortified at her voice sounding weak and womanly.

"I was walking by the store and saw you absolutely enthralled by the map and especially its northeastern corner."

"Are *you* following me?" she asked.

He didn't smile this time. "No. I happen to be traveling in the same direction."

They walked for a while in silence. Emery kept glancing at him furtively. At last, Sebastian stopped in a clearing by a large tree. "Good enough to camp."

She glanced at him uncertainly.

"What, you don't camp at night?"

"Rarely. Not really camp. I just lie down and rest for a bit. That's all."

"Ah. We can camp safely here. You can sleep while I keep watch."

"I don't think I can—"

"I'm not going to attack you, if that's what you're worried about."

"No. I just have a lot on my mind."

"Then lie down and rest," he said, and smiled again.

Sebastian started a fire with a little contraption that created sparks on top of tiny sticks he gathered in just a few moments.

"I've been doing this for a while," he said, noticing her staring at him.

Emery helped him collect branches, and they settled by the crackling fire. Sebastian took a chunk of bread out of his bag and offered it to her. She shook her head. "I'm not hungry. I ate. The trouble with the two guys started because they bought me food at a tavern."

"You agreed to accept food from strange men in an unfamiliar town?"

"I wasn't thinking straight. I was starving, and I didn't have any money."

"It's dangerous to travel by yourself without money."

She shrugged. "What am I supposed to do? Steal it?" she asked with indignation and glanced at Sebastian with scorn. When she saw his embarrassed grin, she opened her eyes wide. "You didn't, did you?"

"I had to. I'm a stranger in this country, and I've been looking for someone for a long time."

"And you haven't gotten caught stealing?"

"I have a knack for this sort of thing," he said, and dazzled her with his smile.

"Who are you looking for?"

"My sister," he said before his smile faded. "And my daughter."

"What happened to them?"

Sebastian waved his hand. "I don't want to talk about it now."

Silence fell between them, separating them with an impenetrable wall of grief, despite their elbows almost touching. Sitting beside him, she felt peaceful and safe. She rested her head on her knees and stared at the fire.

"How long have you been looking for them?"

"For over twenty years."

"Oh, no. That's terrible," she whispered, and thought that he didn't look old enough to have been looking for his family for twenty years. Had she been wrong to trust him?

"I also am looking for someone. My mother," she said after a while to end the silence.

"You know there is nothing here, right? No cities, no towns, nothing. Why are you looking for your mother here?"

"Why are you looking for your sister and daughter here?"

Sebastian stared into her unblinking eyes, and when he did, the golden dots sparkled. Emery noticed him shudder lightly, but he quickly covered it with a cough.

"I'm looking everywhere. I've been looking all over Andalia, and this is the last place to search."

"Right," she said. "I don't believe you. Tell me where you're going."

"Why? You want confirmation that we're heading the same way?"

Emery glared at him. He grinned.

"Fine. I'm going to the airport. How about you?"

Emery nodded. "I am too."

"Why?"

"To get to Sinturija to find my mother."

"Do you speak Sinturijan?"

Emery thought about it, then shook her head.

"How are you planning to get by robotic guns and guards armed to their teeth? And if by some miracle you got through, what would you do in the strange land whose language you don't speak? And how do you know your mother is even there?"

"I know my mother is there because a detective told me. I'll figure it out when I get there. How about you? How are you planning to get to the airport? You are going to Sinturija too, aren't you?"

He laughed. "Just like you, I was going to play it by ear."

"Aha. So, you're giving me a hard time for nothing."

"My ears are much bigger."

She laughed and then grew serious.

"Maybe with both our ears, we'll figure it out," he said quietly.

40

IS SHE BACK?

The next day, Sebastian and Emery continued their journey north, trampling through the woods, crossing a small stream where they refilled their water gourds and splashed water on their faces. They walked until Sebastian stopped, seeing a thin column of smoke on the horizon.

"You said there was nothing up north," Emery said.

"That's what I've heard from people who'd been here before."

"They either lied or didn't know what they were talking about."

"We'll see," Sebastian said, and moved forward cautiously.

It was early afternoon when they arrived at a small town brimming with life. Before they ventured onto its streets, Sebastian stopped and gazed into Emery's eyes. He rubbed his forehead before he spoke in a low voice. "Listen, Emer. No to hurt your feelings, but I've got to tell you about the way you walk before we go into town."

"What's wrong with the way I walk?" She asked, crossing her arms in front of her.

"You move your hips too much. Guys don't do that."

Emery felt her face redden. All this time, she thought she'd had him fooled. How childish and presumptuous of her to think she could mislead everyone with just her clothes and short hair.

"I know you're a girl. I've known that all along. You may pass for a young man, but you have to stop swinging your hips. The men who attacked you knew you were a woman too."

"Why didn't you say something sooner?"

"I didn't want to upset you. It's just your walk. Keep your head low and let the hat cover your face. Don't speak too much or strain your voice. When you try talking in a low voice, it's actually worse. If anyone asks, you're my younger brother. Are you okay with that?"

"Yeah," she nodded. "I feel really stupid."

"It's okay to be stupid," he grinned, and ruffled her hair.

In a noisy bazaar on the fringes of town, vendors shouted and held their wares high on display, trying to outdo each other with their voices and flamboyance. Some were throwing their products, even fish and live rabbits, in midair and catching them just before they reached the ground.

The town's odd architecture was a colorful assortment of different styles. Clean lines met curvy arches and gaudy ornaments slapped on buildings, masterfully carved window shutters, doors, and scary mascarons under the eaves. Shops, restaurants, and bordellos all advertised their businesses in their own austere or glitzy styles.

They navigated through several busy streets and arrived in a much quieter hilly area, away from the vendors and passersby, and stood in front of an inn, deliberating. The old wooden building, grayed with time, boasted a sign claiming the best stew in Andalia. Emery swallowed, reading it. Sebastian grinned and opened the door. A blast of warm air filled with the smell of savory food blew in their faces. A few men sat at the simple wooden tables, eating, clanking their jugs, and spilling malt. Seeing them enter, the men stopped what they were doing and stared at them in silence with an obvious aim of antagonizing the strangers to see how much they could withstand before retreating. Sebastian paid no attention to them and walked to the counter where a tall, skinny man with a mustache and a greasy brown apron was wiping the counter with a frayed rag.

"What can I do for you, young lads?"

"Like a room with a bed and clean sheets," Sebastian said with a commanding ease. Emery regarded him with admiration and a little envy. It was apparent he knew how to talk to people and get what he wanted, foreigner or not. And in that moment, it occurred to Emery that his story made little sense. According to Nora, there were only two continents, and each one was also its own country: Andalia and Sinturija. So, if he was a foreigner, he must have been from Sinturija. What was he doing here, and how did he get here? And why the heck didn't he tell her?

"Fussy, aren't we, huh?" the bartender said with no rancor. "Roy, get over here!" he shouted at the door in the back.

A boy of maybe seventeen came running out of the door with his mouth full of food that he tried to chew and swallow before reaching the counter.

"Take the lads to the honeymoon room. Make sure the bed got clean sheets," he said, and winked.

"Yes, sir," Roy said, swallowing the last bit of food.

Roy walked ahead of them through a hallway and then up a set of steep wooden steps that creaked under their feet. With an iron key, he opened the room at the end of the hallway. It smelled a little dusty, and it was cold, but it was relatively clean. A handmade quilt on the bed and blue curtains with green leaves softened the austerity of the simple wooden furniture.

Roy kept glancing at Emery as if wanting to ask something but lacked the courage. He finally mustered enough to whisper, pointing at her uniform. "Is she back?"

"Is who back?" Emery asked, opening her eyes wide.

"Thank you, Roy. We don't need you anymore," Sebastian quickly interjected, placing a small coin in the boy's hand.

Roy left, throwing one more curious glance at her.

"What was he talking about?"

"I don't know and don't care. The less you interact with the locals, the better. Your voice is not exactly manly."

"He was gawking at my uniform."

Sebastian pointed at the small bathroom. "I'll get us some more supplies and explore the town. Have a blast in there while I'm gone."

And with that, he was gone. Emery glanced at the bag he had left behind.

Just a quick peek.

She swallowed hard, finding an old brown teddy bear among the clothes. She stroked the bear's tired ears, and tears gathered behind her eyes. *He was telling the truth about his daughter.*

She cherished her time alone in the small bathroom, tending to her bruised body that had forgotten what soap or warm water was, and to her feet that for days had suffered abuse in shoes that didn't fit. She noticed her body had an angular appearance, her eyes appeared larger, and her cheeks were hollow.

Sebastian returned, grinning. He brought a round cheese ring, two loaves of bread, carrots, and apples. Emery's mouth watered, and she reached for the bread, but he stopped her. "Let's save this for later. While in town, let's have some proper food. Let's see what the best stew in Andalia tastes like. Cooked food and beer."

"You sure?"

"Yeah, why not?"

She shrugged. "You didn't want me to talk."

"Stuff your face so you won't have to," he said, grinning.

He didn't have to tell her twice. She waited for the bowl of steaming stew with a spoon in her hand and tried not to moan while inhaling her food. Her cheeks were so full they hurt. Sebastian watched her and smiled with his eyes. "I didn't know one could eat so much and so fast."

She swallowed her food. "I'm Emery, by the way, not Emer."

Sebastian nodded, taking a long sip of malt.

When they were almost done with their food, three men rose from their seats at a corner table and walked toward them. Sebastian tensed slightly but remained composed and planted his calm eyes on Emery's. Her pulse quickened.

"May we join you?" The oldest took his hat off, held it in both hands, and spoke in a low voice. None of the men seemed hostile. They acted slightly shy and apologized for disturbing their supper.

Sebastian nodded and pointed to the chairs across the table. They sat in silence, glancing in Emery's direction.

"Are you the new captain?" the older man whispered to Emery.

She tried to swallow the bread but did not have enough saliva to push it through her dry throat. She feared she was going to choke.

"Why're you asking?" Sebastian asked.

The three men looked at each other.

"We have experience," the youngest, in his twenties, blurted.

Sebastian nodded slowly and waited. His expression was friendly, calm, and curious.

"Is she back?" the other younger man asked. "Is *Discovery* back?"

"What if she is?" Sebastian asked.

"You could use us. We have experience. Does the new captain—"

"We'll keep that in mind. Captain Emer and me. Thank you for your interest. Where can we find you?"

"Just ask for Timothy and his bunch."

Now that he had said that, Emery saw a family resemblance: the same sandy hair and firm chins. And the same large hands. Working hands.

Sebastian rose from his seat and shook their hands. They bowed their heads and headed out the door.

Emery swallowed her food. "What was that all about?" she whispered.

"I don't know. Let's go back to the room and talk."

Emery grunted, getting up. The heap of food she ingested felt heavy on her stomach, and she barely made it up the steep stairs, wheezing. Inside the room, she collapsed on the bed and groaned.

Sebastian paced the room.

"Do you know what they were talking about?" Emery asked, massaging her stomach.

"They saw your uniform and think you're a captain. The dead guy you snatched it from must have been a captain."

Emery sat upright, her eyes shining with excitement. "When they asked if she was back, did they say *Discovery*?"

"I think so."

Emery scratched her head. "That was the name of the ship in the painting on that captain's boat. Maybe he was the captain."

"Possibly, but I don't know how it could help us."

"The way they talked about it... like it was some kind of secret."

"Hmm. I don't know."

"Sebastian?"

"Huh? Why are you making such a strange face?"

"I want to ask you something. Don't get mad."

Sebastian scrunched his forehead. "Have I ever? What is it?"

"You said once that you're a foreigner. But there are only Andalia and Sinturija. Are you from there?"

Sebastian rubbed his forehead. "Ugh. No. Actually, I don't know where I'm from."

Emery exhaled, detecting genuine consternation in his voice. But the way he'd said it sent an alarming premonition that what he was about to say would alter their developing bond. Sebastian crossed the room in a few strides, then sat on the bed beside her.

"I'll tell you my story, but know that only one other person knows this about me. For some inexplicable reason, I feel I can trust you the way I trusted her. In some ways, you remind me of her. The way you move and talk and the shape of your eyes."

Sebastian spoke, looking into the distance as if taking inspiration from the drab walls. If he were to glance at Emery, he would have stopped his story immediately upon seeing her face drained of color and mouth moving without uttering a sound. But he was engrossed in his story, telling it for the first time in a long time. Perhaps he wanted to tell it all before seeing his listener's reaction.

41

MEETING MIA

My first memory of Andalia was painful. I felt every muscle and bone bounce and shift as I slammed onto the hard sand. For a long time, I didn't open my eyes. Not out of fear, because I felt none, but because I didn't want to end the utter bliss I was still immersed in after traversing the bright light. I remembered nothing else but the light that carried me. I imagine that's how a newborn must feel—free of memories, fear, or worries. And I probably would have lain there much longer without opening my eyes if it weren't for the cold water that splashed over my body and made its way to my mouth. I sat up, and as I sat spitting out the salty water and looked around, another cold wave washed over my legs and hands, leaving a greenish foam behind.

"The sun had receded from behind the clouds, but I felt no warmth. Wearing only a white cotton shirt and underwear, I shivered when another wave hit. The tide was coming in.

"I rolled away from the water's edge, avoiding another cold splash, and felt so relieved I wasn't hurt. I looked up, but there was no hole in the sky. Nothing showed where I had fallen from. I didn't know my name," Sebastian said, and closed his eyes, remembering.

"All around me was white sand and the ocean. I walked toward the dunes covered in sparse grass. I needed to get warm as the gusts of wind penetrated my body, already cold from the icy water and covered in prickly goosebumps that hurt when the wind hit my skin. I walked through the dunes as the sun made its way down toward the horizon.

"After walking for a long time in total darkness, I saw a light. As I got closer, I realized the light was coming from the window of a small wooden cabin. Shaking uncontrollably, I stood on the small porch, staring at the door, and hesitated before reaching for the handle, glancing at my nearly naked body. Who or what was behind that door? Would they be pleased to see me, or would they be scared? Would they attack me, shun me, or welcome me?

"My teeth clattered as I pressed on the handle and pushed the door in. The gust of warm air that burst out of the cabin pulled me in. As I walked in, a young woman jumped up from a desk loaded with books and papers, glanced around, and grabbed a poker resting next to a lit stone fireplace. She took a step forward, wielding the iron like a weapon, and appraised me. I just stood there unmoving, letting her study me with her golden eyes. I must have been a sorry sight—wearing only wet and sand-covered underwear and a t-shirt and shivering violently. I tried to say something to her, but my clanking mouth produced no intelligible sounds. She looked into my eyes, and, after a moment of hesitation, she lowered the poker to the ground and ambled over to a chair while watching me and grabbed a plaid blanket. She approached me, holding it in front of her.

"'Here, wrap it around you. You look so cold.'"

"Th...th...thank y...y...you," I said, taking the blanket.

"'Come. Sit by the fire,' she said, pointing to an old red velvet chair that looked like it had provided comfort for generations of lost travelers. Her eyes followed my movements as I nodded and walked slowly and sat by the fire. My hands, covered with cuts from the tall grass and purple from the cold, welcomed the heat radiating from the fireplace. My feet were in even worse shape, bleeding from grass cuts.

"'I'm making tea,'" she said. 'Would you like some?'

"I nodded.

"The woman disappeared into the small kitchen, separated from the cozy living room by a short wall. Pots clanked and cupboards opened and closed. Her gentle manner and voice relaxed me, and I sank deeper into the friendly chair and bundled myself tight with the blanket.

The young woman returned with two steaming cups and handed one to me.

"'I'm Mia,' she said, looking at me expectantly.

"It was my turn to say my name, and for a moment, I thought hard, searching my memories for my name, but all I got were the names of some random objects and animals. My face must have reflected distress because she asked tenderly, 'What happened to you?'

"'I don't remember.'

"She asked, 'Were you in a boat accident?'

"'I don't know. I remember the bright light, falling down, and waking up on the beach.'

"'Hmm. You probably should see a doctor. My father will be here to pick me up in four days, but I don't know whether you should wait that long. Are you hurt?'

"'I don't think so,' I said.

"'See, this cabin is very secluded. There is nobody around for miles, so I can't ask for help.'

"'I don't need a doctor. I was just very cold. Thank you for letting a stranger into your home and warming him with your kindness,' I said.

"I think she sensed my sadness and saw my confusion. I detected no fear or pity in her calm eyes, only an inner strength in her that shone through as she looked at me, as if searching my soul. She must've seen something good because she pushed another old chair in front of the fireplace and sat beside me. We sat silently, sipping our tea and staring at the fire for a long time. Her gentle presence, the hot tea, and the fire made me doze off.

"I woke up, sensing her gaze on me. She stood before me, looking at me. Then, she gently removed the empty cup from my hands. She was so beautiful, Emery, so beautiful. I could have stared into her eyes and at her sensuous lips forever. When she caught herself staring at my lips, she flinched and went back to her desk. But she couldn't concentrate on her studies, glancing at me, probably wondering who she had let into her cabin.

"She told me later that she had tossed and turned through the night and had only fallen asleep when dawn was near. I slept little that night but must have dozed off at some point because I awoke to the wonderful smell of something rich and smoky. Mia was in her little kitchen pouring brown liquid into two cups, and handed one to me. I thanked her and couldn't contain a grin, seeing she had misaligned the buttons on her shirt. I guessed she'd dressed hurriedly on account of a stranger sleeping in her cabin."

"'I hope you like coffee,' she said, smiling.

"As I smiled back, a feeling of overwhelming certainty settled on my chest. I'd always remember this moment and this smile that encircled my world in that moment. I would always remember her mesmerizing eyes that gazed at me with curiosity, gentleness, and a hint of an ache, a longing. She told me later she was surprised at herself, at her boldness—she had never openly scrutinized a man before.

"She gasped when her gaze landed on my feet. 'Oh, my. We need to get you some clothes. I'm sure my father had left clothes and maybe shoes in here. They'll be much too small, even though my father is not a small man,' she said, and left.

"She returned shortly with a heap of clothes and a pair of old canvas shoes. 'Try them on.'

"While I took the clothes, the blanket that was draped over my shoulder fell down to the floor, exposing my torso. Mia didn't look away. After I squeezed into the shirt and my head finally made it through the tight opening, and I looked at her, she covered her mouth as she tried to avoid laughing at me. I said, 'It fits. Thank you,' and she burst out laughing.

"The sleeves only covered half of my forearms, and the shirt was tight. Her father's heavy-duty pants only reached half the length of my calf. Mia kept giggling, and I joined her.

"She made a breakfast of scrambled eggs and bread with butter. 'Sorry, I don't have a great selection of food here. I brought only what's easy to make so I can study,' she said when we were eating. I devoured my food to show her how much I loved it.

"When I asked what she was studying, she blushed and hesitated with an answer, long enough for me to raise my hands in a dismissive gesture.

"'I didn't mean to pry,' I said.

"'You're not,' she said sharply and touched her face, which was still flushed.

"I thought stupid humor would make up for my blunder, and I continued to talk when I should've been quiet. 'Hey. If you are studying a touchy subject, like sorcery, I completely understand your hesitation in telling a complete stranger about it. Just don't turn me into a toad.'

"'Yeah. It is sorcery in a way,' she murmured. 'Let's take care of your feet. I'll bring you some bandages and some ointment and socks. The shoes I brought you are way too small. You can't walk in them. You have giant feet.'

"I couldn't take my eyes off Mia while she spoke, transfixed by her pink cheeks, her quick, nervous movements, and the slight vibration in her voice. She turned around and ran out, returning with an armful of supplies and long wool socks. She sat me on the chair by the fireplace and then cleaned and bandaged my feet. I wanted to protest, but I cherished her closeness instead and inhaled the scent of her hair.

"'I'll put some ointment on first, then bandage them. You don't know what stuff was on the grass or the sand,' she said.

"When I asked her if she was a nurse, her face dropped, and she paled. Another blunder. I apologized profusely, wondering why she'd be upset by being called a nurse.

"'I have to go back to studying. On the mantle, there are some of my father's books. You are welcome to them.'

"On her way back to the desk, she said, 'No, I'm not. Not yet, anyway.' She sat, opened her book, and started reading.

"Not wanting to disturb her anymore, I walked to the mantel and read the titles of the hardcover books neatly lined up on the shelf. Most were about the business of making money—banking, investing, selling, profiting. One was different. It was a book about a jungle ecosystem. The photos brought back disjointed memories of trampling through a jungle like that before. I got lost in it for a while, hoping it would bring more memories. At one point, I heard her sighing and wondered if I should just leave. There was that sadness in her, a resignation when she spoke of her studies, so different from when she spoke of anything else.

"'Mia,' I said. 'I don't want to be a burden. I'll leave and try to find a…city…or something that may help me remember who I am.'

"'Nonsense,' she said quietly. 'You are in no position to walk for miles to reach the nearest town. You have no shoes. The terrain once you leave the dunes gets even worse. You wouldn't get very far. My father will be here in four days and will take you to town. I'll make some food. You must be starving.'

"Mia pushed away her book as if it pained her to look at it and went to the kitchen, where she smeared butter on thick bread slices and absentmindedly topped it with copious amounts of cheese slices, while her chest bobbed in little sighs. I ate, glancing curiously at her.

"'Do you have a gun?' I asked her.

"'I don't know what that is.'

"'You mean you've never heard of a gun?'

"'Is it something men use when hunting?'

"'That too—'

"Mia's face reddened. 'Then no. I've little knowledge of men's… dealings.'

"'It's a weapon,' I said. 'A piece of metal that fires bullets at someone who might attack you. You are alone in this remote cabin. Your father wasn't afraid to leave you alone with no weapons?'

"'I have a weapon,' she said, pointing at the poker.

"I must've had a ridiculous expression on my face. She exploded with laughter and could barely swallow her food.

"After we ate, she quickly glanced at her desk but, instead of returning to it, she sank into the chair across the fireplace. We talked for hours. She told me we were in Andalia—one of the two continents in the Galia Ocean, and some smaller islands, mostly unpopulated, scattered in between them. Then she tried to help me remember by asking questions.

"'Do you remember what you did? Were you a doctor, an engineer, an architect?' Mia asked. I must not have reacted because she continued. 'A gravedigger perhaps...?'

"'I think I traveled a lot. I seem to have a lot of glimpses of flying in planes, being in different cities, deserts, forests,' I said.

"'I have an idea. What if I start saying names? Starting with an 'A' all the way to 'Z.' Maybe you'll remember your name.'

"'We could try.'

"'Adam, Alan, Anthony...' she started reciting names and studying my reaction. When she got to 'S' and said 'Sebastian', I gasped.

"'Is that it? Was your name Sebastian?'

"I wasn't certain. 'I don't know,' I remember sighing with exasperation.

"'It will come to you when you are ready. Maybe something traumatized you, and your mind just doesn't want to remember it.'

"'Thank you for trying,' I said and covered her hand with mine. It was such a natural gesture, and yet, she quickly retracted her hand as if a fire touched it.

"'I'm sorry.'

"'No, I'm sorry. I'm anxious about my exam and what comes after...' she said and paused. 'It's the aptitude test,' she whispered and hung her head.

"'What's that?'

"'In Andalia, every girl has to take it before the ...'

"She opened her mouth but then fell silent as if she couldn't find the right words to continue.

"'Before what, Mia?'

"'It's the test to test whether you can be a ... wife and a mother.'

"I thought I had heard wrong. 'You are a woman. Why do you need a test? Isn't it obvious?'

"'No,' she said, and lowered her gaze. 'Not every woman is suitable to be a mother and a wife. You must be both to have a... life... a husband,' Mia said, trying to sound convincing, but her voice was doing the opposite.

"'Do you want to be a mother? Or a wife?'

"'Doesn't every woman?'

"'I don't know. I'm not one. What's on the test? It can't be that difficult, can it?'

"Mia bit her upper lip to stop it from trembling. She looked away to hide the tears welling up in her golden eyes. 'It is. Hard. Very hard. It's tricky. It tricks you into answering the wrong way if you're not right for motherhood ... you know ... the womanly roles and the way of thinking. That's when they get you.'

"She looked so miserable that without thinking, I put my hand on hers again, but this time, she didn't pull it out.

"'Mia, listen to me. Anyone who requires a woman to take a test like that is a total moron. You don't need that stupid test. You will be a wonderful mother and a wife if you choose to be. Screw the test!'

"'I have to take it and pass it with a score above ninety percent ...'

"'Who is making you?'

"'It's a requirement. My parents, the society, and my future husband expect it of me. We know who we'll marry when we are in our teens. We take the compatibility tests—'

"I was too stunned to say anything. I had no memories of my past, but this sounded so wrong. My expression must have said so.

"'How else would you know if you were compatible with another person?' she said defiantly, but her eyes were searching for approval.

"'Chemistry between two people.'

"'Chemistry? Like science?'

"'No, not like science. It's just an expression, for lack of a better one, to explain the attraction between two people. It's like two people meet for the first time and look each other in the eye, they instantly perceive they're meant for each other. They feel each other's...chemistry. No test could ever replace that.' I said and planted my eyes on her. Firmly, unapologetically, intimately, I held her gaze captive.

"'Do you feel that? This is chemistry,' I said. 'You know, that feeling when you're away from home for a long time and when you're returning and you're so close that you recognize the trees and your home and your chest tightens in relief and gratitude. This is how I felt when I first saw you. I've never seen you before, and yet I knew you. And then when I saw your face, I sensed you felt the same. I saw that spark in your eyes when you looked into mine. Right after, you relaxed and dropped the poker because you knew I'd never harm you.'

"She didn't respond but sat frozen in place, unblinking, and not taking her eyes off mine.

"'Tell me I'm wrong, and I'll leave immediately.'

"She shook her head as if in slow motion. Her blonde hair caught a streak of light from the window, and a glow formed around her. 'You're not wrong. But there's no room for chemistry in my world. I'm predestined to marry Gilbert, who was chosen for me by our System, my parents, and his parents. I can't escape my reality because it's the only one I know. The unknown excites me but frightens me more.'

"'I understand. I don't want to frighten you, and I hope you'll find chemistry with your future husband. But I must go now because the longer I wait, the harder it'll be to leave you.'

"My heart and entire body felt heavy. I could barely get up and walk to the door. She sat at the table, staring at her hands. When I opened the door, she stood up abruptly.

"'Don't go. I don't want you to,' she said, and looked into my eyes.

"We became lovers. Mia didn't even glance at her books. She named me Sebastian, and I accepted it. On the third day, our last day together, I woke up to Mia's silent weeping. Her tears soaked her pillow.

"I stroked her cheeks and kissed her eyes. 'Can't you just say you don't want to marry him?'

"She moved her head on the pillow.

"'Don't you have any say about your life?'

"She sobbed harder.

"'You don't have to marry him. We can run away together. Go somewhere else.'

"'Where? Andalia's customs are the same throughout. They'd post my likeness everywhere, and soon they'd find us. I'd spend the rest of my life in prison, and you'd be dead. Taking someone's fiancé is treated as if it's treason. It's punishable by death.'

"'We'll leave Andalia then. What else is there? What other countries border yours?'

"'None. Andalia is a vast continent stretching from the North Pole almost to the South Pole. Another continent is unreachable by regular people's planes. To get on an intercontinental plane, you need permission from the highest council of Andalia. Only diplomats get on those planes,' she said through her sobs. She calmed down, staring at the ceiling for a long time.

"'I can talk to your parents and convince them to change their minds.'

"She sat up and stared at me with enormous eyes. 'You're out of your mind. Nothing will ever change my father's mind,' she said, sounding bitter and almost hysterical. 'Nothing will ever change. It hasn't for centuries. You can't say anything, Sebastian. Or they'll kill you. You must leave in the morning before my father comes. He'll be here in the afternoon. I no longer believe you can go with us because my father will know what's happened between us. He can read me like an open book.'

"The next morning, we awoke in each other's arms to a booming man's voice.

"'Mia, I'm early. The work conference was canceled ...' the voice grew louder.

"I scrambled to get dressed, and Mia fumbled to put a striped gray-blue shirt on and ended up putting it on inside out.

"A tall man overtook the doorway with his broad shoulders. His words trailed off as he tried to understand the sight before him. His blue eyes opened wide, then narrowed as his gaze moved from me to his daughter. He clenched his right fist and smacked it into his left hand.

"'Who the Jester are you?' he spat. 'Mia, what have you done? Who is this Jester?'

"Mia's lips trembled as she tried to button her shirt with shaking hands. She finally gave up and tied one side of the shirt to the other. She moved her mouth, but no sound came from her lips.

"'My name is Sebastian. I'm in love with your daughter.'

"'You are what? In love? You Jesterly blabbering idiot. How dare you? I'm going to kill you!' he hollered, taking a step toward me. His blue eyes shone, his muscular arms bent as he started walking deliberately slowly, preparing to deliver a crushing blow. The delicate blond, almost-white hair, combed to one side when he arrived, now stood up as if he were a cock ready for a fight.

"'Please don't,' I said calmly. 'Let's talk about it. Your daughter doesn't deserve a miserable marriage to a man she—'

"Mia's father lunged at me. Suddenly, I remembered how to fight, or my body did. I sidestepped, avoiding the attack. Mia's father's muscular bulk couldn't stop when it hit no target and plunged into the wall. A pastel seascape behind glass bounced off the wall and landed on him, breaking into a million shimmering pieces covering the wooden planks and his hair. He fell. Although stunned, the big man didn't stay down for long. He stood up and reddened even more. His face stood in stark contrast to his white hair, now gleaming with tiny glass shards.

"'Father, don't. Stop, please.' Mia pleaded.

"'You. Do. Not. Speak,' he hissed. 'I'll deal with you later.'

"'No, you won't. I am taking her with me,' I said, and continued despite Mia's silent plea. 'That's right. If you won't listen to reason, then we'll have to—'

"'To Jester, you will!'

"Her father lurched at me. Anticipating it, I tried to avoid him, but he faked an attack to the right while thrusting his left fist at me. But I was much faster. I bent down and hit him in the stomach. He fell, holding his belly and trying to cough, his face resembling a ripe tomato.

"'Come on. Let's go,' I said to Mia, extending my hand.

"She shook her head. 'Go. Go now, Sebastian. I can't go with you. Go before he kills you.'

"'I'm not leaving without you. He'll hurt you.'

"'He won't. Despite everything, he loves me. He wouldn't hurt me.'

"'But he'll send you to prison. You said so yourself.'

"'No, he won't. He couldn't live with the shame of having a daughter in prison,' she said and approached her father. 'Father. Look at me. Will you send me to prison if he leaves?'

"Her father, struggling to breathe, got up on his knees and looked at Mia, shaking his head.

"She shrugged, pointing at her father. 'See? He won't. Go. Now! I'm not going! I don't want to go anywhere with you! Leave. Now!' she shouted.

"She held my gaze and didn't falter. I left."

"You what?" Emery asked. "You left her with her crazy father? How could you?"

"I was stupid. I thought she wanted me gone. Understand...when I saw her, my life started. When she told me to leave, it ended. I was dead at that moment."

"What did you do next?" Emery asked.

"I ran through the forest feeling no physical pain as the rocks and grass cut my feet, pushed by grief and regret. I ran until my body collapsed to the ground. When I closed my eyes, I saw Mia's eyes watching me, partially smiling and partially soaked in soft melancholy, and that middle cusp of her lip as red as a strawberry. The love and the loss I felt were so profound, unstoppable, and irreparable that I believed I was going to die from grief and guilt that I let her go and didn't know how to find her. The evening came, and then the half-moon slowly made its way through the clouds and settled on my face, caressing it with its cool light. I imagined it to be Mia telling me not to give up but to get up and find her, so I decided to go back to the cabin.

"I walked for hours but at last found the cabin and combed it for clues. When I found her father's name in a book that I threw from the shelf above the fireplace, I sat on the floor and cried, holding it to my chest. I didn't know how I was going to find her, knowing only her father's name and the name of the town, but this sliver of knowledge reignited my hope, and I swore to myself that I would find her even if I had to walk barefoot to the edge of the world."

"Did you ever find her?" Emery asked.

He nodded and grimaced before responding. His voice sounded dull and hollow. "I did. I found her father's house and then after a while, hers."

"What happened?"

"She told me she was happy with her husband and that she had a family that she loved, and she would never leave. And then a little girl holding a bear ran out and looked at me curiously. When I saw her face, my breath was sucked out. I stood there frozen. Her resemblance to me was undeniable—she was my daughter.

"In that moment, her face brought back the most powerful memory since I had dropped onto that beach. I remembered my sister—I had a twin sister. The memories of playing with my sister as a child with pebbles on cobblestone streets flooded my mind as I stood there staring at my daughter. Mia was saying something, but her words didn't reach me. The girl came toward me, and I finally understood that Mia was telling her daughter to go back inside. I considered taking the child and running away with her. I crouched, and the girl showed me her bear. I said something, but I don't know what.

"Mia was pressing me to leave. I stroked the girl's head and took the bear out of her hands. She didn't protest or cry, only observed me with her black eyes. Mia snatched the girl and dashed inside. I left with the brown bear."

"You left her again?" Emery asked.

"She said she loved her husband."

"And you believed her?"

Sebastian hung his head.

"I'm sorry. I shouldn't have judged you."

"It wasn't the uncertainty. I knew she still loved me."

"What then?"

"What could I give her? I was a nobody, a vagabond, a Gypsy, forever a stranger on this unforgiving continent. What could I offer my daughter?"

"Your love," Emery sighed. "I know another idiot who thinks he is unworthy of someone's love," she said, and curled up on the bed, hiding her face in the pillow.

42

PLANNING

Emery awoke early to Sebastian stirring on the bed of blankets he had made for himself on the floor's thick wooden planks. His eyes were red.

"Can I ask you something?" she asked softly.

He waved.

"Did all your memories come back?"

"Some of my memories came back in dreams and sometimes unexpectedly in strange flashes triggered by surroundings, sounds, or smells, but I still don't recall everything and might never. After I saw my daughter, I kept having visions of my sister begging me to find her and release her from a prison. Since then, I have seen her in memory flashes. I sensed we were very close, being twins and surviving the tragedy of our parents' deaths."

Emery dangled her feet while sitting on the edge of the bed. "I woke up in a glass capsule in the middle of the ocean with complete amnesia," Emery said. "Unlike you, I haven't recovered many memories, and the ones I have make no sense. Bits and pieces of places, faces moving in and out of focus. Shit like that," she said, staring him in the eye and observing his reaction.

Sebastian scratched his head. "In the last year, the memory

flashes have been getting more intense and clearer. I remember a crystal capsule, and I also know it was invented by a woman I knew. I can't quite make out who she was, only that I cared about her."

"You're saying someone you know stuck me in this crystal capsule to make me pay for whatever atrocities I'd committed. It makes no sense at all," Emery said.

"What makes you think you've done something atrocious?" Sebastian asked, scratching his head.

"Because someone recognized me, but they wouldn't say anything about my past. It was as if he were afraid of me or hated me for what I'd done."

"Who?"

"You don't know him. His name is Frederick, and he finds missing people," she said and added hesitantly, "He is the one I've glimpsed in my dreams. I think we were close once."

"Do you know that for sure?"

"No. I don't know anything for sure. But he told me that my mother married someone in Sintuirja, moved there, and then disappeared. That's why I'm going there. To find my mother."

"What's your mother's name?"

Emery noticed his lips trembled when he asked. "Why?"

"Because that's what happened to my daughter. She married a diplomat in Sinturija and disappeared. I thought—"

"You thought your daughter was my mother?" she asked and shifted away on the bed. "You don't look old enough to be my father, much less my grandfather."

"I realize how it sounds," he said in a gentle tone, slowly pacing the room. "No, I'm not crazy. I don't know why I haven't aged in twenty years. I think it might be connected to the black shard my sister found in a creek. Or it may be hereditary. If my memory is right, I lived for a long time before I landed on that beach." He turned toward her. "You might be the same way."

"You mean not aging?"

"We both got here in the strangest way."

"That doesn't mean we're related. What's your daughter's name?"

"Her birth name was Zara Ramsey, but she'd been living under a fake name of Edmund Stone," he said, and paused when he noticed her trembling and covering her mouth with both hands. "What's the matter?"

"That was my mother's Andalian name before she married Tirg Igres."

Sebastian's eyes opened so wide, they looked like two bottomless black wells. "You...are my granddaughter."

"If Zara is your daughter and my mother..."

"I'm your grandfather," Sebastian said unsurely, glanced at her, and giggled. "Holy shit!"

As they sat and talked about what they remembered from the past, Emery sensed a tension between them. The possibility that they were related charged the surrounding air with the nervousness of hope. Emery longed to embrace the idea of family, but the tiny voice in her head cautioned her. *What if it's not true? You start loving him only to discover later that he is not your family after all?* She guessed he had similar fears, although on a couple of occasions, he'd moved as if to hug her. He couldn't have known how much she wanted him to embrace her. She said nothing to him, nor attempted to hug him or make it easier, but drank way too much malt instead during late dinner. *I have a grandpa who looks my age.*

Emery woke up late the next morning. The heap of blankets on the floor where Sebastian had slept was hollow. *He must have left when I was sleeping.*

For the first time since she had started the journey, she felt safe enough to yawn and stretch, allowing herself a tiny smile. Sebastian found her with her eyes closed, shifting back to the dreamworld.

"Hey, sleepyhead."

"I didn't realize how tired I was. What now?"

"I learned a few things," Sebastian said, grabbing a chair and sitting across from Emery. She sat up, crossed her legs, and waited.

"I eavesdropped on two guys who do maintenance at the airport. They kept bashing their commanding officers for having to show their badges and permits every time they wanted to go to town and back. Apparently, the government increased security recently. They said that not even rats can get through."

"So, what're we going to do? We're much bigger than rats," Emery said, her face slack with disappointment.

"Once we learn more about it, we'll acquire the badges from the mechanics, or pilots, or whoever else comes to town."

"We'll acquire them?" Emery asked. "Right, I forgot about your talent."

Sebastian looked like a mischievous boy when he smiled.

"How do we learn more?" she asked.

"We'll do some more eavesdropping, and if it doesn't work, we'll make them talk."

"And you have a special talent for that as well?"

"Do you want to get to Sinturija or not?"

"Yes," she sighed. "I just don't want to kill anymore." She covered her mouth, glancing at him.

"You've killed people?" Sebastian asked in a tone she had not heard him use. It was low and chilling.

In that moment, like a scolded child, she felt a desperate urge to justify her actions, but when she imagined explaining her powers she didn't understand herself, it seemed like such a monumental task, she resisted and brushed it off. "I was only protecting myself. It was them or me."

"Who did you kill?"

"I don't want to talk about it," she said.

Sebastian stared at her for a while. "It's okay. I'm sorry."

She lowered her head and worked the blanket with her fingers, fighting tears of self-pity.

"I also learned something more about the ship the guys were asking about. The *Discovery* disappeared a while back, and nobody has seen her since. People believe the government had sunk her because, apparently, she was big enough to sail to Sinturija."

"But she sank, so she's of no use to us."

"Some people believe the captain hid her somewhere."

"The captain? My captain?"

Sebastian got up and stretched, pushing the chair away with his foot. "Possibly."

"Somewhere does not help. Did you hear something else with your special hearing that would narrow it down?"

"No, but we're meeting later tonight with the guys who approached us. Remember the—"

"Of course, I remember the Timothy bunch. Why are we meeting them?"

"Maybe they know where she was last seen?"

"Ugh."

"I'll do the talking."

"Sure, Grandpa," she murmured.

He grinned.

43

THE MAP

The tavern wasn't busy in the early evening. A few men sat at nearby tables, holding their mugs and chatting. The hum of the surrounding conversations and the clanking of the mugs on the wooden tables muffled Emery and Sebastian's conversation with the Timothy bunch. The father and his sons loosened their tongues after a few malts and Sebastian's charm. Emery noticed Timothy's eyes flash and his head nod more vigorously as he listened to Sebastian's commanding tone. My grandpa is a natural leader, Emery thought. She stayed silent, putting immense effort into keeping her face expressionless, feigning importance worthy of her captain's rank.

What Timothy had told them in a muted tone gave Emery hope. Captain Blizzard (that was his nickname; nobody knew his real name) had hidden the love of his life—*Discovery*—in a cave with an underground river running through it.

"And you know where the cave is?" Emery asked.

The Timothy bunch didn't seem to notice her high-pitched voice. Timothy straightened his back, pulling away from the huddle. "We were hoping you'd know. Blizzard drew a map with the location of the ship and hid it somewhere safe, somewhere only his most trustworthy mates or family could find."

Sebastian cocked his head. "Weren't you his trustworthy mate?"

Timothy blinked a few times and looked away for a moment. Then he lowered his voice. "He wanted some time to pass for the government to stop looking for her, and I had to take care of my family."

Sebastian nodded but remained silent, staring at Timothy.

Timothy looked Emery straight in the eye. "Do you have the map? You're his...son, aren't you?"

"We must be sure you're loyal," Sebastian cut in.

"Doesn't get more loyal than the Timothy bunch," Timothy said, furrowing his brow. "I fought alongside Captain Blizzard all the way to Sinturija and back. I was his mate." He said the last words with pride. "Goes both ways. What assurance do we have that you are who you say you are? Maybe you killed the captain and stole his uniform."

As he spoke, he and his two sons rose from their seats as if on an unspoken command and eyed Sebastian and Emery. Their muscular bodies were still and slightly bent, like big cats ready to prance, while their hands jerked in their pockets.

"We're talking to you," Sebastian said. The tone of voice surprised Emery. She hadn't heard him use this icy calm voice before, and she saw him in a different light: as someone who, when provoked, might prove dangerous. She guessed that he might have the same gift she possessed.

"That's your assurance," Sebastian continued. "What other reason would a captain and his first mate have for talking to sailors if not to hire them? And why would we hire them if we didn't know where she was? Tell me, Timothy. But as I mentioned before, we are not letting in potential troublemakers."

The imposing man hovered over the table for a long, silent moment, too long for Emery to bear. She tensed, readying either to escape or to fight. But the tense moment passed. Timothy slid his bulk back into his seat and, with a gruff, conspiratorial voice, asked Emery, "You really have the map? You know where *Discovery* is?"

She could sense Sebastian's gaze on her as she considered her options.

"Dare you doubt me?"

"No, Captain," Timothy said. His sons followed him and confirmed their faith in the young captain, nodding eagerly.

"Are there more of you seeking a spot on *Discovery*?" Sebastian asked.

"There could be," Timothy said with a twinkle in his eyes. "My sons Steven and Maddox have not been on *Discovery*, but they know what to do."

Sebastian regarded him seriously. "Good. We'll meet exactly a week from today in the same spot. In the meantime, get as many as you can, but only strong and healthy. Don't want to have to throw anyone overboard."

Emery clenched her teeth but waited until they were back in their room before accosting Sebastian. The moment the door to their room closed behind them, she faced him. "What the hell? We don't know where the bloody map is or the boat."

"It's not a boat, it's a ship—"

"Whatever. Are you trying to get us killed?"

"We'll pay a visit to your dead captain and search for the map."

"That's your plan? We don't even know if he was the captain or whether the map is in his boat, and, most importantly, Grandpa," she said, and paused to draw breath. "We can't make it to the boat and back in a week."

"We can on horses."

"Where are we going to get horses?"

"I saw horses when I was getting supplies. Don't make faces. Even if we don't find the map or the ship, it's worth trying. If we don't find it, we'll go back to our plan of getting onto the plane."

Emery fiddled with her hands. "We are losing time."

"It's a safer option."

"Suppose we find the boat—"

"Ship."

"Suppose we find the fucking ship. How are we going to get it to Sinturija? You realize that I'm not really a captain."

"We'll figure it out."

"Or get killed by the Timothy bunch."

They set out at dusk, carrying their bags on their backs. Sebastian led them through narrow streets and onto fields. They stopped at an enclosed field with a barn. Three horses and four black-and-white cows stood in their stalls, napping. One horse neighed when they were close enough for it to smell them.

Sebastian looked at Emery. "Are you any good with horses?" he whispered.

The lack of confidence in his voice alerted her. "I don't know. You know I don't remember much. Why are you asking me? Aren't you the one who's gonna steal them? It was your idea."

"Yeah, but I was hoping for a woman's gentle touch. I seem to remember that girls are usually good with horses."

"Ugh. You're not good with horses, are you?"

"I could probably manage."

That sounded neither convincing nor encouraging. Emery sighed, jumped the fence, and plodded toward the barn. As she got close enough to smell the sweet scent of hay and the slightly gamey smell of horses, she straightened her back and evened out her breathing. A little smile danced on her lips when, as she extended her hand and touched the soft black muzzle, the black horse responded with a gentle snort. The black shiny eyes regarded her with curiosity but without fear as the black beauty trotted in place and pushed his head through the metal bars to smell her. She laughed when she felt the hot, moist air as the horse touched her face. She was stroking the strong cheeks and the white between his eyes when Sebastian approached. The horse neighed and shook its head, sending its black mane into a frenzy.

"Shush…It's okay, horsie. It's okay. This is Sebastian, my grandpa, and he is with me. He won't hurt you."

The horse fixed its shiny gaze on Sebastian and regarded him for a moment. Then he continued planting his soft muzzle on her cheek.

"I knew it," Sebastian whispered, grinning. "You are a horse whisperer."

~

"It's not here," Emery said and pouted. "We tore apart the entire boat and haven't found one clue where he hid that damn boat or whether he even was the captain."

She sat on an overturned chair, glooming over the broken furniture and contents of the cupboards and drawers scattered on the floor. "We made a mess of his boat for nothing."

"There is the painting."

"Yeah," Emery mumbled, glaring at the broken frame. "Anyone can have a painting of a boat."

"We go back to our original plan," Sebastian said. "Nothing is lost."

"Except for getting my butt sore."

Sebastian laughed. He walked over to her and seized her chin. "We had to try. I would never forgive myself if anything happened to you."

"Okay," she sighed. "Let's go back." She headed for the door.

Before she reached for the handle, the door swung open, hitting the wooden wall with a loud thud. Three men crowded the narrow doorway. They wore clothes so worn-out and dirty, they had long lost their color and shape. A whiff of unwashed bodies and tobacco drifted inside. Emery's eyes were fixed on the blue flashes on the long blades as they caught the sun peering over the railing. She couldn't look away as she took a step back.

"Give us the map," the man closest to Emery growled. His gray stubble moved on his hollow cheeks as he spoke.

"What map?" Sebastian asked calmly.

"Got no time for jokes. Give us the map, and we may spare your life. Either way, we're gonna get it, so just give it," he said, stepping forward while glaring at Sebastian past Emery.

Her gaze shifted to his face and the worn-out but familiar insignia on his lapels. "Wait," she said in a low voice. "We're after the same thing. We all want to find her, to return to the sea—"

"Sure, except we don't take gurls with us. They distract the mates with their gurly faces, and we need no such thing while we loot."

"But we can have fun now," the second sailor said, peeking from behind the first man.

"You be quiet, Sigil," the first sailor barked, taking another step.

Emery's feet stayed firmly attached to the wooden planks, although every muscle in her body screamed to step back.

Sebastian slid beside her. "Why do you think there is a map here?" he asked politely, as if he were conversing with a friend.

"You think you're so clever. Give me the map," the first man said, raising his voice.

"We didn't find it."

The men pointed their blades at them. Only a few inches separated Emery's chest from the shining blade.

Sebastian sighed. "Leave in peace. I don't want to hurt you."

A powerful smell of garlic and stale tobacco overwhelmed Emery's nostrils as the three men burst into laughter.

"You dainty boy with your dainty gurl was gonna hurt us?"

The man on the left, Sigil, who was closest to Emery, narrowed his eyes and drew breath. Emery blinked. When she opened her eyes, her attacker's face was contorted in pain as Sebastian gripped his hand. Sebastian increased the pressure, and the knife clanked, dropping to the floor. The other two men readied to attack, glaring at Sebastian.

It happened so fast, Emery didn't feel any pain. While Sebastian deflected the knife of the second man lunging at him, the third plunged his knife at her. She shifted to the left to avoid the blade, but not far or quickly enough. It sliced her arm through the thick coat. She felt no pain and thought he missed her, but that didn't stop the anger, which arose instantaneously and so intensely her core was on fire. If she didn't release it, she'd burn, she believed. Her hands, as if acting on their own, flew at him, and his wide eyes reflected the silver of the wave when it hit his chest. He stumbled and fell backward onto the floor. Emery flinched when his skull bounced on the floor, sounding like a splitting melon.

Sigil's face went slack, seeing the wave and his other companion's limp body hung over a broken chair where Sebastian must have thrown him.

Sebastian glanced at her while grasping Sigil's coat with both hands and lifting him up as if he were a toy. Much smaller than Sebastian, Sigil dangled his feet and stared at him with eyes bulging out of their sockets. Saliva dripped out of his open mouth as he struggled to speak, managing only a weak whimper.

"What're we going to do with him?" Emery asked.

"For now, I'm going to tie him up and ask him some questions," Sebastian said, setting Sigil on the only unbroken chair in the salon. "See if you can find something to tie him with," he added, glaring at Sigil, whose skinny body shook along with the rickety chair that wobbled, drumming on the wooden floor. His face was gray and glistened with an unhealthy glow.

"I will not hurt you if you tell me everything," Emery heard Sebastian's calm voice as she ransacked the place for a rope. She finally found a thick orange cord on the deck, but when she brought it back, Sebastian was pounding the man's chest and swearing. "Wake up, you bastard! Goddamn you!"

Thud! The rope fell from her hands. "What happened?"

"He clutched his chest and fell, gasping for air. And now he's not breathing. Shit!"

"Let me see," Emery said, and kneeled by Sigil. She checked his pulse. It was there, but weak. "He's alive. Get some water."

Sebastian brought a bucket of water from the river.

Emery splashed half the contents onto the man's face, and he opened his eyes and coughed the water out as it entered his open mouth. He sat upright, looked at Emery, and shifted his gaze to Sebastian.

"I know nothing, all right? Don't kill me."

"I told you I wasn't going to. I might actually hire you if you're a sailor."

Sigil's eyes darted between Sebastian and Emery.

"How did you know we're looking for a map? Did you follow us?" Sebastian asked.

"Saw you go in," Sigil said and closed his mouth shut.

Sebastian nudged him on the neck with the tip of his knife. "How did you know about the map?"

Sigil tilted his head to avoid the knife. Sebastian moved it and pressed harder. A drop of blood dripped down Sigil's neck from under the knife's blade.

Sigil's eyes went wide. "Everyone is looking for the map now. It's been fifteen years."

Emery and Sebastian looked at each other. Sebastian shrugged and looked back a Sigil. "And that's supposed to mean something?"

"Blizzard said he was gonna hide her for fifteen years."

"So you decided to pay the captain a friendly visit or rob him?"

"Not rob him. Never."

"And you think the map is real?"

"Yes, it's real. He told us he would draw one up."

"The captain did?"

"Yeah."

"Did you know the captain was dead?"

Sigil looked down.

"Did you kill him?"

"No," he murmured and looked up at Sebastian. "He stopped coming to town to buy provisions. My nephew told me." His body became rigid as he sat gazing into Sebastian's eyes. Sebastian opened his mouth to ask him more questions, but the words died in his mouth when his eyes landed on the floor.

He forgot about Sigil. "Are you hurt?" he asked Emery.

"What? No...why..." her voice trailed off as she followed Sebastian's eyes to a red puddle on the wooden floor. "Whose blood is that?" she asked. Sebastian's eyes narrowed as he seized Emery's arm. Once he had done that, she felt the sting. Sebastian helped her take the coat off and then inspected the wound. The long blade had left a deep cut from which blood oozed.

"Oh, Emery. Why didn't you tell me sooner?"

"I didn't know. Honestly."

"Let's take care of that," Sebastian said, and scoured the boat for something to cover the gash. When he returned, her odd expression slowed his gait. "What's wrong?"

"Sigil is gone. He must have escaped when you were looking at my arm. We forgot to tie him."

"Oh, well. I doubt he'd have anything useful to say."

"He is dangerous. He knows I am a girl."

"Doesn't matter. We don't have the map."

Sebastian wrapped straps of the white shirt he tore in pieces. When he was done, he said, "Let's get out of here."

Emery picked up her coat and followed Sebastian out onto the deck. Then she paused, wrinkling her forehead and looking at her arm. Sebastian looked back.

"Wait!" she shouted and ran back.

When she didn't return immediately, Sebastian sighed and walked back. He found her sitting on the floor and removing blood from a piece of yellowed paper with a torn piece of the shirt.

Sebastian's jaw dropped. "Is it...how did you find it?"

She showed him the sleeve of her coat. The knife sliced through the insignia, creating a deep gap. "He must have hidden it under it. It must have fallen out when I removed my coat."

They both sat on the floor, gazing at the map. Emery cleaned most of the blood off, and only a reddish tinge remained.

"Captain Blizzard had quite a talent," Sebastian remarked. "The river and the trees look amazing. Look at the details on the ship."

"Looks like the cave is up in the mountains, right where the river originates. Is that a ..."

"Lake? I think so. Underground lake."

Emery ran her fingers through her hair. Her lips bowed downward and trembled.

"What's the matter?"

"How are we getting this stupid boat out of the lake?"

"There must be a way out. How else would he have hidden it in there?"

"I guess. We're going that way anyway," she said pensively. "If it doesn't work out, we'll go with the original plan."

~

"What you did with your hands...I remember doing that with mine," Sebastian said while they were leading the horses out of the dense thicket where they had hidden them.

"And now you can't?"

"No. I dreamed about it a few times, but since it was so bizarre, I thought it was just a dream, but now that I saw you do it, I realized it was a memory."

"You've tried, right?"

"Yeah...once or twice, but without conviction. Kind of felt stupid."

"Anger fuels it. And fear. You should try it again when you're angry," Emery said, and noticed him grinning bashfully. And in doing so, he looked so young, she again questioned whether he was her grandfather.

~

They rode through the night, avoiding the towns, and by the next evening, the horses' hooves staccatoed on the wooden bridge over the river.

Three days later, where the old forest gave way to short pines and long, thin grasses with their tips swaying like waves in the wind, they veered east. Their ears prickled as the crisp mountain wind blew in their faces, moving the clouds and revealing sharp blue peaks in the distance. When they reached the foothills of the mountains, Emery hopped off the horse and pressed her cheek against its soft muzzle. "Will they survive in the wild if we leave them here?"

Her black horse neighed and moved its head as if trying to answer her question. Sebastian hopped off his brown mare and petted its long, graceful neck. "What do you say, horse? Will you be okay by yourself? Can you handle freedom?"

They took off the saddles, dropped them on the ground, and looked at each other. Emery shrugged while Sebastian clapped his horse on its butt. "Go! Get out of here and be free!"

Emery hesitated and searched her horse's eyes. "Run and be free, horsie." Someone will eventually find and claim them, she thought. Maybe it'd be better for the horses if someone did, but at least they get to taste freedom.

The horses ran alongside each other. Emery's horse looked back but didn't stop.

Despite the great artistic depiction of the area and the details, Blizzard's map included no reference to distance, causing confusion about when and where to turn. As they climbed, the temperature dropped, and in the morning and evening, they could see each other's steamy breath as they spoke. At sunset, they made a small fire and slept close to each other to keep warm. The route was longer than they'd thought, and they had to backtrack a few times, but eventually, one sunny morning, they arrived and stood before the mountain depicted on the map. At its base was the cave that led to the lake.

"It really does look like a hat," Emery said, shielding her eyes with her hands and squinting.

Sebastian nodded. "This is it, Emery. By the day's end, we'll know if the ship is there."

"It's gonna be okay, Grandpa," she said and reached for his hand. "We'll find it and sail out."

He squeezed her hand. "Yeah, we will."

As they climbed down, Emery noticed small white flakes descending slowly and melting when reaching the ground.

"What's that?"

"Snow. Don't you remember snow?"

"I remember the word but not what it meant."

"We need to get moving."

They walked past the cave several times before Sebastian found it, noticing a bird or a bat vanishing into the rock. The dark, narrow tunnel hidden from view by a giant boulder looked ominous, Emery reflected. She followed Sebastian closely, reaching out and touching his back to check that he was still in front of her, as the small torch he carried gave off very little light, terrified of being alone in the tunnel even for one second. The torch licked the dark walls with its faint yellow glow as Sebastian moved his hand.

Sebastian stopped suddenly and brought the torch to the map. "This doesn't show up on the map," he said.

"What?" Emery asked and moved in front of him. Ahead was a fork in the tunnel. The left was narrow and slanted down, and the right was wider and went slightly upward.

"Logically, we ought to follow ..."

"The left one?" Sebastian said. "Yeah, but ..." Sebastian said and shifted his gaze between the tunnels.

"Maybe we should split up," Emery said.

"No, absolutely not!"

"Which one, then?"

"My gut tells me to go right."

"My gut must be pissed at me for not feeding it because it's silent."

"Hmm...What does your brain tell you?"

"Left."

They turned into the left tunnel, which soon grew smaller and sloped dramatically downhill, and eventually they had to crawl on the uneven rocky ground, and, in sections, hold on to rocky protrusions not to slide down. Emery felt the rocks that protruded from the ceiling on her back and her sides as she wriggled her way forward. Despite the damp coldness, sweat dripped from her forehead.

"There is not enough air in here! I can't breathe," she said.

Sebastian shone his torch at her. "Are you claustrophobic?"

"Huh? How should I know?"

"Take short, even breaths and think of something pleasant, something beautiful."

"Sure, like more air." She sucked in air, making more noise than necessary. "I think we should've trusted your gut instead of my brain."

"Let's just go a little farther," he said, and inched forward.

Staying behind in this terrifying black shaft frightened her more than following Sebastian into a passage that seemed even narrower. With her heart pounding, she darted forward on her hands and knees and felt the fabric on her leg split, and then sharp pain as the rocky protrusion sliced her skin through her pants. She sucked more air in and closed her eyes before continuing onward, blinking to stop tears from escaping. Then, she started counting her movements to numb her fear. The air was so full of moisture that drops fell from the ceiling, saturating her hair and clothes.

Nineteen fifty-nine...

"Aha..." Sebastian bellowed ahead. "You were right."

Sebastian stopped. Emery opened her eyes and saw a dim blue light ahead, but she couldn't see anything else past his feet that were right in her face.

"What is it?"

"We found it. We found the lake, Emery!"

The exit from the tunnel was abrupt and steep. A good fifty feet separated them from the lake's surface, illuminated by a faint light that was shining from one side.

"I'll climb down to check out how deep the lake is so you can jump. Stay here."

"Wow!" Emery said. "It's beautiful. So many colors."

The cave enclosing the lake was enormous and complex, with countless smaller caves, alcoves, side channels, and hundreds of long stalactites hanging from the ceiling.

"Looks like the lake is deep. We can jump."

"I'll climb down, thank you very much."

Sebastian watched, nodding, as she descended with ease, hanging on tiny crevices with the tips of her fingers, and supporting her body on the tiniest footholds despite the gash on her thigh. Sebastian jumped into the water, splattering Emery, who, after finishing climbing down, stood admiring the cave.

"You've climbed before," Sebastian said, shaking his head and spreading droplets of water around him. Some landed on Emery, but she didn't notice, looking around the cave.

"I guess so," she said absentmindedly. "Where is it?"

"Good question," Sebastian said, taking out the tattered map. Emery watched over his shoulder. "On the drawing, the lake narrows in the middle, but I don't see it."

"There's light coming from under the lake. Do you think it connects to a second lake?"

"One way to find out. Can you hold your breath underwater?"

"Duh, I'm pretty sure I hold some kind of record. I should go alone and check it out."

"Again, no. We're not splitting up."

"Fine, I'll go first. Hold on to me," Emery said and jumped into the lake.

Emery followed the light, which grew brighter as she dove deeper, and she soon discovered an underground passage. She glanced behind her, and, seeing Sebastian nodding, she continued to follow the passage forward, fighting the current. Just as her chest started hurting, she saw the passage open up to a lake. In her excitement, she hadn't noticed that Sebastia had let go of her leg, and she swam up, nearly reaching the surface. When she realized Sebastian's hand was not tethered to her leg anymore, she looked behind and saw his arms flailing frantically, trying to fight the current. But the current was taking him farther away from her.

Get air! her lungs cried.

Emery reached deep into her mind, seeking strength, ignoring her lungs as they lamented. And from within, a wave of mental and physical strength surged through her veins and into her arms and legs as she swam forward, trying to grab him. His face, with eyes bulging out of their sockets, disappeared from her view. Her hands grabbed only water. She lurched ahead again, seeing only the blue-green whirlpool of furious water, but this time, her hands finally found something to grab onto. For a moment she imagined it to be seaweed and nearly released it, but realizing it was Sebastian's hair, she held it tighter and pulled him with her.

When she pulled him to a flat rock, he was unconscious. She pounded on his chest. "Wake up, dammit!"

He remained still and unbreathing. She turned him to his side and pounded on his back. The gurgling, spitting, and coughing sounds he finally made as he spat the water out sounded heavenly.

"You scared me," she said and spun her head around, following Sebastian's astonished gaze.

The majestic *Discovery*, in all her glory, rested in the middle of the bright green lake.

"She's gorgeous," Sebastian said.

The ship's fore bent elegantly and ended in the body of a carved dolphin. The soaring masts appeared undamaged, and the shiny starboard looked like it had just been polished. A wave came rushing in, stirring the water and reflecting on the ship's shiny surface. And suddenly, the ship looked different, as if *Discovery* were waking up and perceiving herself being rescued, enlivened, readying for a new adventure.

"How do we get her out of here?" Emery asked, taking off her wet coat. Sebastian wasn't listening as he scrutinized the walls. "Wait, where is the light coming from?" he asked, pointing at a far wall.

"I'll go," Emery said, taking off her waterlogged boots and getting ready to jump into the lake.

"Not by yourself."

"I'm not listening to you this time. I don't want to go through a near-drowning incident again. I'll go in and out. If I'm not out in a few minutes...I don't know...you can start searching for me. But I'll be okay," she said, and slid into the green water.

Sebastian's eyes followed her and stayed in that spot the entire time she was gone. She surprised him by resurfacing a few minutes later in a different spot. She swam toward him, and panting, she pulled up onto the slab next to him.

"Well?"

"Well, I couldn't see anything. The water is murky down there," she said. "There is a current stirring the sediment, but I couldn't see where it was coming from."

"We've got to look at all the walls and—"

"I have a better idea. We should check her out," Emery said, pointing at *Discovery*. "We swim to the other side and look for a way in. What do you call the thing that gets you on board such a monstrous ship?"

Sebastian grinned. "You finally said it right. She's no boat—she is a magnificent ship. And it's a ladder. You get on a ladder."

"I wish we had brought the rope with us."

"Maybe we did."

"Seriously? You're clairvoyant?"

Sebastian waved his hand, but the corners of his lips twitched. "I knew we'd have to scale the ship."

The rope proved unnecessary, as a ladder woven out of thick rope and oak planks hung invitingly on the port side of the ship, almost touching the water. Sebastian climbed first and signaled for Emery to follow.

Discovery looked as good up close as she did from afar. The polished teak gleamed throughout as if the crew had just gone inland for a malt. Emery imagined the rowdy, bearded sailors celebrating reaching landfall and boasting about their robberies with loud toasts and laughter. She couldn't see the ends of the soaring masts as they disappeared into the darkness of the cave's ceiling. Their round bases were as thick as a hundred-year-old tree. Only a thin layer of dust covered the railings and the deck. The slow waves splashed against the sides, interrupting the eerie silence as Emery and Sebastian stood awed by the size and the splendor of the wooden beauty.

"They must be some three hundred feet high," Sebastian said, straining his neck. "How the heck did they build this?"

They wandered the ship, taking in the intricate woodworking details and the gold accents.

"This must be the captain's quarters," Emery said. She gushed over the elegance of the large room—the wood moldings, the ornate window frames laced with gold, and a plush red carpet. "So different from his austere boat." Looking at them from a painting enclosed in an ornate gold frame was a man in his fifties.

"It's him. It's Captain Blizzard when he was younger. I see the resemblance," Emery said.

"Really? He was skin and bones when I saw him."

"Handsome," she said, staring at the portrait, mesmerized by his keen brown eyes, while Sebastian opened the drawers and then scoured the gold-engraved books arranged on a shelf fastened to the wall with metal bars.

"What are you looking for?"

"A clue for a way out of the cave."

"Ah," Emery said and peeled her eyes off the captain's image. "I'll help."

"Any luck?" Sebastian asked after a while.

"Nope," Emery said, and sat on the carpet looking around the room, which at the end of the search had undergone significant rearrangement. Furniture had been moved and books and papers lay strewn across the bunched-up plush red rug. Her gaze landed on the painting across from the captain's portrait, then her eyes turned into slits, and her head bobbed to the side.

"We can rest here for a while," Sebastian said.

She curled up on the carpet and slept. Sebastian gazed at her and then curled up beside her.

"Wake up, Grandpa, wake up! I got it!"

"Huh? What?"

Emery stood pointing at the painting. "It came to me in my sleep. At first, I didn't realize the significance of what I saw in my dream, but then I got it. As clearly as I see you now, the image appeared, and I knew it was the answer. You see this structure down here?"

"A structure? No, I don't."

Emery darted to the painting and pointed to two dark rectangles barely visible under the greenish water. "This dark space above the water is the cave, and this is the lake we're on now. These two structures under the water are not natural—they're too even. We must dive and see what they are."

"Fine," he said, took his boots off, and threw them under the desk.

"In my dream, I saw *Discovery* sail out of the cave," Emery said. The golden dots in her eyes brightened.

∼

Emery and Sebastian dove together in search of the dark rectangles. On the third try, Sebastian pointed ahead, and they swam closer. Close enough to touch its firm surface.

"What do you think? Metal?" Emery asked, spitting the water after they emerged.

"It could be carved granite."

"What do you think it is?"

"I think it is a...dam of sorts?"

Emery drew in a deep breath and dove back in.

Sebastian snorted, rubbed his eyes and rumbled before deeply inhaling and diving. "So damn impatient."

He found her barely visible among the sediments she stirred, digging on the side of the dark shape. She saw him through the cloud of fine particles pointing to something on the bottom, where she dug. She had exposed a depression that contained a long handle. As soon as she did, she swam up, and Sebastian followed.

"Did you see that? It's a lever," she said after they emerged.

Sebastian nodded. They looked at each other and swam to the other end to find the second structure. They dove together. An identical lever in a depression was where they expected it would be. Emery reached for the lever, but Sebastian touched her arm, pointing up.

"Should we try?" Emery asked when they surfaced.

"I think we should go back on board and talk about it."

"Why? Why not just do it?"

"Because we might have to move her out quickly if the water

starts dropping fast. Not sure if it would, but if it does, we must be ready."

"The two of us? I don't know how to sail."

"Exactly. And it has been a while for me."

～

Sebastian tended to Emery's arm and leg, wrapping them in strips of cloth he'd ripped from a shirt he found in a drawer.

"Boy, you heal like a cat. Even faster than I do," Sebastian said, shaking his head. "The scratch on the leg is not deep. You'll live. The arm will take a few more days."

Emery and Sebastian spent the night in the captain's quarters on top of the captain's bed with a mattress so comfortable, Emery squealed in delight when she dramatically plopped on it. After studying the boat, Sebastian concluded that they needed at least six men to man *Discovery* and get her ready to sail. After a long debate, they decided to return to town and meet with the Timothy bunch, hoping they could still get in touch despite being a few days late for their meeting. Emery also hoped that Sigil didn't stumble into town, disclosing their secret.

"What if they guess I'm not a captain and not even a man?"

"The alternative of getting safely onboard a plane for you is much worse. We can fool a few pirates, but fooling a few hundred trained soldiers would be much harder."

The next morning before leaving, Emery packed a book on sailing.

～

Timothy and his sons were still in town and still willing to get on board *Discovery* and had lined up three more people eager to join the pirate's life: two younger men, Darnell and Renald, and Timothy's friend Anthony. Emery saw the excitement ooze out of the younger men's eyes when they met them at the tavern. They've heard stories about life at sea and all the adventures. They might have been told about the looting and killing, but not having done it, they probably hadn't thought deeply of what it actually meant. The older men, who remembered what it was like, were enthused, but their excitement was more subdued and carried a weight that showed in their hard eyes.

Timothy and his friend Anthony, who was closer to his age, had been part of the original *Discovery* crew and knew the ship well. They were not surprised to hear about the dam and seemed to have some knowledge of what to expect. Sebastian's caution was justified, Anthony said. The water would drain fast, and *Discovery* had to be ready to sail once they opened the dam. Sebastian trusted the men enough to show them the map in hopes they would know where it drained to and if they should expect government interference when they emerged from the cave. Timothy wasn't concerned about it, but Anthony was more cautious.

"I've heard from a mate of mine that they suspect Blizzard hid her somewhere, and they might be on the lookout for her," he said.

"It's been a while," Timothy said. "Do you think they'd still be searching for her?"

"Might. She was a big deal."

After the men left, Emery and Sebastian went back to their old room in the tavern, which was serendipitously still unoccupied and waiting for them with new sheets.

"How did Blizzard manage to do all this by himself? Build the dam and hide the ship?" Emery asked, yawning.

"He couldn't have. He must have had help."

"I wonder what happened to his helpers."

"I wondered that too."

44

SETTING HER FREE

Loaded with supplies, the six men, Emery, and Sebastian took off for the mountains. They would get more supplies at the port of Madulla, sitting farther up north on an island and known for its affinity for pirates and their lavish spending habits and for its dislike of government.

When they reached the fork in the tunnel, Sebastian and Emery exchanged a glance when they discovered the right tunnel had been obliterated by boulders. Had Sigil followed them, taken the wrong tunnel, and found his last resting place?

Timothy and Anthony's demeanor changed once they boarded *Discovery*. Confident before, they now saturated the surrounding air with coolness and authority. Their voices, sharp and decisive, cut through the air like the blades that hung from their leather belts. It was their home, their work, and probably their love. The younger men followed their orders with ease and efficiency, as if they had done all the tasks associated with setting the sails all their lives.

When they discussed who would dive and release the levers, Emery opened her mouth and was ready to raise her hand to volunteer, but Sebastian must have expected it, because he moved closer to her, then seized and squeezed her hand.

She guessed he didn't fully trust them not to leave her behind as they all glanced at her furtively while carrying out their tasks. She stood on the deck watching the young men dive into the water. Sebastian stayed and worked alongside the remaining sailors rigging the sails. His eyes shone, and the smile on his face was different. Almost dreamy.

When the moment arrived after the sails were hoisted, Emery, clutching the railing, breathed deeply to steady her galloping heart. This was a moment of reckoning: victory or defeat, success or failure.

Soon after the two youngest men, Steven and Maddox, emerged from the water and started climbing up the ladder, there was an enormous swirl, and the water immediately started receding. *Discovery* moved and danced in place as if she were a racehorse ready to gallop but constrained by the reins held by its master. With the water lowering, more light seeped from under the lake, and soon they could see a passage emerging ahead. Soon, *Discovery* would be free after fifteen long years in her underground prison. Her sails came alive when the sun and wind reached them, teasing them with a gentle breeze. Captain Blizzard knew what he was doing anchoring here. Timothy predicted the wind direction just right, and *Discovery* jerked and sailed out eagerly and proudly, flaunting her golden sails.

Emery exhaled. Sebastian smiled his wistful smile.

The sky was clear, the sun was brilliant, and the wind was perfect. Everything was perfect except for the ship waiting for them as soon as they cleared the cave's exit.

It wasn't nearly as big or magnificent or even taken-care-of as *Discovery*, but the gaping holes of the giant cannons mounted on the side and facing them drained the blood from the faces of even the toughest sailors. For a long moment, there was silence. Even the sea quieted, waiting, holding its breath, and betting on who would be victorious if a battle erupted.

Emery pursed her lips to stop a cry from escaping.

Discovery was heading toward the ship, and nobody was stopping her; all stood motionless, held captive by the shock and at the sight before them.

It was Timothy who spoke first. "This is not a government ship. Judging from its build, it was at one time, but the flags are all wrong, and she is just too run-down. It might be a …"

"Pirate ship," Anthony said.

"What could they want from us?" Emery asked. *Pirates don't attack other pirates, do they?* She realized she should be commanding the crew somehow, but she hadn't gotten to that point in the book yet. Instead, she gave Timothy a slight nod and a look that meant "you're in charge."

Timothy nodded. "They could be pirate hunters…bounty hunters," he said, and turned around to face his crew.

Suddenly everyone came back to life as Timothy barked orders to change the course to avoid ramming into the ship. *Discovery* would obliterate the other ship, but not without taking damage herself.

Anthony stood holding a megaphone in one hand and a brass telescope pressed to his eye with the other. "They are waving at us, trying to get our attention," he said. "They don't appear hostile. Maybe they're not after us," he wondered aloud.

"But they're pointing their cannons at us," Steven said.

"Ask them what they want," Emery said in a commanding tone, surprising herself.

Anthony pressed the megaphone to his mouth, glancing at Emery as if asking for confirmation. She nodded and released her breath, relieved that he had asked for her consent.

"What do you want?" Anthony roared through the megaphone.

Because she was standing close to Anthony, the sound was deafening. Emery started reaching for her ears but caught herself.

The sound of the other ship's megaphone reached them, but distorted, and only one word came clearly: "…talk …"

"You want to talk? About what?"

"…aboard…captain…"

"They want to come aboard and talk to us," Anthony said.

"We could just go around them. Isn't *Discovery* the fastest ship ever?" Steven asked.

"What about their cannons? What if they use them?"

"Tell them to send two people. The captain and…the cook," Emery said, and then felt the heavy gazes of eight men on her. She tensed and drew her brows together to hold off the blood rushing to her cheeks. "They won't attack us if the captain is here, and certainly not if the cook is here too," she said. She couldn't be sure if her voice was steady because she couldn't quite hear herself, deafened by fear and self-doubt.

It wasn't a full smile, but Timothy's eyes brightened. Anthony sounded his megaphone, conveying what Emery had said. The mangled message sounded back, but nobody was sure what it said.

Anthony shrugged. "I think they said yes."

"Watch them," Emery said, and turned toward Timothy. "We must be ready to sail if they sound at all hostile. Keep everything set. We'll see what they want first."

A dinghy hit the water with a splash. Anthony kept his eye in the scope and confirmed, sticking two fingers out, that two people had jumped into it.

After they had climbed aboard *Discovery*, they took their hats off and bowed to the crew. Both were stocky and dark-haired, wearing clothes that had lost their newness a long time ago and now were barely presentable. One remained quiet and kept his eyes on his boots, looking up only when asked a question. Emery guessed he was the cook and simply asked what he had prepared for today. He shrugged and answered. "Beans with bacon, rice, and cabbage," he said, and added, looking into her eyes. "Thick bacon slices. Nice and crispy."

She nodded, satisfied, and shifted her gaze to the other man. "Are you the captain?"

"Yeah. It's an honor to be standing on the deck of the Queen of the Sea. I never thought I would live to—"

"What did you want to talk about?" Emery asked. Her eyes burrowed into his, searching for deceit.

"Yeah, he…the thing is, we've got some really good sailors on our *Lady Amada* over there. This here, *Discovery,* is a big ship, and she needs many sailors, many splendid sailors. We offer our help."

He finished and kept his gaze on Emery for a while, then shifted his gaze to Sebastian and then Timothy, but their eyes were focused on Captain Emer, the captain of *Discovery*.

Emery took her time to answer, not letting the intensity of her gaze waver. She wondered if he could see the golden dots light up her eyes under the shade of the hat. "She requires exceptional sailors, not just good ones. Your *Lady Amada* is a tiny vessel. How can you help us?"

He shifted his weight. "I'm Captain Nugget. I had a large ship, but she was taken from me and burned. They feared she could take *Discovery*'s place."

"You're Nugget, the captain of *Lady Storm*?" Anthony asked, coming forward to take a better look at the visitor. "I'll be damned. It is you!" Anthony said, and turned toward Emery, beaming. "Captain Emer, he is telling the truth. We all heard about his ship and his endeavors. And we don't have a proper cook. Our Maddox, if you don't watch him, will turn the best meat into leather."

"How many men do you have?" Emery asked.

"Six of us, captain. And Bert, the cook," Captain Nugget answered quickly and pushed his chest forward.

"Why do you want to join us?"

He opened his mouth but didn't answer right away and glanced at Anthony. "To go pirating. What else?"

"Until you prove yourself, your cut will be half of what my crew will take. Understood?"

"Aye, aye, Captain," Nugget pushed his chest forward and saluted.

They do say aye Captain.

"What were you planning to do with your ship if we accept you?"

"We'll moor her at Madulla."

"Bring all your people over tomorrow evening so I can meet them. Meanwhile, set the sails for Madulla. We will do the same."

"You want all of us to come tomorrow?"

"Is that a problem?"

"No, not at all."

Emery nodded and glanced at *Lady Amada*. "See you later, Captain Nugget."

~

"You did well there. A real captain couldn't have done better," Sebastian said later when they sat in the captain's quarters. His voice sounded thicker and lower. "You reminded me of my sister as I saw her in my dreams. Proud and commanding. When she spoke, everyone paid attention."

"I can't wait to meet her."

Sebastian lowered his gaze. "I'm bunking in the first mate's quarters so it won't look weird. You know where it is if you need to find me," he added, and bent toward her and planted a kiss on her head. She smiled and kissed his cheek. "Your hair is growing out," he said before leaving.

Emery savored the solitude. She exhaled so much stale air out of her lungs, she could extinguish a burning fire. She nibbled on the bread and cheese Sebastian had brought her and glanced at the sailing book. "I'd better finish you, huh?"

She smiled to herself. Sebastian's compliment had left her in a dreamy and lofty mood. But it didn't last long when she remembered Captain Nugget's face, and especially his shrewd eyes when he looked at her. *Does he suspect I'm a woman? Nah, a guy like that wouldn't obey orders from a woman.*

She detected melancholy in Sebastian's voice when he mentioned his sister and thought about Frederick for the first time in days. Safe now, protected by her status as a captain, Emery daydreamed, remembering his eyes and his lips when they pursed in pain. She drew her knees to her chin, wrapped her arms around them, and lay on the bed, trying to remember her past life and the things she could have done to him. She imagined herself stabbing him or betraying him in the worst way, but the actual memories would not come.

They came later, in the deepest darkness of the night. She clutched her throat, gasping for air and remembering leaving Frederick, whose real name was Peter, to fight the Minders alone as she'd fled to find the truth about her mother and to stop the Masters from depriving people of their humanity. He died because of her. Protecting her. But he told her to go. He didn't stop her or even try to. No, Peter wasn't angry at her. The tears that came were hot and burned her cheeks.

My mother invented preontechnology in this world and then disappeared. Does it mean she was behind the change? She really was behind the deaths of billions of people?

She shuddered as the memories of Sebastian and his sister came flooding in. It was as if she were watching a fast-moving movie and being a part of it but not being able to move. Floating from scene to scene. The complex, malevolent, beautiful Zoe. Was Sebastian evil too, or just doing what Zoe had asked of him? Had he been lying to her all this time, secretly leading her to Zoe so she could kill her or do whatever she did to her mother? She oscillated between believing he was acting on Zoe's behalf and believing that he really was her grandfather in this world and cared about her. Could he have faked the affection he had shown her throughout their journey?

She told herself the rocking of the ship, not the burden of not knowing and suspecting Sebastian, whom she'd already loved, had her trapped in the bathroom, vomiting. When there was nothing left in her stomach but bile, she washed her face and looked into the mirror and saw a contorted white face looking back at her. She sighed, splashed more water on her face, and returned to bed. But she realized sleep would not return that night. She covered her face with her hands and rocked on the bed. As she rocked, streams of older memories began flooding her mind. She remembered Sasha and Lev, her loving grandparents, and she remembered Regis, her faithful black dog. When she remembered herself in her mother's arms, a cry muffled by her hands escaped her lips. "It was better not to remember."

Emery avoided Sebastian's gaze and tried to hide her swollen eyes, pulling the hat down to cover her face while she stood holding on to the railing watching *Lady Amada* trail behind them.

"Is something the matter?" he asked, standing beside her.

"I remembered my mother," she said after a long silence.

"Oh, so they were good memories, then?"

She nodded.

"Then why are you crying?"

"I miss her. I didn't remember that I loved her so much."

"It will get easier," Sebastian said and patted her on the back. "You butchered your hair. You should've let me cut it," he said and left, and she watched him covertly as he walked toward Anthony.

Sebastian was winning the crew's hearts and respect with his humor and his knowledge of sailing. He told her that once he engaged in rigging the ship, surrounded by sailors, like-minded vagabonds, his sailing skills resurfaced, and now he felt at home. Oh, how she wanted to believe he wasn't wicked like Zoe.

By evening, her eyes were no longer swollen and red. She had finished her book and headed toward the door. It was time to meet the crew of *Lady Amada,* which was soon to be her crew. Her glance landed on a bottle containing golden liquid inside a glass cabinet. It smelled of old oak, earth, and smoke. Maybe even a hint of the ocean. She took a long sip. It was as strong as it smelled and as good. She wiped her chin and marched out.

A dinghy was approaching. Sebastian was talking to Anthony and Maddox, discussing fixing some sails. Emery held the telescope to her eye. She held her breath, and, certain her mind was seeing things that weren't there, she pressed the lens so tightly to her eye that her knuckles blanched. She moved the instrument away and rubbed her eyes. Then she looked again. She felt the blood drain from her face, which now matched the color of her knuckles, as she watched a familiar figure picking up another familiar figure from the wooden seat and propping him against the *Discovery's* ladder.

Peter, her Peter, known to others in this world as Frederick, climbed the wooden rungs effortlessly with just his hands and arms, hugging the ladder with his torso. He looked up and met Emery's gaze as she finally peeled the lens from her eyes that burned from being opened too wide for too long.

Peter shook his head lightly. She understood.

Next, Thomas, her friend, whose friendship got her through the dreariness of the gray city, known to everyone as Sam, looked at her with the same expression and the same imperceptible head movement. How was she supposed to keep calm when her heart just would not stop pounding, when she wanted to cry out in joy?

He searched for me. He is here for me, so he must not hate me.

She pulled her hat deeper over her face and willed her lips to still and her eyes to stay hard and cold. She thought of Zoe.

Once the first two sailors from the *Lady Amada* appeared on the deck, they helped Frederick up and sat him in a folding chair they had brought with them.

Once they were all aboard, Captain Nugget addressed her, smoothing his jacket.

"We are all here as you requested, Captain Emer."

"I see that," Emery said slowly. Her own voice sounded alien to her but comfortingly steady. "Introduce them and tell me why they deserve to serve *Discovery*," she said and planted her eyes on Frederick. "Why is he here? We need strong and able men."

"Don't be deceived by his appearance, captain. This man has a big brain. He figured out where to find you. And he's as strong and stubborn as an ox, maybe even stronger."

Emery cocked her head and slowly shifted her gaze to Nugget. "Why would we need his brains?"

"He knows all about the cargo ships that cross the ocean between Andalia and Sinturija. He somehow learned and memorized their sailing schedule. With him aboard, we'll know who to loot and when. He even knows when they'll be shipping emeralds to Andalia. Emeralds! Do you know what that means? I'd say he is the second most valuable one. After me, that is," he said, and adjusted his hat.

"Go on, tell me about the rest of your men."

Captain Nugget exhaled and recited with pride the accomplishments of his people. They were all the best robbers in Andalia. Great with their knives and swords. "This one, Nicco," he said proudly, pointing to a scruffy, bearded man whose brown muscles bulged out of his blue vest, "can fight two big men at once as if they were mere children."

Nicco stepped forward and bowed as much as his swollen neck muscles allowed.

Next, he introduced his two younger men, Scott and Renald, and finally Sam as the other smart man, who could mend people's wounds.

After the introductions, everyone gathered in the mess to eat and get to know each other over malt. Emery imagined malt could loosen tongues and build instant camaraderie but could also heighten insecurities and bring out the destructive traits that might otherwise stay hidden until after the new shipmates joined the crew.

Sipping her malt, calm on the outside while scrambling inside, Emery devised ways to meet secretly with Peter and Thomas. She glanced at Sebastian, who seemed not to have recognized Peter. He had only met him once, just before she'd joined Zoe in the chamber, but it was a memorable event. If he recognized him and was hiding it from her, then he is taking her to Zoe. No, she dismissed it quickly. Sebastian couldn't be that deceptive, could he?

Toasts were made, voices grew louder, laughter rose—first coyly, then more energetically as the sailors exchanged their stories of plundering and killing. Emery listened until she heard her name spoken in a deep baritone.

Nicco stared at her, pursing his lips. "Tell us your stories, Captain Emer."

Her mind was blank. For a moment, she couldn't remember her name when the panic darkened everything around her. Out of the shadowy darkness, an image emerged. At first elongated and blurry, then the figure took shape. The beard was first, then the imposing figure of Edward Teach, known as Blackbeard. She inhaled and recounted what she had read about the most famous pirate, telling them about his signature ship, the Queen Anne's Revenge, and the notorious blockade of Charleston. Curious about their reaction, she also fudged and added that her first mate was a woman, Anne Bonny, one of the meanest pirates ever. They listened with interest and cheered her on. Interestingly enough, the mention of Anne stirred no protests or disbelief. She caught Peter's smile.

"What lands are those you speak of?" Nugget asked.

"Lands of unlimited gold and precious stones, riches you never imagined. That's a secret I share only with the most loyal, and time will tell if you're one of them."

"I've heard about those lands," Peter said.

"Where are they?" Nugget asked, leaning toward Peter.

"I will not go against Captain Emer's wishes. He'll tell you if he wants to, but I can tell you this: It's worth the wait."

Peter's unassuming and natural self-assurance, enhanced by years of being a detective and a Minder, immediately curbed everyone's desire to ask more questions. And seeing that flash of confidence in his eyes, and hearing the power in his voice, her chest constricted. She eyed his chest and arms, imagining herself in his embrace.

Sebastian eyed Peter as if he had just noticed him and waited relentlessly for Peter to lock eyes with him. Something passed between them. Emery noticed it but couldn't guess what it was. She couldn't ask Peter, nor Sebastian. The opportunity to see Peter and Thomas would not come before they reached port to stock up and moor *Lady Amada*. Even a day was too much. She inched closer to Peter when they were leaving and inhaled his scent. Suddenly, Thomas, having Peter leaning on him, stumbled and bumped into Emery. She felt a hand quickly slide in and out of her pocket.

Until she was certain Sebastian was not deceiving her, she only exchanged a few words with him, mostly concerning the ship, and told him she had motion sickness. He agreed she should stay in her quarters to avoid detection. "How would a fierce captain look if he were caught puking his guts out?" he said. On her way back to the captain's quarters, she caressed the piece of paper in her pocket as if it were Peter's hand.

With trembling hands, she read the note in which Peter drew a map of Madulla with directions to a meeting spot, marked with an 'X.' Moments later, Sebastian brought her tea and hard biscuits. Whether he believed her, she wasn't sure, but looking at her reflection in the mirror, the lie didn't seem so obvious. The dark rings and gray face would not inspire confidence from her sailors. Confined to her room while awaiting the opportunity to talk to Peter, she read everything she could about ships and navigation. In search of more books, she found a hidden compartment in a bottom drawer, and inside it, a wooden box. Her jaw dropped when she opened it. The box was full of gold coins, rings, and gems that looked like rubies.

Two days later, a small flock of noisy seagulls greeted *Discovery,* circling around the masts and pointing the way to the port of Madulla. And soon the lush island with large rocks flanking it on both sides, buildings taller than Emery had seen anywhere in Andalia, emerged from the sea haze. Another ship, much smaller than *Discovery,* was docked in the harbor. The harbor was surprisingly large for an island. *Lady Amada* docked gracefully ahead of them, and then *Discovery* docked alongside it, taking the rest of the dock with its bulk.

Oh, shit! she thought, stepping out onto the land, which seemed alive, moving under her feet. She glanced around, but nobody seemed to notice that the earth was wobbly. Sebastian must have been expecting it, trotting close behind her and steadying her with a quick tap on the back, while holding her elbow. That was enough for her to regain her balance. After they stepped onto the street, she lied, telling Sebastian she needed some privacy to do some girl shopping with the coins she'd found. The night before, she'd shown him the box, and his eyes flashed. He'd taken a handful of coins to get provisions for the trip and closed the box. "That's a lot of money. Keep it here."

Alone at last, Emery smiled, imagining seeing Peter. Her heart was behaving strangely, one moment skipping beats, another pounding like a rabbit's heart in fast, tiny drums. She followed the handwritten directions on the map Peter had so skillfully planted in her pocket and quickly found an obscure basement tavern at the end of town. It was tucked into a small alley with its aged sign barely legible above the brown door. Peter and Thomas were already there, both wearing dark clothes that made them barely discernible from the drab walls, hunched in a dark corner of a dingy room. But she recognized Peter right away. It was his blue eyes gleaming in the shadows, like a window to the sky that beckoned her.

When she approached them, Thomas smiled, got up, and gave her a quick hug. Peter watched her with such hunger in his eyes that her legs bent under her. She barely made it to the bench, holding on to a weathered old table bearing scratches as deep as if a tiger had clawed them.

"Peter," she whispered.

"You remember?" Thomas and Peter asked at the same time.

"Everything?" Thomas asked.

"Yes. I think so, Thomas."

"You can't call us that on the ship. We're known as Sam and Frederick."

"I'll be careful. How did you find me?"

"Long story," Frederick said. "But the short version is that Narius drove us to the town of Covignon, where we overheard a very interesting conversation between the sailors and learned the whereabouts of Captain Blizzard—"

"But he is long dead."

"Yeah, we noticed. We also noticed that someone ransacked his boat," Frederick said, and cocked his head. "Was it you?"

"Yes, we were looking for the map."

"I was hoping it was you. Actually, we were nearly sure it was you overhearing one of them telling his friends that a witch threw him flying in the air without touching him," Peter said.

"Sigil. How did you even know to look for the ship?"

"Oh, Emery, you underestimate our hound friend. He brought a library with him, much to Narius's annoyance, and was already on *Discovery's* scent even before we overheard Sigil. We knew the captain hid her somewhere in a cave. And then Frederick dug out an ancient story about a subterranean lake," Thomas said.

"But we had to be certain, so we searched the captain's boat one more time and..." Frederick trailed off, smiling.

"And what?"

"We found a map hidden underneath the frame of the—"

"The painting, of course." Emery smacked her forehead with the back of her hand.

Peter exchanged a telling glance with Thomas. Thomas got up and left.

"Emery, I wanted to say how sorry..." Peter started, but his voice faltered.

Emery touched his cheek. "I know why you said what you said and why you behaved like an idiot."

"I did, and I'm sorry," he whispered and grasped her hands. "Tell me about Sebastian. Why are you with him, and how did you find him?"

"He found me. Well, he may have saved my life," Emery said, and told him about the attack.

His blue eyes darkened, and his hands tightened around Emery's as she told the story. Thomas returned as she finished her story. The stillness of Peter's face alarmed him, and Emery had to repeat the story.

"Do you believe him?" Thomas asked.

Emery's face twitched. "I don't know. Sometimes I do, and sometimes I think he is taking me to Zoe."

"You don't think he remembers Zoe tried to kill you and your mother?"

"I don't think so," she said, remembering his eyes when he talked about his daughter and the teddy bear he had carried for so many years. "And if he did, I don't think he would let her hurt me or my mother."

"He recognized you," Thomas said to Peter. "Didn't he? The way he looked at you."

"I'm not sure. There was a question in his eyes when he looked at me. I glared at him intentionally to elicit an acknowledgment, but I didn't get one. And he doesn't strike me as an actor."

"No, he's not," Emery said. "He's spontaneous, not calculated at all."

"You must still be careful," Peter said.

Emery curled up on the bed, hugging the pillow. The tension she had felt since stepping onto *Discovery* disappeared after meeting Peter and Thomas. She returned to the ship, thinking about Peter's carefully crafted plan to sail to Sinturija and ditch the pirates once they got there, and her chest was light again and she could breathe. What was left was a numbing exhaustion, and, like a child, she slept for twelve hours until banging on the door woke her. Sebastian charged in.

"We are ready to sail. Everyone is onboard and ready for your commands. Are you up for it? I tried to wake you twice before, but you were out. I didn't worry, though, because I saw the color returning to your cheeks. Maybe the stable ground helped."

"I am absolutely ready," Emery chirped, and jumped out of the bed.

"Do something about your crow's nest, though." Sebastian grinned, pointing at her head. "Glad you're better."

Getting under sail had gone well, with Emery giving out flawless commands that she had practiced in front of an old mirror, even though they were just perfunctory orders. The crew knew what to do, but the captain's commanding tone boosted the merry atmosphere among the crew. Emery saw the excitement, anticipation, and relief on their faces and the respectful and grateful glances they sent her way. Sebastian told her about the hushed conversations the crew had been having in the galley about the mysterious young captain who had found what others couldn't. The story she told them about the secret lands overflowing with riches only added to the mystery.

"We've got to be on constant alert because the harmony on a pirate ship ebbs just like the sea does," Sebastian said. "Hope the Fred guy knows what he's talking about and we run into some cargo ships so they can loot and be merry."

"Yeah, I worry about that," Emery said.

"What are you worried about?"

"Looting, I could probably live with, but not..."

"Killing?"

Emery nodded. "They've been waiting for this, and I'm afraid of what all that pent-up energy might look like when finally released."

"The older guys like Anthony and Timothy are pretty levelheaded."

Emery's eyes were focused on the carpet as if she were counting its threads. She cleared her throat. "Maybe we could play the Robin Hood card?"

"The what?"

"You seriously don't know who Robin Hood was?"

"No. Another pirate tale?"

Emery searched his face but found his wide eyes blank. "You really don't remember."

"Should I? Did I know this guy?"

"No, but every kid in our world did."

Emery told him the tale of the legendary outlaw.

When she was done, a flash of comprehension lit his eyes. "You want to convince the pirates to give most of what they steal to the poor?"

"Not most, but some—"

"It will never work."

"If we sell it to them as beneficial…"

"How?"

"Payment for keeping their secret. Isn't that what got them caught last time? Didn't the locals alert the government when they were in town? If they were getting a steady stream of gold, they'd never have told on them."

Sebastian got up from his chair. He stretched and scratched his head. "You've got a point. Sort of."

"Do you think you can sell it to them?"

He grinned. "I'll see what I can do."

"Hey, before you leave, what's so special about the emeralds from Sinturija?"

Sebastian rolled his eyes. "Oh, some fools believe they have special properties. Magical and therefore very valuable."

"In what way?"

"I don't know. I paid no attention to those tales, but I can ask if—"

"No, don't bother."

45

THE GREEN SULINA

During the after-dinner celebration of the journey's start, Sebastian successfully implanted the idea of tipping the residents of towns they visited for provisions into the minds of most of the pirates. They grumbled at first. The idea of parting with a portion of the loot seemed abhorrent, but Sebastian finally convinced them with his boyish charm and canine smile.

"Women would love us," he said. "Just imagine them lining up for those jewels, gold, and titanium pieces."

Not everyone seemed to be thrilled with the idea. Nicco narrowed his eyes at Sebastian and lifted his bulk off the chair, sending the wooden thing skidding on the floor and landing behind him with a thud. "For those who want to touch those dirty whores, they can give them their spoils."

As he finished, he set his mug on the table and pushed it down until it shattered. He then pressed his palm into the sharp pieces until his hand bled while glaring at Sebastian. His white teeth studded with gold glistened as his lips tightened around them.

Sebastian leaned back in his chair and grinned. "No need to get upset, mate. You don't have to hang out with girls. There are plenty of boys around."

Roaring laughter. Nicco's cheeks were ablaze. He snatched a broken piece of his glass mug and, so armed, swung his hand at Sebastian. The protruding mass of sculpted muscles blurred. Sebastian, still seated, seized Nicco's burly arm with one hand as if it were a child's and applied pressure to his elbow with the other. Nicco kneeled before Sebastian, exposing his teeth in a scowl. Sebastian increased the pressure. Nicco's brown eyes dulled. The laughter died. Some sailors stood up, watching in silence, but none moved toward them.

Sebastian smiled. "Looks like your mug is broken, mate. What do you say we have a toast? To knowing yourself."

Two mugs full of malt appeared. Sebastian released Nicco and grabbed his mug, pointing at the other with his eyes. The distant crash of waves. A buzzing fly. No one breathed. Nicco's face smoothed out, and he reached for the mug and clanked it against Sebastian's. With the clank, everyone breathed in, sucking out the stale air from the room. The excited sparks died in the eyes of the younger men. The older men nodded and resumed their conversations. Nicco finished his malt in three gulps and left, shuffling his colossal feet as if they were attached to chains, ignored by everyone.

Peter, who sat across from Sebastian, picked up a mug and toasted him.

Later that evening, Emery told Sebastian about Peter and Sam and how much they meant to her. Sebastian nodded as she told the story of meeting Peter in the gray city and befriending Thomas.

"I thought he looked familiar. Now, that you said it, I remember him. He is a good guy and I'm glad that he and Thomas found you."

For Emery, the next few weeks were magical. As a captain, she could spend time with Peter to map out their course to intersect the cargo ships sailing to and from Sinturija. Sometimes, Timothy and Anthony joined them, nodding at the detailed plans drawn by Peter and checking their current course. When that happened, Emery pursed her lips and fought the urge to scream at them to get the hell out of her wheelhouse.

But it wasn't much better when she was alone with him. Their hands never touched, and their smiles died before they left their lips. But they could talk all they wanted. Anyone walking by and looking through the large wheelhouse's windows could see the young captain and the navigator engaged in serious conversations, and it would not occur to them that the two of them were involved in any way other than planning the ship's course. Emery and Peter did not talk about their feelings, knowing that once they did, they'd go over the thin, spiderlike line that allowed them to stay on opposite sides of the charged space between them.

Their secret conversations were always about finding her mother and guessing what Zoe had masterminded this time. Emery convinced Peter that Sebastian was clueless about his sister's intentions, insisting that he didn't remember Zoe's manipulations, malicious actions, and lies. But remembering how close the twins were, she secretly wondered whether she could bear his betrayal if he chose Zoe over her mother or her.

Peter learned roughly where the Igres family lived and assured her that finding them wouldn't take long. They didn't have a plan beyond that point.

After four weeks, they were about to come across a shipment of emeralds from Sinturija to Andalia. Emery crossed her arms, standing on the deck beside Timothy and Sebastian, pressing her lips into a thin line so they would not twitch. Peter sat in his chair outfitted with wheels that Thomas had found during their visit to Madulla, as they'd left his wheelchair sitting in front of Peter's house in their hurry to start the search for her.

When the large container ship appeared on the horizon, Peter searched for her eyes and held them hostage. His eyes were deep blue despite the brightness of the sun already high on the horizon. Emery never imagined blue could be so warm. Her lips stopped twitching, and her chin moved up a few inches. He nodded in encouragement. Her heart smiled.

Maddox and Steven stood ready with grappling hooks to latch onto the ship while Anthony and Timothy stood by the cannons that were ready to fire at Emery's signal. The ship, *Green Sulina*, was full of wood and emeralds, according to Peter. If the *Green Sulina's* crew cooperated, they would not need their cannons. Nonviolent interceptions of goods, according to Timothy, had happened more often than not. Why would the crew risk their lives for other people's riches or the government's property?

The pirate flag hoisted up on the highest mast flopped in the wind, making the bright red irises against the white eyes and black background appear as if they were searching for a target. With steady hands, Sebastian held the megaphone, glanced at Emery, and winked.

True to Timothy's prediction, after a longish megaphone exchange, the crew agreed for the pirates to come aboard. The freight ship was not prepared for an encounter with a pirate ship. None of the commercial ships were prepared for such confrontations anymore, since the *Discovery* was thought to have been destroyed, opting to carry more cargo instead of the heavy cannons. Loaded to the brim with cargo, the ship couldn't outrun the fastest pirate ship in history.

Steven and Darnell operated the grappling device as if they had done it all their lives. Once the gangway, strung together with rope and wooden planks, was lowered into place, Sebastian, accompanied by Anthony, Maddox, and Nicco, walked across. A row of sailors wearing navy uniforms with purple-and-red stripes crossing their chests met them. There was no animosity or fear on the faces of the freighter's crew. Mostly curiosity and perhaps a little awe. After all, what man would not envy the freedom and lawlessness the pirate life offered?

Emery was engrossed in her thoughts, watching her people through the lens of the telescope, sequestering ten wooden containers, and carrying them back to *Discovery* across the rickety walkway. Sebastian and Maddox carried the last box when a skirmish erupted behind them. They tensed, dropped the box, and turned around. Nicco, with his sword unsheathed, shouted at four *Green Sulina* sailors, who were backing away, forming a unified front. Nicco roared, saliva dripping from his open mouth as he, with the agility and the energy of a cougar, lunged at the retreating men. Blood poured as he sliced and thrust his sword into the flesh of the unarmed sailors. One *Green Sulina* sailor came running from the back, wielding an ax above his head. But his ax tasted no flesh. The sailor's eyes bulged and then rapidly blinked when a stream of red liquid covered his face. His arm, firmly attached to the ax, fell onto the wooden planks, then his head, and his body. Nicco had sharpened his sword well.

Through the telescope, Emery saw only the gangway bouncing and Maddox's hand slipping off the thin rope railing, his arms flailing as he plunged into the ocean. She moved her lens to the ship and saw Sebastian coming behind Nicco, who had his sword up, ready to thrust it into another body, kicking his giant feet from under him. The thick legs bent at an odd angle, and Nicco fell on his face, still clutching his sword. Emery saw Sebastian bend toward Nicco and saw Nicco's enormous chest covered with blood, rising and falling, and then his arm thrusting his sword at Sebastian. Her hand flew to her mouth, expecting Sebastian's body to slump by Nicco's, but she didn't see the ending, jerking at a hand touching her shoulder. Emery spun around.

"What's happening?" Anthony asked, taking his hand off her shoulder. "What are they doing?"

"I don't know," she said, wishing she had said nothing because her voice betrayed her and sounded weak and whiny. She turned away and pulled her hat down to hide her face. Anthony tilted his head to see better under the shadow cast by the hat. Emery raised the telescope to her eyes again. The tips of her fingers felt foreign as she held the telescope, watching Nugget bounce on the bridge running toward the *Green Sulina*. The scent of spent tobacco and old leather intensified as Anthony inched closer to her. A hand gripped her shoulder and twisted it. She winced. Anthony held her in a tight grip while studying her face.

"Nugget was right. You're a girl. You're a goddamn girl, not a captain," he hissed.

Emery stayed still, but her mind raced. She could kill him with her power before he could hurt her, but she would reveal her ability, kill a sailor she needed, and face potential mutiny. Her eyes scanned the deck, searching for Peter and Thomas, and saw Timothy, accompanied by Steven, whose knees were buckling under the weight of the thick coiled rope on his shoulders. They were approaching them.

Timothy's face hardened. "What's the matter?" Timothy asked. His eyes darted between Anthony and her. "What're you doing, Anthony?"

"What am I doing? Look at the captain. Look carefully. What do you see?" He increased the pressure while knocking her hat off. Emery grimaced.

"Step away from the captain," Timothy said calmly.

"I tell you what I see, Tim. I see a bloody girl. Our captain is a girl! Just like Nugget said."

Steven shifted his gaze between Emery and Anthony. Suddenly, his lips twisted. "Maddox is in the water, Nicco got crazy and got himself killed, and you bicker about the captain being a girl? Who gives a damn? Isn't she a good captain?" He turned around and ran toward the bridge. He tied the rope to the railing and tossed it into the water. Then he jumped. Darnell, seeing him jump, ran toward the rope and looked down. He didn't pay attention to the confrontation, yelling Maddox's name.

Anthony's jaw dropped. "Who gives a damn? I do. Don't you?" he asked Timothy.

Timothy sighed. "I knew she was a girl the moment I saw her."

"So why didn't you kill her?"

"She gave us *Discovery*...and she *is* a great captain."

Anthony's voice grew an octave higher. "You want to be ordered around by a girl?"

"She's not that bossy."

Still holding her, Anthony grasped his knife.

"Anthony, don't," Timothy said. "We can just drop her off at a port."

"Why bother? We drop her into the sea instead."

As his fingers dug deeper into her muscles, Emery's fear and anger grew. She bit into Anthony's arm. The taste of iron filled her mouth. Screaming, he released her. She kicked him in the groin and backed away a few steps. His face turned scarlet as he clutched his crotch with one hand while walking, half-bent and wailing, toward her, waving the hand that held the knife.

"Don't come any closer. I don't want to hurt you."

"Hurt me? You? I'm gonna show you real hurt."

Timothy grabbed him from behind, but the anger and humiliation infused Anthony with inhuman strength. He pushed his friend away and lunged at him, slicing his chest open. Timothy rolled onto his back, and his head hit the hardwood.

Anthony flashed his eyes and curved his mouth in a menacing grin as he lurched forward. Emery cried out and thrust her hands at him, and the silvery-blue wave hit Anthony in the chest and sent him flying. He landed a few feet from Timothy and stopped moving. Emery watched him in silence for a moment, then shifted her gaze to Timothy's ashen face, tracing the blood oozing from his chest and spreading on the shiny planks. The blood was so dark, Emery hoped it was not real.

Thomas, pushing Peter in his makeshift wheelchair, found her hunched on the deck with her face in her hands.

"What happened?" Peter asked.

"Are you hurt?" Thomas asked, reaching for her hand.

She looked up. "I didn't have a choice. He found out I was a girl and attacked me. When Timothy tried to help me, Anthony sliced his chest and killed him."

"Did anyone see you doing this?" Peter asked.

"Steven heard him say I was a girl, but he didn't seem to care, and, no, he didn't see me do this. He and Darnell jumped into the water to search for Maddox, who had fallen down when..." her voice cracked. "I think Sebastian might be dead...Nicco..."

"He is still alive," Thomas said, kneeling by Timothy, listening to his chest and checking his pulse.

Renald and Scott, Nugget's men, came running from the hold where they hauled the boxes.

"What happened?" Renald asked, wiping his brow.

"Timothy and Anthony got into a skirmish," Thomas said. "Timothy is hurt badly. Can you bring the medical gear?"

"Sure," Scott said unsurely, jerking as if ready to leave, but staying as if waiting for Renald's approval.

"What about?" Renald asked, first eyeing Anthony's bloody sword and then shifting his gaze to Emery, who was sitting on the deck. As he stared at her blue eyes, which in the full sun shone with all their intensity, at her bowed, emotion-crimsoned lips, and at the golden hair ruffled by the breeze, his mouth slowly opened.

"I'm guessing the division of the loot," Thomas said.

"Where is Nugget?" Renald asked, not budging from his spot.

Scott stopped and turned, waiting for him and observing the interaction, apparently sensing it was not amiable, the creases on his forehead deepening the longer he watched.

Emery pointed to the *Green Sulina*.

"Medical gear, please?" Thomas asked Scott, then took off his shirt and pressed it to Timothy's chest.

Scott glanced at Renald, and when his buddy nodded, he disappeared into the wheel room.

Renald's eyes shot between Emery and Peter. Peter clasped his arms on his homemade wheelchair, rolled forward, stopped a foot away from Renald, and slowly regarded him. Soon after, Renald shrugged and ran onto the bridge.

"I need to check on Sebastian," Emery said, standing up.

"No, it's too dangerous," Peter said.

"I agree," Thomas added.

"I can't leave him. He might need help."

"As soon as I patch him up, I'll go," Thomas said.

"We need to come up with a story," Peter said, closing his eyes halfway and rubbing his forehead.

"No use," Emery sighed. "Steven heard it. Nugget suspected I was a woman from the beginning."

"But he didn't care, you said."

"He said he didn't."

"I'm going to check on Steven," Peter said to Emery. "Stay here."

Peter rolled his chair to the railing, pulled his body up from his chair and over the railing, and entered the water with a splash.

Emery heard it and ran toward the railing. "What did you do, you fool?" she screamed.

"I'm a good swimmer," he yelled from the water.

Two heads bobbed in and out of the water. The light blond head belonged to Maddox. Steven's head, the darker of the two, rose a little higher, and then his arm reached up for the rope, while the lighter head bobbed lifelessly. Steven appeared exhausted, holding on to his brother while trying to grab the rope. Darnell was nowhere to be seen. And neither was Renald.

Emery shook her boots off and jumped over the railing and into the water. She dove under and searched for the end of the rope. She found the rope and saw Peter diving toward her. Without surfacing even for a moment, with Peter's help, she tied the rope around Madox's torso and legs. Then she popped her head up and glanced at Steven. His blue lips parted while he was breathing unevenly and spitting water, but he locked eyes with her and a flash of understanding and gratitude passed through his eyes.

"Can you pull yourself up?" Emery asked.

"I think so."

"Then go up and pull your brother up and yell for help. Now!"

"Aye, aye, Captain," Steven said and started pulling himself up. Weighed down with the saltwater that was now pouring out of his clothes, he started slowly, but then his speed increased as if the rope were going up by itself.

Emery looked up. Sebastian was pulling Steven and Maddox up. Her face lit up with a smile as she waved at him.

"Hang on, Captain," he yelled.

Emery reached for Peter. He had no trouble staying above water—his muscular arms moved through the surrounding water, creating deep circles.

"What were you thinking?" she asked.

"He looked like he needed help."

She held on to his arm. Then she touched his chest and felt his beating heart. "If I lose you now, I won't have the strength to continue. Don't you dare scare me like that anymore," she whispered. "I found you and am never letting go of you again. No matter what."

After receiving vigorous chest-pounding from his brother, Maddox spewed tons of seawater and opened his eyes to Steven's smiling face.

Meanwhile, Thomas patched Timothy, stitching his wounds with a thick thread and an equally thick needle, then pouring on it half a bottle of rum, and finally dressing it in bandages. Timothy didn't wake up during this ordeal. His two sons stood silently at his feet, their hands moving nervously in their pockets, watching Thomas jab at their father's flesh.

Meanwhile, Sebastian explained what had happened on board of the *Green Salina*, Nicco's madness, and Nugget's reaction to Sebastian's killing Nicco.

"When Nugget showed up, and I told him what happened, he attacked me, yelling Nicco was acting on his orders."

"Did you kill Nugget?" Emery asked.

"No, I didn't kill Nugget. I didn't have to. The *Green Salina* crew avenged their dead mates. I ran and barely made it to *Discovery* before they cut the ropes."

"Where is Renald?" Sam asked.

"I don't know. I haven't seen him."

Scott stood to the side and said not a word.

Emery found her hat, straightened her back, and faced Scott. "Did Nugget tell you to attack the *Green Sulina* crew?"

Scott looked into the hard eyes of the six people, who watched his lips and eyes, expecting an answer. He sighed and hunched his shoulders. "Not all of us. I overheard him telling Nicco to get two extra boxes and to use any means to get them. Nicco didn't have to be told twice."

"Well, Scott, apparently you are the only one left from Captain Nugget's crew. If you make even one wrong move or give any of us one wrong look, you'll be joining your mates. Understand?"

Scott glanced at Peter and Thomas as if expecting their support. Getting none, he shrugged. A sudden insight flashed through his eyes. "Nugget said you're a girl. Why should I listen to a girl?"

"Because I'm the captain and because this is my ship and my crew," Emery said, and took a step toward him. "And I can kick your ass and throw you to the sharks. Do you want to try me?"

The gold dots in her eyes glowed as she glared at him, a tiny smile dancing on her lips.

He might have tried it, taunted by Emery's smirk, despite her weird, glowing eyes and the threatening pose, but he caught the warning frowns on Sebastian and Peter's faces, and he shuffled a step back. He shrugged again and put up his palms facing Emery. "Whatever."

Steven whispered something in his brother's ear. Maddox looked at his brother, then Emery, and said something under his breath.

"We've got nothing against a woman captain," Steven said. "She jumped into the water to save my brother. I have no qualms about it. Our mother could easily have been a captain the way she bossed us around," he added, and gave Emery a boisterous salute, elbowing his brother.

Maddox saluted too. Then both brothers eyed Scott. Peter and Thomas slid their fingers on the sides of their uncovered heads in a salute. Scott shifted his weight and grimaced, glancing at the vast and dark waters of the ocean.

"Aye, Captain," he said, and touched the brim of his hat.

Steven and Maddox took turns tending to their father, who lay on the bed in sick bay, still unconscious.

Darnell or his body was nowhere to be seen. Nobody knew whether he could swim. What happened to Renald was also a mystery, but no one was particularly interested in investigating his mysterious disappearance. Steven suspected Darnell had slipped and hit his head before hitting the water as he heard a thud and a cry, but he didn't look, trying to save his brother.

That evening, the remaining sailors sang. Holding lit torches, the men stood looking out at the quiet, dark ocean and sang a sea shanty, mourning their fallen mates. She heard herself whimper, listening to their voices descending deeper and deeper into the lowest their throats allowed them to go and extending the notes for as long as they could. She could almost see the air vibrate with their low laments. Her eyes burned, but she didn't cry.

With four people gone and one critically injured, the crew now comprised the cook, who was uninterested in anything that didn't involve food and kept to himself, and seven crew members, including Peter and Emery. All hands went to work, setting a course for Sinturija. According to Peter's calculations, in four weeks, they would reach Morena—a Sinturijan port large enough to accommodate *Discovery* and yet allow for a certain amount of concealment from the government. Sinturijans were not as opposed to pirates as Andalians.

Timothy regained consciousness and was slowly recovering. If he saw Emery kill Anthony without using a weapon, he didn't share it with anyone. Considering he was trying to protect her, she trusted him and told him she had business in Sinturija and would permanently leave the ship, and it was his if he wanted it. His eyes told her he wanted *Discovery*, but he held his response until after she repeated her offer.

"I'll take care of her for you," he said.

She smiled. "It's yours once we reach Sinturija."

"I will keep her and tend to her, but if you ever change your mind, she is yours. You saved my sons' lives. I will forever serve you, young Emer."

Emery could only nod, clearing the obstruction from her throat.

Once they reached the port of Morena and moored at the docks, everyone went ashore to sendoff the captain and her friends. Scott decided to stay with Timothy and his sons and even waved at the end. Maddox picked Emery up and squeezed her until her face turned red. She smiled through the cough.

"Thank you, Captain."

46

SINTURIJA

"Beautiful country," Emery said, looking out the window of a big white van they had bought at the port. "No wonder she moved here."

"She didn't have a choice," Peter said. "She would have been imprisoned or executed if she had stayed. Parts of Andalia are beautiful too."

"Peter?"

"What?"

"Nothing. I just love saying your name. I don't have to pretend and lie anymore."

"How far is it to that Nariana town?" Sebastian asked, tapping on the window.

"Four hours, or maybe less, the way Thomas drives," Peter answered and got a chuckle out of Thomas.

"I remember you driving like a maniac," Emery said. "Thomas drives like a grandpa compared to you."

"Here it is," Peter said, pointing at the enormous mansion. "Igres's family estate."

The house looked imposing from afar, but as they drove close enough to see the gray walls, mossy roof, and the garden overgrown with weeds spreading their green limbs over the sculptures and cracked fountains, its neglect became apparent.

A hunched old man, holding on to a black wooden cane opened the door after Emery's pounding with the iron doorknocker. There was no surprise in his cloudy eyes as he appraised them. Silently. Apathetically. He said something no one understood.

"We're here to see Elenora," Emery said.

"Lady Elenora is not expecting visitors," the man said in Andalian, barely moving his mouth and clasping the door to close it.

"It's about her granddaughter and her son. We must speak with her," Emery said, but hearing her own sharp words, she lowered her voice. "Please tell her it's important and that it is about Emery."

The butler's expression changed. He was no longer apathetic. "You go away now. You're not to dredge up this tragedy again," he said, and pushed on the door.

Thomas put his foot in the doorway. "Just tell her what she said."

A woman's voice sounded behind the man, asking something in Sinturijan.

The butler grumbled back something unintelligible.

"We're here to see Lady Elenora," Emery said. "Could you please tell her it is about her granddaughter?"

A pair of blue eyes peeked from behind the old man. "I'll take it from here, Alfred," she said in Andalian. Alfred shuffled away, striking the floor with his cane; the echo of its clanking died as he disappeared into the house.

An older woman with a silvery bun and webs of wrinkles around her eyes and mouth scrutinized her visitors. Her gaze stopped at Emery. "Who are you?" she whispered.

"Lead us to Lady Elenora, please, and I'll explain everything."

"Come in, but you mustn't stay long. She is not well," she said while leading them through a dark hallway to a large room with the curtains drawn and a smell of old dust and medicine in the air. "I'm Milly. I'll be back shortly. Don't upset her."

Lady Elenora still bore her timeless beauty, despite the creases covering her face, the graying hair, and the hollowness of her cheeks. She lay on a sofa propped up by brocade pillows, holding a white crocheted handkerchief in her thin hands with pulsing, purple veins. At her side, a table held rows of vials of different sizes and colors. She glanced at them without interest or comprehension in her still mesmerizing blue eyes. A drop of drool pooled at the corner of her lips.

Emery moved a chair closer to the sofa. As she moved the chair, a cloud of dust stirred. Emery gazed into Elenora's eyes, searching for a sign of awareness or emotion.

"My name is Emery. I'm looking for my mother, Zara. She disappeared twenty-four years ago. I'm here to find her. Could you help me?"

There was no reaction. The void in her eyes was worse than anger, annoyance, or disbelief would have been, Emery lamented in her mind. Elenora would be of no help to them.

Emery's shoulders drooped. "Please, Elenora. Try to remember," she whispered, and touched her hand. Cold and wet to the touch, her hand was lifeless.

"Where is your son?" Peter asked. "Where is Tirg?"

Drool dropped from her mouth and pooled in a darker and soaked area of her dress. She blinked and grabbed Emery's hand. "Dead," she whispered. "Everyone is dead. Except for me."

She hung her head for a moment, then jerked it back up and found Emery's eyes. "She took everything from me. Everyone."

"Who did?" Emery asked.

"Zoe. She did this. Danuta warned me, but I didn't listen," she said, and closed her eyes.

"You know Zoe?" Sebastian asked, moving closer to Elenora. "Where is she?"

"She's done for," Milly said, returning. "She won't say anything more today."

"What's wrong with her?" Emery asked.

"She's heartbroken. She's been like that since they disappeared."

"She said her son Tirg was dead." Peter said, turning his chair toward Milly.

"We don't know. He vanished even before Zara and her baby and Mister Zmey. Such a tragedy. Such horror."

"Why is she taking so many pills?" Emery asked.

"They calm her down."

"Do you know Zoe?" Sebastian asked Milly.

She shook her head.

"Is she always like that?" Emery asked, gently stroking Elenora's forehead.

Elenora's eyes closed and her breath evened.

"Most of the time, she is. Once in a while, she has moments of clarity. Fortunately, not very often."

"Fortunately?" Emery asked.

"It's worse when she remembers everything. She cries and tugs on her hair and wants to jump out a window. Don't look at me like that. Did you see her wrists?"

Emery turned Elenora's wrist. The entire skin from palms up was covered with scars. Emery swallowed.

"I can't keep up with her. I'm too old."

"Can't you hire more people?" Emery asked.

"There is no money. The family fortune is gone. Alfred and I are not getting paid. We stayed because someone has to help her."

"I am sorry," Emery whispered.

"When was the last time you saw Zara or Tirg?" Peter asked.

"After they moved out, I only saw them a few times for family dinners. I don't remember exactly."

"Are there any other family members left? Friends?" Peter asked.

"Most are dead or have moved back to their own homes. You know, after the money was gone, so was the extended family."

Peter's detective mode was just waking up. "Where did Tirg and Zara live before they disappeared?"

"In the old oak grove. Not far from here, but the house has been empty since…"

"Could you give us directions?"

"I certainly can, but I doubt you'll find anything useful there. Elenora and the police combed the place thoroughly," Milley said, and searched the drawers for something to write on. She found a piece of crumpled paper, straightened it, and, sticking the tip of her tongue out, drew a map on the side that was free of ink.

"The house is probably in poor shape," she said, handing Peter the map.

Thomas and Sebastian were loading Peter in when Emery jumped back out of the van and ran back to the house and pounded on the door. Milly opened the door. Emery grabbed her hand and put a handful of gems in it. "This will help you for a while. Take care of her."

"Thank you, Emery. I hope you'll find them."

"What was that all about?" Peter asked.

"I gave her some emeralds. Maybe they'll cure her."

"Are you okay?" Emery asked Sebastian when she sat back in the van. He appeared to have withdrawn into himself. He shrugged and looked away.

"It might be a different Zoe. Besides, she didn't sound quite sane," Emery said, and added slowly, pensively, "Did you see the pills? There must've been over twenty bottles on that table."

Sebastian kept his gaze away from her and was quiet. Too quiet, she thought.

Her pulse increased at the sight of the house where her mother and father lived. They stopped the car and walked to it, navigating around low-spreading oaks, taking over the driveway. As they neared it, its abandonment became more apparent, oozing a foggy darkness from its lifeless windows. Emery's heart twitched at its gut-wrenching desolation.

Once bright, elegant, and full of young life, the silent structure was grieving at having lost its soul. Dirt, pine needles, and leaves, blown inside through broken windows, accumulated in the corners and at the bases of the scattered furniture and gave off an earthy and moldy scent. Weeds sprouted in the floor cracks. The frayed curtains swayed ghostlike in the breeze wafting through the broken windows.

Thomas wheeled Peter around the kitchen as he searched the cabinets and drawers in search of clues, while Emery, in an emotional fog, drifted deeper into the house, not hearing the leaves and needles crunching under her feet. She entered a room that held a crib. The windows were intact, and the decorations still hung from the ceiling, and ladybugs and butterflies were still bright on the walls in their flight among the yellow daisies.

She touched the crib with the tips of her fingers, wondering if memories would surface. She felt nothing, so she stroked the pink blankets and pressed her hands on the pillow, but neither the crib nor the room brought memories or other sensations. Was she wrong in thinking Zara was her mother in this dimension? But that meant that Peter was wrong. And he was never wrong.

After a while, she stuffed her hands into her pockets and stepped back from the crib, still gazing at it, still hoping for a sliver of memory. She finally shrugged and searched the white cupboards and drawers, and finding baby clothes and blankets, she inhaled their scent. She dropped them—they didn't smell like a baby anymore, but like mold and abandonment.

Emery returned to the kitchen, where Peter leafed through piles of papers he found in the drawers.

"Anything?" she asked.

"Nothing. It's house stuff, designs, and calculations."

She wandered through the rest of the house and found Thomas combing through drawers in the bathroom. Same story here: nothing useful, no clues, nothing personal anywhere. Not even any bills or mail. As if someone had removed it all.

"Where is Sebastian?" she asked.

"I think he is outside. He's in a sour mood."

Emery found Sebastian with his back against a tree. The creases on his forehead made him look tired and older.

She touched his arm. "Talk to me," she said.

He shook his head, and a lonely tear spilled out of his eye.

"My sister did this. She was involved in Zara's disappearance."

"You don't know that. Wait until—"

"I remembered more. She tried to kill your mother before, and you. And I helped her. I've always done what she asked and never asked too many questions. My sister knew better, I told myself. She always wanted to be a hero and make the world a better place. That's what she used to say," Sebastian said. His face warped woefully as he wiped another tear. "You know what? I am not so sure anymore if that's what she really wanted. I don't understand anything anymore."

Emery sighed so deeply, her lungs hurt. It was her turn to be honest.

"You're not the only one doubting the ones you love," Emery said, and stepped away. "I came from a place that was so bleak and horrifying my blood wanted to curdle. The planet was devastated and people were changed against their will into lifeless but immortal puppets. All because of greed and because of…because of the technology invented by my mother. I wasn't entirely sure she was to blame for the change, and I had to know. So, I left the love of my life behind and plunged into the time machine to find my mother, face her, and ask her for the truth: Was she responsible for the deaths of billions of people?"

"And what will you do if she says yes?"

Emery opened her mouth. Then she closed it and bit her lower lip.

"You don't know. I thought so. Neither do I. I don't know what I'll do when I find Zoe."

Shouts coming from the house interrupted their confessions. They looked at each other and ran back. Peter sat on his chair with Thomas resting his hands on his friend's shoulders.

Peter waved a piece of paper. "Found something interesting," he shouted.

"What did you find?"

"See this? This is the map Milly drew, but on the back…"

Emery snatched the paper from him. Her face tightened. "Who is Danuta?"

"I'm not sure, but judging by the last name and the birthday, I'm guessing it's Tirg's sister."

"Moersk Sanatorium. Do you know what it says?"

"My Sinturijan is limited, but I think this is the annual statement, but strangely the balance is zero. This is last year's statement. She might still be in there."

"What's a sanatorium?" Sebastian asked.

"I think it's a place where sick people get better," Thomas answered.

"Well, let's find this sanatorium," Sebastian said.

Emery noticed the creases on his forehead smoothing out, but his grin had not returned.

"This place is enormous. There must be many sick people in this area," Thomas said, scanning the six-story beige building from one end to the other. The morning fog rose from the earth like a breath and enfolded the surrounding trees in gauzy clouds but avoided the structure, which appeared acutely sharp in contrast to its surroundings.

Emery studied the building and did not participate in the conversation, preparing for another she was about to have with someone who might be mentally ill. "I think I should go by myself," she finally said. "If she's unwell, she might be more likely to respond to another woman. And the staff will be less suspicious."

"I don't think it's a good idea," Sebastian protested.

"I agree," Thomas concurred.

"No, she's right. She should go alone," Peter said.

Thomas and Sebastian regarded Peter with surprise.

Sebastian shook his head. "We don't know anything about this place. There might be armed guards."

"Emery can take care of herself. If she's not out in an hour, we'll go in," Peter said, and added to Emery. "Watch the time."

She nodded and walked to the building. The closer she got to the entrance, the smaller and more insignificant she felt. The etched glass panels, intricate in their design and color, adorned the giant double doors. If it weren't for the thick iron bars, they'd have looked stunning, but she was overcome with an animal desire to run from it.

A woman wearing a starched light beige uniform opened the door as soon as Emery grasped the giant iron knocker. Her eyebrows went up, seeing Emery. She spoke Sinurijan. Emery didn't understand her, but from the inflection, she guessed it was a question.

"I don't speak Sinturijan. I'm Emery and am here to see Danuta. Danuta Igres. I'm her niece," Emery said, adjusting her jacket, hoping the woman didn't hear the apprehension in her voice.

Emery showed her the annual statement. "My grandmother, Elenora Igres, gave me this so I could find Danuta. See, I am her niece and need to speak with her. Can you take me to her?"

The woman examined the piece of paper and glanced at Emery. Her expression changed from disinterest to surprise and nearly shock, and she said something else but waved her in and motioned for her to wait at the door.

The interior was even more imposing. Bathed in bright lights from giant fluorescent fixtures, the furniture, the white walls, and the wide cracks in the brown wooden floors looked sharp and uninviting. Emery blinked, closed her eyes, and drew in a breath. When she opened her eyes, she saw the same woman returning with another, older woman trudging beside her.

"Marybell tells me you're a relative of Danuta. Is that true?" she asked in heavily accented Andalian with the slowness of someone who didn't speak it every day and just now tried to recall it from somewhere deep in her mind.

Emery nodded while her lips twitched into a fake smile.

"What's your name?"

"Emery. My name is Emery. Danuta is my aunt. Elenora asked me to visit her daughter. She's ill herself."

"Emery disappeared with her mother, so I've heard."

"I'm back and want to see my aunt."

"Danuta is unwell. It would be unwise for her to have visitors who might upset her. Her health is frail, and besides, she rarely speaks," she said.

"It might be good for her to see a relative," Emery said.

"I doubt it," she said. "A while back, her fraternal aunt came to visit, and Danuta was very upset for a long time afterward."

"Are there rules against visitors? A sanatorium designed to make patients better should—"

"There are no rules," the older woman said. "I'll take you to her. This is not a prison."

The hell it isn't.

"My name is Elisabeth. Sister Elisabeth."

Emery followed Sister Elisabeth down the corridor, watching the sister's calves clad in thick brown stockings move in efficient, even strides below a stiff skirt that barely moved.

Emery unclenched her fists and noticed red marks where her nails had dug into her palms.

"Danuta is still in her room. But soon she'll be going outside and into the garden."

"It's early," Emery said.

"She barely stays inside. Rain or snow, she goes outside. Every day she spends most of her time outside. Wait here while I get her," Sister Elisabeth said, opening a double French door to a lush garden. Emery was surprised at the lack of iron bars on the windows.

Before the sister left, she gazed pensively at Emery. "You have beautiful eyes. When you disappeared, your grandmother posted your image on every street. I remember people commenting on your unusual eyes."

Emery soon understood why there were no bars. The garden was surrounded by a tall iron fence topped with spikes. She walked around the garden, admiring the intricate trimmings on the hedges, cut into shapes of different birds. She breathed out, exhaling clouds of morning mist, and massaged her arms.

The door opened, and Sister Elisabeth wheeled out a frail woman hunched under the weight of countless blankets.

"I told you that you had a visitor, didn't I?" Sister Elisabeth chirped and bundled the woman even more. Emery's heart sank at the sight. If the birthdate on the statement was correct, she was in her forties, but this pale woman looked much older. The morning light only emphasized the ashen, sunken face, and the protruding bones of her forehead and cheeks.

"If you notice she's getting agitated, ring this bell," Sister Elisabeth said, pointing to a silver contraption by the door. "Take her deeper into the garden. She likes it."

The sister left, and Emery had a sudden urge to leave too. Danuta would not tell her anything—the woman was nearly dead in body and soul. Emery's stomach twisted seeing her lifeless hands covered with thick purple veins, clutching at the blanket.

Emery wheeled her to an oak tree and sat on a wooden bench, avoiding looking at the shadow of this woman sitting across from her, uncertain what to ask, or whether she even should. She considered quietly leaving this place. She jerked, hearing a soft, melodic voice. Her heart thumped in her chest.

"I knew you'd come one day."

The transformation of the woman's face took Emery by surprise, and transfixed, she sat staring at her with her mouth wide open. Deepened and shadowed by melancholy, Danuta's eyes were now waking up with tiny sparks of excitement as she studied Emery's face. Then her face lit up and came to life. She had her mother's big blue eyes, shadowed by long, dark gray lashes. "Emery, it's really you. You look just like your mother."

"You know my mother," Emery gasped.

"I tried to warn her."

"About what?"

"My father."

"Your father? He disappeared too, didn't he?" Emery asked, trying to push away a sudden thought. *She is crazy. I should leave.*

"My father was always power-hungry." Danuta spoke in an even tone, surveying the trees swaying in the light breeze. "But I was the only one who saw it. Ever since that woman had appeared, he'd gotten even worse. I tried to warn my mother that he was planning something horrible, but she didn't listen. My mother told my father what I said, and he locked me in the sanatorium, which is just a more elegant and comfortable prison."

No, she's not crazy. "Was her name Zoe?"

Danuta nodded. "She and my father kidnapped you, I'm sure of it."

"Why?"

"My father would never get the power he craved in Sinturija, but with the technology your mother invented, he could do it in the realm Zoe came from. I overhead my father talking to her. And she was beautiful. Something my father can't resist."

"Why aren't you living with your mother?"

Danuta shrugged. "I think my father left strict instructions to keep me here forever."

"Looks like he paid for the sanatorium until—"

"My death."

"But why?"

"I didn't bow to him. I knew his dark side."

Danuta coughed. When she put her hand to her mouth, several white pills escaped her sleeve.

Emery picked them up. "Your pills," she said, handing them to Danuta.

"Oh, don't tell Sister Elisabeth. I stopped taking the pills a long time ago. They made me drowsy, and I couldn't see the trees or hear the birds anymore."

Emery saw a water pitcher through the glass door. "I'll fetch you some water."

"No, there's no time. I must tell you how to find your mother."

"You know how to find my mother?" Emery asked and stood up, crunching the pills in her hand.

"I think I have an idea. I knew about her research and the chamber she built—"

"Perhaps it's time to end the visit, don't you think, Danuta?" Sister Elisabeth said, eyeing Emery from the corner of her eye. "You must be tired."

How did you get here so quietly?

Danuta stayed mute. Emery was biting the inside of her lip, shifting her gaze between her aunt, who sank back into her chair and lowered her gaze, and Sister Elisabeth, who stood with her arms straight down at her sides with fingers stretched out.

"She is not tired. We are still talking," Emery said.

"Was she talking to you?" she asked, pursing her lips and glaring at Danuta.

"Yeah, she was."

"What did you talk about?"

Emery cocked her head and smiled. "Family matters."

"That's enough then for today. You might think she's okay, but you know nothing about her. A slight disturbance that normal people wouldn't even notice might throw her off balance—"

"Normal people? Are you saying she's not normal?"

"No, that's not what I meant."

"Why don't you give us a few more minutes? She doesn't appear to be in distress."

"You don't know her like I do. She is stressed. You must leave before she has an episode," she said, and seized the wheelchair.

"I'm not done."

"Don't make me call the guards," Sister Elisabeth said before pushing Danuta forward.

Emery grabbed the wheelchair. "I'm not done talking to my aunt. Come back later," she said to Elisabeth while pulling the wheelchair toward her and whispering to Danuta. "Are you okay?"

Danuta raised her eyes for a moment and reassured Emery with a quick smile. Then she lowered her eyes again. Emery smiled back, but her smile withered as the sharp sound of a whistle pierced her ears. Sister Elisabeth's eyes and cheeks bulged as she blew the contents of her lungs into a long silver whistle.

"I wish you hadn't done that," Emery said. "I don't want to hurt anyone. I just wanted to talk to my aunt."

"Leave before the guards come," Sister Elisabeth said, trying to get a hold of the wheelchair's handles again. Emery was faster at grabbing them.

Emery grasped the handles and pushed Danuta inside. Sister Elisabeth dug her fingers deep into Emery's arm.

"Get off me and don't follow me. I don't want to hurt you." *You witch*. Emery shook the arm off and sped up. The wheelchair clanked on the uneven brown floor.

As she was entering the corridor, two men in brown uniforms and brown berets headed her way.

She bent and whispered into Danuta's ear. "Do you want to go with me?"

"Really?" The excitement broke her tiny voice. "Yes, I do."

"Close your eyes," Emery whispered, then faced the men. "Don't try to stop me. I don't want to hurt you," Emery said and moved forward.

"You're not allowed to take her," Sister Elisabeth said, trying to grab the wheelchair.

"Why not? You said it wasn't a prison. You won't let me talk to her, so I have to take her with me," she said, pushing Sister Elisabeth's hand away.

"She needs her medication!"

"Yeah, I'm sure she does."

Emery stopped and stepped to the side, extending her palms toward the guards. "Stop and don't come any closer."

The older guard must have heard something in her voice that made him pause and seize the younger guard's arm. "Does the patient want to leave with her?" he asked Sister Elisabeth.

"It doesn't matter," she hissed.

Emery felt the cold hiss of air on her neck and shivered.

"It does," Danuta said, raising her head. "I want to go with my niece."

The guards waited for consent from Sister Elisabeth to let Danuta go, but she stepped in front of Emery and waved at the guards. "Stop her. Danuta cannot leave this place."

The two men moved forward. Emery breathed deeply to lessen her power and thrust her hands, hoping only to incapacitate them. She avoided looking at the silvery-blue waves, the guards, and the sister slumping to the dark floor as she pushed the wheelchair out of the building.

"That was scary and...amazing," Danuta said.

"I thought you had your eyes closed."

When she wheeled Danuta out, the sun had already broken through the fog. Shielding her eyes, Emery walked toward the van, pushing the wheelchair.

Three sets of wide eyes and equally wide mouths greeted them from the open door of the van.

"Let's get out of this shitty place," Emery said

Sebastian and Sam picked up the wheelchair with Danuta in it and positioned it inside beside Peter's wheelchair. Emery slid into a seat opposite Danuta and Peter, but she avoided their glances. Her sullen face discouraged anyone from asking questions.

Thomas drove while Sebastian gazed out the back window watching for pursuers.

Once they drove far enough from the sanatorium and were certain no one had followed them, Thomas stopped the van, and Emery explained what had happened and why she thought kidnapping Danuta was the best option. When she told them about the guards, her voice broke.

"Stop being so hard on yourself," Sebastian said. "She wanted to go with you, but they wouldn't let her. You did what you thought was best for her. Let's figure out what to do next."

Emery sensed what they were thinking. Bringing a frail woman in a wheelchair and involving her in this maddening quest was not one of her most brilliant ideas.

47

THE OLYCETIC LAB

They settled into an inn in Cyper, a small town nestled at the forest's edge. Emery and Danuta shared a cozy room with soft blue blankets, light beige walls, and a window overlooking a cheerful green valley with flowering trees. As soon as Sebastian carefully positioned her aunt on the bed, Emery collapsed beside her. Her heavy eyelids shut as soon as her head reached the pillow.

When she woke up and discovered Danuta wasn't beside her, she darted out of bed, shrieking, and pounded on the walls of the neighboring room. "Peter, Sebastian, Thomas, come here. They kidnapped my aunt!"

Sebastian flew into the room, wiping soap from his chin.

Thomas showed up shortly after Sebastian. "What happened?"

"Someone took her," Emery said, pointing at the empty bed and wheelchair. "They must want us to..." her eyes widened and her words trailed off as Danuta walked into the room.

"Is everything okay?" she asked, probing their shocked faces.

"You can walk?" Thomas asked.

She nodded. "Oh, the wheelchair," she said, tracing his stare to the window, where the abandoned chair sat. "They'd put me in the wheelchair a while back. I never knew why. But I can walk," she said and blushed, glancing at Peter, who had just bumped the door open with his homemade wheelchair. "I used to sneak out at night and walk in the garden."

Emery laughed. "We're definitely related," she said after her laughter subsided and then wrapped her arms around her aunt in a tender embrace.

Danuta smiled, and the room lit up. The old woman transformed into a beautiful and lively woman as her eyes became increasingly blue and sparkled in the sun coming through the slit in the curtains.

Peter closed the door. "Emery said you know how to find Zara."

Danuta's smile faded. "I believe so. Zoe and my father went through the chamber that Emery's mother designed and built. I know where the chamber was, but I don't know whether it's still there."

After everyone left, Emery sat close to Danuta and told her what she remembered about her life. She listened without taking her eyes off Emery, hanging on to each word, nodding thoughtfully, gasping, or shaking her head as if reliving her niece's story.

"You've been through so much," Danuta said.

"So have you. Do you know where my father is?"

"I don't know."

"I'm sorry," Emery said, noticing Danuta's glassy eyes. "I'm bringing all this back."

"No, it's okay. I believe my father did something to him because Tirg wouldn't betray Zara or his daughter. I'm as sure of it as I am sure my father did all this. And that Zoe woman."

Through the local library, Emery, her aunt, and Peter (more mobile in the new wheelchair he had inherited from Danuta) had found that Zara's lab at the outskirts of Nariana was still functioning but specializing in optical research, and was now known as Olycetic Laboratories. The person in charge of the lab was Serena Lorena.

"A woman," Emery said.

"Yes, women can hold leading positions in Sinturija," Danuta said. "Just like your mother."

"So, what do we do? Do we pay her a visit at the lab or find out where she lives?" Sebastian asked, leaning from the front passenger seat as Thomas drove.

"Seems to me the lab is a better option," Danuta said.

When everyone's gaze landed on her, a tiny rosy tinge colored her cheeks. "Sinturija has always been strong in developing science learning programs to encourage kids to want to study it. According to the brochure I found at the library, the lab created a spectacular optical show for kids."

"Yeah, but how—" Sebastian started.

"We can pretend we are teachers setting up a visit for our class," Danuta said. Her voice quivered only slightly.

Emery smiled and squeezed Danuta's hand, secretly promising to avenge her for the years she'd spent in a prison, medicated against her will and forced into a life devoid of purpose, love, or friendship. The bile rose in her throat as the revulsion and hatred for her grandfather grew. She hated him even more than she hated Zoe. She finally realized she was gripping Danuta's hand too hard and let go, wincing when she noticed her fingers leaving red marks on Danuta's hand.

"I'm sorry."

Danuta stroked Emery's hand. "I know what you're feeling, and I'm starting to feel the same. Anger. For stealing my life. I was taught that feeling anger was wrong and not worthy of my status, and I always tried to be a good daughter. For years I squelched it along with other emotions. But because of you, I see things more clearly and am not as afraid of letting my emotions out."

Emery, Danuta, and Thomas entered the lab and waited for the educational coordinator. When a young woman with an abundance of dark curls and serious brown eyes approached, Danuta introduced herself as a science teacher exploring educational opportunities for her students. When she extended her hand, the young woman smiled, and her eyes glowed like amber. She took Danuta's hand and shook it energetically and said her name was Marcella.

Emery and Thomas kept quiet except for the greeting in Sinturijan, which they practiced before the meeting.

Marcella assured them she would show them everything that was designated as educational and safe and answer all Danuta's questions. Her energetic stride was contagious, and soon everyone was almost running to keep up with Marcella, who darted through the labs, showing them the instruments and briefly explaining their functions, not realizing that only Danuta understood her. Emery glanced furtively around, searching, but there were no signs of the chamber.

After exchanging a glance with Emery, Danuta drew a breath and asked, "I've read somewhere that a time travel experiment was conducted here in a secret chamber."

"Which school did you say you represented?" Marcella turned quickly and pierced Danuta with her amber eyes.

"The ..." Danuta said. "I have some gifted kids in my class, and they ask tough questions. I sometimes wonder—"

"There is no secret chamber, Miss Danuta, and if there ever was one, it's long gone. I'd tell your students that there are no secrets at the Olycetic Lab."

"Oh, thank you. I most certainly will."

From the expression on Danuta's face, Emery guessed how the conversation went, but on their way out, she asked. "She didn't know anything about the chamber?"

"No," Danuta said. "But I think she's lying."

"Wait," a woman's voice behind them startled Emery. When they turned around, curious hazel eyes looked at them. The owner of the hazel eyes, a woman in her late forties, stood in a doorway and stepped back when she saw Emery. She pressed her hand to her lips, but a tiny cry escaped. "It can't be," she whispered. "It can't be."

"What's she saying?" Emery whispered to Danuta.

"She is saying it can't be," Danuta blurted, forgetting to whisper.

The woman looked around and, not seeing anyone, grabbed Danuta's arm. "Follow me to my office."

Danuta wiggled her arm, but the grip only tightened.

Emery grasped the woman's hand. "Let her go."

"You're her, aren't you? You're her daughter?" the woman asked in Andalian, gazing into Emery's eyes. "I'd recognize those eyes anywhere. For years, they haunted my dreams. And you look like her."

"People keep telling me that. You knew my mother?" Emery asked.

The woman nodded. "I'm Serena. Let's go to my office."

Serena offered water to everyone. Her hands shook when she poured it into glasses. Water splattered on the glass table. Serena gulped her water.

"Marcela told me you were asking about the chamber. Anytime anyone asks about it, I get suspicious or...optimistic. I guess I never lost hope she'd come back," Serena said, not taking her eyes off Emery. "I was your mother's assistant and blamed myself for her disappearance."

"How so?" Emery asked.

"We weren't careful enough. We were filled with such enthusiasm for what we'd accomplished that we abandoned caution and common sense."

"So, you know what happened to my mother."

Serena sighed so deeply that Emery felt sorry for her.

"Not for certain. Only what I deduced later, knowing your grandfather and after hearing of his visit to the lab the same day Zara disappeared. My colleagues also described a woman accompanying your mother that day," she said, and inhaled. "But nobody knew who she was."

"I know it was all his doing," Emery said. "And I know who the woman was."

"How?"

"Danuta, Zmey's daughter, told me," Emery said, turning toward her aunt. "She tried to warn my mother but was sent to a sanatorium, where she was held prisoner and medicated against her will."

"Oh, I see."

"Does the chamber still exist?" Thomas asked.

Serena regarded him. "And who are you?"

"I'm Thomas, Emery's friend."

"I had it locked and walled off."

"Why?" Emery asked.

"Why do you think? I didn't want anyone to stumble upon it and get lost again."

"But it's still there?" Emery asked, holding her breath.

"It's still there, but it's not functional without dark matter. They took it all with them and burned all the research notes."

Emery's eyes glistened with tears as she stood, folding her hands into fists. "I traveled through bloody black holes and dark hell and a forsaken gray city full of evil wackos and over the ocean from Andalia to find my mother. We must find this stupid dark matter!"

"I might be of help," Danuta said.

"How?" Emery and Serena asked.

Danuta, glancing at Thomas, unbuttoned the top of her shirt and reached inside. In her hand, she held a necklace with a large black stone embedded in gold. "Zara sent it to my mother, asking her to give it to me for my birthday. Along with the necklace, she included a letter. She suspected my father's intentions might not be noble, and she asked me to keep this safe."

"And she told you what it was?" Serena asked. "This stone could be dangerous."

"It's encased in some kind of crystal," Danuta said. "Zara wouldn't put me in danger. The first time I laid my eyes on her, I knew she was good. Troubled maybe, and a little sad, but good."

Emery cleared her throat, but the lump would not dislodge.

"I know you want to find your mother, but there must be another way," Serena said.

"What other way?" Emery asked. Her voice was raspy.

"How did you...where did you come from?" Serena asked. "I thought Zmey took you with him. How did you come back?"

"I don't remember that part or that life. I was just a baby," Emery said and picked up the glass, emptying it in a few sips. "There is no other way," she added in a steady voice, wiping her chin. "I don't want to waste more time. Will you help us?"

"Then you'll disappear again, and I'll have you on my conscience."

"I will not disappear but join my mother. I traveled through a chamber just like that twice already. I wouldn't quite say it was a pleasant experience, but I survived."

"How is that possible?" Serena asked, raising her eyebrows. Her hazel eyes were enlivened by the curiosity of a scientist.

"Help us, and I'll tell you all about it."

Back at the inn, Emery locked herself in a room with Danuta and used all her persuasive power to convince her to stay in Sinturija. Despite the hint of pink on Danuta's cheeks and the luster in her eyes, she was still frail. Or that was what Emery thought. She believed Zoe had taken Zara to create the gray city, and what awaited them there was not something she thought Danuta was prepared to experience. The grayness, the emotionless, cruel Minders, the change extracting humanity from people who would then be ruled by Zoe the empress and Zmey the emperor, would be too much for her frail aunt. Emery repeated what she had already told her, but this time she also told her about the encounter with Master E and his son and described graphically what the change entailed.

"They remove your tissue, blood, all your organs, and replace them with the Essence—the substance my mother invented with preontechnology. You don't eat or drink anymore because your body becomes self-sufficient. And then they suppress your emotions and curiosity with drugs."

Danuta listened, nodding and rubbing her arms, still cold even though the room was already warmed by the afternoon sun.

Emery finished her story, expecting Danuta to agree it was too dangerous for her.

Danuta, however, smiled. She took Emery's hand. "That's all the more reason I should come, Emery."

"Huh? Did you hear what I said about the Masters and the Minders and how dangerous it is? How evil the fuckers are?"

"Yes. And that's why I want to come. For all those years, even before I was sent to the sanatorium, I lived like a ghost. A shadow of my mother, my brother...afraid to live. Damn it! Afraid to even say something out loud. I need this. I want this! I want to stand up to this...what did you say? Fucker? I want to stand up to the fucker for what he did to me, to my mother, and to Tirg."

"You might die," Emery said.

"So what? I dreamed of revenge at night but crushed it during the day. I want my life to finally make sense and to have meaning. I don't want to be a spectator in my own life and watch it drain away. Let me, please. I won't be a burden."

Emery regarded her aunt and saw the excitement paint her eyes the most beautiful blue she's ever seen. "I'd be honored to have you at my side," Emery said.

Dreading similar conversations with Peter and then Thomas, Emery procrastinated; the bile pushing up her throat, threatening revolt when she finally looked into Peter's eyes.

"I know what you're going to say, so don't even bother."

His words hit her like hail on a summer day.

"It's not only your decision. Last time, I made a mistake not coming with you, and I'm not making it this time. I'm coming with even..." Peter's voice faltered.

"Finish," Emery said.

"Even if I were to die immediately. I don't give a shit about my life without you."

"But I do, goddamn you. I don't want anything to happen to you.

Ever since you met me, you have had nothing but near-death encounters. I nearly killed you twice, and you died protecting me."

"Life without you has no meaning. It's shit. I thought I could let you go, but I was just being a dumb idiot. You're not going anywhere without me, even if I have to tie you up."

With the eyes of a lost child, Thomas listened to Emery's speech about why he couldn't go with her. While Emery spoke about his wife waiting for him, her eyes wandered all around the room but never landed on his. "So, don't even try to—"

"Emery," he said.

"I told you, don't even try to convince me."

"Emery," Thomas said and waved his hand in front of her face. "I'm not."

Emery exhaled and looked at him. "Thank you."

"For what?"

"For not making this harder."

"I'm staying so that you know there is a friend waiting...maybe knowing that, you'll make damn sure to come back..."

"Oh, Thomas," Emery said and embraced him. Tears she held behind her eyelids now escaped. "I don't know what's going to happen there. I don't want to lie to you. This is probably a suicide mission for all of us."

Thomas nodded. "It probably is," he said very slowly and paused. He cleared his throat. "But if anyone is going to turn a suicide mission into a victory, it's you. I don't remember my life in the gray city, but from what Peter has told me, and from what I witnessed, you have the heart of a lioness and claws to prove it. So, I'll be waiting. My wife, Anna, really wanted to meet you, and she'll be very disappointed if you don't come back."

"Will you go back to *Discovery*?"

"I think so. I actually enjoyed the sea. I didn't know that about myself."

"Here. Take what's left of the gems and coins. We can't take them with us."

"Are you sure this is where my mother went?" Emery asked after Serena entered the destination into the panel.

"I stared at those coordinates for months before finally walling it off. Those numbers were the only thing I could focus on at night. For years. I'd forget my date of birth before I forgot them."

Emery sat on the floor of the capsule, embracing Peter and kissing his eyes. "You must hold on to me no matter what. When I went with Zoe, I let go of her because I was pissed at her, but I frequently wondered what would have happened if I'd stayed with her. Would we end up in the same place, or were our destinies so different that it didn't matter? Still, hold on to me and don't let go."

"Never."

Danuta and Sebastian were quiet, huddled together in a corner. Emery looked up at Sebastian. In his eyes, and in the way he held Danuta, she was reassured that he would not let go of her.

48

THE GRAY CITY

"C'mon, silly girl, get inside before you turn into a prune."

"What's a prune?"

"Shriveled plum. Oh, I can see your skin is wrinkling."

"No, it's not."

"Get inside, Emery," her mother insisted.

"I don't wanna," Emery said, and opened her mouth to taste the rain.

"Emery, come inside," her mother said. Her voice grew impatient and strangely deep.

"Emery, wake up. Wake up. We must move."

Emery's eyes opened halfway. "What happened to your eyes? They're blue."

"They've always been blue. Look at me. Do you remember me?"

She opened her eyes. For a long moment, Peter held his breath, looking into her vacant eyes. Kneeling beside her, he massaged her hands.

"Tell me, you remember me, Emery. Please."

She sat up so abruptly that her head hit Peter's chin.

"Peter. What happened?"

"We landed in the middle of a storm in some kind of quarry. We need to get out of here before the water rises."

Emery's eyes almost bulged out of their sockets seeing him kneel beside her. "Oh, my God, Peter. You can walk?"

"Yeah," he said, and smiled.

"I haven't seen you smile like this in a long time."

"You remembered me. Get up," Peter said, extending a hand. "We've got to climb up. I can see a way up."

Water came down in sheets. Her feet disappeared into the mud as she tried to walk while holding on to Peter. They were surrounded by steep chalky walls marked with deep gouges as if enormous talons had scratched them. Peter led the way up through an area that was not as steep, but with the torrent escaping the sky, almost every step up ended up in a slide. The outer surface of the rock was strangely spongy, leaving a white residue on their hands.

When they finally made it to the top, Emery burst out laughing. "You look like a prune covered in sticky powdered sugar."

"You think you look better?"

Their skin turned purple as the rain bit into their nearly naked bodies. Above, the terrain didn't look more inviting than below. Endless flats, splattered with rocks, chalky dirt, gravel, and puddles of water, and no trees or shrubs or other signs of vegetation.

"Where is the capsule?" Emery asked.

"I don't know. Maybe it broke midair. I woke up facedown in a puddle. I ran back and forth shouting your name before I realized I could walk. When I finally saw you, I thought my old ticker was going to give up on me."

"We need to find Sebastian and Danuta," Emery said, looking around.

"First, we must find shelter."

"There is nothing around. It's like a wet desert."

"Let's go. We've got to keep moving."

Emery trudged behind Peter, laboring with every step, pulling her feet from the thick mud.

The rain stopped abruptly.

"Look, there is someone waving up ahead. I think it's Sebastian," Emery said.

"Are you sure it's him?"

"Yeah," Emery said. "It's my grandpa."

She tried to take off running, but her left foot stuck deeper in the mud, throwing her off balance, and she fell on her back with a big splash. Sebastian was running toward them. Peter offered her a hand.

"Why are you grinning?" Emery asked.

Peter chuckled.

Emery sat up and tried to wipe her face, but seeing her hands thick with mud, she gave it up and stood up.

They met Sebastian halfway. He lifted Emery and would not let go of her. He carried her and put her down where the corner of a dark gray structure was sticking out of the ground. Emery and Peter stared at the gray, smooth wall as something that didn't belong in this desolate landscape.

"What is it?" Peter asked.

"Where is Danuta?" Emery asked.

"She is inside, and yes, she is okay. I think she is trying to find something to wear. It's a house. Well, kind of."

"A house? Hidden underground in the middle of the desert?" Peter asked.

Sebastian shrugged. "Come on. You look cold," he said, and walked past the gray corner and down the slope along a narrow passageway cut in the rock. One side of the building became visible as they descended, reaching an arched metal door at the bottom. Sebastian pushed it open.

"How did you find it?" Peter asked.

"Danuta was getting tired and not watching her steps. She tripped and fell, and then she bravely tried getting up, but I could tell she was in pain, so I kneeled by her. While I was inspecting her injury, my eyes wandered to the thing she fell on, and guess what I saw?"

"Come on, I'm not in the mood for a guessing game. What?" Emery asked.

"A triangle," Sebastian said, and waved his hands in midair.

The corridor grew brighter with light emanating from the walls. Emery shuddered, recognizing the familiar seamless gray walls and the eerie, sourceless lights.

"I pushed the triangle, the door opened, and then it slid inside the rock," Sebastian said.

The hallway ended in a fairly large room illuminated by the same indistinct lights. To Emery's surprise, it was furnished with sofas, carpets, and even a bookcase full of gold-engraved books. Danuta was lying on the sofa, resting her swollen and purple ankle on the pillows. She raised her head and squealed with joy when she saw Emery enter.

"No, no, don't get up," Emery said, darting toward her. "Oh, my, you really did a number on your foot. Does it hurt?"

"Not so much anymore. I'm so happy you found us."

"What is this place?" Peter asked, looking around.

"I think it may be a bunker," Sebastian said. "The strange thing is that it's stocked with food and water, and it's pretty spacious. Look for yourself."

Emery walked, tracing the walls with her fingers. "It's the same as the walls in the gray city."

"Got to be kidding. Three bedrooms? Full bathroom?" Emery said, then stopped to look at Peter and Sebastian with an odd smile. "You realize what that means?"

"What?" Peter and Sebastian asked.

"This thing was designed for people not yet changed. So maybe we're not too late. Maybe there's still time to stop the change," she said before jumping up to kiss Peter and Sebastian on their cheeks.

"Dinner is served," Peter said, bringing a tray with steaming bowls. "Chicken noodle. I think it's chicken and crackers. You wanna know the weird thing about this food? The tin containers just say 'soup'. No dates, no labels, nothing."

"Smells good," Sebastian said.

Emery started eating as soon as Peter set the bowls on a small coffee table.

"It tastes good too," she said, shoving another spoonful into her mouth. Crackers fell from the corners of her mouth as she inhaled her food. Even Danuta ate all her soup, but she left her crackers untouched.

For the first time since they found each other, Peter and Emery spent a magical night in the same room and the same bed. It's been centuries for Peter and months for Emery since they were together like that, melting their bodies and minds into one dreamlike moment.

"Do you believe we'll find my mother?" Emery asked in the morning.

Peter didn't answer right away but moved a lock of hair off her forehead and kissed it. "I believe you will get your answers this time. Ever since we set foot in this land, I've had this gut feeling that something profound will happen and that you'll be at the center."

Emery snorted. "You didn't answer my question. You sound like a politician, not a straightforward cop."

"Yes, I do," Peter said, and pulled her closer.

She had a similar feeling growing inside her—a premonition of an unavoidable, momentous event that would shatter not only the world but also her heart. Her heart sank into her stomach and twisted into a heavy knot. Her face must have reflected her thoughts, because Peter wrapped his arm around her head and pressed it to his chest, muttering, "Everything is going to be okay."

Sheets bound with large knots into makeshift bags packed with food and water waited at the exit of the bunker. Sebastian sat by the bags, tapping his foot on the floor while Danuta and Peter were engrossed in a quiet conversation. But Emery wasn't ready to go. Unintelligible sounds escaped her mouth as she walked alongside the walls and pushed aside whatever furniture was in her way, tracing the walls with her palms.

"What are you looking for?" Sebastian asked when she came into view.

"Shhh."

Peter smacked his forehead. "Are you looking for a ..."

"Yeah," Emery said. She stopped her search for a moment, looking at Peter. "Why have such a lonely structure in the middle of nowhere? It makes no sense."

Peter dashed to her side and started tracing the walls.

"Could you tell me what the hell you're looking for?" Sebastian asked, getting up from the floor.

"I'll tell you in a minute. You and Danuta get off your butts and start searching for any electronic gadgets, buttons, anything, remotes—"

"What's a remote?" Danuta asked.

"Anything with buttons you can press or glass screens."

"Got it," Danuta said, and with the tip of her tongue out, hobbled from cupboard to cupboard, from cabinet to cabinet. Her foot was still purple, but the swelling had gone down.

An hour later, the search produced no results other than some random objects Danuta and Sebastian had found in various places.

"What do we need this remote for?" Sebastian asked.

"In the gray city, there were invisible doors in the walls, and the tablets could open them. I was sure there'd be such a wall here," Emery said, and slid to the ground. "I was so sure of it I was willing to bet my life on it."

"Why were you so sure?" Danuta asked.

"Because in the gray city, everything was connected, and if this is indeed a bunker, it would make sense if it was tied into the underground city," Peter said.

Emery sighed. "I feel stupid now. We've wasted a lot of time."

"It's not stupid," Peter said. "There were places in the city where the Minders searching for wildlings would stay. And they were connected to lifts."

"It's only been twenty-four years," Emery said. "The city might not be finished yet."

"Maybe not all of it yet, but the thing with this technology is that the construction is lightning fast. The structures that had been started, are most likely finished. You see, the preontechnology not only gave the buildings their extraordinary qualities—it also sped up the construction process. The entire city was built in less than twenty years," Peter said. "But since I was not part of the search for wildlings, I'm not certain all the safe houses were connected to elevators. I've never actually been in one."

"What do we do now?" Emery asked, gazing at her friends.

"We search outside."

"You weren't able to see any weak points in the walls?"

"No," she said and lowered her gaze. "Maybe I'm out of practice, or maybe the ability to see things I once had is now gone."

"We'll stay one more night here, and that will also give Danuta a chance to pamper her foot some more," Sebastian said with a wink at Danuta, and that thing with her eyes happened again. They gained color.

Danuta smiled.

"Things might be different now," Emery said to Peter later, when they were lying in bed. "There is no assurance that the gray city is the same as it was when we were there. I don't know how time travel and dimension-hopping work. I might have caused changes when I went there last time. You know the predestination paradox."

"I thought the paradox would kick in if you went back in time. Or was it the grandfather paradox? I don't remember. You traveled into the future; therefore, you couldn't have caused anything. And now we're transferring into a different dimension, so there shouldn't be any paradoxes or connections," Peter said and kissed her cheek.

"I'm not sure about that. It's a different dimension from Andalia, but I lived there. First in the past and then in the future when I met you. And now I'm going over six hundred years back in time, in a roundabout way. My head hurts when I think about it."

They stopped walking when Danuta started favoring her foot more. With the heavy clouds hanging low, casting everything in gray, the desolate, chalky landscape looked more like a moon, not Earth.

After a short break, Sebastian picked Danuta up despite her protests.

"It's okay. I'm as strong as a horse. You weigh almost nothing. Stop wiggling," he said.

They reached an area with dried-out tree trunks. Most were broken off and covered with ash. Navigating around the ghostly trunks and gnarly, tangled roots, partially hidden in the ground, they slowed their pace. Danuta perched on Sebastian's shoulders; her head bobbed as he hopped over roots, but Emery could tell by the way her eyes closed half-way that she liked the closeness.

Peter was ahead, and at one point he stopped, placed his finger on his lips, and motioned for everyone to stop. Soon, they could see two figures approaching. Sebastian lowered Danuta down and gazed intently into the distance.

"Two men," Sebastian said.

"Yeah," Emery agreed. "And they are moving fast." She looked at Peter. "Minders?"

"I think so."

Sebastian stepped in front of Danuta.

Emery looked him in the eye. "I've got this. There are only two of them. Protect her."

He hesitated but nodded.

Peter and Emery walked toward them. Peter's muscles defined under his jacket, and his eyes narrowed into slits. She didn't argue, knowing he would never agree to stay behind.

"Let's talk to them first, okay?" he asked.

She gave him a sidelong glance. "I was planning on it."

"I meant, let me talk to them. I know how they think and how they're programmed."

The Minders held guns in their gray hands. Emery was surprised to see a slight curiosity in their black eyes as they scanned her face.

"Who are you?" they both asked in unison.

"We are on our way to meet Master E. He's expecting us," Peter said calmly. Emery felt her blood chill, hearing him speak like a Minder.

"Who?"

"Master E. You know your Masters, don't you?" Peter asked. "He's expecting us. We're his spies, searching for wildlings."

The two men exchanged glances and raised their guns. "Searching for who?"

"The...survivors," Peter said.

"We'll take you to the Masters."

Emery looked at Peter. He nodded. She thrust her hands at the two Minders, who fell as soon as the waves hit them and stayed motionless. Peter searched their bodies as Sebastian and Danuta made their way toward them.

"The tablets are different," Emery said, examining a small silver case.

"Assuming Zoe and Zmey were behind creating the Brilliant Genesia and the Diamond Eldorado, we are probably six hundred years earlier than when we met here the first time," Peter said, searching their pockets. "There were several earlier versions of the tablets."

"That's right," Emery said. "That's why everything looks so dead. Maybe the earth is waiting for all the humans to die before waking up."

Sebastian kneeled beside the bodies and studied the gun lying at the feet of the dead Minder.

"Yeah, take one. I'll show you how to use it," Peter said, taking the other gun. "Now let's look at the tablet," he added before inspecting the silver gadget.

"Are they dead?" Danuta asked.

"I didn't have a choice. They would have killed us all without pity or remorse."

"I know," Danuta said. She patted Emery's arm.

Emery glanced at Peter. "Any luck?"

"I've got something. It's not far," he said, turning to the right and pointing ahead. "That way."

"Do you think it's the entrance?" Emery asked.

Peter nodded and then shifted his gaze from Emery to Sebastian and Danuta. "Are we ready?"

Everyone nodded.

"Because once we're inside, the game is on," Peter said. "We don't know what to expect, and we don't have a plan."

"We play it by ear," Emery said, and Sebastian smiled. "Let's go."

Emery feigned courage as every muscle in her body stiffened, screaming to run.

Danuta's gaze was fixed on the dead bodies. "Why don't you and Peter wear their clothes?" she asked, looking at Sebastian. "You could pretend we are wildlings you caught."

"And you said we don't have a plan," Emery said, eyeing Peter.

"I believe the term 'wildlings' was coined much later."

A few minutes later, they looked like Minders except for their skin and Peter's blue eyes.

Emery scooped a handful of the gray soil, which she smeared on Peter's face. Then she stepped back, admiring her deed. "Not bad," she said. "It's dark down there. We might get by."

"Seriously?" Sebastian asked and moved away a few feet, pressing both hands to his cheeks.

Danuta scooped some dirt and stood before Sebastian. He sighed and kneeled so she could apply it to his face. "We're ready now," she said.

Emery noticed the twinkle in Danuta's eyes whenever they landed on Sebastian. Sebastian had been so tender with her.

49

MOTHER

A while later, they stood before a huge rock, where Peter stopped and played with the silver gadget.

"That's just a rock," Sebastian said.

As he said this, the middle section of the rock faltered, revealing a large oval opening.

Just as Emery remembered: The crystal shaft of the elevator opened and came to life with brilliant lights as soon as they stepped in front of it and touched it. Danuta stroked the walls with her fingers in awe. Sebastian's eyes glowed, but Emery's heart dropped.

This is it. I'm back in the gray hellhole for the fourth time in my life. You'd think I'd have learned after the first.

"Fourth time is the charm?" she asked, glancing at Peter.

He barely nodded, studying the tablet.

"Should we find the Master's quarters first, or should we start with the Control Room?" Emery asked.

"Neither," Peter said. "We should start with the Science Center."

Emery pressed a hand to her trembling lips. "Where Mother works."

Peter nodded, opening the door of the elevator, which slowed and stopped moving, reaching the bottom floor without a sound or the slightest bump. "I think there's a chance—"

"That means that Zoe might be there too," Sebastian said.

Danuta said nothing, but her eyes darting from Peter to Sebastian betrayed her nervousness.

"Emery and Danuta," Peter whispered. "Stay behind us and try to keep your blue eyes down."

"You've got blue eyes too."

"That's why Sebastian will go first. Sebastian, I will whisper directions to you. If you see anyone, try not to panic and attract attention. Maybe we can pass through. It's still early in the city's regulatory and monitoring development, and I am hoping they're not as organized or suspicious yet."

Before they took off, Emery squeezed Sebastian's arm. "Remember what I told you about your power? It's triggered by anger and fear. When you feel it building inside you, wait until it's almost unbearable, then release it."

"Right," Sebastian whispered, and touched the pocket that held the gun.

Prompted by Peter, Sebastian led them through a series of corridors. Peter designed a route that avoided larger areas where Minders or Masters might have congregated.

They passed countless corridors and had not come across anyone, and Emery was about to exhale with relief when a voice behind them rumbled, bouncing off the gray walls.

"Are you lost? No civilians are allowed here." Emery nearly gasped, seeing three Minders, one of them vaguely familiar.

"We're not lost," Peter said. "We're delivering the survivors to the lab. Wait. Sylvester?"

"How do you know me?" one of the three Minders asked. "Who are you?" As he asked, a gun materialized in his hand. The other two men also pointed their guns at them.

"I'm Konrad. We were in training together. You must remember me."

"No. I don't," Sylvester said. He lowered his gun slightly. "Which training?"

"The martial arts training. You threw that guy against the glass wall, and it broke."

"Yeah, he was lighter than I thought, but I still don't remember you," he said, but placed the gun back into his holster. "You'd better get going then."

"Phew," Danuta exhaled after they were far enough for them not to hear. "You really knew him?"

"In my previous life."

Peter stopped by a double door. The doors lacked knobs or any other way to open them, but at least there were doors, Emery thought. Would the silver gadget open it? He tried pressing buttons, but the door remained shut.

"They must not have the clearance to open the lab."

"Now what?" Sebastian asked.

Emery scratched her forehead and then approached the door, folding her hand to knock. She glanced at Peter. He nodded. She knocked. When no one answered, Emery knocked again and again, harder and harder, until her knuckles were red.

"We might have to find other Minders. Maybe Sylvester..." His words trailed off as the door opened slowly, revealing a young man wearing navy scrubs and white goggles sitting lopsided on his head. From his blond hair, his posture, and the way he cocked his head, Emery guessed that he hadn't been changed.

"Yes?" he asked.

"We came to deliver these survivors to Doctor Zara Igres. She is expecting us."

"Who? There is no Zara here. Are you sure you've got the right lab?"

"Physics lab?"

"Yeah, you are at the physics lab, but nobody named Zara works here."

"How about Olesya Solensky?" Emery asked, stepping forward, pushing the door slightly.

"Oh, Dr. Solensky is busy right now. And I know nothing about wildling, and I am her assistant."

"Well, I'm her daughter!" Emery shouted before pushing her way inside.

"And I'm her father," Sebastian said, following her.

The assistant staggered and held onto the doorframe to keep his balance as Peter and Danuta walked in. Danuta stopped for a moment and straightened the goggles on his head. "I'm sorry," she murmured. "She hasn't seen her mother in a long time."

"Where is she?" Emery asked, looking around. The monstrous monitors were alive with schematics, chemical formulas, and genetic codes. A woman with her back to them sat staring into the eyepiece of an enormous microscope. Her black hair was chopped short, but Emery recognized the familiar curve of her neck and her straight back and the way she sat and moved her hands, manipulating the handles on the microscope. Emery's heart stopped beating. Words died in her mouth. Sebastian stood by her side, also silent, wringing his hands.

"Zara!" Danuta shouted, and darted toward her.

The woman turned and, seeing approaching Danuta, stood up. A glass tube rolled out of her hand and shattered on the floor.

"Who are you?"

"Oh, Zara. You're okay," Danuta said. "It's me, Danuta. You must recognize me. I'm a little older but—"

"Oh, Danuta, Tirg's sister. It's you. How?"

"Look who is here." Danuta turned toward Emery, extending her arm in a dramatic arch.

Emery stood speechless. She had searched for her for so long, and now that she stood before her, she couldn't think of anything to say. And even if she could have, her mouth was numb. Her mother walked toward her slowly, dropping her arms as she got closer. When her eyes landed on Emery's golden specks floating inside sky-colored orbs, she gasped.

"It can't be. You're dead. It can't be...you can't possibly be her. My daughter died."

"What are you talking about?" Sebastian stepped forward. "Emery is right here. She searched the world looking for you. Nearly did die a few times."

Emery barely breathed as Olesya, her mother, beautiful and poised, just as she remembered her, and unchanged, scrutinized her face.

"Is it really you? How?" she asked, and reached for Emery's cheek, touching it gently.

Emery moved her cheek onto her shoulder, pressing her mother's hand to it and closing her eyes. Tears sprang from her eyes. Tears she couldn't shed before. Tears she had saved for so many years. For this moment.

Olesya carefully stroked Emery's head.

"Mother," Emery said between sobs that shook her chest. Emery folded into her mother's arms, dotting her navy scrubs with hot tears.

"We came through the time machine you built," Danuta said. "Serena helped us, and I used the black shard you sent me."

"How did Emery die in this world?" Peter asked.

Olesya gazed at him for a long time, wrinkling her forehead. "You look so familiar. Who are you?"

"Peter. We used to know each other."

"Oh, Zoe told me my daughter didn't make it. She said she...disintegrated in her hands into golden specks," Olesya said.

Emery pulled out of the embrace and looked at her mother. "And you believed her? You didn't search for me?"

Olesya's face twisted as Emery studied it. Something about her mother's face was off. Something she hadn't seen or perhaps not remembered from before. An odd angularity to her cheeks. After all, she was only twelve when her mother disappeared into the capsule.

"You remember nothing from your previous life. When I was your daughter, and we lived in Seattle, and Sasha was your mother, and Grandpa Lev was your dad. You don't remember any of that?" Emery asked.

Olesya shook her head. "I'm sorry. I don't."

Emery hung her head, walked away, and slumped at a nearby desk.

Olesya's gaze landed on Sebastian. "You look familiar too. Who are you?"

Sebastian stepped closer. He reached for Olesya but hesitated and pulled his hand back. His voice was hoarse when he spoke. "I carried the bear with me for twenty-three years," he said while retrieving the tired old bear from the makeshift bag. "The plastic eyes and the tie didn't make it through the travel, but the cotton bear did," Sebastian said and handed Olesya the bear.

She took the bear, staring into Sebastian's face. "You're my father."

"You know?"

"My mother told me when I was leaving," she said as she studied the bear. "It's much smaller than I remember it. I remember you coming to our house and taking the bear. How I wished I had known you sooner. Why didn't you stay?"

"I couldn't, you know that. That would've endangered both of you. I left when she told me to leave, but when I found out you'd disappeared, I started looking for you."

"You look like Zoe."

"She's my twin sister. Where is she?"

"She never mentioned a brother. She's in her quarters, I suppose," she said to him and then glanced at Emery, who sat with her hands covering her face and muttered to herself. "I'm sorry I don't remember our previous life, my baby, but I still love you. For years I mourned you, wishing I had made different choices in life. Wishing I had never invented the damn time machine and the preontechnology. I could have just lived happily ever after with Tirg and you—"

"Is my brother here? Is Tirg here?" Danuta asked.

Olesya opened her eyes wide and faced Danuta. "Here? Why would he be here? Did he come looking for us?"

"I don't know where he is. He disappeared. I thought maybe I'd find him here. That he came with my father and you."

Olesya's arms flopped to her sides. "Noooo...not him too."

Danuta's eyes grew colder. She seemed taller and stronger when she asked. "Where is my father? Where is that monster?"

"I don't know. I try to stay away from him."

"Are you afraid of him?" Danuta asked.

"No. When he is near, I want to kill him."

"Zoe probably knows where he is. Let's go to her quarters."

While Danuta was talking to Olesya, Peter walked to Emery and stroked her shoulder. "What's wrong?"

She looked up at him in utter confusion. "I don't understand any of it. I thought she was being held here against her will," she whispered. "I thought I'd be rescuing her and that she'd be happy to see me."

"She is happy to see you, I'm sure," he whispered back. "But she's also in shock. You were dead to her for many years. Give her some time."

"Yeah," Emery whispered, gazing at Olesya with teary eyes. She wiped her eyes and touched Peter's hand. "I love you, Peter," she whispered, still looking at her mother.

"I love you more."

Sebastian was pacing the lab when he noticed the assistant hunkered down in the corner. "Where is Zoe Brie? Do you know her?"

The assistant, clutching a large tablet to his chest, cowered under Sebastian's gaze from above. "I know her, but I don't know where she is. Probably somewhere in the Master's quarters."

Sebastian looked at Olesya.

She met his gaze and asked, "Does she know she has a brother?"

"She'll recognize me. How could she not?"

"I can call her, but..." Olesya said. Her voice trailed off as she shifted her gaze between her visitors. "She's not going to like seeing the rest of you."

"We could hide," Danuta said.

"I'm not hiding from her!" Emery shouted.

Peter touched her elbow. "Just until we're certain how she'll react to Sebastian."

"No!" Emery said. "Call her."

Olesya sighed. "She can be dangerous when startled, or when she feels cornered."

"So am I," Emery said, and then burrowed her eyes into her mother's before continuing. "You used to be dangerous too. She kidnapped and killed your daughter. You shouldn't be afraid of her. You should be furious."

"It's not that simple."

"Why isn't it? It should be."

"Zoe was heartbroken when she told me. She really was. And she convinced me to work on the time machine and figure out how to trick the paradox and go back in time. Then I could go back in time and save you."

"Did you? Build the time machine?"

"I did, but I haven't—"

"She lied to you. Traveling back in time is not possible."

Olesya opened her mouth to say something but paused.

"What?" Emery asked.

"I'm close. Very close," Olesya whispered into Emery's ear. "But I don't want anyone to know. I've discovered the secret of traveling back in time."

"I don't believe you," Emery said.

Olesya sighed, taking Emery's hands into hers. "I understand that you don't trust me. For years, I thought you were dead, and now you stand before me. A tiny part of me thinks you're not real, but my heart knows it's you," she said, looking into Emery's eyes and smiling the smile Emery remembered from her dreams and her life before. Then Olesya reached behind her neck and unclasped a gold necklace, which she quickly took off and placed in Emery's hands, closing them with hers and whispering. "It's my legacy and secret I carried with me for years. Take good care of it. Protect it, as it may save you and the world. It's the key to the universe's balance. Hide it from those you don't trust. You'll know what to do when the time comes."

"Do what and how?"

"You're part of it. It will guide you."

Emery's fingers wrapped around the necklace, and she felt the smoothness and heaviness of the stone as she put it in her pocket. The last thing she wanted from her mother was jewelry.

She glanced at her mother, drawing her brows together. "Call her."

Olesya's black eyes moistened as she gazed into her daughter's eyes. Then she nodded, pressed a few buttons on her pad, and waited for an answer. After a moment, she looked up. "She is not picking up."

"Lead us to her, then," Emery said.

Olesya regarded her daughter, and something flashed in her eyes. Perhaps she remembered her daughter's stubbornness from a previous life. She sighed. "Stay behind me."

"Sure," Emery said. *Yeah, right.*

They moved through a dimly lit corridor and into an elevator, then through several other corridors and rooms. Although the passing Minders noticed them, they didn't stop them, noticing Olesya among them.

Olesya stopped at a door and turned around. "Are you sure?"

All heads moved. She swiped the face of her tablet against the door.

The door opened silently to reveal the brightness of diamond-studded walls. Emery shivered, remembering Master E. She stepped back only to be pushed by Sebastian.

"Let's go," Sebastian said, moving past Emery. "Which way?"

"Turn left into the hallway and then find a door with the initials 'Z.B.'"

Sebastian darted forward, found the door, and stood there, tapping his fingers on the silver frame.

"My tablet can't open it. You must knock."

"Knock?" Emery and Sebastian asked.

"Don't you have something more sophisticated? A bell, at least?" Emery asked.

"People don't visit each other here," Olesya said.

Peter shook his head, stepped forward, and pounded on the door. Sebastian grinned and kicked the door.

The door opened to a surprised Zoe. Her eyes darted from face to face, lingered on Sebastian's, and rested on Emery's.

"It can't be," she said, and grasped the door. "You died in my arms, disintegrating into millions of golden dots. You can't be her."

"Well, it is me. And I came to avenge myself," Emery hissed. "And my mother."

"Wait," Sebastian said, tapping Emery on the shoulder.

Emery's first reaction was to attack Zoe. Pour all the anger and resentment into instant revenge. She could almost taste its sweetness, imagining thrusting her hands at her and seeing the silvery blue waves reaching Zoe's chest in slow motion and ripping it open. She imagined Zoe's scared eyes as she begged for her life. But she let Sebastian talk to her.

"And who the hell are you?" Zoe asked, staring at Sebastian.

"You know who I am, Zoe."

"No, I don't."

"You remembered Olesya and Emery and the fucking chambers, but you don't remember your own twin brother. What were the visions you sent me, then? Begging to find you and rescue you from a prison."

"You're crazy. I never had a brother, and I certainly never sent you any visions."

"What? Why are you doing this?" Sebastian grimaced and reached for her hand.

Zoe intercepted his hand and pushed him. Not expecting it, Sebastian lost his footing and staggered backward. Zoe's eyes shone as she glared at him, raising her hands.

"What are you doing?" Emery stepped between her and Sebastian. "He is your brother. He told me all about your parents' deaths during the French Revolution and the two of you having to fend for yourselves, stealing and begging. And how you found the black shards that gave you the power and immortality."

The hollowness of his eyes as he gazed at Zoe, the sister who'd rejected him, jabbed at Emery's heart.

"I never had a brother. I was an only child."

"He looks just like you," Danuta said.

Emery shifted her gaze from Sebastian to Zoe. "Sebastian is your twin brother. I knew you in your previous life. You were so close. Think. Try to remember. Talk to him and ask questions." Emery's anger at Zoe was nearly gone, replaced by a desperation for Zoe to recognize and accept Sebastian.

"Can we go inside first?" Danuta asked. "I need to sit down."

Zoe shifted slightly, but the opening still wasn't wide enough for anyone to walk through.

Anyone but Danuta, who, smiling politely, bumped past Peter and squeezed her thin frame through the sliver of space, apologizing.

Zoe ignored her, looking at Sebastian.

"Zoe," he whispered. "We were inseparable. Remember that time when..."

As Zoe listened to Sebastian telling the story of when they first realized that they had powers, Peter noticed Danuta searching the room and then disappearing deeper into Zoe's lavish apartment, where diamonds and emeralds formed elaborate designs. He tensed when his hand didn't find the gun in his pocket as he went inside, brushing past Zoe. She reached to stop him, but not convincingly. Her hand flopped by her side, not reaching him.

"...we fought the Nazis in Berlin—remember how we made the entire squadron disappear? And that time in Egypt," Sebastian continued.

Zoe listened, grimacing.

"What are you doing?" Peter asked, seizing Danuta's elbow before she could disappear into a hallway leading deeper into the diamond-studded apartment.

"Looking for my father. You stay here. This is my battle."

"Before you do something you'll regret, give me the gun."

"No," Danuta said and moved forward, freeing her elbow.

"How do you know he is even here?"

"My father and Zoe are close. I walked in on them. He cheated on my mother with her. He is here, or close by."

Danuta pushed forward and disappeared behind a silver-framed door. Peter reached for the door, but upon hearing a stranger's angry voice coming from the front door, he stopped and ran back. He gasped when he saw an imposing man standing there. The stranger's mouth hung open, an unfinished shout of fury dying in the air.

Zmey's now-black eyes shot icy daggers at Sebastian. He roared, demanding to know who he was. Then he turned toward Olesya and shouted in Sinturijan, pointing at the hallway where they came from.

Then, Emery shouted at him to leave her mother alone and stood between them. "You're Zmey, aren't you?" she asked. *He used the black shard on himself, but his skin is not gray. He didn't want the complete change, only immortality.*

The anger within her grew as all the pieces fell together. He, her grandfather, was the one responsible for the change. He'd used her mother and maybe even Zoe to build the city and rule it alongside the gray minions he'd deprived of emotions and self-awareness. Emery's eyes were glued to his as she tried to claw her way into his soul and understand what had made him into this grotesque, power-hungry creature that now stood before her.

"Can't be. You died," Zmey said, and glanced at Zoe. "You said she died."

Zoe nodded, not taking her unblinking eyes off Sebastian.

"You brought them here, didn't you?" Zmey shouted at Olesya. "You found a way to get her back and get help."

"She is your family, your granddaughter. And so am I," Olesya said. "Don't you care for us at all? Aren't you happy she's alive? When you cried after you'd found out she died, were those tears a lie? Was the sorrow you carried on your face not real?"

Zmey glanced at her and opened his eyes wide as if he had just seen a stranger as she stood with raised eyebrows and hands up in the air.

"No, that was real," Zoe said. "His tears were real. He was broken for a while. Maybe still is," she added, glaring at him.

He met Zoe's eyes, and his eyes flashed. He turned to Olesya, his lips twitched, and he laughed, tilting his head back. Then he stopped laughing abruptly. "You're brilliant in the way you do science, but not in real life. In real life, you were stupid and naïve. You think that Tirg just happened to fall in love with you? I picked you before he met you." He paused, looking at Emery, and sighed. He opened his mouth to say something, but Zoe interrupted.

"Why are you doing this? What the hell is wrong with you?" she screamed in his face.

"It's not that I don't care about my granddaughter, but if she's anything like her mother, she will never accept Brilliant Genesia and will fight me on it. Isn't that right, Emery?" he said, glancing at Emery. In his hard eyes, she detected a tiny flash, a sparkle of emotion, and she felt hope that she had found a way through his dark soul.

"You were right; I wouldn't have," Emery said. "Explain to me how changing people into mindless machines is brilliant?"

"I give people immortality while taking away the mundane and unnecessary aspects of life."

"Mundane. Like love, empathy, curiosity?"

"How about getting rid of hate, killing and eating animals, all the disgusting bathroom mess?"

"Tell her, Zmey," Zoe said.

"Why did you say you picked me?" Olesya interrupted.

"Didn't he recognize you when you first saw him?" Zmey asked.

"The painting," Olesya said. "But how could you've known I would invent what you wanted?"

Zmey smiled.

Olesya's face convulsed. "How? Aras wouldn't ..."

Zmey's grin widened.

"Answer me! How did you get my notes?"

Sebastian stepped forward. "Tell her, you bastard."

"Who are you? I asked you that already," Zmey said, the grin fading from his face.

"I'm her father," Sebastian simply said.

"No, you're not. I know her father."

"And who is stupid and naïve now, big shot? Look at me closely. Then look at her and... Zoe. What do you see, huh?" Sebastian said, mushing the words in his mouth.

Zoe stepped forward, grabbing Sebastian's hand. "He is lying. I don't have a brother."

"I met her mother when I washed up ashore and fell in love with her," Sebastian said, glaring at Zmey.

"You betrayed me!" Zoe shouted, spilling her words in a fast, sharp rhythm. "You're supposed to love only me. You must leave now. I don't want you around."

"So, you do remember me. Why did you lie?" Sebastian asked, grabbing both her arms. "Why, Zoe?"

Zoe grimaced and shook her arms to free herself from his grip. "Let me go."

"To protect you, you idiot," Zmey said, pulling a gun and pointing it at Sebastian's chest. "Three would be a crowd. I wouldn't have let you live."

Emery cleared her throat. "Put your gun down, Zmey. It's no good here. We'll just take my mother and leave you to rule your kingdom all you want. There is no reason to kill him or anyone else. Zoe would never forgive you," Emery said calmly as if she were talking to a good friend. "We'll leave. You don't want the time machine anyway, do you? It's Zoe's pet mission, isn't it? You got what you wanted, and you don't need my mother anymore."

Zmey steadied his hand. "I don't want anyone hunting me," he said, and fired the gun, but he didn't expect Zoe to react so fast. She lurched in front of Sebastian. Blood poured out of her chest as she fell.

Emery clenched her jaw and readied to thrust her hands at Zmey, but Sebastian stood in her way, frozen, watching his sister's life draining from her. She tried to push Sebastian aside, but his rigid body was like a boulder. This was happening fast, but for Emery, time slowed as she tried to clear her way to get to Zmey. In her mind, she was screaming at Sebastian.

"Where is my brother?" Danuta's voice was shrill and loud when it sounded in the absolute silence that Sebastian had created with his terror, anguish, sorrow, and growing fury.

She appeared behind Sebastian quietly, like a ghost, and like a ghost moved forward, holding the gun in her trembling hands and pointing it at her father. "What did you do to him?"

Zmey stared at Zoe's blood-splattered face, gazing at him with surprise and hurt, slowly shifted his gaze to Danuta. His lips pulled back, revealing his teeth grinning in a cruel grimace. "You're not dead yet? What are you going to do with that gun? You don't have the guts. Always full of ill morals and afraid of everything and everyone. I can't believe you're my daughter. Stupid—"

The bullet ripped through his left arm, almost tearing it off. Danuta's face turned ashen. She dropped the gun, which Peter immediately lunged for.

"Mom, get down," Emery shouted.

Peter readied the gun and pointed it at Zmey at the same time as Sebastian threw his arms out at Zmey, screaming at the top of his lungs, and as Emery raised her hands, ready to thrust them at Zmey. The silvery-blue wave left Sebastian's hands and hit Zmey in his chest and head, and he fell, landing close to Zoe. His head was twisted at an odd angle with his black eyes focused on Zoe, as if just now realizing the horrors of his deeds.

Sebastian lunged forward and kicked his body out of the way and kneeled by his sister, seizing her hands. "Zoe, please don't die. Please," he said, sobbing. "I finally found you."

"I shouldn't have sent you a vision. That was...before I knew Zmey. Tell Emery, Tirg is...in a...cell. He might still be...alive." And with that, Zoe breathed her last breath.

Sebastian picked her limp body up into his arms and rocked her, whispering in her ear.

Emery watched Sebastian in horror, only partially understanding the grief of losing part of himself. She moved toward him to console him when she noticed her mother slumped on the floor, her arms outstretched.

"Mom!" Emery yelled, dropping onto the floor by her and shaking her mother's shoulders. "I told you to get down. Why didn't you listen to me?"

Olesya's black eyes looked up at the ceiling, unmoving, unblinking. Her face was pale and rigid. Peter slid beside Emery and checked Olesya's pulse and put his head on her chest to listen to her heart. He met Emery's eyes and shook his head.

"What happened?" Peter asked.

"Sebastian's wave must have hit her," Emery whispered. "I just found her, and now she's gone. It's not fair. It's not right."

Danuta sat on the floor, staring blankly at the bodies. Peter held Emery in his arms for a long time.

Emery didn't cry or even weep. She pulled out of Peter's arms and crawled to Sebastian, who still held Zoe's limp body to his chest. "She's gone," she said, stroking his hand. He looked at her but didn't seem to understand her.

She tugged on his arm. "My mother, your daughter, is gone too. The people we loved and came to find are both dead."

Sebastian closed Zoe's eyes, accepting that she was gone, and shifted his flat eyes to Olesya's body. He gently laid Zoe on the ground, then scooped up Olesya, holding her to his chest and kissing her head. "I'm so sorry," he whispered. "I should've protected you instead of…"

"I'm sorry, Sebastian. For both of us," Emery said and stroked his shoulder. He laid his daughter on the ground and extended his arms to Emery. She folded herself into his arms, which were damp with Zoe's blood.

He kissed her head. "We still have each other," he whispered into her ear.

She pressed her body deeper into his arms, and they sat like that for a long moment.

Emery averted her eyes and paced the living room when Sebastian and Peter picked up the bodies and carried them into a bedroom at the back of the apartment. When Emery saw Sebastian picking up the brown bear along with Olesya's body, her chest heaved in dry sobs. Peter met her eyes when he closed the bedroom door behind him.

Emery headed for the bedroom and reached for the door only to withdraw quickly, as if the door were on fire. The heaviness in her stomach she had felt since her mother died had increased, and now it threatened to revolt. *I can't now. I just can't.*

⁓

Tirg was unresponsive when they found him in a tiny cell in the musty, dark basement. His thin, pale body, bearing hundreds of scars, lay curled on the floor. Danuta pressed herself against his body and covered it with her tears.

"Danuta, we must take him out of here," Emery said, peeling Danuta off Tirg, surprised at the strength of her bony arms. "You want him to live?"

Danuta looked at her and nodded through tears.

"We must get him out then."

"Let's go back to Zoe's place. I doubt anyone would disturb us there. At least not for a while," Peter said.

Sebastian picked Tirg up and carried him, following Peter, who walked first with his gun ready to fire. Emery took the back, making sure nobody could sneak up behind them. They went back to Zoe's apartment and placed Tirg on the sofa.

Tirg swallowed some food and water but otherwise remained unresponsive. Danuta sat by him, stroking his head and talking to him gently, as if she were a mother soothing her sick child. Emery paced the room, stopping by Tirg at every other turn. She didn't remember him, didn't know him, but he was her father, her blood, and she didn't want him to die. And each time she looked at him, the more she needed him alive.

Tending to Tirg for the rest of the day and night granted everyone an excuse to avoid addressing the future. But the next morning, when

Tirg swallowed some food and water and opened his blue eyes, they realized they would have to talk about what to do next.

"Danuta?" Tirg whispered. "Am I finally dead?"

"No, you're not. We found you just in time. Our father did this to you?"

"No, he only watched," Tirg whispered.

"Your daughter is here too."

Tirg's eyes twitched. "My daughter died," he said, and clenched his teeth.

Danuta took his hand in hers and kissed it, then pressed it to her cheek. When she pulled it away from her face, it was wet with her tears. "I believe something happened to her, and she disappeared before getting into this realm, but somehow she found her way back, and she is alive and well."

Tirg shook his head, but seeing Emery approach and smile at him, his eyes widened. He clasped his emaciated hands together.

Emery trembled, watching this shadow of a man, a pile of bones underneath scar-covered skin, and questioning whether he really was her father. But when her eyes landed on his, her body calmed. She recognized his eyes—they were the same sky-blue eyes as hers. Eyes that had not lost their color, strength, love, or compassion despite seeing only the gray walls for years. Eyes that now sparked with understanding and the love for his daughter.

"My baby. It is you. It really is you," he whispered.

Tirg tried to see past Emery, searching for someone. "Where is Zara?"

"She's gone," Emery said, taking his hand. "I'm sorry. I tried to save her, but I couldn't." As she said that, tears poured from her eyes. She sobbed and then smiled through her tears. "But I'm here. Father."

Emery sat by her father's side, telling him about her journey. He listened, smiling and furrowing his brow as she told him about her fortunate and not-so-fortunate adventures. He'll be okay, she thought when she finished, seeing the blood return to his cheeks and the shine to his eyes. She hadn't known him in her previous life and had almost lost him in this, but now desperately wished he'd stay in her life forever. As she neared the end of her story, his eyelids closed, and soon he fell asleep. The look on his face was peaceful, and his breath even.

Emery wiped her eyes, got up, and searched for Peter. She found him taking apart Zmey's tablet. "You've been busy."

"Yeah," he said, and put away the tablet when he saw her face. "He'll be okay."

"I know," she said as she sat by him on the sofa. He wrapped his arm around her and pulled her closer.

"Ouch," she said, pulling out.

"What's wrong?"

Emery reached into her pocket, curious about what had poked her. The necklace her mother had given her shone in her hand. What she thought was a stone set in gold did not resemble a jewel when she inspected it. The gold substance looked like nothing she'd seen before. It shone and glimmered as if it had its own power source.

"What is it?"

"My mother gave it to me, saying it was her legacy and a secret to restoring balance to the universe, and that I needed to protect it," Emery said and put the necklace on. She held it between her fingers, studying it. "She also said she was close, and I think she meant the time machine. I don't know what she was trying to say, and now I will never know. I wish…I wish…I could have protected her. I wish I could go back in time."

Emery wept. Peter pulled her close, and she fell asleep in his arms.

When she woke up two hours later, Tirg was awake and hungrily swallowing the food that Danuta had brought him. Emery's face lit up when she saw him eating. When he saw her gazing at him, he beckoned for her to come close.

"I must tell you something. I don't want you to think that your mother knew I was held captive and did nothing about it. Zoe told me Zara didn't know I was here, and I asked Zoe not to tell her, fearing she'd try to get me out and that my father would hurt her. I was such an idiot for not listening to my sister," Tirg said, glancing at Danuta. "Danuta saw through him and warned me, but I didn't listen."

"He said something about picking her mother for her brilliant ideas and making you fall for her, but how did he know about them? Who told him?"

"Aras's assistant, Isaac. My father paid him a fortune for the copy of the notebooks."

"You knew about it?" Emery asked.

Tirg grimaced. "Of course not. I loved your mother and would have given my life for her. I would never, ever have betrayed her. He told me everything after his people threw me in prison. From the other side of the bars. Coward!"

"Nobody knew what happened to you."

"He drugged and imprisoned me in Sinturija, then Zak brought me here and my father tried to convince me to join him. When I found out he'd kidnapped Zara and murdered you, I tried to kill him, but his people overpowered me."

Sebastian stood by, listening, wringing his hands. "You spoke to Zoe?" Sebastian interrupted.

"She only found out a few months ago that Zmey had imprisoned me here. I'd probably be dead already if it hadn't been for her bringing me food and water. She promised to get me out when the time machine was ready."

Sebastian's chest moved in sobs. "Why did she need this stupid time machine, anyway?"

"To go back in time and save your parents."

Sebastian turned on his heel and bolted out of the room. His chest heaved violently.

When he returned a while later, he stood in the middle of the room, shifting his gaze from person to person.

"Now what?" he asked.

"Now we'll free all the changed people and destroy Zmey's empire," Emery said. "Help the planet recover."

Peter nodded and smiled at her.

Sebastian clenched his hands into fists. "Sounds like a plan."

ALSO BY EVA BARBER

The dark world series

(BOOK I)

UNBORN

Unborn tells a tale that feels like a dreamy collision of family bonds, mystery, and the tug of destiny. It opens with the discovery of a mysterious infant in the forest, devoid of a belly button, by a couple in rural Russia. Sasha and Lev, battling their own heartbreak over childlessness, decide to keep the child despite its otherworldly origins. What unfolds is an exploration of the girl Olesya's extraordinary nature, her struggles with identity, and the looming forces seeking to claim her.

Unborn is an atmospheric and thought-provoking read for anyone who enjoys stories about family, identity, and the intersection of science and the fantastical. Fans of speculative fiction with a strong emotional core, think *The Midnight Library* meets *The Giver*, will find much to love here.

-Literary Titan Book Review

THE DARK WORLD SERIES

(BOOK II)

THE GIFT

The Gift is a genre-bending blend of science fiction, fantasy, and metaphysical adventure, perfect for readers who enjoy character-driven journeys, time travel, and philosophical explorations of love, purpose, and destiny. Think "The Time Traveler's Wife" meets "Interstellar", with a touch of spiritual myth. It's beautifully written and emotional, ideal for fans of romantic sci-fi, cosmic or multiverse fiction, and stories where imagination meets heart.

-Likely Story

MISUNDERSTANDING

Eva Barber's *Misunderstanding* is a gut-wrenching, beautifully layered novel that fearlessly explores trauma, friendship, betrayal, and the long, painful road to healing. At the center of it is Alice Williams—a girl raised in poverty and brutality, whose fight for survival becomes both physical and emotional. This isn't just a story about abuse. It's a story about what happens after—the aftermath, the unearthing of dark truths, and the question of who you become when the world breaks you and expects you to stay broken.

Barber writes with fearless clarity and emotional depth. Her prose is sharp, poetic, and unflinching. *Misunderstanding* doesn't offer easy redemption or tidy closure. Instead, it offers something more powerful: truth. Hard-won, painful truth—and the strength to face it.

Alice grows up in a suffocating trailer with her alcoholic, violent father and a mother who is more ghost than guardian. The trauma begins early and leaves no part of her untouched. Her only escape is her imagination—turning old playing cards into characters and narratives to distract from the chaos—and eventually, a friendship that will define her life: Lilly Labarre.

Lilly lives in a different kind of prison. Outwardly wealthy, stylish, and picture-perfect, her world is one of emotional starvation and cold neglect. Her mother, Chloe, is obsessed with appearances and perfection. Her father is passive, always caving to Chloe's icy authority. But in Alice, Lilly finds not just a friend, but someone who sees her. And in Lilly, Alice discovers safety and joy for the first time.

Their bond is immediate, intense, and unwavering. Despite coming from opposite worlds, they recognize each other's pain and fill the gaps their families have carved into them. This friendship is the emotional center of the novel—and the compass by which Alice navigates everything that follows.

Misunderstanding is not just a great story—it's a roar!

-Book Viral Review

For more information about upcoming books and excerpts, visit:

evalidiabarber.com

www.ingramcontent.com/pod-product-compliance
Lightning Source LLC
LaVergne TN
LVHW010147070526
838199LV00062B/4281